MEASURE
OF DEVOTION

What Reviewers Say About CF Frizzell's Work

Exchange

"CF Frizzell really knows how to write tension! A great read, a real roller coaster of emotions with a sensational love story."—*Kitty Kat's Book Review Blog*

Night Voice

"CF Frizzell has written a beautiful love story, a romantic tale that will have you cheering on Murphy and the lady who has stolen her heart. …There was just enough angst and plenty of hot sex in this excellent book to keep anyone hooked. Emotions ran high and how all of those involved communicated their feelings made for a very interesting read. I loved it."
—*Kitty Kat's Book Review Blog*

"I very much enjoyed it. The main characters felt real and likeable. The connection between them was palpable and the slow build-up was a pleasure to read. The supporting characters were also well developed. …I liked the author's writing style and will keep an eye out for her future works."—Melina Bickard, Librarian, Waterloo Library (UK)

Stick McLaughlin: The Prohibition Years

"[E]xciting reading and a story well told!"—*Golden Threads*

By the Author

Stick McLaughlin: The Prohibition Years

Exchange

Night Voice

Nantucket Rose

Crossing the Line

Measure of Devotion

MEASURE
OF DEVOTION

by
CF Frizzell

2021

MEASURE OF DEVOTION

ISBN 13: 978-1-63555-951-4

THIS TRADE PAPERBACK ORIGINAL IS PUBLISHED BY
BOLD STROKES BOOKS, INC.
P.O. BOX 249
VALLEY FALLS, NY 12185

FIRST EDITION: JUNE 2021

CREDITS
EDITOR: CINDY CRESAP
PRODUCTION DESIGN: SUSAN RAMUNDO
COVER DESIGN BY JEANINE HENNING

Acknowledgments

Being a die-hard history buff, I always hoped to visit Gettysburg National Military Park, but it took the Golden Crown Literary Society's 2019 conference in Pittsburgh to get me there. My ever-understanding wife, Kathy, and I took a roundabout vacation that included three days at the historic site, and that, of course, set off a cannonade of storylines in my head.

One idea kept recurring and, during a Pride Festival that summer, fellow BSB author Jesse Thoma pressed me for specifics, pen and paper poised to record details as they fell out of my imagination. The story probably would have evolved eventually, but *Measure of Devotion* is due in very large part to her dogged insistence and unfailing support. So, a heartfelt thank-you goes to Jesse, an author who lends as much of herself to others as she devotes to her own remarkable novels.

I extend hugs to best bud and award-winning BSB'er, Kris Bryant, and readers Deb, Nadine, Val, and Jesse for all the enthusiastic encouragement and invaluable feedback. I hope you're pleased with this end result.

A thank-you also goes to my gracious brother-in-law Frank Creedon who landed at auction a priceless 1866 volume of Massachusetts military info. One of dozens of references I accumulated for this project, the book provided remarkable detail (and required a cautious, delicate touch).

No BSB novel gets into a reader's hands without a ridiculously talented editor having waved her magic wand over each word, and, once again, I am ever so grateful for the wizardry that is Cindy Cresap, my personal Merlin.

But Kathy took every step with me, lovingly and with superhuman patience. No matter how many times I *just had* to read her an author's quote that became six tedious pages; or drew battle maps on the kitchen counter; or spewed TMI about disgusting camp conditions, her support held strong. I'm sure it must have wavered now and then, but even though I fought my way to victory on this campaign, she's my Medal of Honor winner.

Dedication

To the women and men, very young to very old, who lent
their full measure of devotion to American democracy.

And, always and forever, to my wife, Kathy,
truly one of this world's better angels.

To the Reader

The trouble with writing historical fiction is, well, history. It's demanding. It's a copilot, not a backseat driver. The author is obligated to remain respectfully attuned throughout, to look history in the eye, and to hear its voice. When I stood on the actual site of this novel, history sized me up like a stern parent and demanded I respect, remember, and learn. *This* place is not a simple backdrop for fictional escape. What happened here to families, citizens, and governments in 1863 is just as critically important today. A viscerally divided nation, feverish with patriotic fire, fell upon itself here in the Battle of Gettysburg, a climactic death match between one hundred fifty thousand Americans.

Measure of Devotion is a fictional tale of a fictional woman soldier, Catherine "Cooper" Samson, who happens upon love through the course of very real battles, including the greatest engagement ever fought on American soil. At stake, that July 1-3, 1863, is her very survival, not to mention the preservation of American democracy. Her courage is tested like never before. Our nation's identity begins turning on this vast, bucolic farmland.

Building a story around the Battle of Gettysburg in America's Civil War often felt like an overwhelming constitutional challenge unto itself—*my* constitution. While the storyline and main characters are my creations, all locations, action, dates, and conditions, as well as the majority of events, characters, and details, are as accurate as my research-addled mind could handle. There are no embellishments or exaggerations.

Many of the thirty-eight farms on and around the battlefield at the time are now the property of the Gettysburg National Military Park, and some are private residences, but the Bauer farm in *Measure of Devotion* is a fictional property. It is an incorporation of location and construction held by several farms of that day. Caught "in the middle of it all" during the battle, farming families and their homes were subjected to horrific conditions far beyond what any of us could imagine today. I have woven some of their experiences into those of the Bauer family.

Measure of Devotion is no lighthearted romp through sunny wheat fields. It details two women's hope and courage through hellish times and their discovery of lasting love. Civil War realities of hunger, fear, and danger, and societal realities of conformity, family, and propriety are all *their* realities.

I have sought to deliver a unique experience through these characters, and to share how they are changed forever by the profound significance of this event and place. Today, as back then, walking onto the battlefield itself, some two miles wide and a mile across, the vista beckons you with a church-like reverence and humbles you where you stand.

Fellow citizens marched across this plain, actually thirteen thousand of them, elbow to elbow, on July 3, 1863. Along the distant tree line, you can picture them coming, shouldered guns glistening, flags fluttering, advancing on drummer boy beats too faint for your ears. Determination to dominate, to carve their own nation from yours, to sacrifice their last breath, is evident in their rigid, methodical pace. And here, behind a stone wall that hardly reaches your knees, you stand awestruck by the sight, barely cognizant of what it all means.

One hundred and fifty-six years later, I set foot on that wall and an honest-to-God lump formed in my throat. Why? Not because I recalled something from history class or was eager to see the movie setting. But because I—and every American should—know that "Fore score and seven years ago" *originated here for a reason.* I looked down at my comfy walking shoes on the rock and meadow grass where dead soldiers fell, piled four or five bodies high. The magnitude of where I stood rumbled through me. Maybe it was the touch of spirits forever cast in this stone.

The soil of this miles-wide acreage is enriched with blood—literally. For several growing seasons after the battle, some crops flourished like never before, grasses grew greener, oats darker, corn more luxuriant than ever. Many years later, a simple shovel could still turn up belt buckles, bullets, bones. Reportedly, bodies remain to this day.

For at least seven months, resident farmers and their children witnessed gruesome work on their land, as human remains were moved from backyards, wheat fields, drinking wells, and shallow battlefield graves to the new national cemetery. There would never be another Civil War battle on northern soil, but the Confederacy fought on for two years, defensively, until it expended all its limited resources.

Today, *Measure of Devotion* feels complete at last, and, admittedly, timely. For reasons beyond this author's gratification, I hope it leaves the indelible mark on you that it has left on me. Never again will I be an innocent Gettysburg tourist. I have walked and slept here and crawled through its wheat. I have bled and cried here, faced and delivered death, and, ultimately, found love and eternal peace here.

Truly, hallowed ground. It has been an honor.

CHAPTER ONE

D ying wasn't unthinkable, but today would *not* be that day.
Catherine Samson's heart pummeled her rib cage as if trying to escape, as if it knew better than to challenge death again.

The bayonet at the tip of her long gun glinted with bravado in the sunshine, undaunted by swirling clouds of smoke. As much as it represented a last line of defense, it always seemed so eager to lead the way, dutifully blind.

She tightened her sweaty grip as she tramped across another unfortunate farmer's second-growth hay crop. Part of a human wave of blue uniforms, she advanced on the wall of Confederate guns, thinking she probably should be praying right now, because on this steamy September day, she was in hell.

Lead minié balls the size of acorns whistled by. Continuous cannon fire shook the ground, buffeted her body, and made her flinch. Dirt and rocks erupted, balls and chunks of iron rained from the azure sky. She counted her blessings to be only staggered, nicked thus far. Purpose and duty drove her forward, outranking fear and exhaustion. She'd overcome so much to fight for the Union cause, kept her gender hidden for more than a year, and refused to consider her luck changing now.

Better to focus on love of country, to stand tall for it, as tall as any man, just as resolved as her late twin brother, Cooper, had been when he enlisted. She knew she risked everything by adopting his identity, but she saw it as the only significant means available to defend her nation. After all, American freedoms hung in the balance, and she fully intended to pursue happiness in a life of her own choosing. No matter how great the cost.

As Cooper of the 19th Massachusetts Volunteers, she quick-stepped through clouds of gunpowder and narrowed her itchy, watery eyes against the sting. Smoke clogged her nostrils, so she sipped at the air, even though it soured the back of her throat and caused her to spit. Grit clung to her heated face and neck. Sweat compounded the burden of her regulation wool frock, the blouse beneath it, and the ever-present undershirt tight against her skin.

Shells splattered against the sky, piercing and concussing soldiers in groups, slaying them beneath hailstorms of shrapnel. Screams rang out amidst shouts, commands, and bugle signals as chaos intensified.

Just ahead, two comrades in the 19th regiment fell. Friends, men she knew lay motionless. *Keep going.*

Dodging them on the run, she focused on a target through the haze, paused for a half-beat, fired, and strode on. The rebel soldier jerked and disappeared behind his stone wall. She picked another cartridge from her pouch and stopped to reload, her body bent into as much of a crouch as her Springfield rifle musket would allow.

Dozens of bluecoats pounded past her as she bit off the paper tip and poured. Bullets swarmed in all directions, and, with barely a pop, one pierced the tail of her frock. With a furious thrust, she rammed a minié ball down her gun barrel. Another comrade spun to the ground within her reach and Coop fought the distraction of his grotesque, fatal head wound.

Outnumbered two to one, the Confederates deserved credit for their valor, but she knew the federals would win the day and take this sunken Maryland road. After three hours, and a fourth assault, this *must* settle things.

Cooper fired again, slammed a rebel officer from his horse, and paused to reload.

Faster.

Now, at less than one hundred yards, she was an easy target. She thanked the fates that, somehow, her steady hands, her marksmanship, and her luck continued to serve her. With practiced speed, she reloaded, took aim through the drifting smoke, and spun another rebel from his battle line.

Hustling on, she again reached for a cartridge, but came up empty-handed. Her heart skipped. The moment had arrived when she faced the most vicious element of combat, the last resort. She eyed the bayonet, knowing it would force her close enough to deliver shock and agony with her very hands, to see a life stop forever as she shivved her blade into a human body. Flashing upon her own mortality, she rushed through the smoke.

The Union's screaming charge crashed upon the enemy, leaped onto the wall, shooting, thrusting, batting away rebel rifles. Cooper's ears rang from the close proximity of gunshots. Stricken comrades tumbled against her. Blood splattered against her cheeks. She hurdled the wall, prepared to lunge, just as the entire Confederate line fell back with hands raised. In what seemed to be the first time all day, she took a breath.

That night, Cooper and others from her exhausted regiment sat around a cookfire and mourned the missing. Her friend Timothy Doten was among the absent, and her heart ached for him. With mixed feelings, she pictured that surrender scene: a moment's jubilation, quashed just as emotionally when word came of the day's other engagements. The list of casualties ballooned to unimaginable numbers, far greater than any battle she'd fought to date, and made this conflict at Antietam Creek feel like a draw instead of a victory.

Fellow soldiers debated this outcome long into the night, as a temporary truce allowed for the wounded to be collected and the dead buried. Cooper knew she'd never unsee the hundreds of bodies strewn about the fields. Talk around camp indicated Confederate Gen. Robert E. Lee soon would withdraw his army and leave the Union as the victor, but thousands had been killed or disabled in the multiple battles of the day. She considered herself incredibly fortunate to have emerged unscathed, again. Tim, it seemed, had not been as lucky. Spiritually and physically drawn, she left the camaraderie for her tent. It probably was time to write a letter to the family of a fallen friend.

She stopped her regiment's hospital steward as he hurried by. "Hey, Paddy. Any word on Doten? We were separated this afternoon and I haven't heard a thing."

"Haven't seen him." He pointed to the sea of hospital tents at the rear of their encampment. "Stretchers are still coming into C tent, though. That's where I'm headed. A few of ours could be there."

"I'll join you."

Although bone tired, she kept up with Paddy's speedy pace and struggled to be patient.

Tim had become her dearest friend in the army, and to lose his down-home wit and bear-like presence would knock her spirit sideways. The confidences and family orientation he offered so freely had tempted her to share her true identity, but too often she lacked the courage to broach the subject. His had been the first true, look-her-in-the-eye test of her disguise, back when they had mustered in together fourteen months ago.

Inside the medical tent, she felt the crisp, subdued autumn night surrender to the frenetic atmosphere of urgent care and the agonized cries of the wounded. The air was heavy and thick, too warm, and the scents of chloroform, blood, and scores of candle lanterns hung in the humidity, enveloping everyone. Cooper rubbed her nose and, as she scanned the dozens of injured soldiers, their protruding bones and oozing tissue, their terrified and tortured faces, she had to fight the impulse to run.

The setting's grim aura aside, the threat it posed to Cooper's participation in this war bore down upon her. Hospitals made her nervous and skittish, after many months of hiding inside her twin brother's persona. Obviously, disrobing for wound care was out of the question, but these days, just being a visitor was a challenge.

With steadied nerve, she offered handshakes and encouraging words as she wandered between the cots and makeshift resting places arranged by stewards, nurses, and volunteers.

"Who are you looking for, soldier?"

The woman questioned her with a soft voice and vibrant eyes that belied her weariness. A spritely emerald green, they soothed Cooper's edginess as surely as a soft palm to her cheek. The mussed blond hair framed a striking heart-shaped face, far too lovely for such a setting as this, and her curious look reached so deeply, Cooper's nerves twitched.

"I…um…" Much to her own relief, she remembered her manners and yanked the cap off her head, then swiped at her hair when it fell forward. "Ah, Tim," she offered, hoping this woman's intuition hadn't somehow detected hers. "I-I mean, I'm looking for Pvt. Timothy Doten, 19th Massachusetts. Do you know if he's here?"

The woman held Cooper's gaze for an extra moment, before her inquiring expression faded to one of concern. She beckoned with a finger. "Come with me."

Cooper maneuvered along behind her toward the far end of the long tent, a melding of two to accommodate operating zones. She was glad to be led on a circuitous route around the surgeons at work, but bustling personnel and pools of blood on the plank floor made walking difficult. She tried to concentrate on the view before her, the woman's slim figure in the long, blood-stained dress, its dirty hem frequently skimming the floor.

"I hope we can help you," the woman said over her shoulder. She looked back and her hair flared into a golden veil against her cheek. Distracted, Cooper almost missed the woman's words. "We'll inquire of

Clara. She's a one-woman machine here, thank heavens. She's keeping us organized, and we'd be lost without her."

"Is she a volunteer like you?"

The woman nodded as they walked. "She is, yes. From Washington. I'm here with a group from our town, Gettysburg. It's north of here. Perhaps you've heard of it?"

"Seen it on a map."

"By the way, I'm Sophie."

"Pvt. Cooper Samson, ma'am, 19th Massachusetts. I appreciate this."

They arrived at a table littered with papers. An older, stern-looking woman stood bent over the mess, obviously busy.

"Clara?" Sophie called, and the woman straightened, her frown dissipating. "This is Private Samson. He's looking for a Pvt. Timothy Doten, 19th Massachusetts."

Cooper stepped up to the table and her anxiety mounted as Clara turned from one page to the next. *So many wounded.*

"Now, don't despair if he's not here," Sophie told Cooper, and set her fingers on her arm. "Try the other tents."

Cooper tried not to think about any other alternative. If Tim hadn't been logged in for treatment yet... She cleared her throat and let Sophie's compassionate touch redirect her thoughts. "I'll do that. Thank you. And thank *you* for all you're doing here. It means everything, you know."

Sophie smiled a bit sadly. "We do what we can."

"I'm sorry," Clara said, and set down her papers. "Private Doten is not with us. Not here," she added.

Cooper felt her chest tighten. Sophie touched her arm again and that seemed to ease breath back into her lungs.

"Don't forget there are A and B tents," Sophie reminded her, "and dozens of smaller ones."

Cooper simply stared at Clara's papers, exhaustion threatening to overtake her rational thought. Sadness rushed at her spirit like the 19th had charged the rebel line today.

"Cooper?"

Cooper managed to nod toward the table.

Sophie tugged at her sleeve. "Let's get over to A tent."

Parting the heavy tent flaps, Sophie led them outside, and Cooper halted at the scene. Wounded were everywhere, on stretchers, blankets, propped against trees, simply lying on the ground, waiting, crying, bleeding, praying, dying. She peered through the darkness for a familiar face.

Sophie turned to her. "Take a good look around, then I'll walk you over to A tent."

"No. I mean, that's okay. You don't have to. Your work is more—"

"Hush. I'm done for today. Clara's sent me 'to the rear,' as she put it."

"Then you must need to rest. Bet you've been at this all day."

"And I thank you for your thoughtfulness." Sophie patted Cooper's shoulder. "Now, please take a breath of this air. Take a few." She stepped away to snatch a lantern off a tree branch and Cooper marveled at her energy, her generosity.

The lantern shed little light on Cooper's search for Tim among the wounded. Instead, its dim glow shone brilliantly on the scores of grotesque injuries, the suffering. She swallowed hard, hoping Tim already had been doctored and released. It was highly unlikely, but the best she could hope for.

"I imagine you have experienced this before," Sophie said as they left the area.

"Never in numbers like this." No previous battle she'd seen had taken so many men from so many units. And all in far less than a day. Inconceivable. She figured this amounted to a living nightmare for Sophie. Yet this woman's kind spirit still seemed to prevail undaunted. With growing respect, Cooper considered Sophie's deportment, her calm and steady approach to work of this magnitude. "You handle yourself so well."

"Thank you, but all the volunteers owe a great debt to Clara for her patience and instruction."

"She's your teacher?"

"You could say that." Sophie leaned closer. "We've heard that folks in Washington call her Miss Clarissa Barton. Knowing they lend her that courtesy makes us all quite proud."

"Well, your work is vital, to say the least, ma'am. How long have you been volunteering?"

"Hm. Almost a month now, I suppose. We all had some training with Clara first, and then we were split up and some went to Harper's Ferry and some to South Mountain. That's where I was before coming here to Sharpsburg."

"We were at South Mountain, too, although held in reserve. The men had a tough time of it. Being your first action, it must have been hard for you, too. Dealing with all this isn't easy."

"I think, next to the passing of my mother, those first hours at South Mountain were the worst experiences of my life. Sights I never imagined seeing, the sadness." Sophie's voice softened. "I confess, we frequently cried on each other's shoulders, and I'd like to say it helped prepare us for something like this, but nothing could have done that. This… You just have to… to train your focus. A tragedy like this, it's almost impossible to keep count, the numbers are so great."

"Today was very bad, you're right. Makes us all miss peacetime."

"I definitely do. My father and Greta and Karl, my younger sister and brother, weren't keen on my leaving, but so many women want to do what they can for the cause. I trusted that my siblings would fare well, helping Papa in my absence, so when the Ladies' Aid Society formed, I joined." She sent Cooper a quick, proud smile. "We filled a wagon with ladies and four more with donations."

"Four? Gettysburg sounds like a very generous town. Will you continue with the army now, after this?"

"Some of us will. I haven't decided yet. A lot of us are needed at home for harvest, and even though Papa would prefer to have me there, I know he and the children can manage. Here, though… If I can provide comfort, maybe even some medical assistance, I feel compelled to do so." She released a slow sigh. "I *do* know that I need to make up my mind soon."

Cooper nodded. She'd certainly enjoy having Sophie in the volunteer group that accompanied the army. Spending time with her seemed to reinvigorate Cooper's spirit, warmed her blood from the flat, lifeless cold that empowered her soldier livelihood. What a gift it would be, to have more of her company beyond this dark moment.

She could remember only once in her life, being so moved by such a compassionate friend, although Peggy had been much more than that. Their friendship had blossomed into a love each believed would last a lifetime. That is, until Peggy's father took a railroad job and moved them out west. How vividly Coop recollected the months of heartbreak that ensued, and how her late twin brother had somehow understood.

Now as they walked by lantern light, Cooper sensed Sophie, too, would understand, and she wondered if this Gettysburg lady had a special friend of her own. *Are you betrothed? Do you entertain gentlemen callers at home? Would you renounce a woman in uniform?*

She shook herself mentally. How unearthly is this moment, she wondered, to be here on such a classic autumn night, strolling across a grassy field, an ocean of sadness, all in the company of a charitable soul as fetching and graceful as Sophie.

"And what about you, Cooper? What's home like in Massachusetts? Are you a fisherman?"

Cooper snickered. So many teased Massachusetts soldiers that way.

"Farmer," she said. "Mostly wheat and hay. In Plymouth, south of Boston."

"Is there a Mrs. Cooper Samson and little ones?"

"Unattached," she mumbled, and flashed upon the image she frequently concocted of her late brother. In it, he ultimately survived this enlistment to enjoy married life on the family farm.

She thought of him so often—in fact, every time someone called her name. It was his name. The name she screamed until her voice broke on that fateful day, climbing through the rubble of the barn to find the bodies. She still fought the heartache, the horrific loss of both parents and her twin. The day after he'd enlisted.

She hadn't hesitated to abandon her own name, to honor him by fulfilling his obligation, and take up the cause in which they both fervently believed. It was a duty she, Catherine Samson, had ached to accept but from which women were legally barred. As twins practically inseparable since birth, their spirits soulfully blended, their likenesses had always been virtually indistinguishable, even as they entered adulthood. Carrying on in his name kept him alive in her soul, would make them both proud.

Cooper tensed as she geared up to offer the tale she'd come to live by. "There was a…Well, right after I enlisted, I-I lost…See, there was a barn collapse." She took a breath. *This is so hard for so many reasons.* "I lost both parents and my twin sister."

Sophie reared back. "Oh, good heavens, Cooper! I'm so sorry."

"It was really difficult at first, but army training and action came fast." She waved a hand at the scene of wounded surrounding A tent ahead. "You have to concentrate elsewhere or die."

Sophie stopped them before entering the tent. "I can see why you're determined to find your friend. We'll find him, Coop."

Sophie's compassion, her familial use of Coop's shortened name, struck a warm chord.

They held open the tent flaps for a steward exiting with a two-wheel cart, his load a heap of severed hands, feet, arms, and legs, and Coop appreciated Sophie tugging her away from the sight.

CHAPTER TWO

Sophie Bauer had seen so much in her month volunteering, she could write a book about the tragedies she had encountered, but she couldn't relegate Cooper Samson to "another experience." She sought success for him and his search, and despite the late hour and the sixteen she'd already spent on her feet, she focused harder on his quest.

The A tent search proved unsuccessful, however, and it pained her to see defeat shadow his face. He appeared to be a thoughtful sort, considerate and kind, selfless at this horrendous time when self-preservation was one's top priority and far from guaranteed. Alone now, without a family, his heart deserved at least the victory of finding his friend.

"Let's get over to B tent," she said, pausing to let him take one more desperate look around. "There are lots of tents out there. Don't lose hope."

Coop nodded and followed her out.

Sophie raised the lantern and its candle flickered madly in the breeze. Coop moved to her side, and they carefully worked their way through the maze of wounded. His scrutiny of every face slowed their progress.

"You said he wore a red neckerchief?" Sophie asked.

"And has a wide beard, not quite to his chest."

"Sorry, Coop, but half the men here have those beards."

"Oh. Yeah."

Sophie smiled at the ground as they completed a trek around the tent. "You prefer not to grow a beard?"

"Eh." Coop removed his cap and wiped his brow with his sleeve. Sophie watched his dark hair dangle at his shoulders and wondered if he'd done the rough cut himself. When it swung toward his face, he combed it back with his fingers and held it in place with his cap. "A family trait, I guess," he added and shrugged. "The guys tease me, but I don't mind."

"Makes you look young."

"So I'm told."

"How old are you?"

"Twenty-four. How old are you?"

Sophie raised an eyebrow. "Asking a lady her age, are you?"

"Forgot my place, ma'am. No offense. My apologies."

Sophie almost giggled. "I'm just teasing. I'm twenty-three. Contrary to custom—and I am quite often, I dare say—I do not take offense at most direct questions."

"Well, then." Coop stopped walking. His face brightened, the weariness lifted slightly. "I-I wish to say, ah, that is, I'd like you to know how much I appreciate your kindness to me tonight. Um…" He looked away as if searching for the proper words. "Forgive me, but, there must be someone special in Gettysburg clamoring for your return."

Sophie's emotions swelled and she almost relented and set them free. She longed to express them, to ease her heart's demand, but this definitely was not the place, and she certainly didn't know this Cooper Samson well enough to speak of such intimacies. Besides, she simply couldn't even consider confiding anything to a man. But the honesty in his eyes drew her in, his sincerity and humble manner, even the set of his mouth with that silly dirt mustache below his nose. He was as compelling as his query.

Undoubtedly, Coop was a handsome soldier, perhaps the most alluring man she'd ever met. He stood slightly taller than she, his wiry build unimposing yet projecting strength in his battle-worn uniform, and she enjoyed gazing upon him. Ragged and dusty, he wore his cap low over his forehead, deepening the depths of his brown eyes, and despite the day's grit and smudge that blunted his sharp features, Sophie found herself intrigued and longing for a smile. She imagined it would be dazzling.

"I think you used the most appropriate term earlier," she said. "I, too, am unattached."

"I hope that is by your choice, Sophie."

"It is." A choice freely made, she thought, for while many gentlemen callers had tried, none had succeeded in stirring her romantic interest. Her closest companions through the years had been women, and Sophie had no regrets. "My mother, rest her soul, would have had me married at sixteen, I'm afraid. Thankfully, Papa just lets me be."

"You choose not to marry?"

"Do you?"

Coop squared his shoulders. Maybe the question probed too deeply.

"I-I take each day as it's given. No more, no less."

"Then I see we are kindred souls." She extended her hand. "I'm honored to meet you, Private Samson."

Coop smiled, finally, a slash of white against his gritty, sun-stained skin. The sight caused a surge of warm, unexpected pleasure to course through her. Then, absent the expected dominant grip, the tenderness with which his hand enclosed hers sent heat shimmering up Sophie's arm.

"Coop! That you?" a gruff voice shouted from the trees at B tent.

They spotted the scruffy soldier waving his arm from where he sat.

"It's Tim!" Coop said and spun to Sophie. "Let's go!"

He hurried ahead, and Sophie did her best to keep up, lantern and hem of her dress in her hands. She hopped over the handles of a stretcher but lost her balance and teetered precariously over an unconscious soldier. Suddenly, Coop's arm wrapped her firmly about the waist and swept her forward.

"Can't lose you now," he said, and Sophie exhaled a thank you, relieved to be saved, taken by his thoughtfulness.

They dropped to their knees beside Tim, who pushed himself with one arm into a taller sitting position against the tree. Naked from the waist up, his upper chest and right bicep were bound together by a long, filthy strip of blood-stained bandage, and a ribbon of caked blood disappeared at his waistband.

"Took you long enough," Tim said, and socked Coop's arm but almost toppled onto his side.

"Quit whining," Coop said, setting him upright. "You're lucky I had help."

Tim grinned at Sophie and pulled off his cap. "Ma'am. Pvt. Timothy Doten. Pardon my present attire."

"You hush about that. We're just glad to find you. I'm sure the doctors will get to you soon."

Tim sent Coop a sideways look. "With such a fine lady, I'd have taken my time, too."

Sophie felt her face heat, but the brotherly interaction made her grin.

Coop gestured to her. "This is Sophie, you mule butt. She's been nursing all damn day and if it weren't for her, you'd be out here crying like a baby. Now, what's going on with you?"

"Ah, horseshit." Tim's eyes then flashed at Sophie. "Apologies for the cursing, ma'am. Caught a bayonet across the arm, halfway across the chest. Just deep enough to bleed like a stuck pig. Confounded thing won't stop unless it's wrapped up tight."

Sophie handed the lantern to Coop and inspected Tim's bandage. "Not too bad for a field dressing, but surely soaked through and needs to be changed. Can you move your arm all right? Your hand?"

Tim swayed where he sat and tried to catch himself with his good arm. Again, Coop straightened him.

"Hurts, but things still move." He winced as he flexed his arm and fingers.

"Good. Very good, in fact." As she tightened the knot of cloth at his chest, Sophie could feel his eyes roaming her face. "This is still bleeding badly. When were you wounded?"

"Late afternoon."

"By the looks of this—and you, I'd say you've lost a lot of blood. But you're a lucky man."

"Oh, I am a *very* lucky man, indeed."

"A very *married* man," Coop added, still holding Tim in place. He swung his own canteen from around his neck and pulled the cork with his teeth. "Here. You're going to need help for a while now. Lucky we're not chasing those rebs. And did you hear? We think Lee's pulling out. A truce is on."

"Truce?"

"They're still bringing in wounded. We'll all be on burial detail for a while, but I think you'll be fit to march when we move out."

"I imagine a large part of our hospital complex will have to follow along later," Sophie said.

Tim stared down at his chest and nodded. The solemnity of his situation obviously struck him. "So, where to next?" he asked Coop.

"Never you mind," Sophie answered, and glanced toward the hospital entry. "Once they tend to you, you'll be moved to the healing tents. You might even warrant wagon transport when the time comes."

"And here I've been wishing for new shoes."

"You're stuck with your old flappers, I think," Coop said.

"Looks like they're coming for you now." Sophie stood, and Coop sat back on his haunches as two drummer boys set down a stretcher. Coop helped them situate him onto it, over Tim's objections. "Stop your fussing," Sophie said. "You're too woozy to walk. Be a good patient."

She knew he might spend a chilly night under the stars once his wounds were treated and bandaged, and she felt bad about that. The smaller tents for the recuperating had been filling up at suppertime, so there might not be room for him now.

Coop must have been considering the same thing as he studied the distant acreage, where torches and cookfires lit pathways throughout the tent settlement. Abruptly, he turned back when the two boys grunted, lifting Tim for transport.

"I'll wait for you," Coop told him, "get you back to our unit." Tim raised a hand in acknowledgement as they took him away. "Somehow," Coop added under his breath.

"He won't be out for a while," Sophie said, "and they won't let him go right away."

"If he's able to pull on a shirt and walk, the army will give him back to us."

Sophie frowned. "He won't be able to load his rifle."

"He'll manage."

"One step at a time, soldier."

Coop shook his head. "No. He'll be back with our company soon. Sorry to sound bitter. Guess I'm just tired."

"I certainly understand. Honestly, I don't know how you have any energy left at all, after what you've been through today."

Coop flexed his shoulders, as if he'd just realized he needed it. "The same goes for you." He took the lantern off the ground and offered his arm. "May I escort you to your quarters? Um…Wherever they might be."

Sophie linked their arms. "Very chivalrous of you, Private Samson."

The compliment appeared to take Coop back, for he fell silent during their walk, studying the ground, the matted grass, the trees, the passing horses and wagons, even the stars. Sophie wondered if he pondered the setting, the tragedy of the day and its aftermath, or the triumph of locating Tim not too seriously wounded. Truly, all those things struck Sophie deeply, but, for her, this moment in particular registered in a special place. And it was remarkably welcome.

Maybe her own weariness had set her mind adrift, she thought, had made her emotionally susceptible to a man's supportive gesture. Considering she'd always deferred, maintained her self-sufficiency and avoided unwelcome advances, her acceptance of Coop's offer left her rather confused. But he posed no threat or insinuation. Quite the contrary. He fostered comfort and honesty, compassion and respect in a combination Sophie had never before encountered in male acquaintances. All of which rattled her constitution. She enjoyed Coop's company, that much she knew, but he *was* a man, after all.

"It's that one," she said. She pointed to the covered wagon ahead and drew them to a stop. "At the outset, we were assured of lodging in town, but apparently every boarding house, every home not filled with soldiers was taken by other groups, so we're making the best of things in our wagons. I imagine the ladies are asleep inside now, so..."

"It is very late," he said, nodding, and handed her the lantern. "This is yours."

"You keep it for the walk back."

"No, ma'am. I insist. The hospital will need it, anyway."

Sophie accepted. "I'm happy we found Tim. It's been a successful night."

"Thanks to you. I don't know if I would have had the spirit to keep looking."

Sophie smiled at his hapless expression. "Oh, I do. I think you would've walked through your shoes till you found him. But I'm glad that wasn't necessary."

"And I'm glad I met you." He removed his cap and his hair again shadowed his face. "I don't know your last name, Sophie, so... May I inquire?"

Sophie bit back a smile, taken by his propriety. "It's Bauer, Private Samson. Sophie Bauer. And it's been my honor to assist a valiant soldier such as yourself." She offered a quick curtsey.

Coop bowed slightly. "The pleasure has been mine, Miss Sophie Bauer. You've been my personal angel on this battlefield, the brightest light that's shone upon me in many a day, and I'm sincerely thankful."

Sophie knew a blush had overtaken her cheeks and she appreciated the lantern's dim light. Her heart thumped at the sentiment. *Oh, how he could turn my head. A man, no less.*

"Perhaps," she began, immediately wary of emotion pouring forth, "we could meet again to sit and talk."

He fumbled with his cap. "I'd like that very much."

Sophie delighted in the hint of shyness rarely seen in men. "We ladies brought along plenty of coffee beans for roasting. You might like that."

"There's no limit to your kindness. Yes, I'd enjoy that almost as much as your company." Coop's earnest, forthright gaze held Sophie in place, lost for words. She couldn't look away, even when he reached out and squeezed her hand. The gesture threatened her composure. "So," he added, and edged back a step, "Well, if it's at all possible, if we're not breaking camp, that is, I-I'll call upon you."

"I look forward to it."

CHAPTER THREE

Her basket of supplies refilled for the third time since breakfast, Sophie continued to administer to soldiers resting in the village of small tents. Visiting one after another, row upon row through the day's constant drizzle, she wiped brows, checked bandages, emptied buckets, wrote letters home for those who couldn't, and jotted notes for the doctors, all while patients groaned, flirted, or offered tales of home, of bravery beyond imagination. She smiled throughout, maintained an optimistic attitude, and soldiered on. And more than once during the day's labor, she wondered if she'd cross paths with Coop again.

As darkness fell and she doled out coffee, bread, and cups of broth to those who could partake, she heard the news that the army would break camp at dawn. Already, artillery batteries limbered into formation along the main road, while orderlies and stewards packed miscellaneous items from the medical tents, dismantled whatever could be spared in advance. A considerable number of patients had left since the supper meal, either transported to hospitals or released to their units, and she hoped Private Doten had been returned to his because she hadn't come across him yet. Coop's smile came to mind and she wished she could see it again but doubted that would happen now.

Back at C tent of the 3rd Brigade's hospital, to which her Ladies' Aid Society had been assigned, Sophie found activity persevered uninterrupted from the previous night. Surgeons still worked doggedly, stewards shuffled patients in and out, nurses and volunteers administered care, and privates still dug graves behind the site. Rumor circulated that, although the army would move out tomorrow, the hospital would remain in operation here for some time, until every wound had been addressed and the last wagon train of the most seriously injured had left for the major hospitals in Frederick City or closer to Washington.

She still hadn't decided if she would take a leave or continue with the Society when the hospital moved on. No one spoke of the army's next destination, so she had no idea how far away or for how long she'd be from home if she stayed. Regardless, there was so much still to do, so much life-or-death work that mattered. And an inkling of the right decision began to emerge.

Beneath a canvas three-walled tent, she stoked the firebox of a bulky iron cookstove and set about roasting pans of coffee beans. The all-quiet bugle sounded from the army encampment, affecting all soldiers, except officers, special details, and the medical teams who, like everyone else, existed on gallons of this coffee. The volunteers welcomed time assisting the hospital cooks, especially when field equipment rated as luxurious as this. Stove smoke elbowed its way around and above the canvas ceiling, while warmth radiated toward the open end of the hospital tent nearby.

"A chilly night tonight, Miss Bauer." A fellow Society member, Mrs. Eliza Schmidt, appeared at Sophie's side and rubbed her hands together over the cooktop. Lantern light cast her jowls and short, stout frame in silhouette. She'd been delivering water buckets to the surgeries for the past several hours, and Sophie knew that, for a woman along in age, Mrs. Schmidt had to be worn and wet clean through. "I just never thought army hospitals brought along stoves like this. I don't recall ever being told so, anyway."

"I was surprised to see it, too," Sophie said. "Glad it's here, though. Maj. Letterman has made such a difference since South Mountain."

Mrs. Schmidt drew her shawl across her chest. "And couldn't we have used this beast then?"

Sophie groaned in agreement as she shimmied the browning beans. Mrs. Schmidt hailed from Gettysburg's neighboring town, Taneytown, Maryland, and made sure everyone knew that she had recruited two of her friends to their group. Although generally well-intentioned, Mrs. Schmidt rarely had no opinion or nothing to say. Sophie mourned the loss of her solitude and forced a bit of polite conversation.

"These beans are almost ready. There'll be more coffee for everyone soon."

"Lovely, my dear. You're remarkably efficient, always thinking ahead. No one's had a chance even to dream of coffee lately over at A and B tents." With due caution, she settled her weight on a short keg of salt and sighed toward Sophie's pans. "You know, Dr. Hathaway predicted two more weeks before we're ready to go."

"Two more? Did he say where to then?"

"South is what I heard, but there was a whisper of Falmouth."

"Isn't that the little town outside Fredericksburg?" Sophie stopped and stared at her, hoping she'd misheard. She had hoped their next assignment would bring her closer to home, not some one hundred miles farther south. "That's what he said?"

"I happened to pass by as he was speaking to a doctor I didn't know. Dr. Hathaway's a captain, so I expect he knows *something*."

As Sophie prepared the coffee pots, her shaky decision to remain with the Society, a debate she had put to rest only today, resurfaced in full force. *It will take days to get there and then all the way back. And who knows how long we'll stay? Being away from home for at least another month is a lot to ask of Papa, Greta, and Karl.*

Mrs. Schmidt rose with a moan and began gathering tin cups onto a tray. "I'm sure your siblings will be of great help to your father in your absence. I bumped into him at the train depot prior to our departure, did you know? He expects your fall harvest to be lighter than the summer's, so that should ease the children's workload, don't you think?"

Sophie could only nod. Her mind insisted on wandering. Yes, the summer's harvest of wheat and rye had been hardy and thankfully so, but the family always doubled its efforts to replicate the crop in the fall. She really didn't know if Karl and Greta were up to the task, and worried about Papa overextending himself.

"I'm still concerned for them."

"Ah, Sophie. Such a devoted daughter you are." She patted Sophie's cheek. "Your father is a wise man, not one to overlook the needs of his children or work them like slaves. Don't fret so."

Sophie hoped Mrs. Schmidt wouldn't resort to the "if only you had a husband" rationale. The various ladies' circles at home wallowed in such discussions, which kept Sophie from regularly attending any of their meetings. Fleetingly, she wondered how many Gettysburg single ladies would become soldiers' wives, driven by novelty, desperation, loneliness, or social pressure. She knew of two who had wed hurriedly as their men prepared to march off.

But her choice—of a woman as a life partner—would be different, she believed without hesitation. She didn't care how many saw her as resigned to a spinster's life, not even courting at her advancing age. She would have her independence, freedom from the constraints of marriage to make her own choices, to be her own person, not a husband's accessory or property. Her father seemed to respect that, and she was helping raise her siblings to do the same.

"They're young, Mrs. Schmidt, and always aiming to please."

"Sweet children, certainly, but you must be practical, dear. They are safe, healthy, well fed, and enjoy the comforts of a fine home. And thousands of men are giving of themselves to preserve that way of life. Their efforts must be at the forefront of your concern right now."

Sophie lacked the energy for debate. Perhaps because Mrs. Schmidt was right.

At the sound of footsteps, Sophie stopped filling coffee cups to see Coop emerge from the shadows. He doffed his cap quickly, a sly grin offered to both of them.

"Good evening, ladies."

"This is a pleasant surprise." Sophie gestured with the coffee pot. "Mrs. Eliza Schmidt, this is Pvt. Cooper Samson, 19th Massachusetts Volunteers."

"How do you do, Private Samson?" She offered her hand and Coop stepped forward and shook it.

"One of the lucky ones so far, ma'am," Coop said. "I'm honored to meet another of the hard-working battlefield angels."

"We met last night," Sophie explained to Mrs. Schmidt, "located his wounded friend."

"I see."

Sophie turned to Coop, his appearance still disheveled and dusty. No doubt he'd slept in his uniform, if he'd had much time to sleep at all. "I hope Tim's back with your regiment."

"He is and doing much better. He's weak but plodding along, trying to keep up. Our sergeant let him lay low for much of today so he'll be ready to go tomorrow."

Without moving her head, Sophie could tell Mrs. Schmidt looked back and forth between them. "Tomorrow is the day, then?" She opened the stove and jabbed a poker into the waning coals. She added two logs and returned to filling cups on Mrs. Schmidt's tray.

"It is," Coop said, "and that's why, tonight, I...um..."

As Sophie finished pouring, Mrs. Schmidt adjusted her grip on the tray and caught Sophie's eye with a wink.

"I'll go deliver all these before they cool," she said. "Nice to meet you, Private Samson. May the Lord keep you safe."

"Thank you, ma'am. Thank you for your service."

Sophie quickly poured coffee for him. "We wondered about tomorrow. I really didn't expect to see you."

He tucked his cap behind his belt buckle and accepted the cup with both hands. "This is a fine treat, Sophie. Thanks. Such a damp day makes for a cold night." Their eyes met as he drank. "I'd love to spend the time, you know, sit and talk a bit as you suggested, but I'm afraid I've already been gone a while."

"I heard the night bugle. You'll be in trouble if they find you missing."

"Everyone sneaks out now and then. It just took a while to get here. This hospital camp that Letterman set up is huge and poking around brigade tents so close to division headquarters is risky." He set the empty cup down and looked around nervously. "But I wanted to say good-bye."

Sophie immediately shook her head, surprising herself with the impulsive response. "No, not 'good-bye.' Something tells me we'll meet again."

"You're staying with the army?"

"I had thought so, until Mrs. Schmidt said she heard Second Corps is headed quite a distance south. Is that what you've heard?" Coop's nod made Sophie sigh. "So, I haven't decided yet."

"I understand your family must need you."

"It's true, but I know the army does as well. That's why it's such a difficult decision."

He nodded at the ground and Sophie wondered if he reflected on his own lack of family, having no one yearning for his return. The impulse to hug him almost pushed Sophie closer, and the reflexive nature of such an intimate gesture rocked her. *How does this man elicit so much from me?* She busied herself with another check of the fire.

He scanned the area again, obviously concerned that a sentry or, worse, an officer would find him out of place. "Well, if you do decide to stay on," he said, "I'll do what I can to say hello. Maybe we'll have another coffee chat after all."

Sophie bit her lip at the finality in his voice. "Perhaps we could correspond?"

"I'd like that."

"As would I." And she meant it, even if still taken aback at hearing the suggestion pop out. Volunteers wrote many letters *for* the wounded, but she had never initiated correspondence *with* a soldier. The furrows across his brow dissipated and his expression relaxed, an easy curl formed at his mouth, and Sophie took note of how the simple offer of a letter could lift a soldier's spirit.

But now he fumbled with his cap again. "I need to go, I'm afraid."

Without thought, Sophie placed her hand over his. "I'm very glad you came. I've enjoyed seeing you."

He entwined their fingers with a gentle grip. "Maybe we'll meet again, Miss Bauer?"

CHAPTER FOUR

Unlike most of her comrades, Coop took gleeful satisfaction this time at being deployed in advance of the main army. She counted her winnings proudly, having collected on a bet that II Corps would reach Falmouth in record time.

"Twenty-nine," she told Tim as the downpour pummeled their tent. "Good money."

"Tell you what's good. Good to be here already. The muck 'n' mire that's going to be stewed up out there..." He whistled. "Hey, how many oceans of mud can eighty thousand men, ten miles of wagons, and all their horses make?"

"Twenty-nine!" Coop repeated, laughing and waving the army's paper money at him.

He kicked back and roared. "And they're still coming in, poor sods. Mud's as thick as molasses *everywhere*."

Coop handed him fifteen dollars and put the rest in her billfold and buried that in her knapsack.

"What's this for?"

"The way my luck's been running, it's about time you took a salary," she said, and sat back with her writing paraphernalia.

"Salary? I didn't convince those knuckleheads to put money on it, *you* did."

"But who threw that ugly cuss in the trough? *You* did. It's settled, and first leave we get, I'm buying. Maybe it'll be right here, once we cross over to Fredericksburg."

"If we don't flatten the place first." He tucked his bills away as well. "This is mighty generous, Coop. Beats a month of army pay. Thank you.

Mary will feed the family for days. I'll send her twelve from this." He stared blankly at the paper Coop held to her knee, obviously stuck on a thought. "Maybe nine."

She snorted at him. "Write your letter. I've decided to try one of my own."

"Still nothing from that pretty lady, Sophie? The volunteer at Antietam?"

"No. I'm sure she's long-since back on her farm by now. And probably plenty busy with her family and harvest."

"Uh-huh. And suitors, y'think?"

"Probably." Although she easily could, Coop didn't want to picture it.

As usual, Tim went on. "I know she's bound to have them lining up, but, I don't know, she seemed genuine, I guess, like she wouldn't forget you." He began writing his standard every-other-night letter home. "I think she took a shine to you, my friend."

"She was very thoughtful, considerate, like most of the volunteers."

"Oh, bull." Tim lifted the hem of their shelter and spit into the rain. "She's not like them and you know it. You're not fooling me. Those eyes, those luscious pink lips, a smile that makes y'heart thump? And such pretty hands. You see her hands?"

"Will you quit?" She battled back the tangible memories, the ones that visited her sleep every night and accompanied her on daily marches.

Not smart to dwell on that creamy complexion, the way she bites her lip nervously. Such strength and confidence, whether she's soothing a grumbling soldier or stoking a stubborn cookfire. Hell, I can still feel her fingers, slight and tender, returning my squeeze.

"She's worth dreaming about day and night," Tim added, "and I bet you do."

"You sound like every old crow at the commissary, too busy blabbing to hear what he's saying."

"Bah. Go on and write—"

"I'm going to if—"

"You know, it's about time. You've put it off for weeks."

Too much friendly correspondence will lead to trouble, an attachment that definitely wouldn't end well, and I can't talk about why. I refuse to lead her on, to deceive her. Your heart's as big as your block head, Tim Doten, but you're not making this easy.

"I'm not expecting anything, mind you, just hope she's fared well since Antietam."

"That's a great approach. Took your sweet time figuring that out."

"It's not an 'approach' to anything. I'm just going to write a little something. I don't know what yet."

Coop focused on her paper and wished the proper words would just trickle out of her pencil. This dilemma, she pondered, well, she hadn't signed up for this. The cold, the aches, the hunger, all such woes came with the job, that much she accepted, but this concern simmered unabated no matter how much logic she applied.

The urge to communicate with Sophie again, to whatever degree, felt almost like *need*, and *why* was a question she didn't want to face. She certainly hadn't expected her heart to latch on to a woman and not let go. *Really mustn't allow that.* She recalled so clearly, casting aside her self-centered longings to parade off and quash the rebellion. *Thought I buried them deep.*

"You know," Tim rattled on, not bothering to look up from his letter, "I'm relieved you're finally writing to her. You're too young to be such a staid ol' Yankee."

"So, what? I should be married and have a dozen children by now?"

"Hey, we're both twenty-four. I got two and there'll be more when I get home." Coop shook her head at his goofy grin. "Be reasonable, Coop. Miss Sophie's a fine looking woman. Your children would—"

"Enough already. I'm just dropping her a note. Don't be getting all heated up on the subject."

Coop closed her eyes and assessed what little she knew of Sophie Bauer: committed and warmhearted, with a selfless, independent bent so deeply ingrained she had sacrificed her homelife for a greater calling. Coop opened her eyes at the realization she'd done the same.

And if I tell her the truth? Will she respect the lengths to which I've gone? Will she feel embarrassed, humiliated, having shown attention to a woman? Will her devotion to Union regimen obligate her to report me? Maybe. Maybe not.

Tension across her shoulders had grown into an ache and Coop stretched her back in the cold. The blank paper on her knee, soft now in the dampness, begged for content.

We're only acquaintances, for heaven's sake. Relax. Just an innocent note. Not the place to risk so much confidentiality.

"Do you even know where she's at?"

Coop looked up. She had almost forgotten he was there. "Gettysburg, pretty sure."

"Hm. Well, just put 'Ladies' Aid, Second Corps' on the envelope and it should reach her. And do you good."

Coop started scribbling. She had no idea if it would ever reach Sophie but enjoyed hoping.

November 20, 1862
Sophie. A most gracious hello.

I hope this correspondence finds you well and looking forward to a Thanksgiving Day gathering of your loving family and friends. I imagine you will enjoy a sumptuous spread of royal proportion on your Gettysburg table, with slathered breads and plump pies, the thoughts of which make my mouth water as I write.

We have been told to expect roasted beef for the occasion and, already, we argue about sneaking second turns in the food line. There will be whole brigades of smiling faces on that day, a welcomed change from the sourpusses moping here in Falmouth. If you could spare a moment, please feel free to share a tale of your special day or any day, for I hope to hear that happy times and good fortune follow someone so deserving.

Today, after weeks of waiting, we finally heard that General Burnside is on the move to join us with the entire army. They say he has a mandate from President Lincoln to advance upon Richmond with all haste, so his arrival could bring an end to our monotonous waiting. However, now we hope not to spend the upcoming festive respite crossing the Rappahannock or clearing rebs out of Fredericksburg.

The crossing, itself, poses some risk, as Johnnies on the far shore take full advantage of our pause here and continue to strengthen their position by the day. Curious times, our delay, with blue and gray picketers close enough to chatter back and forth over this narrow point on the river. They even float tiny sailboats to each other, exchanging goods, tobacco, coffee, and such. I refrain from participating, for the irony strikes me deeply, brothers one minute, deadly enemies the next.

It is with lingering fondness and gratitude that I frequently revisit our meetings at Antietam. I recollect your tireless labor, your encouragements, and your inspiration remains with me still. Thank you for taking this letter, for I am overdue in extending appreciation and sincerely wish only the best of times for you and your family.

A kindred soul,
Pvt. Cooper Samson
19th Reg., Massachusetts Volunteers
3rd Brig., 2nd Div., II Corps

❖

Sophie scooted under the canvas shelter that teamsters had erected off the Society's personal wagon and hung her just-rinsed dress and apron close to the edge. A sizeable, defiant bonfire, grown from a cookfire only feet away, roared against the rain and lent warmth to the shelter, the wagon, and her chilled, aching bones. She gathered her shawl tighter around her shoulders and held her palms to the heat.

Maybe there will be word from home. She expected the second of her twice-weekly letters to be authored by Greta, full of talk of the family's Thanksgiving Day preparations. Unable to participate for the first time, Sophie and all her compatriots mourned the coming event and passed the entire journey here by mixing tales of Thanksgivings past with plans for their own, together in Falmouth. She vowed to celebrate a special Thanksgiving with Papa, Greta, and Karl upon her return.

But, to lift her spirit through tomorrow's festivities, she *so* looked forward to a letter from Greta. Karl rarely wrote his own, preferring instead to scribble a note somewhere on Greta's, but between Greta and Papa, she could rely on plenty of entertaining news.

"Your vegetable soup was heaven-sent, Sophie. Mine never turns out so well." Laura, the Society's youngest member, joined her beneath the shelter and also rubbed her hands in the warmth. "Perfect on such a night, especially after this miserable day."

"It was a group effort. Rather surprised myself, to tell you the truth, throwing it together so hurriedly, but I do think it was just what we all needed."

"Hard to imagine we set out before dawn and we are just now settled. Being staged to the rear of the Army of the Potomac certainly makes one appreciate its size. I think it goes on forever."

Sophie smiled. After twelve hours of travel, too frequently interrupted by mud pits and obstinate mules, and another four hours inching along in queue, Sophie couldn't disagree. "At least we completed the last leg of the journey. There is much to be said for being warm and dry and motionless."

Laura dropped her voice to a whisper. "My backside insists that I stand till sunup."

Sophie bumped her shoulder. "Mine, too."

"Oh, Felicity has returned with mail. Sorry, I forgot to say earlier."

"Bless her for enduring such a trek," Sophie said on a sigh. "To go through this rain and mud, through all that army chaos over there, and somehow locate the camp's mail office? I might have given up until tomorrow."

"Oh, I agree. Felicity has such a sturdy constitution. She told me once that having six children made her strong and I believe her."

Sophie laughed. "I would as well. I'm sure it helped in navigating through an encampment that size."

"Surely, no one can build an entire city faster than the United States Army. Did you know that, from the top step of our wagon, you cannot see the end of it? So many tents whiten whole tracts of land, as if after a snow. There are roads, cookfires, and torches, horses and wagons going every which way."

"Well, I'm glad we're here on the outskirts, with trees to block the wind and for firewood. I'm sure the army will move us around the camp as needed, but I'm so grateful to be settled at the moment." She turned from the fire. "Shall we check on the mail?"

"Yes!"

They hurried to the wagon and joined others from the Society, already tucked into their bedrolls and reading by lantern light.

"For you, Sophie Bauer." Mrs. Schmidt pointed at two little envelopes on Sophie's blanket.

Eager to recognize the handwriting, Sophie lit a candle and Greta's young script jumped out at her, but the other she didn't know. Intrigued, she turned her back to the ladies, removed her dress and corset, and slipped promptly beneath the blanket. Finally comfortable, she leaned toward the light to read.

Coop. Of course he is here, somewhere. And sent this quite some time ago...to Gettysburg.

A confusing combination of emotions trickled through her as she scanned the pages of pencil scratching, and her pulse quickened. How touching that Coop would write, she mused with an odd, rising apprehension. *Hadn't it been my idea, after all?* How sweet his consideration for her and her family. *And I have shown none in return, resisted, in fact, each time the urge has risen.*

She pressed the pages to her chest and stared at the arched ceiling, wondering where her courage had gone. A slight mist floated through the canvas into her eyes and she wiped them with the blanket.

Shame on me. He deserves as much from me as he has given. And here he writes, believing I no longer accompany the army. But what appearance might I risk? I dare say you, Cooper Samson, could very well answer my heart's calling if it did not yearn as it does for a woman's love.

Caution, she thought, caution in each sentence of her response. In no way, should an appreciative thought, a fond declaration be misconstrued. She still considered it wise to maintain distance between them and prevent misconceptions from ruining this friendship.

And what of this...flicker of attraction, this fondness I hold for your compassionate voice, your endearing smile? Oh, such a riddle. Perhaps only shared time will properly light the subject, bring resolution to each of us.

Saving Greta's letter for a Thanksgiving treat tomorrow, Sophie tucked both envelopes under her pillow and extinguished the candle. She curled on her side, eyes closed, and decided against responding to Coop in writing. He was here, after all, and tomorrow was Thanksgiving Day.

If the army is taking the occasion to celebrate, I will get a message to him.

CHAPTER FIVE

Coop evaluated the Thanksgiving meal and the socializing it created as a desperately needed escape for everyone. Spirits were high for the first time in too long, and no one complained about the long lines at each company's cookery. Like everyone else, she held out her tin plate with great anticipation as hunks of freshly fired bread, rations of roasted beef, and boiled potatoes, onions, and turnips were slapped down. A feast, for sure, far from the routine chunks of salt pork and boiled beans of camp life—and miles better than the rock-solid hardtack and bitter, watery coffee they endured on the march.

Mixed with a dash of sugar lent by a friend, Coop's coffee settled into her happy stomach just fine, and didn't stop her from dozing off that afternoon. She actually smiled when a chorus of "The Battle Cry of Freedom" woke her, even though the singers were terrible. But the banjo player was good, and before long, card games folded, naps ended, and lively conversations turned to singing, and the entire 19th was bellowing loud enough to carry across the river. Coop joined in until a rather tipsy messenger from the quartermaster trotted up to her.

"Samson?" She took the note he extended. "Guess it came in this morning from the aide camp. They said she was a *real* pretty one."

Her spirit rising, Coop noted the graceful sweep of the handwriting and smiled. *The aide camp?* The absence of a postmark struck her, and she glared at him.

"It's taken this long to reach me?"

He shrugged. "Better late than never, ay?" He ran off and Coop absently sat on the nearest box.

Trailing fingertips across the lettering, she caught her mind wandering and ripped open the envelope.

November 27, 1862
Greetings, Coop.
Happy Thanksgiving to you. Received your letter late yesterday, here,
as it seems it traveled even farther than we did, to Gettysburg and back.
We are camped at the northern edge of the army, at least for now, so please
feel welcome to stop by when duty permits. I am sure you will relish all the
amazing dishes the ladies are planning. I so enjoyed hearing from you and
hope we have time to visit, especially on this holiday.
Sincerely,
Sophie

Coop stood and looked north into the land of army tents. She wondered if she could hike to the aide camp, visit, and make it back in time for her picket duty, which began in a few hours. *It's closer than she is. Hope you had a fine Thanksgiving, Sophie.*

"Y'lookin' like a sailor lost at sea." Tim appeared at her side, finishing the last of a cookie. He produced three more from his pocket as he hung a heavy arm off her shoulder. "So, what's that?" He nodded toward her note. "Trouble?" His breath colored with whiskey, he handed her two cookies and jammed the last one into his mouth, whole. "Shortbread," he told her, crumbs blowing everywhere as he spoke. "You missed out." He backhanded his mouth. "So...y'getting promoted?"

"No, but still good news. There's just no time to see it through."

He bent severely to squint at the envelope. "Whoa, now! Is it from her?" He took the envelope and sniffed it.

Coop grabbed it back. "They're set up to the north."

"Hm." Tim straightened to his full height. Tugging on his beard, he could be in deep thought, Coop figured, if his current condition allowed. "Y'won't make it on foot. We got duty soon." Impressed he remembered, she hoped he would be capable by then. "So," he added, and slapped her on the back, "let's go get you a horse."

Coop laughed. "Right. 'Excuse me, Captain. Borrowing your ride for an hour or so. Be back soon.'"

"No. No. No. Y'don't ask, dummy. Y'just slip one off the line."

"Tempting, but I don't want a month's night picket tacked on as punishment. Besides, those wranglers in charge of the animals are so bored, they'll shoot me just for sport."

"Hm. Yup, that they would. Well..." He tossed his hands in futility. "Use the time to rest up. See her tomorrow." He dropped to his knees and crawled into the tent. "We'll probably still be sittin' here at Christmas, anyway, waiting for ol' Burns to figure out what to do."

Coop returned to staring north. Dusk seemed in too much of a hurry these days, chasing away the twilight, and definitely didn't enhance her view.

Surely would have made Thanksgiving special. Tomorrow, then.

At dawn, puffing life into the little cookfire, Coop still groused about lost time. If only those hours on picket and the restless sleep that followed had passed as fast as darkness descended nowadays. *She wouldn't seem so far away.*

As usual, Captain Weymouth consumed most of their morning with drilling, the endless maneuvers and skill tests, while Coop counted the minutes until she would be free to hike across camp. *At least we don't appear to be going anywhere yet. Still.*

The pontoons needed to bridge the river had finally arrived but, in Coop's opinion, and that of her comrades, ol' Burns was sitting on his hands, putting their well-being in serious jeopardy by stalling. Rebs continued to cajole from across the river, and she thought they sounded increasingly impatient for action. *Burns needs drilling on proper tactics.*

Just after midday, Coop entered the tidy acreage of volunteer wagons, a grand representation of social, religious, civic, and humanitarian groups from as far away as Kansas and Vermont. Coop was impressed to see everyone gathering Thanksgiving leftovers, compiling mass quantities of goods for the army. Baking or frying went on feverishly at the clusters of wagons, and Coop graciously accepted every delectable handout as she strolled by, searching.

Women strode purposefully from one chore to the next, quite the pleasant sight, considering what she routinely saw. Coop recalled these varying fashions all too clearly, the cinched waistlines, long sleeves, the lighter, softer colors distinguishing young single ladies from the "married women." Although such uncomfortable memories made her shudder, this world of women felt empowering, relaxing.

Everywhere, women bustled about, calling instructions, laughing, some singing as they tended the fires, rolled lint for wounds, knitted and mended, swept and scrubbed, washed and hung clothes and blankets. Quite a busy place, Coop mused, and knew it would disperse among the brigade hospitals once hostilities began. But, at least for now, they appeared to toil with a happy excitement, and Coop enjoyed returning the greetings and smiles, and tipping her cap.

Ahead, a little wooden sign dangling from the crown of a wagon caught her eye. The burnt-in lettering read, "Gettysburg," and Coop stopped short on the spongy field. Sophie stirred a large iron cauldron hanging above the flames.

Just the sight of her raised heat beneath Coop's collar. The pale green dress hugged her shoulders and back, outlined her waist, flared at her hips as she bent and sampled her concoction. A matching bonnet covered her hair, appropriate in this chilly weather, Coop knew, but she would have preferred to see sunshine glinting in Sophie's hair. Wisps of it now drifted from beneath the headpiece and teased Sophie's cheeks.

Coop walked on, wondering if she dared embrace her. *Probably should avoid that.*

Sophie turned, and the brilliant smile seized Coop's breath. She snatched her cap off her head.

"Coop! You *did* get my note!" Sophie offered her hand and Coop squeezed it, worried her voice would crack. Sophie stepped closer, scanned her face, that smile pressing joy into Coop's veins with every thump of her pulse. "I'm happy to see you," Sophie said, leading her to a seat. "Please come and sit. Are you a tad thinner than when last we met? Let me get you some cider." Coop was grateful Sophie hadn't waited for her to speak.

She watched her hustle to a nearby table and pour from a heavy crock.

"We made this batch before breakfast," Sophie explained as she returned with the cup. "Tell me what you think. Be honest, now." Coop took a tentative sip, then gulped down the rest. Sophie clapped her hands. "That's all the answer we need."

"Is it good?" Laura asked, passing with a basket of potatoes. She looked from Coop to Sophie. "I think he likes it."

"I do, yes. It's delicious. I can't remember the last time I had cider. Thank you." Laura moved on and Coop searched Sophie's eyes, possibly for too long. "Sophie, I'm glad—surprised—you're here. I-I'm happy to see you too."

"Your letter caught up to me just the other night and there really was no time to contact you until yesterday morning."

"Quartermaster was slow sending it down to me, I apologize. If I had known you were with the army, I-I would have…I don't know, but I would have greeted you upon arrival."

"Oh, that's very sweet, but the weather was horrendous. You would have had to swim here, so I'm glad you didn't." She pressed her palm to Coop's sleeve and the pressure tingled into her shoulder. "You've been well? How was your Thanksgiving?"

Coop didn't care about health or holidays. She wanted to taste her lips, feel Sophie kiss her in return, to be in each other's arms. *Stop it!*

"I-I've been well, thank you, and Thanksgiving was good, considering. I'm sure the food didn't come close to what you had here, but for us it was special. And there was silliness and music, and no thoughts of our mission."

"I'll be honest. I had hopes of you joining us, with your friend Tim."

"Thank you for thinking of us. Your Thanksgiving was good?"

"Being away from family had us all a bit blue, but I must say yes, it was enjoyable. The Ohio ladies next door," she nodded toward the adjacent group of wagons, "they shared roasted turkeys and several organizations contributed to make quite the feast."

"We still have plenty of cornbread," Mrs. Schmidt injected and stopped at Coop's side. "Lovely to see you again, Private. Sophie, don't forget to send him off with enough to share."

"I'll make sure he has plenty," Sophie answered, watching her depart. "So thoughtful," she added, and cast a grin toward the ground.

Coop agreed the woman was considerate but seemed nosy. She stood and offered Sophie her elbow. "Can they spare you for a time?" Sophie accepted and Coop tried not to stand too tall as they strolled away.

"Mrs. Schmidt is the motherly sort," Sophie said quietly, and waved to friends as they passed. "Occasionally, an overbearing mother."

"How are you, Sophie? You seem to never stop working. Do you get frequent letters from home to keep your spirit up?"

Sophie didn't speak for some time and Coop watched her keenly, wished she could read her mind. *You miss your family. I know you do.* Sophie looked at the road as they walked and finally lifted her eyes to Coop's. Neither of them turned away for several steps. *Whatever you are thinking appears serious. And now, I'm thinking serious thoughts. Are you seeing something in me you shouldn't? Something unexpected? Unwanted?*

"You're a very special man, Coop Samson. I feel I would have liked your family."

Coop took a breath, felt a weight lift from her shoulders. "They would have liked you as well."

"Tell me about your twin sister, would you?"

"Er...My sister? Well..." Coop's conscience gnarled within her. "Let's see. Um...Catherine. She loved being outdoors and often tangled about that with Mother. She learned her mending and such just fine but, well, looking so much alike, we instigated some serious mischief over the years."

"She preferred doing what you did?"

"Indeed." Coop leaned closer. "Outshone me too often." She enjoyed this liberated feeling, speaking truth, especially to Sophie, and bringing that little smile to her face gave Coop a thrill.

"So, she enjoyed farming, tending the animals?"

"And riding and hunting. Both Father and Mother reprimanded her constantly, but she was determined. You might even say, rebellious."

With a little grin, Sophie asked, "That trait runs in a twin's blood?"

"I suppose you're correct. We had significant influence upon each other, sharing adventures, but she always paid the price."

"Quite the independent one, your sister. I wish I could have met her. I think we would have been fast friends."

Coop smiled. *Imagine if we had known each other growing up.*

"I can still hear Mother warning Catherine, 'Spinsterhood and misery await the woman who doddles in such pastimes.'"

"Forgive me," Sophie said, stopping their walk, "but I do not share your mother's sentiment. Do you?"

If I kissed you right here and now, would you faint? I might.

"No, dear Sophie. I do not agree with Mother. A woman must be free to achieve anything to which she sets her mind. I witnessed this in Catherine. *You* demonstrate that determination to succeed every day, in all the ways you care for your family." She waved her arm broadly. "In all you give to our cause."

"Thank you for that." Sophie clutched Coop's arm to her side and began leading them back. "Credit to your Massachusetts roots, possibly, but I am heartened by such free thinking, particularly coming from you. Women deserve equal opportunity to live the lives they wish. Not marrying at my age, I know I must frustrate Papa sometimes, as your sister frustrated your mother, but marriage is a choice for me to make, not a requisite for enlistment."

I could not agree more.

Sophie blew out a breath. "Forgive me for rambling so. I had simply sought insight into your family, your twin. The opportunity to speak my... Well, I should not have run off, speak—"

"Of course, you should." Coop tugged her arm closer. "That's what our chats are all about. Time well spent, learning to know you, Miss Bauer."

Sophie glanced at Coop and shook her head. "You *do* impress me, Private Samson."

Back in the bustle of activity, Coop watched her cut a huge block of cornbread and wrap it in paper, then produce a small crock from a crate by the wagon. "This has a sturdy ring you can attach to your belt," she said, "instead of lugging it all the way back. And please don't eat all this cornbread and leave nothing for Tim."

Grinning, Coop tied the crock at her hip. "Could I stop by another time?"

Too soon wouldn't be smart, but...tomorrow?

"Please do. Any time."

Coop willed her nerves to settle. Standing like this before Sophie, the impulse to caress her face pounded dangerously strong. Sophie's eyes, glittering as she smiled, had some undeniable, magnetic pull.

Coop swallowed hard, and whispered, "I miss your company already."

Did I say that out loud? Sophie's blush told her she had.

"Come back soon, won't you?"

Coop took a step forward, thankful when Sophie did the same. They reached for each other and the hug was friendly, brief, but long enough for Coop to know she was in trouble.

CHAPTER SIX

Assembly sounded at dawn, actually later than Coop or anyone else expected, because dead of night would have been considerably better than daylight for what the 19th was about to undertake. In an instant, the six-week respite became frenzied activity, packing gear and striking camp. But, thanks to the army's continued delay after Thanksgiving, Coop countered her anxiety with memories of subsequent meetings with Sophie. Remembering those hours in her company would keep her sane.

The Rappahannock awaited, and she cursed whichever officer had lost his sensibilities and volunteered the 19th to lead this crossing at daybreak.

"What," Tim posed as they hurried into formation, "you expected to decorate for Christmas?"

"You're the one who built us that oven. Hate leaving—"

"Was good, wasn't it?" He grinned but his shoulders sagged. "At least we had hot meals off it."

"And warmed our bones. Good job you did. I'll miss it."

Gear crisscrossing their overcoats, they lined up with the rest of the 19th and the 7th Michigan. The 20th Massachusetts was summoned to bring up the rear, which put hundreds of men at the edge of the road in one ridiculous bottleneck. Coop figured that, even in this poor light, the enemy couldn't possibly miss hitting such a plentiful target. She sighed hard, tried to force that from her mind.

"You have all your letters from home?"

"I do. Tucked away snug."

Coop could feel her most treasured possession between her shirts, almost at her belt buckle. A thin leather flap enclosed the small, matted tintype of her parents flanked by Cooper and herself. Other necessities were either stuffed into her knapsack or tied on top of it, rolled up in her bedding.

"Keep 'em dry," she said as they stared at the underbrush, knowing the black swells of the river passed by just out of sight.

"We best keep *us* dry."

Coop took a breath to steady her rising heartbeat. *If only we'd crossed weeks ago when we arrived, we wouldn't be facing rebs now, wouldn't need to take the town from them.* Everyone groused under his breath about Burnside.

Now, standing with her rifle resting on her shoulder, she mourned last night's failed effort to bridge the river. So many engineers had been picked off as they aligned the pontoons, she didn't blame them for refusing to continue, but now Burnside planned to throw the 19th and others right through rebel fire to clear the way. Her chest tightened at the prospect of a point-blank challenge.

"Y'know," Tim thought aloud, "if we'd drawn *daylight* picket duty a while back, me and you could have taken out those Mississippi boys over there."

Coop knew the keen-eyed Southerners in their floppy hats were a cocky sort, eager for more target practice.

Coop tilted her head toward Tim and kept her voice hushed. "Pushing a sandbox across the Rappahannock with them waiting up there doesn't thrill me."

"Fish in a barrel."

"Yankees on a raft."

"They say it's only four hundred feet, this narrow point."

"Just keep your head down."

Suddenly, two cannon batteries behind them erupted with covering fire, ten guns shaking the ground and belching smoke past them, through the woods, and onto the river. With orders to keep low, she rushed forward with her unit, through the brush, down the banking, and into the boat.

Packed in, kneeling and squatting, they shoved off and caught glimpses of the artillery's devastation on their objective. Exploding case shot sprayed cast iron marbles everywhere, kicked up dirt, shredded foliage, and splintered log breastworks. Rebel shooting paused, then came at a frenetic rate. Minié balls whizzed by, zipped into the water, snapped into the sides of the boats, and Coop, like her comrades, folded herself as far down onto her thighs as she could, rifle at her side.

Union cannon responded in full. Dozens of guns fired over their heads onto the banking and into the town itself. The bombardment set homes, barns, and shops ablaze, visible through the woods ahead, and the incessant pounding echoed off the river. But enemy fire continued from the banking, causing Coop to wonder where the rebs would retreat to, if the town was being demolished behind them. She banished the thought to concentrate on her own survival.

Crouched nearby, Pvt. Henry "Spud" Russet strained to drive their boat forward with a push pole off the river bottom. He was a Boston luthier, a devoted father of three, and she'd often marveled at his strength, and now willed him to heave harder, faster. His counterpart on the opposite side suddenly took a bullet in the eye and collapsed into the river. There was no time to reach for his body, nor was it safe. Someone grabbed his push pole and took his place.

Abruptly, Tim toppled against her hip and Coop spun to help.

"Just nicked me," he said, his voice clipped. Readjusting the bedroll over his shoulder, he grumbled, "Another hole in my blanket."

"'Cause you're just too damn tall."

Then Spud screamed and fell, both hands to his throat. Flattening Coop atop the soldier behind her, he writhed pitifully across her lower body, his warm blood soaking her leg. In seconds, his motion ceased and Tim and others freed her by sliding his body onto the boat's wooden deck.

"Damn them!" she cried, returning to her position. "And we can't even get off a shot."

Tim pointed to the sky. "Cover fire has stopped." He spared a quick peek over the soldiers ahead of him to the shoreline. "Less than fifty yards."

Lt. John Adams yelled at everyone. "Keep down!"

A minié ball sliced through Coop's cap and as it flipped off, she heard the man behind her gasp. He collapsed at her heels.

Coop's boat slipped into shallow water and Adams brazenly stood and slashed the air with his saber. "Bayonets!" He drew his pistol and set a boot on the forward rail. "Look at 'em run! Under a black flag, by companies now, have at 'em!"

Coop clicked her bayonet into place. Although relieved to scramble up this embankment free of enemy fire, she wasn't a fan of "black flag" rules. Men always interpreted it as freedom to plunder, and though she harbored a fiery anger toward these rebs, she knew her comrades would hold nothing back. Having watched helplessly as friends were killed for four hundred yards, her Yankee brethren would take vengeful advantage of such leeway.

Within five minutes, Coop had her first look at the popular market town of Fredericksburg, half of which lay in ruin. But the emptiness, the eerie quiet filled her with a trepidation she knew they all shared. The rebels had fled somewhere.

As they crept through the streets, Coop maintained a steady eye on the blank windows, rooftops, building corners, sensing an ambush at every step. And then gunfire came from all directions. Blue uniforms jerked violently, crumbled, spun down into the dust. She dove for cover.

For over an hour, fighting raged throughout the town. Union troops split into small groups, and Coop and Tim accompanied Adams as he led the sweep through the settlement, darting from building to building, kicking in doors, racing to every room in search of enemy shooters. She wished army training had included this "hide-and-seek" strategy, considering death could be waiting behind any door. But she preferred this challenge, relying on her physical abilities, to what she had endured thus far. Always seemed to her that those in-line battles, being a sitting duck striding toward blazing guns, simply surrendered her life to fate.

From an attic window, Coop pointed to the church steeple across the road. Two Confederate sharpshooters pinned down federal units desperate to secure the center of town.

"I'll take the one facing east."

Tim knelt by her side and they leveled their rifles out the window. "Ready?"

"Ready," Coop said, her eye glued to her target.

They fired in unison and both sharpshooters fell. Immediately, Union troops stormed the street and shops.

From their perch, Coop and Tim watched resentful comrades smash windows and shatter doors, and turn what was left of the town inside out. They emerged from buildings, hollering about victory, tossing paperwork and trimmings into the air. They claimed anything they could carry, either to use or to sell. A few clutched scraps of leather and other fabric, some carried leaking sacks of flour or their slouch caps full of loose goods like salt or oats. Some lugged stools, small carpets, even wooden shelving. One soldier ripped a broken door off its hinges and carted away the pieces.

Tim mumbled, "I could've used a new blanket."

"Let's go." Coop turned to leave, disheartened by the looting. "They're taking everything the rebs didn't. Poor shopkeepers are dead-empty now."

❖

Coop helped bring the last of the wounded into an empty house and would have headed back to her unit, if not for the nasty scuffle underway on the street.

A soldier of the 7th Michigan wrestled with a white-haired Negro, tried to tie his hands, and screamed about his lack of cooperation.

"Your reb master's loss is my gain, damn you!"

The elderly man deflected a blow to his stomach, and the soldier tackled him.

The sight threw Coop's memory back to her youth, and she stood mesmerized by the savage emotions playing out on the street. She saw her own father, wispy and soft-spoken, raising his arms in futility, and heard his voice crack in desperation as he struggled in vain to sway his eldest son from his ill-thought position.

She hadn't thought of Sonny in years and now saw him too clearly. At seventeen, he had disowned their family and set out to make his own way. Only ten years old at the time, she and Cooper had played with, learned from, and generally harassed their older brother as most younger siblings did, until his stubborn restlessness led him away, never to return.

"I know you shoot as good as Coop, but he'll be Father's lacky when I'm gone. You are better off helping Mother around the house. You're sure the spitting image of him, Cath, but be thankful you ain't Coop."

Sonny would be thirty-one now. She doubted he would even care to know that his parents and brother were dead. He had abandoned their family, after all; his feelings no longer mattered to her.

Here, this soldier from the 7th asserted himself over the runaway with as much righteous might as Sonny had thrown at their father. And, like her father had too many times, the Negro cowered beneath the younger, more physically dominant man.

The Michigander yanked the Negro's arms from across his face and punched him repeatedly.

"Stupid, boy! You'll do as I say!" They fell to the ground again.

"Leave him be!" Coop shouted, words jumping out of her heart.

Two others from the 7th arrived and looked on. "Another reb's runaway," one muttered.

"He's coming with me," the soldier in the dirt stated. He jerked the Negro upright, spun him around, and bound his wrists. "Good money in shipping back darkies like this one." He yanked him around again to sneer into his bloodied, wide-eyed face. "We got a few of you already."

Coop pushed at the soldier's shoulder. "You're no better than the damn rebs. Untie him."

"Take a walk," he said, and grabbed the man's arm. "This way, boy."

"I said, no." Coop shoved the soldier aside. "He's a free man. Lincoln said so and you know it." She hated that so many Union soldiers' motivation for war had changed since the Emancipation Proclamation was first announced. Their tolerance of slavery ground at her civility, her morality.

The Michigander pointed at her. "Ain't the law yet." He glanced at his mates with what seemed like an appeal for support. But a passing handful of soldiers then joined the scene, and Coop took a little strength in recognizing them from her 19th and the 20th Massachusetts. She cringed when one of her fellow statesmen stepped up and lightheartedly elbowed the 7th's irate soldier.

"What's one more?" the soldier from the 20th asked the group and encouraged the Michigander. "Go on. Take him."

"What?" Coop felt her face flame with outrage. "No! Untie him!" She glared at the 20th's soldier. "A Massachusetts man. You dishonor the claim, sir."

"Oh, shut your yap," he fired back, smirking. "Did you sign up to fight the darkies' war? Damnation, you didn't. We all joined for the Union cause. Just because Lincoln changed the rules mid-fight, doesn't mean he changed *our* purpose."

Coop stepped into his face, glad she towered over this haughty *Harvard* man. "The Union we fight for grants liberty to everyone! You somehow forget that?" She shoved his chest, he staggered back, and she pursued him. "You wanna *sell* this man?" She turned to the 7th's fuming soldier. "You, too? Seems to me y'both should be in gray not blue."

The Michigander seized the Negro's arm again and pulled him along. "I ain't playing games with no stupid Boston blowhard!"

"Stop!" Coop yelled. "He's a free man."

"Don't look that way to me," he retorted, not turning back. "Worth plenty."

Hefting her rifle to her hip, Coop plucked a percussion cap from her pouch and swiftly set it in place. She cocked the hammer and leveled the gun at him. Everyone backed away.

"You free that man or I'll take your foot clean off!"

Now he stopped and turned, an eyebrow raised at the sight. He pushed the Negro into the arms of his 7th comrades and stormed toward Coop.

Startled by his rapid approach, she lowered the gun barrel to the dirt just before he lunged. The harmless blast rocked the quiet street, and they fell in a heap, rolling in a dust cloud, fists swinging wildly.

Coop managed to split his lip with a punch, but his glancing blow nearly broke her nose, blinded her with pain. A hit to her gut sent the air from her lungs. As she doubled over, she slammed her fist upward, into his throat, and he reared away, gagging.

"You men!" a sharp voice cracked. "Break that up now!"

Firm hands gripped her arm and back and flung her to the ground. Her opponent similarly was laid off. Coop took satisfaction in seeing him dab at his mouth, pant as hard as she. Blood trickled from her nose and she backhanded it away, angry at herself, at him, at the divisiveness of this damn war.

A pair of officers stared down at them. Capt. George Macy of the 20th stood with arms crossed, while her own, Captain Weymouth, tilted his hat back and frowned.

"Both of you, on your feet."

Macy looked to the pair of his men nearby. "Untie that Negro. Regardless of our politics, gentlemen, our president prefers he be set free."

Coop knew the pro-slavery attitude or at least an indifference to the practice permeated many Union regiments, but she wanted an officer—especially an officer from staunchly abolitionist Massachusetts—to deliver a severe admonition for this. The Negro rubbed his wrists and hurriedly bowed, thanked Macy, and then did the same to Coop. Silently, she wished him well as he ran down the street and into the woods.

She dusted herself off and retrieved her cap and rifle, awaiting reprimand from her captain. Regardless of purpose, fighting within the ranks was a serious offense.

Weymouth grilled her with his eyes, then turned to the Michigan soldiers. "You men best heed Captain Macy." He blew out a breath. "All of you, get out of our sight." Watching them leave, he added, "Samson, you stay."

She shouldered her rifle and stood by obediently, angered by their casual response to their men. The officers glanced at each other before Macy walked away, shaking his head.

At last, Weymouth turned to her. "Gun went off when you struggled?"

Coop couldn't tell if it was a question or a statement. "Yes, sir. I didn't shoot at him."

"Would you have?"

"Just toward his feet, sir."

"I see." Weymouth toyed with his beard. "Look, Samson, as we punch them back, the rebs are losing their Negro servants in droves, and a lot of our units are turning in the runaways. It's mighty difficult to balance, I'm afraid. But firing a weapon? That makes for a bigger mess." He waved his hand at the scene. "And with so many witnesses."

"Yes, sir."

"I should give you twenty-four hours on the wheel, or at least a month's night picket." He paced away, looking at the dirt, then paced back. Coop could deal with the night duty but not being lashed to the quartermaster's wagon wheel for any amount of time. Weymouth stalled, surveyed the street. "We'll probably be moving out tomorrow, once the whole army crosses, and I'll need your accuracy on the line. Consider your punishment delayed for now."

"Yes, sir. Thank you, sir."

"Thank me by taking out as many rebs as you can. They're gathering on the heights outside of town, waiting for us."

"Yes, sir. I'll do my best, sir."

He sent her a sideways glance. "Next time, just knock him out cold, okay?"

She saluted and thought he grinned as he returned it, before leaving her in the street.

CHAPTER SEVEN

Word traveled fast through the ranks the next morning: disaster had struck 3rd Division assaulting Marye's Heights, and now 1st Division was bogging down. Anxious regiments rumbled about who would be selected next, and spotting the courier hustle into Captain Weymouth's tent, Coop knew the answer. Minutes later, she and all regiments of 2nd Division's three brigades moved out, solemn and guarded, but determined to somehow succeed where two previous divisions had not.

"I thought General French was better than that," Tim muttered, his words almost inaudible as they marched toward the raging battle. "For the whole 3rd to get whipped..."

"I was rooting for Hancock," Coop said. "His profanity alone should've sent the 1st right over those righteous rebs."

Their snickering was interrupted by an exploding shell in the woods nearby. Everyone flinched as they marched. The concussion knocked over several ranks of men, but they staggered back into line.

"They've got our distance," Coop said, knowing enemy batteries had fine-tuned their aim to this location. She jutted her chin forward. "Those wounded up there. Hancock's men."

Captain Weymouth strode past shouting encouragement over the din of shells dropping ever closer to their column. Coop tried to concentrate on the intrepid flags ahead, their II Corps designation in swallow-tail blue and Massachusetts's white with blue state seal. As much as they represented the unit's pride, defiance, and bravery, they guided the soldiers through the smoke of battle, and were hard for *anyone* to miss. As always, she was glad *not* to be a color-bearer.

An explosion behind her sent shards of metal into the ranks and she glanced back to see four from the 19th strewn across the road, some screaming, some silent. Facing front, marching on, the view proved no better. Bodies littered the road, many moaning and reaching for help among others garishly disfigured. Stretcher-bearers hurried wounded men in the opposite direction; soldiers by the dozen hobbled to the rear, supported by others or their rifles. Coop tried to steel herself for what lay ahead and called on what remained of her good fortune to prevail.

The field of battle presented a scene she had hoped never to see after Antietam. Confederates lined an impressive stone wall that crested a rising, relatively narrow field some five hundred yards deep, all of it dotted with fallen blue-clad bodies. *Not again.* Before she could voice a thought to Tim, he offered his own.

"God help them *and us.*" He rubbed his bristly cheeks. "Not wide enough for us to get up there in line. Need to go…maybe by companies."

"Best of luck to you, my friend."

In one blue wave after another, broken into slimmer groups, regiments streamed onto the field on the double-quick. Immediately, destruction rained from the Heights, as well as from the right, and Coop wished the 19th would divert to take out that battery. But no such order came and they hustled forward, taking every punch the rebels delivered. Men of all regiments began to drop. Weymouth fell, shot in the leg, and she ground her teeth at the loss.

All her senses tingled in alarm, suffocating beneath booming cannon, whistling shells, exploding iron, and the dreaded hiss of sprayed case shot. Every few seconds, another comrade fell, some in multiples. Officers yelled to thin out their clusters.

An iron shard ripped through the hem of Coop's frock as she ran forward. *A narrow miss.* Ahead, solid shot plunged into a soldier, sending his arm whirling into the sky. The cannonball continued, ricocheted across the meadow and felled another man.

Return fire. Breach the wall. Coop concentrated on her objective, desperate to reach it.

A blast from a percussion shell kicked her in the back, slammed her face-down into the turf, breathless and stunned. Slow recovery of her lungs led to rising panic, but she fought off the tension and sucked desperately at the air. Coughing hard against its smoky content, Coop gathered her limbs beneath her, grabbed her gun off the ground, and hustled forward.

Another explosion staggered her, and Coop heard the ominous sizzle of case shot just as it struck. Fire blazed across her forearm, burned a patch along her shin, and tore through her wool clothing as if it didn't exist. Knocked to the ground, she counted her blessings. These minor wounds would bleed profusely but were a far cry from the shattered bones—or death—the cast-iron marbles were designed to levy.

When a cannonball pounded nearby, she scrambled out of its path and advanced. To her left, Captain Weymouth's replacement jerked sideways then backwards, shot in the arm and side.

The regimental colors called her, as they did every soldier, and she took a quick breath when they fell. But instantly, they reappeared. *Strength to the brave who show the way.* The courage of soldiers never ceased to amaze her.

Several yards ahead, Tim stumbled, and her heart leaped to her throat. But he forged on. The colors fell again, and not far to the right, the Stars and Stripes disappeared. From the rear, cries rang out with the explosion of more metal fragments.

She spit out the soot of smoke that blanketed the field. Breathing came hard and her legs wobbled with exhaustion. Easily within rifle range, she summoned all her strength for faster footwork and steady aim. And luck. She fired toward the wall and her target collapsed onto it. She crouched to reload, holding her breath that a shot wouldn't finish her where she stood.

Cannon continued the barrage and unending waves of smoke billowed over the wall, down onto the field. Rebels fired blindly, one volley after another, and minié balls peppered men and ground like a vicious New England hailstorm.

Suddenly, their banners reappeared through the roiling haze. This time, one lone color-bearer waved both the Massachusetts flag and the Stars and Stripes in the face of sure death. She scurried toward the colors, relieved to see many of the 19th still able to do the same. Closer now, everyone could see the color-bearer was none other than Lieutenant Adams himself, rallying the troops. Somehow, he ran forward to the remnants of a rail fence, and Coop and the rest of the 19th managed to join him at the only semblance of cover on the field.

Pinned only fifty yards from the wall, they hugged the ground and waited to be hit. No one dared rise to shoot. As it was, one man lifted himself on an elbow and then spun onto his back, a bullet in his forehead.

Coop pressed her face into the matted meadow grass, tried to concentrate on what remained of its naturally sweet scent, and listened to her heart pound. Even on this cold December day, sweat trickled from her scalp to her cheeks. Cautiously, she dragged her arm to her face and wiped it away. Her wounds burned with each brush of her uniform but, lying here surrounded by hundreds of dead and wounded, she considered herself beyond lucky.

What they would do now, however, worried her greatly. She wished she could commiserate with Tim. After carefully rolling her head left and right, she knew she wouldn't spot him, not with such a minimal field of vision. Resigned, she concentrated on recovering her muscle strength, and willing her frayed nerves to settle.

Time passed incalculably. Curling her body somewhat to scan a bit of the field behind her again, she quickly wished she hadn't. The sight was sorrowful. Thankfully, there remained men of their brigades fit to retreat, and they hurried back to the road and tree line as best they could, but just as many victims lay upon the field. And that was only the small portion of it she could see.

As firing from the wall dissipated, laughing among the Southerners could be heard across the meager distance to where the 19th hovered. Adams passed a whisper that everyone was to stay low and maintain their tenuous position, isolated as they were, with no possibility of forward or backward movement. Coop knew he feared—that they *all* feared—rebels would pour over the wall and make prisoners of everyone left alive. There would be little if anything they could do to repulse them. She wondered if her comrades trapped here had already loaded their guns. Hers was and she was thankful she'd been able to survive loading it when she did, because such motion certainly wasn't wise now. She didn't want to envision their defense when the rebels came.

Hours passed, and, mercifully, nightfall brought a stillness to the battlefield as both forces awaited any move by the other. She figured the hushed setting ate at everyone just as much as the numbing cold. She listened to the jolly ramblings of the rebels, cruelly intermingled with the desperate cries of the Union wounded and dying who lay unreachable between the lines.

Smoke soon rose from small Confederate fires behind the wall and had Coop yearning for warmth. Harsh whispers around her told of similar longings, and of fear of being captured or found frozen to the ground by dawn.

"Samson!" Adams grunted under his breath. Coop slid her cheek over the frosty grass to see him. He waved her to where he lay behind a post.

Hoping most Southerners had dozed off, she dragged herself around two sleeping comrades and the final ten feet to his side. He pointed beneath the fence rail toward the enemy, and whispered, "There."

Coop straightened her head and peered into the dimness. A rebel crept soundlessly down to a wounded Union soldier.

"He touches that man, you pick him off."

With guarded movement, Coop slid her rifle up her side and set a percussion cap in place. She took aim from her prone position and followed the rebel's progress. She sensed Adams sighting right along with her, as well as everyone in the regiment still awake.

The wounded man raised a beckoning hand to the approaching rebel, said something in a failing voice. Coop concentrated on sighting the rebel's chest. She wouldn't miss. Too many rebs pilfered fallen Union soldiers for money, food, or souvenirs. Not this time. She cocked the hammer.

But he swung a canteen from his hip, cupped the Northerner's head, and gave him water. Several drinks, before carefully setting the man's head back down.

Coop looked to Adams and found him just as astonished as she. The rebel moved on, providing water to another Union man, and then others, until he emptied all four canteens he carried. Coop eyed the Southerners watching along the wall, and when the reb hopped back onto his side, no one said a word to him.

"Well, don't that beat all?" Adams said on a breathy sigh.

Coop put her rifle down. "Wouldn't have believed it if I hadn't seen it myself, sir." She rubbed her eyes. "The only decent thing that's happened in Fredericksburg."

Sophie brushed back the hair tickling her cheek and fed more wood to fires beneath the kettles. She checked the closed iron pots inside the fire rings, found the bread ready, and carried each pot to a large stump. She'd been laboring at this for hours now and longed for sleep. The uprooting and hurried resettlement at 3rd Division took much of the society ladies' energy, and now the wounded pouring into camp demanded whatever the volunteers had left to give.

A surgeon interrupted his brisk walk between the large hospital tents to grab a ladle of coffee.

"Thank you, madam," he said before drinking.

Sophie winced, watching him swallow the hot liquid. "Careful, Doctor."

He shrugged. "No time," he said, scooping another. "Night time is a savior, I guess. We're withdrawing." He gestured with the ladle. "If you think you've been busy today, just wait till they all start back over the river."

Envisioning the inevitable onslaught, Sophie looked off into the darkness that shrouded the brush and riverbank. "We've lost?"

The surgeon grunted as he set the ladle down. "No one even got close. A horrible day." He wiped his mouth and mustache with his sleeve. "Going to be rough for us these next few days and nights." He pointed at the fire. "Thank you for that. Try to pace yourself, madam."

Now, Sophie understood the scope of activity around her. This would hardly be the brief layover she had anticipated and explained why all their means were being deployed right here. Hospital, cook, and recovery tents were going up everywhere. Nurses, aides, stewards, and volunteers hauled gear in every direction, distributing equipment and supplies, restocking as fast as they could. In the forest, chopping went on tirelessly, and heaps of logs for building and fires grew nearby.

Heading into a tent already filled with wounded, Sophie paused and turned her tray of soup bowls aside. Mrs. Schmidt barreled out and, as usual, didn't see her until the last minute.

"Oh, my dear woman!"

Sophie had to smile at the surprise on the wrinkly face. "We almost had ourselves quite the disaster."

"Indeed. That soup will be taken off your hands promptly by the eight or so gents in the rear right. They're whining a bit much, I dare say, considering the lot of most others, poor souls, and what you have should hush the din in there considerably." She examined Sophie's face a bit longer than Sophie appreciated, then urged her away from the tent opening. "You look worn, dear. I found myself a little respite an hour ago and you should do the same."

"Thank you, Mrs. Schmidt. I just might." She started for the tent. "It might be wise for everyone concerned."

Sophie had hardly emptied her tray when an assistant surgeon stopped her among the patients. "Have they instructed you ladies about the incoming wounded?" He blinked and the hopeful expression on his cherubic face seemed to waver. "I mean, the major wanted me to make sure you knew."

She glanced briefly out toward the operating tent where division surgeons were hard at work. "Knew what?"

"You're the Gettysburg group, right?"

"We are."

"You're to move to one-three."

"I'm sorry. I don't und—"

He squeezed his eyes shut and shook his head as if to clear it. "That is, you're assigned to 1st Division, 3rd Brigade. The facilities are being expanded."

"Oh. Well, of course. I'll make sure the others know. We'll be there promptly."

"Thank you, ma'am. I'll inform the major."

Sophie exhaled when she stepped outside and wondered where she would find the strength. But when she pictured the arrival of another brigade, at this, nearly the two o'clock hour, her heart ached for the men who would soon trudge back for care—and for those who could not trudge at all.

This *was* why she was here, after all, she pondered. It was why she made the excruciating decision to serve with her heart, and forego a return to family, forego Thanksgiving, and even risk spending Christmas in camp. Writing her decision to Papa, Karl, and Greta had been so difficult and taken several days, but she prayed they would agree that the army's need surpassed everything. She knew it would be hard for them to understand, for who could, unless they had experienced this firsthand. She awaited a return letter with great anxiety and wished the mail didn't take so long.

She located Mrs. Schmidt and several other Society workers and spread the word to begin packing, then managed to convince a teamster to move their wagons again, closer to where additional tents for her brigade were being hurriedly erected. After another hour of dishevelment, supplies were reorganized, and Sophie set about building multiple cookfires.

She had barely drawn flames, had just finished pounding in uprights to hold the kettles, when another assistant surgeon called her away to his tent. Someone else, offhand she didn't know who, would have to finish her setup. Hurrying to him, images of what awaited flashed through her mind. This was the surgical tent and she never relished being inside. It always took time to adjust to the smells, not to mention the agony of the wounded, the anxiety in doctors' voices, the grating of saws on bone. She wished she could return to the cookfires.

At the entrance, Sophie washed her hands in the basin, took the tray of bandages the surgeon offered, and spared a few seconds to inhale and exhale some fresh air, then moved inside.

A sea of bodies lay before her, the dozen or so cots swallowed up by soldiers prone on blankets or hay around them, and nearly all of them voicing something. Far too many were here, where surgeons did their work, but other tents just weren't going up fast enough to house all the incoming wounded. No man wanted to lie here, a captive audience to what happened on those tables.

"This way," the round-faced surgeon said, and led her through the maze of bodies. Stopping on a patch of dirt floor, he set down a pail of water for her and indicated the dozen soldiers in the immediate vicinity. "If you could dress wounds in this group, we'd be grateful."

"Right away," she answered, and knelt at the nearest soldier.

"It's my shin, ma'am," the man moaned. He ripped his trouser leg farther open at the bullet hole.

Sophie began washing the gaping wound, and although she still found the sight of exposed bone disturbing, she was relieved to see this one had not been shattered. "You left a chunk of you out there, didn't you?"

"Feels like I left the whole leg." He hissed as she applied lint padding.

"You're a lucky one. What's your name? Your unit?"

"Cpl. Jacob Hinchley, ma'am, 66th New York, 3rd Brigade, Hancock's 1st."

Sophie wrapped his leg and he twisted in pain. "Try to stay still, Jacob. Tell me about home."

"New...New York City's my home-hometown," he said through clenched teeth. "Y-you ever been?"

Sophie shook her head and offered a smile. "Can't say as I have. I don't know what I'd do with myself in such a grand place."

"Lots to do and...and see," he added, now watching as she tied off the bandage. "A crowded commotion but...a far sight better than here."

"No doubt."

"We lost Lieutenant Colonel Chapman first thing this morning, then Captain Wehle. He got us through Antietam, y'know. And then, Captain Hammell went down." He sat up, frowning while Sophie wrapped his torn trouser leg closed over the wound. "All we got is Lieutenant Derrickson now, ma'am, but maybe he's gone, too. I don't know."

Sophie leaned back and patted his shoulder. She tried not to look too deeply into his weary face. "Be strong, Corporal Hinchley. We need you."

"Yes, ma'am. Thank you."

She beckoned for an orderly to help Hinchley outside. "There'll be coffee, bread, and soup soon. You go out now and rest."

She worked her way through the others, hours passing unnoticed, except for complaints from her legs and back. She refilled her tray four times, moved from one patient to the next, relieved to send many outside to rest. The majority, however, required surgery, and three of them, amputations.

By dawn, Sophie sat on a log by the fire at the Society wagons. Beyond tired, she wiped her face with a wet cloth and finished a bowl of broth. Not much of a meal, and she had missed out on the latest round of bread, but she didn't have the energy to chew anyway. Nor could she continue to watch the endless stream of defeated soldiers still returning from the battlefield.

She climbed into the group's personal wagon, wrapped a blanket around herself, and stretched out among four other sleeping women. Mrs. Schmidt snored in the corner, but not loudly enough to keep Sophie from nodding off.

It seemed that in no time at all, a severe knocking and a man's coarse voice sounded at the rear of the wagon. "Ladies? We could use you now, ladies."

Sophie forced her eyes open. Sunshine glowed through the wagon's canvas. *A few hours' sleep is better than nothing.* Rustling and grumbling, the women tossed aside their blankets and tried to tidy themselves before climbing out. Priscilla, their organizer and affectionately appointed "sergeant," primped her mussed hair and folded her blanket properly, then turned from Mrs. Schmidt to Sophie.

"Felicity and Mary will be coming inside to sleep, so we need to get back to work. I believe we're to return to our originally assigned area this morning but could be moved again."

Sophie stood and stretched, bent and touched the toes of her dusty shoes. Her legs and back wouldn't appreciate returning to work so soon. She set her dress aside, its hem dark with dirt, the sleeves spotted with blood, and folded her corset on top. Down to only her chemise, she draped a long shawl around her shoulders and joined the other ladies at the wash-basins behind the wagon.

She'd helped cordon off this private area for their toileting by stringing old blankets between trees and around the washbasins' stumps and clotheslines. Soon they would have to start doing this in a wagon, out of the brutal chill, but today, she was grateful for the sunshine.

Tending to one's personal hygiene proved a constant challenge, regardless of the weather, and Sophie understood why even the men usually took to the woods to relieve themselves rather than use the long ditches they dug. Those latrine trenches couldn't be set far enough away. Ironically, the December cold helped minimize the stench and insects; in warmer weather, they had been intolerable and put too many people down with illness. She fervently preferred the forest to such facilities.

Sophie viewed toileting, in general, a particularly difficult chore, especially with only a washcloth, bar of soap, and small towel. Early on, she shipped back most of what she had brought because there simply wasn't room in the wagon, and then, upon leaving Antietam, had to toss out what remained because of wear. Now they had what they'd scrounged and were lucky to have it because deliveries from the north had become as unreliable as the weather.

She washed her face and neck, discretely lowered the top of her chemise to wash her arms and bosom, and then quickly dried with her little towel. Then, when opportunity allowed, she reached beneath her chemise, changed her drawers, and hurriedly washed her feminine parts. *Someday I will enjoy a tub again.* When finished, she washed cloth, towel, and undergarment and hung them to dry, and rushed back inside to dress. Thankfully, the aprons Priscilla handed out today were freshly laundered, although they were the last of the lot. Sophie was glad her turn as laundress wasn't due for two days.

Felicity had prepared porridge for the ladies before she retired, and Sophie enjoyed every mouthful in her tiny bowl before they packed and rushed to their original location. She liked this spot better, where 2nd Division, 3rd Brigade was camped. They were in among the pines where lines could be strung and the forest floor was far less dirty and easier on her feet. However, she found that her fire rings—in which she took great pride—needed some restoration. And, within moments, "Sergeant Priscilla" began directing construction of their privacy screen.

A regimental nurse assigned them tasks and Sophie soon saw herself loaded with coffee tins, entering a crowd of wounded sprawled outside the medical tents. She reminded herself that she did, indeed, just finish four hours of sleep, while her weary bones insisted that she had not.

Small groups straggled back across the river throughout the day, companies, they were called, supposedly around one hundred in number but now so much smaller. They had been among the first into battle, men of the first and third divisions, and she hoped the size of these early returns didn't reflect the total cost. That would tell a disastrous tale.

By late afternoon, the army showed in full retreat. Sophie gathered that it had used this day after engagement to gather itself and then used nightfall to withdraw because, much to her dismay, beleaguered brigades in both divisions began pouring in. She also heard that 2nd Division, last into the fray, would be recalled last.

Sophie took advantage of her late sleep shift and dozed off to images of haggard men shuffling in broken formations. She knew they would still be filing in when someone woke her in a few hours. The 2nd probably wouldn't start arriving till well after that, and she sighed at the hours of work ahead.

With exhaustion taking hold, thoughts of that division lingered. It encompassed Coop's brigade and she fell asleep hoping to hear he survived this ordeal.

CHAPTER EIGHT

L aura woke her with a slight hand on her shoulder. "Time to rise, Miss Sophie."

"Already?"

Laura pouted as she nodded. "We've had our three hours, I'm afraid." As she refastened the tip of her long red braid, she offered a grin. "Best hurry before our sergeant calls on us."

"True. Priscilla is nothing if not dutiful." Sophie sat up, hating to cast her blanket aside. "They're still coming, I assume?"

"Oh, yes, ma'am. Talk outside is of many more arriving."

Sophie imprinted that information at the back of her mind, 2nd Division, 3rd Brigade, as she promptly straightened herself. *Coop.* She freshened her face in the washbasin's icy water and took in the cacophony of camp noise.

Nothing had changed since she'd been at rest. Officers, stewards, teamsters, all shouted while the wounded cried, wagons clattered, and mules protested. Around her, everything continued in relentless motion. She immediately sought coffee at the cookfire and stretched her back as she watched the horrific parade transporting the injured, dying, and dead.

At the riverbank, she found an unending procession of infantry making way across the pontoon bridge, scarcely lit by torches. The line stretched up the far banking, all the way back to town. A dark and dreary production several days in the making, she thought, and wished she knew how to heal such defeat. She believed it to be the deepest wound these brave soldiers would endure.

Stretcher-bearers struggled continuously, heading to tents or simply open patches of ground near them with bloodied, often disfigured soldiers.

Two drummer boys, hardly older than fourteen, rushed past her to join the effort, and Sophie tried to imagine them leaving home at their age. Maybe they ran away. For this.

She focused on her task and filled a tray with cups of broth, then made her way to the wounded lying outside the assigned tent. They called out every sort of request as she served one after another. Their injuries were wide-ranging, their spirits fatigued and beaten. She'd witnessed destruction at Antietam but never such a defeat of morale. Talk was sour, demoralized. Comrades whispered about faulty Union leadership, about temptation to abandon the cause.

Hearing that Gen. George Meade's effort farther south had failed for lack of support, and that Major Gen. Darius Couch had sent brigades of regiments in futile waves against Marye's Heights, Sophie was hard-pressed to muster encouraging words.

She reloaded her tray with bandages, lint, and other medical items and returned to the field. An assistant surgeon and a lieutenant walked among the men, sorting by need. Glancing around, Sophie thought the sorting impossible.

"Miss Bauer?"

She turned at her name and nearly dropped her tray. "Coop!"

He limped closer, a bedraggled but welcomed sight. What looked like dried blood blackened the light blue of his left leg, and dust and meadow grass covered his frock from shoulder to hem—part of which dangled behind him. But, cap askew, he smiled through the dirt on his face and extended a grubby hand.

"Sophie." He stood his rifle on its butt and enclosed her hand with both of his. "You never fail to make me smile."

"Oh, Coop. My goodness."

"You look wonderful."

"And I'm happy to see you're well."

"Some nasty scrapes but..." He squeezed her hand. "The fates were kind."

"Come." Sophie waved him to a nearby tree but could tell he was reluctant. "Sit here so I can look at these scrapes."

"There are far more who—"

"Sit. I'll be quick."

She knelt beside him, her heart still reveling in the first happy moment in far too long. He pulled up his pant leg to offer his wound.

Sophie frowned hard at the elongated swath carved along his calf. Fresh blood glimmered around the edges, trickled from beneath what had already dried over the surface, and followed a preexisting trail into his stocking.

"Did a bayonet do this? A saber?"

"Case shot. Miserable things go everywhere." He grimaced when she turned his leg slightly. "Stings and still bleeds." He lifted his left arm. "Same over here, I'm afraid. Like a burn. But mostly, they're nuisances."

"Nuisances? They'll be a tad more than that once I start cleaning them." She set to work, unwilling to meet his eyes. Somehow, she had to accept the fact that Coop stirred her senses, even the most sensitive ones, and she couldn't stem their reaction. Certainly, there wasn't time to ponder it, but she vowed to find some, because there was just something about him that spoke to her. No man had so reached her before.

He jerked and inhaled sharply when she dabbed the dirt and woolen thread from his wound.

"Sorry," Sophie said just as Coop said it, and she forced her concentration back to the task at hand. Focused on being thorough, she couldn't help but notice the undamaged skin around the raw tissue, so pale and smooth, even with grit clinging to the hair on his leg. Such remarkably fine hair for a man.

She prepared a roll of bandage. "Show me your arm next, won't you?"

Coop swung his cartridge box and canteen over his head, then shrugged out of his knapsack and bedroll, and unbuttoned his frock. He withdrew his wounded arm and held it out.

Finished wrapping his leg, Sophie took his wrist and moved up what had once been a white shirt sleeve to look at his forearm. "Good gracious, this is just as messy." Blood caked over the broad gash and had dried in a path through more of his delicate hair to the back of his hand.

"Sophie, I shouldn't keep you. I…I appreciate this special treatment, but there are—"

"It's not special treatment."

Coop raised his arm with her hand on it and looked directly at her. "Yes, it is."

"No, it's not," she countered, equally determined, and urged his arm down to rest on his leg.

Okay, yes, it is.

But she wasn't about to stop. "I wish all the wounds here were as easily tended as yours."

Thankfully, Coop stopped pressing the subject. He studied her every move and probably a lot more of her as she worked. She could feel his eyes stroking as tenderly as fingers, on her hands, neck, and face. Those intimate sensations tingled again. "You nearly had both arm and leg broken beyond repair."

He didn't respond. The concept probably unnerved him.

"We should have written more to each other," he said at last, his voice shy.

She looked up, taken by the little smile, the slim lips pressed tightly together as if holding back words. "You write eloquently. Has anyone ever told you?"

"I do? Well, no. That is, I don't write much."

Now, Sophie sat back on her heels, recalling her own debate about writing at all. She wouldn't mislead such a sweet man into thinking something might come of their correspondence, not when he was alone in this world, not when her heart ached for female companionship.

"I'm sorry I didn't write more, Coop. I promised to, I know, and I'm embarrassed—"

"Don't be. Nothing could be better than our times together. And this is better than a letter."

Sophie swallowed hard. *Is this what friends do?*

"It's hard to see being hit by cannon fire as a lucky stroke," she said, "but I'll admit that saying hello in person outweighs a piece of paper."

"Agreed." With his free hand, he drew Sophie's drooping shawl farther up her shoulder. "Do you have warmer clothes? There's enough sickness in the army, Sophie. Don't let it claim you, too."

She had to smile as she worked. "I'm cautious of that, yes. Thank you. And I do have a heavier shawl as well as a coat, but I'm in such constant motion, in and out of those hot stuffy tents, leaning over cookfires. I'm usually warm enough."

"Hm…Well, good. You have enough blankets in your wagon? I could get you more if you'd like. The quartermaster owes me."

"That's awfully kind of you, but you mustn't worry. So far, the weather has been bearable."

"It's hardly that, Sophie. We were frozen to the grass the other night before we slid away. Surely you could use another blanket." He sat forward urgently. "You know, if you set a bucket of hot rocks among you, it would warm the wagon."

Sophie grinned at him. "Well, that sounds worth trying. Now sit back, Private Samson, and let me work." His thoughtfulness and eagerness to please had her pulse running high. He definitely wore his heart on his sleeve. "How is Tim?"

"He's well, I think. He was unconscious for a while and they hauled him into a wagon, but I heard he walked most of the way here with a headache. I haven't seen him for two days and it's hard to get word with so many injured."

"They say it was bad out there, the worst of the war."

"You can only ram your head against rock so many times. Never seen such slaughter. Needless. And all for naught."

"To think, three days of it."

"No, really all in one day. Yesterday, we grouped in town and thought Burnside was just crazy enough to send us back at them in the dark."

"After such loss, he'd do that?"

"Nobody wanted to believe it, not a night assault and not with our numbers down so badly. We just returned to the field to cover the retreat." He pinched his eyes with his free hand, inadvertently smeared the gunpowder on his cheek. In Sophie's opinion, the streak, combined with his other smudges, lent him quite the roguish air. When he spoke again, his voice was distant, tired, and he did not look up. "We withdrew all the way. Lost it all."

"But I'm glad you made it through, Coop. I know the army will recover from this." Wishing she had something less hollow to say, she slid his tattered sleeve down over his bandage and watched as he redressed. "I know that's easy for me to say, but we all believe in the cause and must let it drive us forward."

He pursed his lips as if he doubted her. "Burnside practically invited Longstreet's entire corps to dig in all nice and comfy over there." He draped his canteen and cartridge box over his shoulders and sagged back against the tree, cushioned by his knapsack. "The man's a fool," he said in a low grumble, and reset his cap. "You'll find no one disagrees now. Probably not even Mr. Lincoln himself, once he hears of this catastrophe." Suddenly, he leaned forward and pointed far up the Rappahannock. "Did you know, the man stayed at headquarters, never once stuck his head out to see what was happening? Never even crossed the damn river."

"Hush," she whispered, a hand on his arm. "You mustn't be overheard."

Maybe recalling his words, Coop stared back at her for a long moment, and Sophie felt the heat of his agony seep into her. She wished she could assuage the despair, erase the disillusion.

At last, his eyelids lowered. "You're right. I'm sorry I—"

"Do not apologize," she said softly, and bent closer. "Talking's good for the spirit, and I believe you and I are good at it, but men are whispering of desertion now. Morale is terrible."

He nodded as he looked around. "I think Ol' Burns will end up paying for this one."

Cloak covering her shoulders, Coop sat cross-legged on her bedding, thankful to be back in one piece, back in the stockaded tent they abandoned before the battle. Coop endured these days of army recovery and tedious drilling, particularly with the vile bayonet, by appreciating the accompanying hours of prolonged rest.

Not only could she devote more than a half-minute to cooking salt pork for supper, but she had time to enjoy Silas Benning's harmonica at the 42nd New York, and even tolerate the Harvard boys long enough to listen to Red McIntyre's poetry. Playing cards lost its luster because she often won, and gossiping around the fire held little appeal, although she did learn tidbits of fact sprinkled in those conversations. Today's highlight had been hearing of Lieutenant Adams's promotion; she had witnessed his heart-stopping bravery, a flag in each hand amidst the tumult and smoke, and knew the image would never leave her. Nor would she forget the carnage.

But she found comfort in thoughts of Sophie, the main reason Coop appreciated this abundance of free time. In contrast to her relatively subdued army encampment, the medical area still bustled, treating battle wounds and a multitude of ailments, and Coop pictured Sophie scurrying among surgeons, nurses, stewards, and other aides, relentless at her labor. Her hair would be awry, her apron soiled, her winning eyes weary.

From her brief visit several evenings ago, Coop knew Sophie had little free time to socialize, but felt they enjoyed those few minutes together, shared over warm cider. It had been a snowy night, as cold as tonight, she thought, and hoped Sophie didn't regret her decision to stay with the army this long. Christmas with family, home cooking, and a real bed had such allure, and Coop believed Sophie's presence spoke volumes about her character, her dedication to the troops and the cause.

Coping with memories of her own past Christmases seemed a bit easier this year, occupied as she was with preparing a gift for someone who mattered. Last year, Coop's first without her parents and brother, had been tortuous, and she would have bypassed the holiday completely if Tim hadn't included her in his reverie.

A stick fire in her tent's tiny rock stove provided just enough warmth to keep her fingers nimble, and by candlelight, she checked the materials she just acquired at the sutler's wagon. Grumpy Mixon typically overcharged her for the three blankets, one for Tim, and two others for Sophie. Coop planned to create a useful gift for her by attaching the light blue flannel blanket to the one of dark gray wool.

She paired the blankets and began stitching them together, gathering the yards of material onto her bedding to keep it off the tent's dirt floor. Sewing brought back recollections of hearth-side work with her mother, as many years spent creating and mending as Coop had managed to put toward shooting and riding. Stitchery always served a cathartic purpose, allowed her to escape into youthful, fanciful thoughts and grown-up dreams. And as a soldier, helping her comrades with mending kept the lurid images of war at bay and allowed for those of Sophie, sitting beside her, sipping coffee, her voice as sweet as her manner.

Tim called her name from just outside and lifted the tent flap. "There you are. What's that you're up to?"

"A Christmas present." Coop's candle flame bucked against the sudden breeze.

"You're sewing. As if our entire company hasn't given you enough things to mend."

"Guess I'm good at it." She shrugged. "Look, squeeze in if you're ready, but drop that flap. The stove's going in here."

"Have to call on Mother Nature first," he said, and dropped the flap. "For your Sophie, isn't it?"

"She's not *my* Sophie. But yeah. She works hard for everyone and won't be home for Christmas."

"Her family will probably send her presents. I hope to get a box from mine in the next few days, and we'll eat well, my friend."

Coop believed Tim to be a husband and father of the highest caliber, he cared so much for others. He knew Coop had no family, that there'd be no one sending presents, and here, as they approached another holiday in camp, he planned to share his bounty with her again. If they ever received a furlough near a decent town, Coop vowed to treat him to a dinner he'd have to crawl away from.

She liked hearing the uplift in his voice. Knowing his family stayed in frequent contact empowered him, and that bolstered her spirit. "You think Mary will send her fruit cake?"

"I'm counting on it. Nobody makes a better one. It's what I married her for." She sensed him grinning at his own words, standing out there in the cold. "You know," he went on, "she might send some jars of jam, and maybe those pickled onions I told you about."

"Stop. You're making me hungry."

Coop jumped when he jerked back the tent flap again and leaned in. He scanned the blankets across her lap.

"So, when you giving it to her?"

"I don't—"

"Less than a week 'fore Christmas, Coop."

"I know. I know."

"Y'think she'll give you something? Like a few good Christmas kisses?"

She jabbed her thumb toward the outside. "Go do your business."

He laughed as he left Coop with excited thoughts.

My *Sophie.*

"Christmas kisses."

Coop chortled as she worked. "Wouldn't *that* be something? I'd kiss you right back, Miss Sophie Bauer." She shook her head at herself. "I shouldn't, because…Well, just because. But be crazy not to, and downright impolite. But *you,* pretty Sophie, you shouldn't kiss me because…" She stopped and stared off at the candle. "But it'd be downright impolite if you didn't."

She shifted on her bedding to make room for Tim's return, and tried to fold the yards of fabric into some semblance of neatness. With a little luck and another night's work, she'd finish this project in time, thanks to the needle and thread in her housewife, the tiny kit of basics given to everyone by the Christian Commission many months ago. She'd have to buy more thread from the sutler but looked forward to that moment on Christmas Day when she'd see Sophie's eyes dance with delight.

A thrashing noise behind the tent distracted her. She looked up at the canvas ceiling when something scratched across it. Then, Tim's grumbling sounded from the front.

"There!" he proclaimed and poked his head inside. "Ain't much to look at, but…Get out here and see what I got us."

Coop set her blankets aside and joined him. The top five feet of a pine tree sat stuck in the dirt outside their tent flaps, a little tilted, but nonetheless upright. Hands on his hips and a smile lifting his beard, Tim studied his acquisition with pride.

"A Christmas tree," Coop declared and clapped him on the shoulder. "Excellent job."

"Better than that branch the 42nd put up."

"Sure is." Coop walked around to examine the tree's far side. "Bet those Harvard boys find themselves something bigger."

Tim snorted. "The mighty 20th will probably have one shipped to them."

"Y'know, we'll have to decorate it with things that won't be stolen."

"The 42nd strung hardtack on theirs. No risk with that."

"We could hang a few worn socks on ours. They'd be safe."

Tim turned to her abruptly. "Thought you were gonna mend them?"

"I will. *After* Christmas."

"Hm. There's talk now of moving out after Christmas, so ol' Burns can get even."

"Cross the river again?"

"A ways farther up."

Coop folded her arms and shivered. "In the dead of winter." She shook her head. "I'd rather stay right here till the crocus bloom, thanks very much."

CHAPTER NINE

Sophie added wood to her cookfire and watched Coop stack rocks into a knee-high crescent around it, touched by his effort to direct more heat toward her wagon. Most of her fellow Society workers dozed inside now, having sent off some of the last transport wagons to the area hospital, and Sophie relished having this Christmas Eve to herself—and Coop.

His arrival through the thin veil of falling snow brought a smile to her heart. He said regiments in his brigade had spent the entire day drilling, which made his mile-long trek across the snowpack to her all the more special.

"Do not try to convince me you ate supper, not that I care to even *picture* what that might have been." Sophie placed a bowl of hearty vegetable soup into his hands and sat beside him at the fire. His eager acceptance pleased her immensely.

"Most generous of you, madam, but ye have little faith in military cuisine."

"*Ye* speaketh truth," she replied with a light laugh.

Sophie hummed along to a distant Christmas carol, content to watch the flames as he ate. She admitted to herself that she treasured his company, his easy humor, and thoughtfulness, and that his presence brightened this special night in ways beyond those of a good friend. She'd miss him when the Society ended its term of service next week. And she fretted over how to break the news.

Coop pointed to the army encampment. "That's Captain Pierce," he said, and smiled into his soup. "One of many decent voices in Mr. Lincoln's army, I do say. The pride of New Hampshire."

Sophie looked toward the settlement of tents, silhouetted against the glow of hundreds of tiny fires, and listened to the smooth tenor sing "It Came Upon A Midnight Clear." "I don't believe it's ever sounded more beautiful."

"Do you sing at home with your family?"

"We sing often, actually. Years after Mama died, Greta and Karl developed sweet voices that she would've loved."

He set the empty bowl at his feet and turned to face her. "I bet they're hard workers like their big sister."

Sophie tilted her head. "Most times. Compared to others around us, ours is a small farm but every part of it is necessary so we all work hard at it. But those young ones do get into their share of mischief."

"I'm sure. You're lucky to have them."

"Absolutely. I often consider the day one of us finally leaves the nest. Being the eldest, that probably will be me."

"If they're like you, they'll carry on strong."

Sophie chuckled. "Oh, I believe they will, but will *I*?"

"From what I've seen, there's no doubt you'll succeed in whatever you do. I bet your brother and sister are just like you."

"Our German heritage comes with a strict upbringing, but we're all rather independent and stubborn. Papa prefers that Karl learn by his side and that Greta master domestic chores, although I've managed to persuade him otherwise." Sophie sat back, knowing her pride was showing. "Karl is only nine but bakes a biscuits-and-ham supper that would make Mama smile. And Greta, she's a finagler, she is. Just twelve years old and she can haul our produce to town and wrangle prices as shrewdly as Papa."

"And big sister Sophie holds everything together, doesn't she?"

"Well, let's just say I've tilled, cleaned, cooked, and hammered enough nails in my day. I'm a firm believer in being at least a little skilled in as many things as possible. Thankfully, Papa has seen the wisdom in that. And I'm pleased that Greta and Karl respect and lean on each other's skills."

"So admirable of you, Sophie. You foresee owning a farm yourself one day?"

"Oh, maybe. A small place, possibly, one I can handle into old age."

"I must admit, I'm surprised to hear you speak of leaving, of... solitude."

"Well, I expect one of my siblings will take over our homestead once Papa's gone, and I can't imagine staying, living the life I choose and intruding on Greta's or Karl's family."

"I understand that," he said. "I'd often pondered the same things, that is, until the accident. Our homestead is mine now, to work and live as I choose." He doffed his cap and settled it back over his hair. "Daunting, sometimes."

"I have no doubt you'll do well, Coop." Sophie flicked snow off his shoulder and gave it a little squeeze. "You just make sure you get back to it in one piece."

"Doing my best. But even if I leave a leg here in Virginia, I'm going to make the homestead work."

"Your family would be proud."

"I try to do right by the Samson name. I left the homestead in the hands of a dear family friend my father met many years ago. He's done well for himself and his family and has a little place above his *very successful* leather goods shop in town. He and his boys have helped us on the farm a lot over the years, so I think Father would have approved of leaving it in his care."

"Sounds like he would. I imagine your enlistment was difficult for him."

"Well...I know they were surprised—and worried."

"To see an only son go off to war must be..."

Coop poked at the coals and added another log. He seemed lost in thought. "They'd already lost a son, you see."

"An older brother passed?"

"His name was Sonny. Well, that's what we all called him. Honestly, I don't know of his well-being today. He set out to seek his fortune at seventeen, and only once did we hear from him again. I think I was maybe fourteen when he sent his only letter, a farewell of sorts. Sonny had started his life anew, was interested in the frontier, but offered nothing specific. And as the years passed, we became a family of four."

"My gracious, Coop. You haven't heard from him in...ten years?"

"Fourteen since I've seen him."

"How sad that he left you all, the family that raised him. I'm sorry to hear this."

"We were his typical pesky little brother and sister, and he meant the world to us, although we struggled mightily whenever he and Father fought. They had many violent clashes, about chores, politics, patriotism. Sonny made Mother cry all the time, which was why a part of us was glad when he left. Of course, we never thought he'd shun us, but as years passed, we knew he was gone forever."

"Do you, today…Um, considering your parents and sister are gone, do you—"

"Do I wish to reconnect? No." Coop shook his head firmly and jabbed at the coals. "He'd hardly be an acquaintance today. And one I can do without."

Sophie patted his shoulder as she tried to muster a response. "I've no doubt you have developed far more solid acquaintances in the army—and are better for them." She went to the wagon and returned with a small tin flask. "Here," she offered, removing the cork and tipping it over Coop's empty coffee cup. "For the holiday."

"Well," he said, grinning. "Thank you kindly. Can't say as I ever expected the Ladies' Aid Society to offer this kind of spirits to a soldier."

"We know officers have their share of whiskey," she whispered, leaning closer, "but we have our own brandy." She poured some for herself and set the flask aside.

"Much appreciated." Coop reached out to the scarf covering Sophie's head and hesitated. "Allow me." She wiped off the snow with light strokes of her hand. "Hopefully, we won't get buried where we sit."

"Not with such warmth from this wonderful fire you've built."

She drew her gaze from the fire and caught him studying her hands. His had delivered a comforting touch that still simmered along her nerves, a pleasant sensation she didn't know how to handle. She raised her cup and his eyes followed, glinting with firelight as they met hers.

"A toast?" he said, and an easy smile grew across his lips.

A most handsome man, Sophie mused, and gentle and polite, so remarkable as to lead her to question her heart as never before. She would miss him dearly, would worry about his safety. And more than any friend she had ever made, she would yearn to see him again.

What does this mean?

He held his cup against hers. "I remember the night you aptly named us kindred souls, Miss Sophie Bauer. Let's toast to them."

Sophie pressed her cup to his and let her smile convey her pleasure. "Indeed, Private Samson. To kindred souls. May we lend the full measure of devotion to our hopes and dreams."

They sipped the brandy and Coop groaned with approval. "Warms the soul, it does. Thank you."

"The pleasure is mine."

Coop gestured around them and sighed. "So many wounded have been transported out, the hospital camp has shrunk. Your work must be less stressful."

Sophie nodded, sensing the time had come to deliver her news. "The army now is capable of handling the hospital work. The surgeon-in-chief notified all aide groups two days ago." She sipped more brandy. "Ours will leave for Gettysburg on Saturday."

"This Saturday?" He waited for her nod, then turned back to the fire. "Oh."

"Priscilla, our leader, she chose the date. She says we could reach home by the New Year." Coop looked at her over his shoulder and Sophie sensed his skepticism. "I don't think we'll make it in time, either. Several groups will leave together, and the train could be thirty wagons long, so, considering the snow and all..."

"I think you're right. I'm glad for you, though. All of you. You've worked so hard for us, endured so much, missed out on holidays with family." He turned back to her and smiled. "Really, I'm happy for you. But I'll miss you."

Sophie felt her throat tighten. "Depending on the army's needs, I could be back for another tour of duty." She had only vaguely considered that option and questioned her motivation in speaking it aloud now. She poured another round of brandy for them. "But, Coop, most certainly, I'll miss you, too. I...I promise to write."

Coop sent her a sideways look. "I promise, too."

Sophie tapped their cups together. "An accord between us then," she said, and they drank. "The army is staying here for the winter, isn't it? Have you heard anything?"

"Just rumor, as always. We might cross the river again. Depends on whether ol' Burns gets his whiskers in a twitch."

"Oh, Coop, I hope not. You're all settled in now. Why—"

He shrugged. "I can write you when I learn anything."

"Oh...Yes. Write. Good."

A deep pause fell over their conversation, and Sophie felt it weighed as heavily on him as it did her. Sadness, a tinge of finality crept into her bones and she blinked several times to keep tears at bay. She watched as he finished his brandy in one gulp and stood, snow sprinkling off the back of his overcoat.

"I probably should sneak back now." He pushed the embers around and stacked several logs on her fire. "That should provide you some warmth for a while." He removed his cap, slapped the snow off it against his leg, and wiggled it back on. "Sophie," he began, turning to face her, "tomorrow's Christmas Day. May I call on you?"

Backlit by the fire, his expression couldn't be read, but Sophie figured she was better off not knowing what it revealed.

"Of course you may. Friends should share Christmas Day whenever they can." Impulse nearly drove her to hug him. Instead, she brushed the snow off his shoulders.

Coop caught her hand and edged closer, and she could smell the scent of snow and earth off his coat, the sweet smell of brandy on his frosty breath.

"I do not wish to overspeak," he whispered, "but I think of you often and always with a smile, a rousing beat to my heart. I'd be most grateful to share even a few minutes with you tomorrow."

Without a second thought, Sophie set a palm to his smooth cheek, his jawline firm and cold. "And my heart would pain me, Coop, if my Christmas passed without you."

His shadow enveloped her when he bent forward, and, without reservation, Sophie lifted her face and welcomed his kiss. His chilled lips drew lightly on hers and hovered against them for a moment before kissing her once more.

She opened her eyes as he drew away and recognized a longing that rang deep into her soul. She squeezed his hand, wished he would kiss her again, felt the instinctive urge to kiss him. But Coop stepped back with a hint of that easy smile.

Sophie took a deep breath, as subtly as she could. Yes, she would miss this *man* terribly.

CHAPTER TEN

Coop and Tim devoured half the fruit cake Mary sent as they ran to answer roll call on Christmas morning. And lined up on the snowpack in forty-degree sunshine, they whooped with everyone else, elated when officers canceled the day's drilling. Activity jumped into high gear, as Coop fried real bacon and the smells of cookfire breakfasts blanketed the encampment.

Enthusiastic socializing filled the morning hours, with troops crowded into groups, opening boxes from home, and sharing discoveries and spirits with friends. Tim presented Coop with two pairs of socks and summarily ordered her old ones deposited in the latrine sink an acre away.

Coop gifted him the blanket to replace the holey rag he insisted she mend every week. He hugged her hard and handed over a jar of pickled beets—adding that they had to share it.

Before long, loud crazy games broke out between companies, regiments, and entire brigades. After the 19th lost an abbreviated marathon to Battery B of the 1st Rhode Island artillery, Coop and Tim redeemed their regiment by outshooting the Harvard boys and then trouncing their 1st Brigade counterparts. Everywhere, raucous entertainments prevailed. Coop spent a light-hearted hour drinking sugared coffee and watching officers of the 72nd Pennsylvania catch a greased pig someone had found roaming the woods.

After all the lunch lines had filed through the cookeries, liquid spirits spread seriously throughout the camp and activities took a wild turn. Coop, Tim, and several others downed less than their share before heading out on foraging detail. No one disputed the necessity of firewood, but on this day, Coop and the others hoped to make short work of the chore.

She hacked a log in half and dragged it onto the pile, knowing she couldn't ignore Mother Nature's calling any longer. Deeper into the forest, she found a secluded spot to relieve herself, and, after repeated, keen scans into the brush, unbuckled her belt, unbuttoned her trousers, and dropped her drawers.

The distant sounds of the work detail carried through the woods, but some raucous laughter sounded too close for comfort. She hurried to finish as the voices grew louder, drunken revelers, she thought, and her nerves tightened.

"You got my spot!" one yelled, obviously having seen her.

Hurry.

"Warm it up for us!" shouted a second man. "Let's plant us one big patch of lily-white Union asses in these Virginny woods!"

Coop yanked up her drawers as they thrashed their way to her. "A man can't find privacy in this entire godforsaken state!" she griped at them, tying her drawers as fast as her fingers could work.

Reaching into his trousers, the New Yorker eyed her private area. "Y'get everything collected in there, slick?" The nickname used by a few from the 42nd always unsettled her, reminded her that some fellows took note of her clean-shaven face and slim build.

His friend laughed over his shoulder as he squatted. "Maybe slick don't have enough to pack." The men laughed.

Buttoning her trousers, Coop sent the first man a knowing look. "You best watch yourself. Next thing you know, your friend will take an interest in *your* parts."

He looked sharply at his comrade, eyes narrowed.

Coop adjusted her belt buckle and hustled back to her detail, her heart rate returning to normal.

Tim waved her to help him finish limbing a fallen tree and she joined in, eager to expend nervous energy. She hacked off branches and alternated with his cuts to chop the log into manageable lengths.

The wagon loaded, they led the horse back to camp and Coop worked her way through the crowd surrounding the "beauty pageant," staged by several costumed, highly inebriated "ladies." Although she initially found the frolicking comical, she soon soured on the production. No doubt they had looted the embellished hats and dresses from innocent Fredericksburg families, and the demeaning demonstrations, suggestive gestures, and exaggerated dancing and mocking, just became insulting.

"Ho, there, Samson. Merry Christmas." The cheerful voice came from Henry, her absurdly smart young friend in the 20th Massachusetts. A high-bred Harvard-educated fellow, of course, he nevertheless displayed enough dignity to accept defeat each time she beat him at cards. At times, Coop wrestled with opinions espoused by this twenty-one-year-old with deep Democratic roots. Opposed to Lincoln's politics, Henry did fervently believe in preservation of the Union, but professed that slavery should be allowed to wither away on its own, and Coop often engaged him in lively debate.

She offered a handshake. "Same to you, Captain Abbott. How's that arm?"

"Eh, slow healing, but it will suffice." He offered his tin cup. "Here, have some."

"Much obliged." Being friends with an officer cost her some ribbing from fellow enlisted men, even though she kept things as confidential as possible. Privately, they bypassed military protocol altogether. She sipped his refined, smooth bourbon, and handed back the cup.

He gestured to the pageant and the laughing crowd. "They're outdoing themselves, this holiday. Maybe a bit too much fire water."

"A lot gets through the mail at Christmas. Did your father send you that good stuff?"

"He did." Henry dipped his head. "Any time you feel the urge, Coop, look me up. There's plenty more."

"Thanks. I prefer to go easy on the spirits, keep a clearer head."

"Commendable. I usually rein in the temptation as well, but there's an ample supply among our officers."

Coop wasn't surprised. Like Henry, many of the 20th's soldiers claimed well-to-do Boston families who made sure their sons enjoyed comforts from home. Thankfully, Henry wasn't one to flaunt his status and she liked that about him.

"We're putting up an extra table tonight and you're welcome to join us," he said with a nudge of his elbow. "Come with a full pocket, because I intend to empty it this time."

"Bah. I'd join your game with empty pockets to be filled," she answered with a laugh. "But I'm visiting a friend tonight and will have to clean you out another time."

Eyeing her sideways, Henry smoothed his thumb and forefinger over his slim mustache. "A stroll to the hospital camp as I've seen you take before? Visiting a lady friend, perhaps?"

"Nothing escapes you. She's leaving with the Gettysburg volunteers on Saturday, I'm afraid."

He straightened into his command posture. "Then, by all means, go."

"I doubt I'll see her again, so…"

"One never knows, Coop. The aid groups come and go for varying periods. You intend to correspond, at least?"

"Yes."

"Very good. They are a special breed those ladies, full of heart, and if she has moved yours, do not fail to respond." He clapped her shoulder.

Laura showed Coop to a seat by the fire, then bid her adieu. The little camp at the Ladies' Aid Society appeared deserted but especially tidy, and Coop sensed it was prepared for tomorrow's departure. The thought weighed upon her spirit.

She jumped to her feet when Sophie emerged from the wagon, angelic in a crimson dress Coop had never seen before. An evergreen shawl provided the perfect backdrop to the glimmering hair that cascaded over her shoulders.

Coop caught her jaw dropping and cleared excitement from her throat. She absently ran her palms down the front of her frock, hoping the effort she had lent her uniform showed, that her buttons and buckles shone, and that she had mended her frock in decent fashion.

"You are a Christmas angel, Miss Sophie Bauer."

"You flatter me, Private Samson." Sophie reached for Coop's hands, drew them to her bosom, and heat raced so fast to Coop's head, she thought she would faint.

"Y-you deserve it and so much more. Sophie, you're…" So many complimentary words came to mind, Coop couldn't choose one. "You are lovely beyond words—and I'm beyond honored."

"And I'm so very happy you could come." She led Coop around the wagon to a three-walled tent where a small table sat with place settings for two. "I've made a supper for us that I hope you'll enjoy."

"Supper?" Coop took in the porcelain plates and cups, the white napkins, the tiny bowls of apple butter, salt, and pepper. "Look at all this. It's spectacular. You did all this for…for us?"

"I most certainly did. We Gettysburg ladies are quite resourceful." A bottle of wine in one hand, Sophie slid the cups across the table. "Now, if you'd please pour, I'll fetch our supper." With a cute little grin, she was gone.

Coop hurried out of her knapsack and set it aside. The gift inside could come later because, right now, none of this seemed real. By flickering lantern light, she poured the wine. Where did all this come from? And where were the other ladies? Obviously, Sophie had gone to considerable lengths. Coop couldn't help but believe the attraction she felt was mutual, and that sent a tremor of apprehension through her. *How dishonorable am I?*

Sophie set a cast iron pot on a stump nearby, removed the lid, and sent steam and aroma floating over the table, flooding Coop's senses. Sophie spooned plump biscuits out of the pot and set two on each plate, then added scoops of roasted chicken, potatoes, onions, carrots, and turnips, all in a lusciously thick gravy. Coop knew she gawked and tried not to drool. Not only had she not *seen* such a meal in ages, *never* had one been prepared for her to share intimately with another woman.

Finally, Sophie joined her, beaming across the table, a vision Coop believed stolen from her personal fantasy.

"I-I can't begin to thank you, Sophie. You are an amazing woman."

"Hush, now. This was a joy for me, Coop. I wanted to make your Christmas special, and this was something I could do."

"All this…Well, it's no easy feat. I raise a toast to you. You've made this a *very* special Christmas—for us both." She lifted her cup and Sophie set hers against it.

"And I raise one to you, for your selfless friendship. Despite all a soldier endures, you've helped me cope with some extremely difficult times."

"That's worked both ways," Coop said.

"It's what friends do," Sophie replied, and they drank. "Now, don't you dare let this meal get cold. Eat."

Coop took her time but devoured the feast with serious intent, conscious of her manners yet all-too-aware of how Sophie expected a famished soldier to behave. Throughout, however, the lantern-lit vision opposite her begged for attention.

"I see that… It looks like your group is prepared to leave tomorrow."

"We're ready, yes." Sophie's eating slowed and she poked at her food. "Everyone's eager to return to family."

"I'm sure. Do you think you'll be back?" Hoping to disguise her longing, she waved her cup toward the wagon and winked before taking a sip. "I mean, how could all this ever lose its appeal?"

"Believe it or not, there's a great deal that I'll miss...and knowing that the war is still being fought while we're at home..."

"With any luck, we'll wait out the winter months, maybe even stay camped right here."

"You don't think General Burnside will try again to catch Lee?"

Coop emptied her plate and sighed. "Our numbers are down badly, with all the wounded and desertions, so I'd say that's unlikely. We think we're in for a boring winter camp."

"Well, at least that's safer." Sophie took Coop's plate and refilled it. "I want you to stuff yourself, Private Samson. I enjoy seeing you eat."

"Lord, Sophie. I can't remember when I've eaten so well."

Sophie added a scoop of vegetables to her own plate before sitting down. "I'm glad I had the chance to do this. I've missed cooking a full meal."

"Well, I'm happy that things will return to normal for you, Sophie, but you'll be sorely missed."

"When the need arises, another group will take our place. I'm sure."

"No one could take your place."

Sophie set her fork down and dabbed her mouth with her napkin. Her silken complexion darkened in a blush. "You're very sweet to say."

"I'll miss you." Coop slid her cup against Sophie's. "I'll miss your gay spirit, your kindness. You are an inspiration, Sophie. Forgive me, but... you're as beautiful inside as out."

"Hush, please. Oh, how I will miss you, too." Sophie wrapped her fingers around Coop's on the cup. "I confess that through all our travails thus far, through the harrowing and the tragic, I have never been as touched by a soldier as I have by you. Our acquaintance has been so unexpected, so remarkable to me, and I treasure it deeply. You, Private Samson, just might be the most thoughtful, the most honorable person I've ever met."

Coop swallowed hard against the dishonor in her throat. *Is this the time to lay my "honor" on the table?*

"Do you think we'll meet again?" she dared ask.

Sophie's twinkling eyes fluttered closed and she sat back in her chair. "I suppose it is unlikely, isn't it?"

Coop could only nod. If this was their last moment together, there was no need to bare any secret, least of all one that would spoil the memory of such a glorious Christmas night.

She rose from the table and retrieved her knapsack.

"I have something for you, something I hope you'll find useful on the journey home and, maybe, thereafter."

Sophie turned in her chair and watched. "Something for me? But that's not necess—" Her eyes widened when Coop pulled out the folded blanket. "Good heavens! A blanket?"

"Merry Christmas, Miss Bauer." Coop set it in her hands and Sophie stood to unfold it.

"It's so thick and warm. It's wonderful!" Her eyes flashed with surprise as she turned it over. "And so soft! Oh, Coop. Thank you." She clutched it to her chest.

"I lined that side in flannel so it'd be warmer and softer."

"*You* stitched these together?"

Coop straightened. "I did. Massachusetts Yankees are resourceful, too."

Sophie swung the blanket over her shoulders as she rushed forward and wrapped Coop in a hug. Coop seized the fleeting intimacy and drew her closer.

"Something to remember me by," she whispered. A hint of lemon reached her as she pressed her cheek to Sophie's hair. She closed her eyes and relished the scent, the feel of Sophie's firm torso, the lithe form warm against her chest.

"Remember you?" Sophie said, her tone incredulous. She leaned back, made no effort to relinquish her hold. "Always, Coop. Always."

Coop took one more chance. She lowered her face to Sophie's, brushed the tip of her nose with her own, and when Sophie didn't withdraw, mustered her bravery and set a tentative kiss on her lips.

In that instant, the outside world vanished, reality, their tent, the war, her honor. Absolute tranquility hummed the length of her spine to somewhere her feet were supposed to be. She lost contact with them yet somehow felt quite grounded by a fulfillment she had never experienced. And feeling Sophie return the kiss, Coop fought back the onset of wondrous tears.

Sophie rested her cheek on Coop's shoulder. "We *will* correspond. Won't we?"

"I think we'll both do a better job of it this time."

"Last time, our correspondence fell shamefully inadequate." Sophie raised her head and looked down at Coop's brass buttons, laid her palm over one. "I can't identify my feelings right now. There are just…just so many…but something says my days would not be complete without some connection to you."

Coop cupped her cheek. "How have you managed to speak my thoughts?"

"I don't know what it all means, Coop, but…it's true." She leaned up on her toes, surprised Coop by initiating another kiss.

Coop drew her in, and the sheer thrill of holding her this way, snug and tight, made Coop's arms tremble, her knees weak. In all the hours spent dreaming of such a moment, Coop hadn't come close to conjuring such a heady state. A heart swirling in joyous surrender, she figured.

They kissed longer this time, and as Sophie reached farther around Coop's neck, Coop splayed her palms across Sophie's back, grazed a hand between her shoulders, another to her waist. Her heart thrummed, yearning flared through her chest, her hips, sensations she felt embed into her soul.

Sophie withdrew just enough to speak against Coop's mouth. "When this rebellion nightmare ends, you'll visit me in Gettysburg before going home, won't you? Please say you will."

CHAPTER ELEVEN

Sophie hadn't expected difficulties adjusting to life back on the farm. The habits of wagon life, the regimen of hospital duties, the cooking, washing, and sleeping routines lingered for days, as did emotional memories, the horrors and the triumphs. But none proved more disruptive than Cooper Samson.

A simple morning coffee brought his delight to mind, and Papa often caught her adrift in thought. Published lists of the dead and wounded had Sophie commandeering every newspaper from Karl, who spent hours consuming every exciting battle article. And Greta simply couldn't let a day pass without teasing her older sister about the *special soldier's blanket* on Sophie's bed.

Sophie sat on it now, a comforting place on this cold rainy day, made infinitely warmer by the envelope she held. As with Coop's previous letters, she could feel his hands, broad and strong along the fingers as they traversed her back. How earnestly they must have held pencil to paper in writing this, she pondered, as earnestly as he held me to his chest.

Recalling the sheen of his frock buttons made her smile and she could feel one still, as if ingrained in her palm where she had set it upon him. A gesture she initiated. The moment she conveyed intimate feelings. The moment she kissed him. *Him.*

Sophie thrust the letter onto her lap and dropped her head back with a frustrated, bewildered sigh.

Since when do I reveal my private thoughts to a man or...or seek his kiss? Since when do I daydream over a man's touch, recollect with such fondness the press of his mouth to mine?

She had kissed men before. Preferred not to, never enjoyed it, but she had done it and preserved her reputation as "one of those sad cases who needs a good man," the subject of back-of-the-hand gossip about her spinsterhood. Secretly, she valued that reputation, for it allowed her the freedom to live as she chose—eventually with a woman "companion," a fairly commonplace arrangement in and around Adams County. However, she kept highly guarded her desire for a woman to stir her senses the way the *Bible* insisted only a man could and should. *My fulfillment will come with a woman, not a man.*

But she'd welcomed Coop's kiss and then kissed him of her own volition. *Why?* Her reputation wasn't at issue. *Would anyone's kiss have been as enjoyable, considering their circumstances?* She doubted that. The idea of such intimacy with any other soldier made her cringe.

Sophie looked at Coop's letter and her vision blurred.

"What is it about you, Cooper Samson?" She pulled a handkerchief from her apron pocket and wiped her eyes. "You've got me all kinds of confused, you know." She leaned back against the headboard as she unfolded the letter. "Just please be well."

January 24, 1863

Warmest greetings, Sophie, and well wishes to you and your family.

Well, you might be interested (or amused) to learn that we here are repeating ourselves. It has taken half of January, but we expect to leave familiar Falmouth soon and deal with the Rappahannock again. It is possible ol' Burns will have us hiking this time. Considering we have had snow for several days now, please wish us fair weather and lots of luck.

Not too chilly inside as I write, snow outside is six inches deep and melts through our roof, but the little stove is a blessing. Tim and I will be sad to leave it and our stockaded tent-works behind. He sends his regards.

I was happy to hear that your group was properly welcomed home by townsfolks at the hotel's special Christmas/New Year soiree. Thoughts of all that food made me hungry. So glad you received lovely much-deserved gifts.

Speaking of gifts, I hope your blanket is proving warm on these cold nights. I pass the time with thoughts that you are cozy and content. And I frequently relive memories of our glorious Christmas supper, your beautiful smile by lantern light, the intimacy of you in my arms, and the tenderness of our kisses. The finest of Christmas gifts. No soldier was luckier than I.

Please take care and remain safe and well. Eagerly awaiting your next letter, I remain,

A kindred soul,

Coop

"And no lady thrust into this ghastly war could have received more heartfelt companionship," Sophie murmured. "It seems our crossed paths have created a truly unique intersection, Private Samson, but…are we not destined to continue along our individual roads? Who knows what the future holds, when or where a special woman will claim each of our hearts?" She folded the letter and returned it to the envelope. "Yet, I somehow feel you will always have a special place in mine."

"Are you talking to yourself again, Sophie?" Greta held the bedroom door open an inch and spoke through the gap. Her adolescent grin said she hadn't overheard much.

"And are you eavesdropping again, Miss Busybody?"

Greta waltzed in and sat beside her on the bed. "So, what's new with Cooper?" She eyed the envelope on the night table. "I already saw that you got another letter today."

"And it's private."

"Well, is he okay? Or maybe he got shot up and wants you to come back and nurse him."

"Quit your scheming. He's fine. He thinks they could be going into battle soon, though."

Greta stretched out, her arms crossed beneath her head on the pillow. "How do they keep warm out there, in tents in the woods and snow?"

"They've been camped in one place long enough to fashion little log walls to put tents on, and they build small ovens out of rock and mud. Some are just outside the openings and others, like Coop's, are in a corner with a chimney."

"And then they just march off and leave them?"

Sophie nodded. "When the order comes, yes."

"Do they have to march at night?"

"Sometimes."

"But what happens to the wounded?"

"My, you're full of questions, aren't you?"

"Just curious."

"Well, the wounded who are well enough to transport—and that is *not* luxurious—they are sent off to big hospitals, then the medical camps pack up and follow the army."

"Like you and the Ladies' Aid Society did."

"Yes. We set up wherever the army medical people need help. Another group will leave from here once the army sends word."

"Hm. So if Cooper is going into battle soon, will you be leaving again?"

"I won't be going with the Society next time."

Greta sat up, worry etched across her face. "You won't? But what if Cooper gets shot up?"

"Stop saying that. The Society will go, if and when it's needed, but I'm going to pass this round. My group was away for almost four months, or did you forget? That's twice as long as most groups stay, and I'm needed here at home, too, remember. I thought you missed me."

Greta lurched forward and squeezed her around the neck. "Oh, but we did! We missed you terribly. I'm glad you'll stay home this time." She lay back and swiped at an errant tear.

Sophie stroked her cheek. "I certainly missed you all terribly, too, Greta, but my work was vitally important."

"I know. Everyone talks about the rebellion."

They looked up when Karl entered, eating a hunk of buttered bread. "Even at school, they talk about it," he said. "Papa says it's important like family."

"He's right," Sophie told him as he sat on the bed with a bounce. "Imagine if our town was its own country and we all, us families, were the states. We live our own little family lives, but together we make up Gettysburg. Well, America is a collection of different family-states, too, and we work together so every person can live the life they want. Back when our country was new, all the states came together, they *united* as a big family, and agreed to a list of rules called the Constitution. That's called democracy, our American type of government."

Karl nodded as he inspected his bread and took another bite. "Democracy. That's what Papa said."

Greta sighed. "Well, I think Southerners are wrong. You don't go back on your word. They agreed to join with us so they shouldn't have their own government too."

"And I agree with you, Greta, but Southern states think they're entitled to do otherwise because they claim Northern states aren't being fair. The problem is, if states go solving their disagreements this way, we will wind up with no country left at all. It would be as if you moved away." She turned to Karl. "And then you. Then me. We'd get nothing done as a family, would we?"

"Wouldn't be much of a family," Karl said.

"That's exactly right. And if families moved out of town, would there still be a Gettysburg? No. We should be getting together, working on our disagreements." She raised a finger to make her point. "Remember, though: deep inside, just like blood makes us family, we're all Americans to our roots. That's why President Lincoln insists the states stay united."

Greta's thin golden eyebrows lowered with concern. "But Southerners are stubborn."

Sophie withheld a grin. "Well, when you believe you're right…"

"Well, I think they're mean to start a whole war over it, making our soldiers go down there and fight them when we should agree to talk—"

"And they started it," Karl said, quick to remind her. "They shot at us first."

Greta turned sharply to Sophie. "And they *are* mean. They *sell* Negroes. They make sure Negroes get no democracy. How can they treat people like they're not people?"

"It's an old way of living, Greta, one that some still believe is right."

"But it's not right," Karl injected. "Papa says rebels hitch up Negroes like oxen to till the fields." He shook his head. "I don't see how a different skin color makes that right."

"Me neither," Greta added.

"Slavery has always been wrong," Sophie said. "We didn't put a stop to it right from the start when we should have, back when we agreed in the Constitution that all men are created equal. And so, nowadays, it has come to be that Southern states with their big plantations need the workers to—"

"But they ought to hire them, fair and square," Karl stated. "All farms around here do that. When you need help, you hire somebody, like Papa hires Mr. Robinson when he needs help."

"The South is fighting against being told what to do."

"I hope our soldiers set them straight." Greta sat up. "You know, last fall when you were away, and the churches had that big party for the Negroes in town? Remember when I wrote you about it?" Sophie nodded. "It was such a grand time because everyone came, the Robinsons, the Wickers, the Trembleys. We celebrated the freedom proclamation President Lincoln wrote. Did I tell you that Mr. Wickers has relations who are still slaves in Alabama? He talked about seeing them someday."

"It is a sad thing, Greta. So many Negroes can't escape. Hopefully, that will end—"

"When we put down the rebellion and make everyone talk sense again."

"Yes. But, unfortunately, many, many lives are being lost."

"Know what Tassie said?" Greta asked, back on her elbows. "She said Mr. Trembley's brother was a slave in Mississippi and he stowed away on a steamer and escaped. He wants to fight with us, she said."

"I'm happy for him. And our soldiers could use the help."

"Is your friend Cooper a good fighter?" Karl asked, brushing crumbs off Sophie's blanket.

"One of the best in his regiment."

Greta brightened with a new thought. "Do you think we'll meet him someday?"

"We'll see, honey. He might pay us a visit on his way home."

Coop wiped her hands on her frock and flexed her fingers around the rope again, ready to clench it with all her strength. She hitched her shoulders, wiggled her shoes into the mud until they disappeared, and lowered her head against the wind-whipped downpour.

The sergeant shouted, "Heave!"

Along with a dozen men, and a dozen more on their own rope, she threw her weight and muscle into moving the brass Napoleon cannon, but it wouldn't budge. She toppled sideways into the quagmire, some others fell flat.

"Get up, you bunch of hogs! Move this gun!"

Again they tried, as they had for two hours now, but, like the five cannon in line behind it and, no doubt, the scores of guns, limbers, caissons, and wagons farther back along their train, this Napoleon sat hopelessly entrenched up to its wheel hubs.

Coop spit through the goop splattered across her mouth and struggled to free her feet from the suction. "This is hopeless."

Tim swore under his breath. "This isn't going to work, either," he said, pointing to the artillery crew. Desperate to free their prized possession, the gunners added a third team of horses between the pull ropes.

On command, the teamsters shouted and whipped the horses, and Coop added her effort to the manpower hauling on the ropes. Horses sank, men slipped, and angry, exasperated orders blew away in the deluge.

"What is it about this damn river?" Tim shouted against the torrent. "Took an act of God to cross it last month, and it'll take another one now."

Coop scraped handfuls of mud off her elbow, hip, and leg, slinging each one into the wind with disgust. "If it'd only stop raining for a day or so."

"Well, I've seen three days of rain but never like this." He waved at the riverbank ahead. "Figures. This time we have the pontoons when we need them, just can't get to the confounded river." He squinted ahead and then to the rear. The miles-long wagon train snaked into the darkness in both directions. "Well, they're out there somewhere."

Coop shivered. Standing around in wind-driven rain, soaked from head to toe, and caked in mud had her itching to do something. Anything. "Has to be close to freezing now," she said, and shrugged deeper into her frock. "Back home, this would be a blizzard."

"Shh. Don't even conjure the thought of snow."

"It'd be easier to get around in snow." She pulled her feet from the ooze and reset them, only to feel herself sinking again. A gunshot from somewhere in the rear took everyone by surprise. "Revolver," she said, and nodded when a second shot sounded. "That sutler Mixon, the weasel, bet he shot his old mule. He always said he would."

"More than a few will have to be put down in this."

"Look. Now, they're sending up the 7th to help." She snickered. "You think adding another regiment will get us moving?"

Coop scowled when the order finally came to settle in for the night. She silently cursed the Napoleon as much as Tim did outwardly, flabbergasted that as many as one hundred and fifty artillerists and infantry couldn't move one stupid gun. At least they'd managed to save all eight exhausted horses that ultimately had been brought to bear.

Beneath the trees, she and her comrades unrolled their rubber blankets and laid down. They covered themselves with wool blankets and canvas sheeting and curled up, eager for whatever warmth they could generate.

But morning came within a few hours and Coop hustled to light a cookfire, glad to be mobile and not rotting away, cocooned in muddy wet wool. Raising the fire took longer than usual in the steady mist, and everyone had to gulp down lukewarm coffee when they were ordered back to the line.

She swung her axe with purpose, her entire brigade transformed into lumberjacks. The four regiments deforested the vicinity, collecting logs to corduroy the road, a chore usually left to the pioneers or engineers for bridging streams and ditches. Word had it that this morning every division had a brigade in the woods because there were miles of road in need of this resurfacing.

The discouraging news traveled. Coop learned of over-eager divisions knotting into massive traffic jams as they bogged down on inadequate roads. She knew the less ambitious lumberjacks among them chose slimmer trees and wasn't surprised to hear that such construction buckled beneath tons of cannon and wagons.

"If it weren't so maddening, it'd be funny," Coop said, standing back as she dropped another tree. Tim and others closed in to help her trim the limbs and haul it to their pile.

"According to the New York skirmishers," Tim said on a sigh, "Johnnies are all along the far bank already."

Coop stretched her back and grimaced as the mist turned heavy. "Here we go again."

"Sounds like it. For miles. They said reb sharpshooters are laughing at us, being stuck like we are."

"If we cross against them, they will need to pay."

"Those boys were pretty good last time, but I still say you and me, we would've done far better shooting, had the shoe been on the other foot."

Coop removed her cap to scratch her head and peered up. "Rain's coming back, too." No sooner had she reset her cap, the downpour began. "Y'think ol' Burns has any idea what's going on?"

"Why would he change now?"

"Right. I think my toes have shriveled up."

Tim laughed. "One less thing to wash."

"Wash? What's that?" She'd give everything she owned for a warm bath. The last time she cleaned herself was the night before they broke camp in Falmouth, now more than a week and ten tons of mud ago. It had been just a pan of cook water she and Tim boiled for those four quail eggs, but it felt great and did the trick. He even disappeared for a card game, which allowed her time to give her privates a good cleaning. But a bath?

Coop sliced into another tree trunk, her mind on hot water, honeysuckle soap, and a soft clean bed. *How long has it been? That furlough before Antietam in early September.*

She swung the axe again and smiled. That Virginia redhead, Marietta, had provided a surprising evening of insatiable, if rather unpolished kisses. But a hotel room to herself, a luxurious bath, and good food dominated that furlough—until Coop's monthlies arrived on the last day.

As had become her strategy since enlisting, Coop relied on small well-placed towels and frequent visits to the privy to hide her monthly condition. When the furlough ended, she reported back to her unit well stocked for months to come.

That was five months ago, and she considered herself fortunate that her monthlies had come and gone before this march. *Such a plague upon women. We endure so much more than men will ever appreciate.*

She stopped chopping to catch her breath and immediately thought of Sophie's energy and enthusiasm, all given so freely, so eagerly to others. *You battle through your own tribulations. I would return that care and concern, but I doubt you would take me as I am.*

Christmas memories of sweet, lingering kisses threatened to sweep Coop away.

"Samson." The call came from so close she jumped. "Let's go. We're moving out."

Tim approached from her other side. "Sarge caught you daydreaming."

"We're moving out?"

"Back to Falmouth. Where else?"

"Ah. Guess another day of rain made Burns take notice."

"Oh, this is another notch on his failure belt. Bet he isn't the only general who noticed."

"Well, I hope so because this running up and down the river isn't getting us anywhere."

Tim chucked her arm. "Seemed like it took you somewhere just then. Where'd you dream off to?" He leaned against her shoulder. "Gettysburg?"

Coop grinned. "You think we'll ever get up that way?"

"Pennsylvania doesn't want grubby hordes stomping through its fields, so it's not likely...unless, of course, you run away to see your gal."

"Hm. I'm not the runaway type."

"You're an honorable man, Samson. I know that." He gave her a pat on the back. "I'm sorry, my friend, but we need to keep the war in the south."

CHAPTER TWELVE

May 27, 1863

My dear Coop,
Almost a month has passed since your last letter and I worry for your well-being. June is not far off now, the spring season is bursting with all its bluster and promise, and I feel you would share my delight at such flourish. I sincerely hope this correspondence finds you well and able to put words to paper.

Newspapers still recount the army's profound difficulties at Chancellorsville and listings of sacrifice continue to appear in each edition. I read them all with great apprehension, not wanting to see your name.

Please know that Greta, Karl, and Papa send their best wishes to you and smile fondly upon our friendship. Like me, they eagerly anticipate your letters, although I do keep them to myself and only recount your tales.

Papa has us all hard at work here, with the rye and wheat doing well and the bountiful vegetable gardens in constant need of tending. He added a third milk cow to our little menagerie last week and has hired on Eldus Robinson to help repair our hay loft. Eldus is a supremely blessed carpenter, much in demand in town, and we are excited to have him. Twice he has brought along his little family to pass the time with us and Greta has made a sweet friend of Tassie, his daughter, as have I of his wife, Rose.

Speaking of Greta, you should be most flattered to know that she has taken to swooning about the Yankee soldier who writes me letters. She finds you quite romantically mysterious. She is growing too fast for her twelve years. Karl fancies himself a sharpshooter, having heard of your accuracy—from whom, I simply cannot imagine, and has shown talent playing the banjo, as well, thanks to Eldus who is a superior musician. And Papa reminds me constantly that he needs to shake your hand for being the gallant soldier you are. I confess that I blush with pride each time.

As I said in my last letter, our Ladies' Aid Society left for Chancellorsville at the end of April, and I am told it arrived at the peak of the battle and will remain with the army for several more weeks. Felicity Ruggles from my group is with the Society again and has my explicit instructions to keep a watchful eye for you. Of course, it is my deepest hope that you never need to avail yourself of the Society's medical assistance but know that she is a special friend among those at the ready.

As for myself, I have become an attentive, eager student of quilting under Rose's wise guidance. We visit each other often and she encourages me through the sewing with laughter, delicious little cakes, and sweet tea. She is possibly ten years my senior, a hard-working mother, wife, and seamstress, and hers is a friendship, a confidence I treasure. I am quite proud that her Negro family is one of us. Adams County does have its dissenters, but I am thankful to see nary a sign of rebellion here in town.

Also, I announce that, finally, I completed the parlor rug that has taken nearly three years of my life. Hurrah! With the weather so warm now, I was glad to finish the project, one my dear mother always urged me to attempt, and now it will adorn our worn floorboards with lovely color. Next, I intend to repair the cracked leg of Greta's bedside table, a task I am excited to undertake. Hopefully, Papa or Eldus will lend some guidance—for Greta's sake.

In short, we are well here and hungrily following news of the rebellion, wishing it would end without another shot. I am sure you and your fellows wish the same. I further wish you good fortune, Coop, and hope you are able to write soon. Oh, how I do miss our exchanges.

> *With warm regards,*
> *Your kindred soul,*
> *Sophie*

❖

June 9, 1863
Dear Sophie,

All is well in familiar Virginia and I hope it is for you and your family. My days of recuperation seem ages behind me now, as I am back to the monotonous drilling and chores of daily soldiering with only minor difficulty. Marching at length still serves as a faithful reminder, however, that a person should avoid having one's foot fractured at all costs.

Please forgive my correspondence delays and the heavily medicated prose that accompanied those earlier weeks of incapacity and discomfort. Medication and exhaustion did lay me low, and my thinking too often so hazy as to preempt putting pencil to paper. The fellow charged with helping me unload that munitions wagon suffered a mean broken leg when the pile toppled upon us, so I consider myself lucky to have sustained the more minor injury. I have learned that life on crutches is as grueling as on the march, and my arms and shoulders currently rejoice at having retired such demonic contraptions.

I am deeply touched by your attention to the Chancellorsville accounts. It was amidst that disastrous engagement that a rebel blast led to my accident and thereby removed me from further action. Although General Hooker replaced ol' Burns with attentiveness and restructuring, and boosted our general health and morale, his tactical skill failed us miserably. It is my opinion that too many logistical opportunities were missed; likewise, some advances, including that of my 19th, should have been rethought. You may not have read that a reb shell knocked Hooker cold during the battle. Considerable optimism then flowed among the ranks, that we might see a change in command—again, but there came widespread disappointment when we learned it was not to be.

Overall, however, we are rebounding, and our numbers are on the rise once more. The president's call for more troops is already paying dividends and, even though that process is slow, we are in no immediate need that I can tell. It is possible we soon will advance up the Shenandoah in search of Lee's army and many of us look forward to the change in scenery. I am not alone in my weariness of Fredericksburg and its environs, the contentious Rappahannock, these beaten farmlands. As long as we ensure the rebs get no farther north, we are eager to head for someplace new.

But I have learned that Mr. Lincoln's army sometimes works in mysterious ways. Two days ago, I received approval for the furlough I requested last month when I was injured. Then today, I received word that it has been canceled. No explanation was provided, but Tim suspects the army is planning to move, while I suspect the army simply believed my foot had healed sufficiently enough to put me back to work. My emotions suffered some knocking around at that good-then-bad news, for I had contemplated a surprise trip to Gettysburg.

I do still hope to visit when I can. I feel that your letters already have me well acquainted with the town and your family. I thank your father, Greta, and Karl for their kind thoughts and please convey my eagerness to meet them. I long to shake your father's hand as well, and I wish him and Mr. Robinson success with the loft. May their work be swift and secure and only done on cool days.

I take heart to learn that Gettysburg embraces the Robinsons. I have always believed that defending the solidarity of our nation and the liberties it represents should be everyone's paramount concern. How these screaming rebs can give their very lives to shatter our beloved country, to brutalize fellow human beings is beyond my understanding. Their blind insistence confounds me, and their fervor is infuriating. I perform my duty proudly and have no regrets, only the longings for home and for loved ones I have lost.

I learned last week of repairs performed on my home and, like you, am greatly relieved to know a trusted friend helped tend to the task. Sam Henderson and his sons patched storm damage to my roof, and he wrote with pride of their enlistment in our navy. My heart goes out to Sam and his wife and the boys I have known since childhood.

Won't you give a hello to young Karl for me? Suggest to him for me that patience and practice are required to refine one's craft, be it sharpshooting or playing the banjo. Please tell him further, that I began shooting at the age of five and, at twenty-four, I know there is always plenty to learn. (I soon hope to hear his banjo ring across the hills.)

Please inquire of Greta how she already knows me so well. Yes, I suppose there is mystery and romance in this Yankee, as I believe exists in most people, and one day she will discover this in herself. Greta has been blessed with a truly remarkable sister to guide and nurture her, to be the closest of friends. Tell her for me that I know how treasured a big sister can be, for my sister always wished she had one. Greta is a very lucky girl.

And congratulations, Miss Bauer, on completing your parlor rug! A weighty chore, indeed, and a wonderful accomplishment. I look forward to someday seeing it grace your home. I imagine your father is quite proud. And now you eye a woodworking challenge for Greta? This confirms for me your boundless courage. Charge on undaunted, lovely lady! Knowing your determination, I will bet my month's wages that the finished project will become a treasured heirloom.

On a different note, the generous package you sent arrived yesterday, battered but unopened, and I required a private moment in my tent. After nearly two years with the army, yours is the first package I have received, and I am mature enough to admit that tears were shed.

Know that within minutes I found the bottle of wine among the new socks you made. Oh, what treasures, all! I toasted you immediately and then Tim and I did it again, several times. I have stashed away your peach preserves for the next time we have any decent fried pork, which might be in a week or so. I only hope I can wait that long before gobbling it all up in one sitting. I drool anticipating its scrumptious taste and rich texture, a sweetness only you surpass. Thank you sincerely for your thoughtfulness.

Writing to you is such a grand pleasure. It warms me to know your gentle touch will caress these little pages. I envision your sparkling smile as you read—and here, now, I feel my own smile broaden.

I am eager to see you, Sophie. I miss our time together, as I miss your comforting voice and tender touch and everything about you. There is so much we have not shared and maybe things we never will, but our special friendship is of the highest value to me. Maybe one day you will consider a visit to my home, or maybe each year we could visit one another in turn.

Of course, I have no idea what each day holds, nor when I will be able to visit or how long I might stay, but I am certain that all memories we make will be ever-lasting. Somehow, this connection we share must never fade.

Thinking of you, I remain,
Your kindred soul,
Coop

CHAPTER THIRTEEN

Clearing the breakfast dishes onto Greta's tray, Sophie thought Papa's worried look too contrary for such a classically beautiful June morning.

"Now what have you found in that newspaper?"

He plopped the *Stars and Banner* onto the space his plate had occupied. "Militia units are assembling everywhere since Governor Curtin called for volunteers."

"They will keep the rebels from coming north," Greta stated.

He shook his head as he stood and tugged absently on his suspenders. "Unfortunately, no militia will stop an army the size of Robert E. Lee's. If he's of a mind to sweep through here, he will."

"So, you believe the rebels will come?" Greta froze before leaving for the summer kitchen, tray in hand. "Do you, Papa? Whatever will we do?"

Sophie hoped he would choose his words wisely and not heighten the anxiety filling the room.

Karl raised his fist. "Our army will stop them," he said with blind confidence.

"Yes, son," Papa said, "as long as it gets here in time. Those Confederates are already too close. They were in Winchester and Harper's Ferry over a week ago, probably coming back up through Sharpsburg again, and I don't like the direction they're taking."

Sophie wiped her hands on her apron. His evaluation provided little comfort and the idea of their happy, bustling town being overrun made her heart race. Noting the alarm on Greta's face, she risked asking more of him. "You really don't think they'll come back across Antietam Creek, do you?"

"I'm no army tactician, Sophie." He shrugged. "But I worry about our militia fellows, so eager to take up arms. They aren't trained soldiers. Some are old coots like me, and most of the town's young fellows, well, they're naive boys." He moved to Karl's chair and stopped. "You know the savings bank on the Chambersburg Pike?" Karl nodded, looking up at him, wide-eyed. "A teller there boasted that his son intends to serve as a drummer boy." He gripped Karl's chin. "He's just two years older than you. Do not entertain such ideas."

"But, Papa," Greta insisted, "what should we do? Are our soldiers coming?"

"I'm sure they are, child." He took a cleansing breath as he scanned the table, possibly searching for a new topic. "Now, you and Karl take these dishes outside to the summer kitchen and finish cleaning up. Then, Karl, I'll meet you at the barn."

Sophie studied the dark concern with which he supervised Greta and Karl's departure. Gone was his easygoing demeanor. "We have reason to worry, don't we?"

He half-turned to her, hands supported by his pockets, his bearing resigned. "Last I heard, Sophie, no one knew exactly where our army was or if it's even en route. There's serious doubt it can get here in time. Tomorrow afternoon, I'm going to a meeting in town. Folks are gathering to decide what measures to take."

Sophie gripped the chairback. "How can we possibly withstand rebel forces? They will...I can't bear to consider it."

"It's been suggested that our merchants gather their inventories and send them off for safekeeping. Farmers want to start herding livestock out of town."

"Rose Robinson fears the worst, Papa. She's raised the subject several times and I have tried to lessen her concern, to be reassuring, but it seems she could be right. That family...All the Negro families..."

"She is right to worry. Eldus has talked of moving them in with friends in Taneytown if necessary. Those rebs will hunt down every Negro they can. It won't matter if they're our fellow free citizens. They'll be sent into Southern slavery."

Sophie pulled out the chair and sat hard. "Somehow, I never dreamed it would happen here."

He stepped to her side and rubbed her shoulder. "This is all speculation right now, remember, but worthy of serious consideration. Be strong, child. We must be, especially for the young ones."

"I've seen the horrors of battle, Papa. You've read the articles. Children shouldn't be exposed to war. And armies devastate the land. What of our crops? Our homestead?"

"Nothing matters more than our safety, Sophie. Our land, our belongings, our home, they are worthless compared to our well-being." He gestured toward the trap door to the cellar. "I believe it would be wise to consider some protection for ourselves. When you have a moment, please see to the cellar, its suitability as a refuge, and consider the necessities we might require."

"Yes, Papa."

He gave her shoulder a squeeze and ambled out the back door.

Her thoughts wandering wildly, Sophie hefted the hinged square of floorboards and stared down into the blackness of the root cellar. Not a welcoming place to stay for any length of time, with its cobwebs and dust, the cool air smelling of rock and dirt. She lit a lantern, gathered the folds of her dress in her free hand, and edged down the rickety steps.

"How has it come to this?" she said on a sigh, shining the light around the small room.

The little worktable required serious scrubbing, and more than that old stool should be available for seating. Perhaps an old rug from the attic would do well on this dirt floor.

Crates on the plank shelves held a meager supply of root vegetables, primarily purchased in town, because, like most families, the majority of their own crops had yet to produce. Thankfully, there were some canned goods and jars of preserves put up last fall and winter. She blessed Papa, Karl, and Greta for laboring in her stead, performing this tedious but vital chore during her tenure with the Society.

Their family *could* survive down here if necessary, she thought, but certainly a thorough cleaning was needed. She hung the lantern on a nail and went up for a broom and wash bucket. But worries quickly consumed her, thoughts of clothing, hygiene, and when and for how long their little family could be required to exist in such a space.

She gathered cleaning necessities with rote effort, all the while picturing the Union army streaming northward along the Emmitsburg Road just outside, arriving heroically to the town's defense. She hoped Papa would return from his meeting tomorrow with mail from Coop. *Are you on the march, Private Samson? We grow fearful. You might be surprised to learn of the precautions everyone is entertaining.*

Sophie stood at the sink and pumped water into her bucket. Her mind drifted to her siblings' worries, the rumors from their friends, the half-heard adult conversations that planted seeds of uncertainty and fear in young imaginations. She set aside the bucket and ventured out to the summer kitchen.

Greta worked at the table, her back to Sophie as she kneaded a mound of dough. How devoted she is, taking the initiative at her age on such a hot day, Sophie mused. Just a stone's throw from the back door, the summer kitchen spared the main house from the heat of cooking and washing during the hottest season, and here was Greta, valiantly laboring to provide bread for supper.

"Honey, let me do that." Sophie turned Greta from the table.

Bedraggled curls stuck to Greta's forehead and cheeks, and when she raised her face to Sophie, droplets of perspiration slithered along her neck. "I thought I could—"

"So I see. And you do, exceptionally well, I might add. But let me take a turn now. It's time to cool yourself." She hurried to fill a glass of water for her. "Have this, please, and step outside. There is still some shade to be had at the back door."

Greta sipped as she went. "I stoked the oven so it will be ready when the dough rises."

Wiping her own wet forehead, Sophie could tell. "You grow smarter by the day, Greta. I'm so proud of you."

Sophie finished the kneading, laid the dough aside, then prepared the beans she had soaked since last night and set the pot on the back of the stove. Chicken would complete their supper, she decided, after considering the supply of meat hanging in the smokehouse. Finally satisfied she could escape for a while, Sophie eagerly departed the sweltering little building.

She dried her face with the hem of her apron and took a moment to gaze across the placid landscape. Distant homesteads baked just like hers in this unforgiving sunshine, hardly a shade tree to be seen across the two miles of farmland to the north and south. Likewise, to the east and west, the plain spanned a mile between rises of land. Only the Emmitsburg Road, zig-zagging worm fences, and stone walls disrupted the bucolic expanse of green and gold, delineating crops, pastures, corrals, and property lines.

With a palm flat above her eyes, Sophie squinted to discern the trees of the Sherfy peach orchard to the south and grinned at the tactile memory of its sweet-scented shade. Fresh peach tea would be such a treat today. Too bad this heat would make the trek to the Sherfeys unbearable. Woods to the west presented similar discouragement. That forested ridgeline, extending from the Lutheran Seminary in town, sat a half-mile away, not worth a stroll when she already felt so damp and sticky.

Hammering in the barn caught her ear and she spotted Greta chatting with Tassie at the nearby well. The girls giggled in the sun, took turns splashing each other from the bucket. A pleasure to watch, considering the town's pressing dilemma, and Sophie waved a greeting to Tassie before returning to the house and work in the cellar. At least it would be cooler there.

❖

The following evening, sitting on the porch in the humid, still air of sunset, Sophie debated the idea of retiring to her room to read Coop's latest letter. Surrounded by family after a hearty supper, so at ease and comfortable like this, she finally opted to treasure the moment and read later. Besides, Papa had yet to tell of his meeting in town this afternoon. He had been late for supper, therefore the meeting must have been substantial.

"A fellow from Greencastle came into the meeting," he started, rocking in his favorite chair. Karl hushed his banjo and Greta drew her chair closer to Sophie's. "The news isn't good, I'm afraid." He looked from Greta to Karl. "Don't either of you start fretting and lose your senses. Time now demands we be smart. You understand?"

Both children nodded, hanging on his every word. Sophie knew what was coming and her attention piqued. She sat back and braced her will and spirit for whatever he had to say.

"Advance units of Lee's army are in Greencastle, cleaning it out. Everyone's fairly sure that Chambersburg is next."

"Really? And then where?" Karl leaned his banjo against the house and rubbed his palms along his thighs. "Then here?"

"Oh no." Greta's voice cracked. "They're really coming?"

Papa stalled. He scratched a stick match to life and relit his pipe. This was hard for him, scaring the children.

Sophie skipped ahead. "What's the plan in town, Papa?"

"An urgent telegram went off to the governor, asking that he immediately post militia units here. We all have faith he will be prompt." He met her eyes, and she knew they both were equally aware of the futility of militia protection.

"And the shops, the banks, the tradesmen?"

"Well, everyone will begin packing to transport inventories to the depot. The station manager said extra train runs should be arranged tomorrow to start getting things out of town."

"Will the rebels steal all the money in the banks?" Greta wanted to know.

"Anything they can get their hands on, child. Anything to help the Confederacy."

"And everybody's animals, too?" Karl asked. "What about our cows and chickens?"

Greta turned to him. "Tassie told me if they have to move to Taneytown, they'll take the cows but her father's only letting her take a few chickens."

Karl frowned. "Well, what about the rest?"

"Maybe…" Greta turned to Papa, then Sophie. "Maybe we could take them?"

"We'll see, Greta," Sophie said. "Right now, I don't see why not."

Papa puffed thoughtfully. "You see, my thinking is the rebels are headed to the river, to Washington, probably dead-set on staying ahead of our army. So, I believe they'll move through our crossroads quickly and continue on to Wrightsville."

"After they take everything," Greta finished.

"In town, yes."

Sophie hoped Greta and Karl felt at least somewhat reassured that an invasion would not reach this far south of town. They sat in silent contemplation, their youthful complexions drawn, their thoughts no doubt somewhere children's thoughts should never have to go.

Sophie, however, fought the trembling in her hands. She knew of army foraging, that a force the size of Lee's Army of Northern Virginia could smother an entire countryside. Last she'd heard, it numbered seventy, maybe eighty thousand strong, and bore a much-feared reputation for replenishing its supplies any way it wanted. Now, this far from home, it would have many desperate needs.

She sought Papa's eyes, but he fussed with his pipe.

"We need to take care of ourselves," she said, sounding as confident as possible, and set a palm on Greta's shoulder and looked at Karl. "Tomorrow, let's take stock of everything, okay? I will tally our stores of flour, sugar, molasses, salt, all those necessities. You two do the same for the animals, with the hay and feed, and then the smokehouse. Make lists and if we have to go into town and buy some things, we will, before inventories are taken away. We could be stuck here for several days, so let's make sure we have enough to last. Are you two up for that? It's a big responsibility, you know."

"Sure we are," Karl said. "I'll check the loft and—"

"*I'll* check the loft," Greta insisted.

Karl thumbed his chest. "*I'll* do it."

"Oh, no," Greta said. "I will. I'm a better judge. Did you forget how to write?"

"Hey! Of course I—"

"Stop." Sophie shook her head. "Greta checks, Karl writes. The end. And no lollygagging around. Remember: merchants will be closing in a few days and then there can be no more shopping. Make no mistakes."

"Could I visit Tassie if we go to town?"

Papa rocked forward. "Greta, child. The Robinsons will be busier than we will be. They'll need to move everything they own."

"Oh, yes." Her shoulders drooped. "If she moves, when will I see her again?"

"We have to wait for all this to pass," Sophie said. "Like Papa said, maybe it won't be long."

Greta sighed. "It's like a blizzard is coming."

"Yeah." Karl nudged her with an elbow. "A big gray one."

"We have important work tomorrow." Sophie shooed everyone off to bed and gave Papa an extra-long hug. "We'll get through this," she whispered.

He leaned back and stroked her hair. Seldom emotional, Papa had hardened after two infant deaths and Mama's passing, so the gesture brought a lump to Sophie's throat. She remembered his and Mama's laughter in her very early years, and how it had nearly vanished after two brothers were lost. Greta's arrival and then Karl's restored Papa's spirit but losing Mama took a serious toll. Although he worked just as diligently for his children as he did for the farm, only rarely did Papa spare a tender touch.

"You are my brightest star, Sophie. The love in your mama's heart shines in your eyes." He surprised her with a peck on the cheek and left her standing on the porch.

Sophie settled into his rocker, stunned to see the depth of his concern expressed in affection. She drew Coop's letter from her apron pocket and held it in both hands on her lap. Her eyes closed in the slow, rising breeze off the meadow, Sophie wondered if she ever would be so honored with a love such as that between her parents. She pondered whether either of them would appreciate her devotion to a woman, and then dismissed the thought, doubting they would.

Oh, but they would feel differently about Coop.

The envelope she held fluttered in the breeze and she stared at the script on its face and smiled. "Your strong penmanship speaks for you, Private Samson."

June 20, 1863
My dear Sophie,

Greetings to you from a wheat field north of Aldie in ever-present Virginia. I am beginning to wonder if any other state in our nation exists, for this is all I have seen in far too long. I hope you are well and finding more pleasure in this weather than I am. Heat here is oppressive. I never thought I would long so badly for my cooler New England climes.

Are you kept busy with gardening by now? I imagine fruits of Bauer labors are quite visible. Or maybe you have begun Greta's table project? I expect to see a perfect product someday. Take care wielding the hammer and that you don't cut yourself with a saw! I am too far removed from Gettysburg to nurse you back to health, regardless of my desire to do so.

Well wishes to your family, as always. I hope everyone still follows news of this rebellion with patriotic enthusiasm. We advance methodically northward on the word that rebs are somewhere nearby, and never know if one day we will head east to Washington or the next day march west into the mountains. We fervently hope General Hooker has skilled scouts plotting our course.

Several days ago, we learned of the rigorous battle in the gaps around Aldie. It was mostly a cavalry engagement, but I was quite saddened to hear that my fellow statesmen of the 1st Artillery were all but wiped out. Our side was overrun, three to one, we are told, and the rebs withdrew to places unknown. We believe they were a screen for the larger army, which must roam somewhere nearby. And so we march on.

I apologize for the brevity here, for I am worn to the nub from the heat. None of us has difficulty sleeping each night, whether we bed on pine boughs or riverbed rock. I promise to write again in a few days. Please write of any news, any thoughts you wish to share. Your words are of more comfort than I can express.

Wishing I had more energy to correspond, I remain,
Your kindred soul,
Coop

Chapter Fourteen

Y ou can start bringing things out to the wagon now, Karl." Sophie paid for her pile of supplies at the Fahnestock Brothers Store and spotted him eyeing the large candy jar on the counter. "Okay. I'll get peppermint sticks, but we cannot have any before supper." She grinned when he dashed out to their wagon with a keg of salt. "Please add four sticks to my total," she told the clerk. "Um...Better make that eight. I don't imagine you'll have much of a supply after tomorrow."

"You're right," he said, and put the candies into a paper sack. "In fact, tonight we're clearing the shelves."

Karl hurried back. "Some commotion on the corner," he reported. "Let's go see."

"Make another trip here first," she said, and collected more items off the counter. Weighted down with sugar and coffee, Karl followed her outside.

Nearly a dozen men and women huddled in the light rain across the town square, actually a diamond-shaped convergence of many roads. More citizens hurrying to the gathering raised Sophie's curiosity.

"One last trip, Karl," she said, and sent him back inside. As she eyed the growing crowd, a neighbor she knew left the group and shuffled in her direction.

"Good morning, Martha. What's going on?"

"Oh, Sophie! Morning to you. No time to chat, I'm afraid. Must get home." She stopped and shook her head. "Our militia has raced back— to safety, we hear. They encountered a force of Confederates this side of Cashtown, out on the Chambersburg Pike."

Sophie's breath caught. She looked back to the gathering across the diamond, only to find it had dispersed already. No one was wasting any time.

"Oh, no." Her mind spun with multiple worries.

Martha gripped her arm. "Must go, dear, and you should get home." She glanced at Karl, who now stood surveying the area. "Yes," Martha added, stepping away, "get the young ones home. Move along, dear."

As she scurried off, Karl promptly set the keg of molasses in the wagon and pointed to the corner. "We have to get Greta at the Robinsons."

Sophie agreed. Martha was right to urge haste. This news needed to travel fast, to Papa and Eldus, who probably was with him finishing the loft. No time to waste now.

She shook an old blanket over the supplies in the wagon and dusted it with hay.

"Can't take a chance that our things might appeal to some rebel," she told Karl, and waved him up onto the wagon and snapped the horse into motion. "Papa and Eldus need to know what's happening."

"Glad the Robinsons live right over here," he said as they rounded the corner onto Chambersburg.

Sophie knew "this side of Cashtown" placed the rebels only seven or so miles away. Her palms wet with fear, she focused on the distant end of the popular road, hoping she wouldn't see what she now believed was coming. Thankfully, she saw no sign of advancing troops.

She drew the wagon to a stop at the white picket fence and Karl was off and running to the Robinsons' front door before she set feet on the ground.

Rose greeted him with her usual broad smile, but it disappeared when she saw Sophie shake her head.

"It's time, Rose," Sophie said as she neared the front steps.

"The rebs are coming!" Karl announced, and peered through the screen door. "Hey, Greta! Come on out! We have to go!"

Sophie squeezed his shoulder. "Hush. Where are our manners, young man?" She brushed the hat off his head and handed it to him. "Did you even greet Mrs. Robinson?"

Hat in hand, Karl hung his head. "Sorry, ma'am. Good morning, Mrs. Robinson."

Rose ruffled his mussed hair. "Mornin' to you, handsome Karl Bauer." She looked to Sophie. "You're sure?"

"The uproar has begun, it seems." They turned to check the road, the diamond. People moved quickly on the boardwalks, dashing in and out of shops that had begun closing. A bevy of schoolgirls ran crying into the Eagle Hotel lobby. Wagons and horses dodged each other in their haste.

Greta and Tassie joined them on the porch and Karl couldn't wait to deliver the news.

"Rebs are coming."

"Mama?" Tassie's frightened eyes filled and Rose drew her to her hip.

Greta stared up at Sophie. "It's time to go, isn't it?" She took Tassie's hand. "We'll all just go and hide a while, okay? My papa thinks it won't be long."

Sophie swallowed hard at Greta's care for her friend. "That sounds like a solid plan," she offered, and lifted Tassie's chin. "We all need to be strong, children and parents alike. That's what families do, right?" Tassie nodded as a tear dribbled down her cheek. Sophie wiped it away with a fingertip, so tempted to scream about the war and its unfathomable Southern politic. "No tears, honey. We all have work to do. You're such a smart young lady. Are you ready to be strong like your mama and papa?"

"Yes, ma'am."

"Good girl." Sophie spread her arms across Greta and Karl's shoulders. "Rose, we'll send Eldus back as soon as we get home."

"Thank you," she said in a tight voice, and tugged Tassie closer. "We have plenty to do now and best get after it. Ain't that right, my girl?"

Someone yelled from a house far up the pike.

Pounding hooves could be heard then, growing ever louder, and Sophie finally spotted the onrushing horses. Numbed by the sight, she watched as they swept by, headed for the diamond, mounted soldiers screeching, waving their hats. Then they began shooting wildly into the air.

Sophie sensed her blood chill when another group arrived bearing the lead flags of an army unit. Ahead, the few townspeople left on the street fell motionless and gawked.

She spun to Rose, who clutched Tassie to her side.

"You two, inside. Hurry." She pulled the door closed after them and addressed Greta and Karl. "Let's just calmly watch this rebel show, okay?"

Uniformed in muted butternut gray, some with embroidered insignia adorning their sleeves, officers paraded by and pranced about on their horses in the center of town. Primped and well dressed, they sat in stark contrast to the infantry that now marched in their wake.

"Such a scruffy lot," Sophie groused. "How do they manage to give us such trouble?"

Few soldiers displayed the formal uniform. Many were barefoot, most wore aging floppy-brimmed cloth hats, and all were covered by the grime and wear of war. Rifles at their shoulders, they were high spirited, however, calling out victory cheers and singing songs of the Confederacy. Sophie refused to wave back, and she wasn't alone. Already, the first units assembled at each connected road in the diamond.

An adjutant shifted his horse next to a tall, distinguished officer, and shouted, "Major Gen. Jubal Early!" The general urged his horse a few steps forward, took his time scanning the storefronts, and then called out a lengthy list of "tribute" items townspeople were expected to bring forward.

Sophie glanced at Karl. "You think there's seven thousand pounds of bacon available in town right now?" She shook her head at Early's bombast.

Greta looked up at her. "A thousand pairs of shoes? Don't they know better?"

It's what they'll do when they don't get them.

The large regiment continued to pass, and an officer tipped his hat to them. Sophie glared at him until he rode on.

With eyes still on him, she backed up and spoke through the door to Rose. "Do you need help gathering your things?"

Rose's voice trembled. "We are prepared, Sophie, but thank you."

"Then we will hurry off. Eldus needs to be here. We'll tell him to approach with all caution."

Abruptly, Rose opened the door enough to extend her arm. "Please, yes," she said, taking Sophie's hand. "He must take care. Let him know we will wait in the cellar for him."

"It's likely they'll demand goods and be gone, you know."

Rose whispered as she peeked out at the passing soldiers. "We all know what they'll take."

"But it's possible that a brief stay in the cellar will be enough for now." Sophie covered Rose's hand with hers. "When this group leaves, your family should be able to get to Taneytown safely."

Rose took a breath and appeared somewhat inspired. Perhaps, Sophie mused, she summons her strength for Tassie.

"We'll do our best," Rose answered, and patted Tassie's shoulder. "Won't we, child?"

"Yes, ma'am."

"Lock the doors now, and shutter and lock your windows. Our thoughts are with you all. Take care." She squeezed into the narrow opening and hugged Tassie and then Rose. "Good luck, dearest Rose."

Greta and Tassie hugged and Tassie came away with tears again welling in her big brown eyes. Sophie noticed Greta swipe away some of her own.

"Here," Greta said, untying the red bandana from around her hair. "You have this. I know you like it." She picked up Tassie's hand and stuffed the bandana into it. "You keep it for good luck, okay? And promise you'll come visit soon as you can?"

Tassie nodded and dropped her head, crying.

Sophie took a circuitous route out of town, daring to race the wagon home on rougher, lesser used roads. Eldus would have a grave time returning to his family. Soldiers would spread through the streets like a plague, but the sooner he made the attempt, the better his odds. She couldn't bear to envision her friends' fate if those rebels captured them.

She heard a multitude of gunshots ring out from back in town, a celebratory salute, she figured, and wondered what rebel achievement had warranted the display. Securing a trove of bacon? The opening of a bank vault? Discovering champagne at the Eagle Hotel?

"Whoa!" Sophie stopped the wagon when a small herd of cows meandered across the road. "Hurry up, ladies," she said, sighing. "Such bad timing."

Beside her on the seat, Greta looked back.

"I see Mr. Trembley!" she exclaimed, and leapt up, hands to her mouth.

Sophie turned in her seat. The Trembley barn stood open and a group of soldiers clustered around the opening.

Karl stood. "They're taking him," he said, sounding dazed.

"Poor Mr. Trembley! His family…" Greta practically fell back to the seat. With the heels of her hands to her eyes, she tried to stem her tears. "They'll make him a slave, won't they?"

Sophie wished she could say something that wouldn't deepen Greta's despair. But she couldn't. "I'm afraid so, yes."

"And how will Mr. Robinson ever get home now?"

"Very carefully, honey." She inched the wagon through the cows and picked up speed.

❖

Sophie emptied most of the goods they purchased into small containers for stacking in the cellar. With Greta and Karl assigned to trim the vegetable gardens of any produce remotely grown, she took the opportunity to speak with Papa.

"On the Baltimore Pike, you say?"

"Apparently, our militia met more than its match," he said, not looking up as he cleaned an old pistol he rarely took from his bedroom. "Rebels killed one of our boys on the spot. In fact," finally he paused to look at her, "you might know him. George Sandoe. He was about your age."

Sophie stopped working. "George? We worked together at the Globe Inn when we were young. Oh, Papa, how sad."

"The first of us to fall," he muttered, back inspecting his gun.

"So the rebels are moving south of town, then?"

"Hopefully not this far. That's why I sent Eldus off right away, in case they're of a mind to explore out here. He went as soon as we got word from Mrs. Leister about Sandoe." He rubbed the pistol clean with a rag. "I want you to know the feel of this." He handed her the weapon and pulled a tiny pouch from his pocket. "No bullets. They're in this sack, but you test the weight of the gun."

"Papa, I couldn't—"

"You never know, Sophie. I want you able to defend yourself or the young ones if necessary."

Sophie gripped the pistol, held it at arm's length as if shooting at the floor. "It's heavy."

"Think you could pull the trigger?"

She handed it back to him. "Well, if someone intended to hurt one of us, I suppose I could."

"Good. Let's take all this to the cellar and stash it away."

He piled jars and small crocks in his arms and managed the steps without holding on to anything. Sophie followed with an armload but took extra care on each step.

Papa arranged his load on the shelves and went to the far corner of the room. "Set yours down and come over here." He pulled several large stones out of the back wall just above the floor and revealed a space some four feet square. "A special hiding place," he said, one Sophie had never seen.

He wrapped burlap around the gun and sack of bullets and set it in a small crate. Then he produced a thick envelope from his back pocket. "Almost three hundred dollars here, Sophie." Her jaw dropped. "Every cent I had hidden in the house is going right here. Nearly broke my back saving this, with hopes of adding that southern acreage, not of donating it to some dammed treasonous…No, sir." He dropped that into the crate, too, and next, placed a tiny velvet-covered box in Sophie's hand. "Open it."

Lifting the lid, Sophie fought back a sob. "It's Mama's wedding…"

"She even kept the box." He shuffled in place. Sophie kissed his cheek, and he scratched the back of his head awkwardly. "I wanted you to know I'm putting it here."

She kissed the gold ring and handed it back. "I should put my keepsakes here as well, shouldn't I?"

"For now, anyway. Do it soon."

"Right away."

"There's not much room, and we should fill it with food, maybe a blanket or two, but our irreplaceables are a must."

"Well, we *are* done stowing food, so I'll gather other things now."

He slid the crate into the safe space and reset the rocks in the wall. "Just until you're ready. I'll go check on our gardeners."

Sophie led the way upstairs. "Too bad what they're picking now won't last us long."

"Hopefully, long enough for those rebs to leave."

"I wish we could hide the rye and wheat. Those crops might be the first to go."

"You just get your necessities together. Concern yourself with that."

Sophie set out her few treasures on her bed: her mother's necklace, a framed tintype of the Liberty Bell taken just for her, a ticket stub from her first solo trip on a train, the five-dollar gold piece that was her first month's salary at the Globe, and several letters from teenaged girlfriends. To that she added a ribbon-bound bundle of Coop's letters.

Having gathered everything into an old cigar box, she stared down at the bed and its special blanket. "No rebel hands will ever touch this." To be sure, she folded it as compactly as possible, wrapped a sheet around it, and returned to the cellar with her treasures.

Resetting the rocks in the wall proved difficult once she stuffed everything inside. She labored to account for everyone's needs, the spare clothing, blankets, jugs of water, a short barrel of smoked meats, and every canned and jarred product they could spare. She even secreted away four sweet sticks.

With the space secure and looking undisturbed, she assessed the cellar and hoped these stores wouldn't be touched. Maybe rebels would just take what they found in the smokehouse and go. She chortled at herself. This underground pantry, like every farmer's, would be a target. If—when—the rebels came, they would take everything. She walked to the safe space and patted the rocks, grateful.

Sophie passed the evening on the porch with family again, although tonight's anxiety prompted little conversation at first. Even supper had been subdued. She'd managed to create a tasty supper of very young vegetables and remnants of last night's pork, along with Greta's outstanding bread, even though both the main and summer kitchens had been reduced to bare bones. Despite the pleasant meal, the household mood remained somber.

"I wish we knew if Mr. Robinson made it home," Greta said.

"We just have to wait and see, child."

"But, Papa, for how long? What if—"

"Greta, we have no way of knowing."

"Well," Karl said, and swung a leg over the railing, "just wait till our army marches right into town and captures all them rebs. That's what I'm wishing."

Greta said, "Me, too."

"Me, three," Sophie added.

Papa began the methodical process of packing his pipe for a smoke. "In his last letter, where did Coop say he was?"

"North of Aldie, but that was almost a week ago."

He put his tobacco pouch away and chose a stick match. "Hm."

"What are you thinking, Papa?" Karl asked, searching Papa's face. "You look to be calculating."

Papa's lips curled around his pipe. "You're right, my boy. Our United States Army can march a good twenty-five, maybe thirty miles in a day. At least, that's what it claims. So, could be it's closing in on Frederick City or thereabouts. Just a guess."

"Could they come tomorrow?"

"I doubt it, unless they're closer right now than we think." He drew on the flame and puffed out smoke. "Couple days. Maybe."

"Those rebels better leave soon," Greta said.

"If they know what's good for them, they will," Karl said. "Yankees will give 'em what for." He glanced at Sophie. "I bet Cooper will take out *more* than his share of them."

Sophie grinned. "He'll do his duty. Yes, I'm sure he will try."

"I wonder if we will have a chance to meet him," Greta said. Sophie thought it was the first time Greta had smiled all day. "He *will* come here, won't he?"

"I'm fairly sure, yes, but who knows what will happen when our army gets here or how long it will stay? I'm sure he'll visit us if he can."

"What's it like in Massachusetts? Has he told you?"

And, as usual, Karl showed interest in Coop as well. He brought his leg back over the rail to lean on his knees. "Does he have a boat?"

Thankfully, their minds are off the Confederacy, at least for the moment.

"That, I don't know for sure. I don't recall him ever saying so, though. He's a farmer."

"How come he's not married?" Karl persisted. "Did his wife die?"

"No. He just hasn't cared to marry."

"Not yet," Papa chipped in. "Probably looking for just the right gal." He puffed again and winked at Greta, who immediately turned to Sophie.

"Stop." Sophie raised a palm to silence whatever was about to spring from Greta's conniving mind. "Stop that thinking. I've told you all, Coop and I are just good friends. That's all, so—"

"I think 'Coop' sounds funny," Karl said. "Reminds me of chickens."

Greta smirked at Sophie. "You think he's handsome. You told me so when you came home in January."

"Well, he is. He's tall and has dark hair and very brown eyes."

"How long is he in for, has he said?" Now, Papa joined the interrogation. "Is he a one-year man?"

"Three."

"Three?" Papa straightened in the rocker. "You don't say. Hm."

"He enlisted shortly after Lincoln first put out the call."

"Well now." Papa stared off toward the dark fields, puffed twice, and looked back at her. "You know, that's highly commendable. A right honorable fellow, this Cooper, your *friend*. I need to shake his hand."

Sophie sipped her coffee and enjoyed the tranquility of everyone in deep thought about something other than rebel invasion. Her family's sweet attachment to Coop seemed to grow by the day, much like her own, although the family knew nothing of her confusion.

A serious, lasting relationship with a man? It still escapes me as much as it has for years, still rattles uncomfortably inside. Except when it comes to you, Coop Samson. How baffling. Dare I believe you have opened my heart wider than I thought possible and raised its voice?

Quiet settled in around them and across the fields, occasionally spoiled by gunshots in town. She gave thanks that at least this area south of town seemed at ease and hoped tomorrow brought more of the same. The days couldn't pass fast enough.

CHAPTER FIFTEEN

If there was any consolation for the endless routine of marching and skirmishing, Coop found it in the army's proximity to Sophie in Gettysburg. She wrote that much in yesterday's letter and planned to finish her composition today. However, now camped just a day's march away in Taneytown, she pondered the necessity of writing at all.

"We could be there before the mail delivers my letter."

"You heard the talk last night," Tim said, poking and making a mess of their little cookfire. "Hate to say it because I know what you're hoping, but chances are we're headed elsewhere—if anywhere at all. Headquarters are set up here. Finish your letter and mail it." He added a scrap of wood to heat their coffee to a boil. "Can't say as I mind sitting around, though. Can you? Really?"

Coop saw opportunity for time with Sophie slipping away. Ever since Hooker resigned and Gen. George Meade took over two days ago, II Corps seemed to have no strategic purpose other than "sitting in reserve" here in Maryland, awaiting orders, and Coop grew impatient.

"Of course, I don't mind resting. Who would? Except that we should be doing *something*." She unwrapped two sizeable chunks of stringy beef and pierced them with sticks. She handed one to Tim, and together they roasted their late breakfast over the fire. "Sometimes I wish I joined the cavalry. They're always on the move."

"Chicken thieves, all of them," Tim said with a snort. "I cannot see you serving under the likes of Kilpatrick. You would have shot him long ago."

Coop conceded that point. General Kilpatrick had had his share of bad luck; his poor tactical skills preceded him. "Now, Buford. I'd like to serve under him, tough nut that he is." She assessed her meat and extended it back over the flames. "They say he's up in Gettysburg right now."

"Bah. I know what you're itching for, Samson. You just want to see a certain pretty farmer's daughter."

"True. I do."

Tim eyed her sideways. "You really up for answering your heart? Could be some time before we squash all these reb vermin. You'll bust open if we go another year doing this."

"I made it these six months since I've seen her, haven't I?" Coop checked her meat again, this time satisfied it was cooked through. She sat back and blew on it before tugging off a bite. "Besides, it's not like we would ever get married."

Tim scowled at her, his wooly mustache drooping over his lower lip. "Why not? She wouldn't wait for you?"

"Well, she's mighty independent. So am I."

"Don't you want her for your bride? Bring her back home and make yourselves some dandy looking young'uns? What's wrong with that?"

"That would be her choice, to go anywhere with anyone, especially having a young sister and brother to look after. You're getting too far ahead in your thinking."

"*I'm* not the one getting too far ahead of himself."

Coop looked out along the row of tents. "Eat while you can. Sarge is coming. I'm guessing our midday rest is about to end."

The bugle call and orders for heavy marching came loud and clear, unexpected and urgent. Coop jerked to her feet, shoved the rest of her beef into her mouth, and splashed some coffee into their cups.

Tim plucked off his meat and threw his stick aside. "I'll go get us stocked up. Do the fire last and save my coffee." He took off to acquire their rations of food and ammunition.

Coop dove into the tent and began rolling blankets and stuffing personal items into their knapsacks. Heavy marching meant everything must go, so she knew they wouldn't be back. And, apparently, had to get wherever they were going in a hurry.

Rapid deployment for an entire corps always consumed the better part of a day, like trying to push a railroad train into motion by hand, but on this, July's first day, Coop found herself back on the march in less than three hours. She had jammed some hardtack into her trouser pocket to munch along the route but soon realized their pace wouldn't allow it.

The push northward was a frenetic march for II Corps, and Coop began wiping away the dripping sweat after less than five minutes. Sergeants and lieutenants hustled alongside the column, barking about speed and closing ranks. Separation between companies and then regiments disappeared, and Coop thought the 19th looked far larger this way than regularly arranged.

They closed in on the wagons ahead, those of the 20th, and directly into their dust, which settled upon everyone and everything.

Coop pinched at her eyes. Grit coated her wet face, weighed down her eyelids, and worked its way into her mouth. She ground it between her teeth, then took a sip from her canteen and spit between the men ahead.

"Wish we had more coffee," Tim said.

"Too hot for coffee." She slapped her cap against her thigh to remove the dust. "Damn. We're looking like rebs."

Coop started to notice discarded knapsacks and other gear along the road as troops lightened their loads, and she shook her head. *They'll regret that later.* She refused to relinquish any of hers, no matter the weight or the sweat it sent trickling down to her backside.

All along the line, troops coughed, sneezed, spit, and succumbed to the heat and lack of clean air. Men stepped out more frequently by the third hour, some dropped to their knees, others fell at the roadside.

"You see Tinderman?" Coop asked, unbuttoning her frock beneath the crossed straps of her haversack and canteen. "That was Tinderman back there, laid out." She peered up at the cloudless sky.

Tim looked up as well. "If this march doesn't kill us, the heat will."

When the order to rest finally came thirty minutes later, Coop didn't bother to catch the scene of thousands of men hitting the dirt at once. She crawled beneath a tree and scrambled for her canteen.

Tim hailed Lieutenant Adams as he strode along the line. "Lieutenant! Are we there yet?"

Adams took a step closer and frowned down at them. "Guess I'll put it to you the way it was put to me: When we get there, you'll know it."

"Gettysburg?" Coop tried.

"Before sunset, per General Gibbon."

"Gibbon?" Tim asked. "Where's General Hancock?"

"Meade sent him on ahead and turned Second Corps over to Gibbon. General Hancock's got command of the field now."

Someone behind Coop asked, "Big doings in Gettysburg, Lieutenant?"

Adams wiped his face with a handkerchief. "You could say. General Buford sent for help and now two corps are into it up there, First and Eleventh. By the sounds of things, they might have met the whole damn rebel army. We lost General Reynolds early this morning."

Coop and the men around her groaned at the news, especially at the loss of Reynolds, the hardened, respected commander of I Corps. Obviously, this didn't bode well, and she understood the imperative to arrive on the battlefield. No one complained when they resumed their hard march.

Just past the supper hour, filthy and exhausted, Coop and the rest of the 19th gladly made temporary camp still several miles south of Gettysburg, in the shadow of a hill called Big Round Top. Gunshots and cannon fire could be heard from somewhere far ahead. An overheated courier stopped at Coop's offer of a canteen and shared dire news: rebs were chasing Yanks back through town to hills at the northern end of the Union line.

Learning the 19th had arrived at its southern end, and that high ground named Cemetery Ridge connected the two, Coop reclined onto a patch of tall grass. *At least there's no action here. I hope to never move again.*

"The following pickets fall in!"

Soldiers rose on elbows, most too worn to complain, some barely lifting their heads to watch as names were called for the night picket detail. Coop sat up and every muscle protested when she heard her name. She grabbed her Springfield, lumbered back to her aching feet, and heard Tim's name in the background. Having him alongside would probably be the best thing about this night. It looked to be a long one.

Their assigned territory for picket duty lay farther north, more than a mile closer to the fighting, beyond Big Round Top and the next hill, Little Round Top, and near the center of the long Union line. Once there, they marched due west until positioned a half mile deep onto an enormous plain of farms, fields, and pastures. Considering pickets were being posted out here, Coop figured the rest of the 19th ultimately would be positioned along the line directly behind them, and she took comfort in knowing that support would not be too far away.

She stifled a growl at the Southern forces facing her. From their own high ground—that Tim somehow knew to be Seminary Ridge, the long rebel line enjoyed an unobstructed view of this open terrain, which offered the pickets virtually no cover in any direction.

Only parallel fencing lining the road cut through these fields, and Coop assessed the meager strategic value of the post-and-plank fence on her side and the post-and-rail on the other. Although she didn't appreciate being so exposed, she knew the fencing at least was *something*: The plank version closer to her provided a measure of concealment, and the west-side fence provided an obstacle five rails high, certain to slow any enemy advance.

Prone on the ground in the tall wheat, Coop and others in the detail listened to distant firing to the north and took in their surroundings, lucky to do so before darkness fell. She whispered to Tim, who lay several yards away, that it appeared they had been assigned the dead-center of neutral ground.

Only a scattering of farmhouses dotted this mile-deep swath of land, unfortunately located—with Coop and the rest of the 19th pickets—squarely between rebel and Yankee lines. In fact, her current position had her only a few hundred yards from one such house and she sympathized with the innocents caught inside. Like all the others, the homestead no doubt sheltered a family behind those shuttered windows and closed doors. A reluctant bystander, helpless in its predicament.

Tim uttered a soft hiss, caught Coop's attention, and nodded toward an oncoming wagon. Coop lay still, her Springfield loaded and capped, and watched an elderly couple hurry its weary horse along the road. Tim shook his head at the sight and Coop agreed, civilians best stay off this road.

She rubbed dust from her eyes, did her best to swipe at her face with the less-dusty underside of her sleeve. She wondered if those travelers even noticed the row of dirt-covered soldiers lying in the field. With hours of high heat having baked the dust onto her uniform, she blended rather well into the wheat that flourished around her. Now, with the sun setting, her sweat-soaked wool grew damp and cool. A chill might set in after dark, she mused, and allowed herself the fantasy of a soft blanket under the stars.

Which spun her thoughts to Sophie.

Do you use my blanket still? Do you live around here? In which direction is your farm from town? Are you near that battle to the north? Have you and your family left for safer lodging?

The idea that Sophie could have left town, as so many townspeople did when an army arrived, threatened to bring on a headache. Cooper shuddered to think she'd finally reached Gettysburg only to discover Sophie may be gone. *Totally unacceptable.*

Exhaustion preyed upon her faculties, made every thought a chore. Peering dutifully into the trees along Seminary Ridge a half mile away, she took note of rebel riders passing to and fro, wagons and artillery rolling into position, dozens of Negros in white shirts carrying supplies, wisps of smoke rising from the hundreds of cookfires. *Won't be long now before reb pickets come out to play.* She couldn't afford to let exhaustion steal her focus.

She dropped her face into the turf and took a breath. Hours on this picket shift could be difficult. She had to stay sharp.

❖

"I'd never seen anything so glorious as I did this morning," Sophie said, refilling Papa's coffee cup. "Did you see when they unfurled those colors passing by right outside?"

Papa sipped and nodded. "What a grand sight. We went to the roadside, didn't we, Karl?"

"We surely did! Cheered them right along. A soldier saluted me, said he was from Michigan's Iron Brigade."

"When we heard the band start up, we went out, too," Greta said with a glance at Sophie. "The Iron Brigade wears funny tall black hats."

"I was so relieved to see them all. They said they were First Corps," Papa added. "Have to say, though, I didn't appreciate them hacking through that fence of ours or flattening half our corn. It was knee-high. Such a shame."

"They were in a heap of a hurry, short-cutted over Seminary out toward McPhearson's," Karl told Sophie.

"Unfortunately," Papa added, "those boys had a hard time of it. Judging by the sound of things, the rebels pushed them right back to this side of town."

"Lots of folks left town today, headed south," Karl said, and folded his arms on the table. "Their wagons were loaded heavy. Some even led their stock down the road."

"I'm sure rebels have taken the town," Papa said. "All the noise these past hours has been from Cemetery Hill. That's very close by." He sighed and stared into his cup. "Sorry to say, I think our crops, our stock are in jeopardy, but there's nothing we can do about it now." He looked at Greta. "They won't hurt us, child. They just want supplies."

Sophie said, "It just happened so fast, being surrounded like this. I...I never thought..."

Papa's shoulders appeared to slouch in despair. "I had hoped that raiding party you saw come in the other day would be the end of it, but now there's one big mess brewing out here."

"They're all lined up on both sides, Papa," Karl said. "I watched the ridges fill up."

"So many of them." Greta sat down with a piece of bread and buttered it slowly, lost in thought. "Their fires stretch as far as you can see."

"I *am* mad about their thievery," Papa said, and his free hand curled into a fist. "Not even dark an hour and we lost a cow and several chickens.

Those rebs… My guess is the horse will be gone before sunup, if it hasn't been taken already. Rebels better show some mercy."

Sophie sat beside him and patted his hand. "I object to the shooting so close around the house."

"It's scary." Greta refused to look up. "And getting worse. There's so much of it now and it's loud."

"Earlier," Karl began, his voice rising with excitement, "I could see them out by the road, all hunkered down, eyeballing each other. Saw some shooting, too, but didn't seem as if anybody could hit a target. If I had a gun, I could have shot those rebs myself."

Sophie told him, "You keep those windows shuttered, young man."

As if on cue, a lone rifle shot sounded from the direction of the barn and startled everyone. Then another rang out, followed by a lengthy exchange of shots. After a pause of a few seconds, another exchange broke the silence. Sophie looked around at the rapt faces when cries for help in Southern accents reached them.

"They're *very* close."

Pounding on the kitchen door made them leap to their feet.

"Hello?" came the panicked voice, then more pounding. "Y'all in there? Need a hand here!"

Papa held up a finger. "You three stay put." But they followed him to the door anyway.

It flew open when he reached for the handle and two rebels dragged in a wounded comrade. Unconscious, with a chunk of his bicep torn away, he bled across the floor as they laid him in the corner.

"Appreciate your help, sir," the lead soldier said, eyes flicking to Sophie. "Ma'am. Billy here could use some tending."

Irked beyond measure, Sophie stepped forward and caught the odor of body and clothing rarely washed. She wanted no part of these men, their clothes, or whatever crawled through them in her house. "This is not a field hospital. I've worked in them and obviously know better than you what they look like."

"Then we're lucky we brought our brother to the right place, ma'am." He grinned wildly, all too confident in his faded sweat-stained shirt and dirty trousers.

She slammed her hands to her hips. "This a private home, a *Union* home. Certainly not *your* field hospital."

"Remove this man at once," Papa ordered.

The soldiers backed away from their comrade. "War changes things, folks." The lead rebel tipped his hat. "The fine citizens of Virginia extend their appreciation." He pivoted and the pair ran out into the darkness.

Sophie flung the door shut after them, and they all stared at the tall, bearded rebel on the floor.

"What do we do now?" Greta asked.

Karl wandered closer and wrinkled his nose. "Do they all smell this bad?"

Papa drew him back. "You and Greta go clear the table and get to bed."

"But—"

"No arguing, son."

Sophie knelt at the soldier's side with a towel and bowl of warm water. "I'll clean this wound best I can. Papa, if you would, please, we have some bandages in the credenza."

Greta stood glued to the floor, still staring at him. "What happens when he wakes up?"

"I doubt he'll feel up to rising anytime soon, honey. He's lost a lot of blood. Rest assured, we'll send him on his way as soon as possible."

"Off to bed," Papa insisted, holding strips of clean cotton at the ready. "I can't sleep with one of *them* in our house."

Sophie finished wiping the wound and looked up at her. "Karl will be upstairs with you, and we're right down here. No need to worry."

Papa took Karl by the shoulder. "Be brave for your sister. Both of you, upstairs now."

With her siblings gone, Sophie grumbled at the situation. "How could they just storm in here, although I suppose armies do it all the time. But we don't have the medicine or equipment necessary for this. And in his condition, he'll need nourishment, too."

"Maybe a cup or two of the broth from supper?"

Sophie nodded, grateful when he went to the stove and ladled some into a cup.

The soldier groaned as she worked.

"This wound should be packed but we don't have much to offer." She wiped away more blood and quickly wadded a cotton strip. His eyes still closed, the rebel raised his good arm, but it dropped back to the floor. "Can't believe I'm tending wounded in my own home."

Papa set the cup of broth on the table to cool. "Your experience is invaluable, Sophie."

She considered herself lucky in that regard, but feared for the neighbors who probably would be forced into situations like this, none of them practiced in medicine to any degree, none familiar with or able to stomach grotesque battle wounds, or to counter the intensity in an enemy's eyes. Maybe farmers closer to Cemetery Ridge would fare better with Union casualties, being their own soldiers, but farmers closer to Seminary Ridge dealing primarily with Confederate wounded surely would be hard-pressed to cope. *And here we are, just as likely to see friend as foe.*

She set the cotton into the wound and wrapped it in place, wishing she had the correct supplies. She so resented this, aiding a treasonous soldier, but felt a deep sense of humanity at play, and didn't hesitate to do what she could. She did wonder, however, if Union soldiers received as much consideration from Southern civilians. Confederate attitude stirred her blood to a boil.

She dreaded the idea of rebels coming to collect this man, more of their ilk in her home, and questions she couldn't answer threatened to overwhelm her. Would more wounded seek this house? Union as well? Would an officer suddenly appear and designate their home a field hospital? For which side?

Again, the rebel groaned, a wince creasing his brow. Gazing down at his ragged clothing, she imagined him as quite imposing, being of considerable height, barrel-chested, and with black hair and beard both seriously overgrown. And most likely full of Southern attitude. Had he barged able-bodied into their home, she would have feared for her safety.

"He'll probably be alert enough to take nourishment soon," she mumbled.

Behind her, Papa silently mopped the floor, much to Sophie's surprise. At the sound of more gunshots, he stopped, looked at the door, and muttered, "Why do I believe this is just the first of them?"

CHAPTER SIXTEEN

Crouched in the wheat, Coop steadied her Springfield on the fence plank and searched the dark field ahead for activity. Tim whispered her name, and she tilted her head toward him, the most critical motion she ever made. A gunshot split the night—and her scalp—and hurled her onto her back.

Stunned, Coop struggled through the shock to catch her breath, then registered the ringing in her head, the searing heat of a slice above her right ear. *But I'm still alive.* Her mates in the 19th fired into the field, distracting her self-assessment. She damn well wanted to retaliate, too, but now blood flowed to the back of her head toward the ground.

She rolled onto her side, her head spinning, and instinctively reached inside her frock for her emergency roll of bandage. Pain lanced through her brain, forced her to grit her teeth. No one, least of all Coop, wanted to visit the medical tent. She fumbled with the lengthy strip of cloth as blood reached the back of her neck.

Tim suddenly threw himself flat on the ground beside her. "Holy smokes, man. Where'd they get you?"

"Skimmed my head. Luck's with us tonight, Tim."

"Lemme help." Studying the gash, he set aside his rifle and took the bandage.

"Thanks," she said as he slid closer. "You need to reload."

"I will." He squinted through the darkness and labored to wrap her head without rising to his knees.

"Damn, it's like someone hit me with a shovel. My whole head hurts."

"You're one lucky guy." He rapidly wound the cloth around her head. "Hey, maybe your innards will get shook up now and you'll grow a beard."

"Shut up."

"Least then you'd look less like a drummer boy."

Bless him, she thought, teasing to lift her spirit. "Not every guy in Lincoln's army has to be a hairy bear like you." She rubbed a backhand against her eyes, trying to correct her blurry vision.

He shrugged as he worked. "Mary loves this beard. Can't wait for her to see how long it's grown when I get back."

"Better trim it or she'll run off with the children."

"We'll see about that. How you feeling now?"

"Dizzy, but it should pass, right?"

"I think so. You got a tough noggin'." He sent her a dubious look. "No fakin' now. You sure you can manage?"

"I'm sure."

"We don't want to lose our best rifleman, but you could head to the rear. They'll send out a replace—"

"Hell no. I'll be just fine in a minute or so." She carefully maneuvered into a low, crawling position. "Thanks for the help. Now, load up." The wound's intense throbbing made her blink as she made her way through the wheat and retrieved her gun and cap. "I owe the shot in this to at least one reb out there."

Tim grinned and bit off the end of the cartridge to reload. "Get yourself situated then. And keep your head down." He rammed the minié down the barrel and scooted back to his position.

She strained to sharpen her focus, eager to detect movement. They were out there, damn rebs, beyond this fence and that on the other side of the road. Edginess ate at her patience as minutes ticked away. She closed her eyes for a moment to force back a stabbing pain. Wetness at her collar said blood must have soaked through the bandage already.

She blamed the wound on a lucky shot. Or maybe it was her own fault. The day's forced march probably dulled her instincts. *Let the guard down and left the head up. Should have been more aware.* Surely didn't appear that anyone else in the 19th had been hit, and she kicked herself for having earned the distinction.

She grew angrier, more disappointed with herself by the second. Frustration with a fractured foot had only recently abated; she'd returned to active duty not that long ago. How many more times could she press her luck before she ended up in a hospital bed, naked enough to be shipped home in disgrace?

If only that reb had missed.

She almost chuckled at herself, thinking if she'd dozed off at that moment, he might have. But at least she had just been grazed. *How lucky was that?* And she was up and conscious and able to load and shoot. That's what mattered. And for the millionth time since she first donned her brother's uniform, she thanked the fates for being on her side.

Coop steadied herself with a slow, deep inhale and exhaled the same way. The back of her head and neck, her collar, now they irritated her, so wet and tacky, but at least the dizziness seemed to have passed.

She scanned the darkness, a bit worried by her fuzzy vision. Too bad there was virtually no light. Granted, in the scattering of farmhouses on this common ground, a lamp glowed from an open window or two, but that didn't lend any help spotting the phantom rebs. However, in the summer kitchen of the closest home, a lantern *did* furnish their silhouettes.

A handful of rebels scampered around the little building and Coop and the rest of her line fired through the fence. A few shadow figures dropped, and the frantic return fire went wide. Reloading, Coop saw two dark forms help another toward the main house. *Those poor folks don't know what they're in for.*

The 19th blasted another volley and surged through and over the near fence. Coop staggered, suddenly dizzy again, but managed to cross the low roadbed and climb the banking and get through the second fence. They all paused and fired.

A tidal wave of weakness suddenly overtook her. Leg muscles slackened, shoulders sagged, arms fell limp, and her upper body snapped back at the gun's recoil. In a flicker of cognition, she knew all support had given way and she was going down. She heard her head hit the ground, a thunderous bang through her brain, and all the sights and sounds of the night vanished.

"Not quite so much flour, Greta. I know we've cut back already but let's see how we do with even less." Sophie gave her a reassuring squeeze. Unable to sleep, Greta had reappeared in the summer kitchen and Sophie hoped this familiar chore might help wear her out. Thankfully, Karl slept through what somehow had quickly become a commotion of soldiers from both armies and medical personnel in the parlor.

Back stirring the boiling pot of bandages, which had been the doctor's primary request, Sophie wondered how things had degenerated to this point so fast. Only two hours ago, when the Union captain appeared at the front door, she knew her fears had been realized. She hadn't even registered his name or unit before he waved in a regimental surgeon, an assistant, a nurse, soldiers lugging equipment, and followed them with three wounded privates.

The war definitely had come home. Not that there was anything she could do about it or been given any choice.

She shook her head as she worked. The parlor hardly resembled its quaint self now, and she pictured the whirlwind that transformed the room. While the surgeon tended to his instruments, his crew rearranged furniture, settled the wounded onto cots and blankets laid over her newly-sewn rug, placed medical paraphernalia everywhere, and stacked crates of supplies along the wall into the kitchen.

She was impressed when the doctor, without hesitation, finished with a Union patient and started on one of three rebels. They hadn't been his first priority, and a part of her was glad about that, but he provided equal care to the enemy. Again, Sophie wished the Bauer home needn't comfort Southerners.

"How much more bread do we have to make for them?" Greta's slight frame slumped over the table on outstretched arms. "I'm tired."

"That's the end of it for tonight, honey. Hopefully, we won't be receiving any more *guests*."

"Guests." Greta humphed out the word and pressed both hands into the dough. "Don't see why we have to take in those rebs anyway. Our boys shot them fair 'n' square, so let them take care of their own."

How a twelve-year-old now sees the world, Sophie mourned. With deepening dread, she considered how bad their situation would become. *God forbid, these two huge armies around us unleash their full force. They'll crush us between them.*

She could only hope Greta didn't see the big picture, didn't recognize how they and their neighbors were trapped here, destined at the least to serve either side and show mercy while their world crashed around them. *How hypocritical this war is, taking so many lives in a fight about humanity. How shameful, caring only for victory at any cost, regardless of lives changed forever, showing no regard for the innocent.*

Sophie kept her concerns and reservations to herself. She would set a proper example for her siblings. They would show kindness to the wounded now occupying their home, to Yank and rebel alike, for all their pain and suffering were beyond measure, often beyond relief.

His cheeks flushed, sandy brown hair clinging to his neck with perspiration, Karl hurried into the summer kitchen. "They need another cleaver."

Greta stopped kneading and gaped.

"The only one we have is in that drawer," Sophie told him, and he darted across the room to retrieve it. "What are you doing out of bed?"

"I heard them say they needed one. I-I was listening."

Sophie sighed. "Well, since you're up, we *will* need more wood for the stove soon."

"Okay, before it's all stolen," he mumbled, riffling through the drawer. "Y'know, we got five Yanks now. One's losing a leg. Another fella, well..." Hefting the large knife, his voice trailed off. "But we got four of them damn rebs, too. Just ain't fitting, helping invaders heal."

"We have to remember that doctoring is all about mercy, not politics."

"So's it's okay they come and take over our house? Steal from us?" Karl steamed. "Papa said he convinced them not to take our last cow, but they already took the others and the horse. Now, we *can't* leave even if we tried. The Aldens did already. Soldiers ain't showing mercy to us, that's how I see it."

"The Aldens are gone?" Sophie knew about the thievery, a crushing blow to their family. Papa had been furious. And she'd just visited the Aldens last week, and now her dear childhood friend, Elizabeth, was gone.

"Midday," Karl said, nodding. "The Wickers said so when they went by. They were headed somewhere outside of Taneytown. Everything they owned was on their backs and little Maisie was in the wheelbarrow."

Greta straightened at the oven. "In the wheelbarrow?"

"Yup." He nodded with emphasis. "I hate them damn rebs."

"I do, too." Greta shoved the last loaves of bread into the oven. "And I hate cooking for them."

"Stop, both of you. It's why our soldiers are fighting this war. To make things right. We mustn't allow meanness into our own hearts. Having men who are enemies of each other in our home is bad enough, I know, but we," she pointed at each of them, "you and you and I, we're in charge of our hearts. Remember that. We're the bosses of that." Karl frowned at his bare feet and Greta appeared to ponder the concept. "And no more curse words, either of you. You know what Papa says about that."

"He's not back yet," Karl said, conveniently changing the subject.

Greta's eyebrows rose. "He's been gone too long."

Sophie tried not to worry about that, Papa going off with some soldiers, down to Little Round Top to help acclimate a signal team. And now Greta looked to be near tears.

"Takes time, you know, being so careful in the dark. I know I would have a hard time showing somebody the lay of the land when I couldn't even see it. Wouldn't you?"

Greta nodded but Karl just shrugged. He wandered to the doorway and stopped, the heavy cleaver nearly tipping his slim form sideways. "Doctor said they're low on bandages again. Are those dry yet?" He pointed to the window and the clothesline of stained linens outside in the dark.

"They should be. Greta, would you please gather those off the line?" At the thought of them venturing out, Sophie added a caution to both siblings. "We must be quick going outside, purposeful, and take special care. Remember, there are soldiers lying about in our fields, so be sure to carry a lantern at all times. It will signal that you're not the enemy."

At Greta's weary nod, Sophie spoke to Karl. "Please tell Dr. Taylor I'll bring more bandages very soon. Then I'll hang these." She indicated the boiling pot she stirred. Karl spun on a heel and left. "Don't go out without a lantern!" she yelled after him. "And please don't forget about the firewood!"

Once Greta stepped out, Sophie dried her heated face and changed her apron. She poured herself a cup of water from the pitcher and made a note to refill it at the well. How long their spring would last was anyone's guess now. Soldiers had been helping themselves since dawn.

The other huge pot of water on the stove had reached its boiling point and she knew another armload of soiled linens would arrive any second. All this baking and washing were taking their toll. Greta and Karl were strong, farm-raised, but young and fairly built nonetheless, and in need of sleep. And, up since dawn, Sophie felt the pressure bearing down on her shoulders, back, and feet. And her spirit. She hoped the work in the main house would subside soon.

With a lantern dangling from her little finger, she lugged the heavy pot of steaming linens outside and relieved Greta of the clean pile.

"I'll take these to them, honey. Thank you. Head on up now and try extra hard to sleep. And tell Karl I said to go, too." She cupped her chin. "Thank you so much. You did the work of two women, you know. I'm so proud you're my sister." She squeezed her in a quick hug. "I know Papa's proud, too."

"And Mama?" Fatigue tinged the hope in her voice.

"Oh, honey." Sophie fought the onset of tears. "Don't ever forget that Mama watches over us. Always. I *know* she's the proudest of all."

Greta hurried off to her bedroom and Sophie finished hanging the bandages before heading to the house. Stepping inside, she tried not to recoil at the familiar smell already emanating from the parlor.

Gone was the earthen scent of tilled fields on fresh air, the sweetness of Papa's pipe smoke that the gathering room always carried, all now smothered by shuttered windows in humid July heat. Instead, the acrid odor of chemicals, blood, and soiled clothes greeted her as she stepped into the bustle of activity, and the memories of Fredericksburg washed over her. Dr. Taylor, his white coat already spattered with blood, waved her through the maze of crates, make-shift tables, and patients. A Union nurse thanked her as he took away the basket of linens.

Two Union soldiers struggled with the weight of a dead comrade in a blanket as they carried him out the front door, and Sophie wondered where they would take the body. Rumors from town told of burials in front and back yards, in gardens. She hoped this madness wouldn't turn their sweet farm into a cemetery.

"Miss Sophie?" Dr. Taylor dipped his hands in a basin of pink water. "You think you could help Nurse Johnson over there with a bandage change? Just for a moment or two." She looked where he indicated, at the nurse bent over the rebel Billy, the first one brought to their home hours ago. Dr. Taylor arrived at her side, drying his hands. "You have no idea how lucky I feel, having someone from the Ladies' Aid Society here with us. Your father was quite proud to tell me. We greatly appreciate your help."

Oh, Papa. Most boasting is uncalled for.

She crossed the room and saw that the rebel still bled from his wound. "Nurse Johnson? I'm Sophie Bauer. I'm here to help."

He looked back without straightening. "Okay. Hold his arm up this-a-way and we can make quick work of this one."

Sophie looked down at the soldier's gritty face. He was awake now, although his dark eyes fluttered in pain. She held his wrist and he jerked as his wound was addressed. Sophie tightened her hold.

"Where are you from?"

His vision sharpened on her. "Well, I must be in heaven already, ma'am, because you surely are the most beautiful angel I ever did see."

"You're not in heaven, I assure you."

"Nelson County, Virginia, ma'am."

"I see. You've come a long way."

"Yes, ma'am. My aching feet agree." He tapped his forehead with a quick salute. "Corporal Billy, that's what they call me, of the 22nd Virginia, at your service, ma'am." He grimaced hard.

"Keep still now."

"I'm afraid I missed your name."

"I'm Sophie Bauer and you're in my home."

"Mighty appreciative, ma'am."

"Gettysburg is my town."

"Well, we won't—" He inhaled sharply as the nurse wrapped his arm. "Won't be holding it long now. Once we're done showin' General Meade we mean business, we'll be moving on."

"Is that right?" She bit back a comment.

"Yes, ma'am. Got him where we want him now. All of them. Be right smart of him to step aside and let us march on through."

"To where?"

"To Washington, of course. Going to show your President Lincoln that the South's not to be reckoned with. We're to be left alone."

"Left alone to split our great country in two? To treat fellow human beings like animals? Where's your humanity, Corporal Billy?"

He ran his tongue along his parched lips and grinned up at her. "You're quite the lady, aren't you, Miss Sophie Bauer? A most lovely spitfire, if you'll allow me. You have to agree that states have rights, ma'am, that's why we're not all one big state. We're separate for a reason."

"First of all, we *are* 'one big state,' in a way. Your Virginia, Georgia, Alabama, the Carolinas…Once upon a time—not that long ago, I might add—we all fought and died together to become these *United* States, so we *are* one, going way back. And second, no one, no country or state or farmer, no person has a God-given right to enslave another. Those are facts as I know them."

Nurse Johnson straightened and wiped his hands on a blood-stained rag. "Spare your breath, Miss Sophie." She scolded herself for letting exhaustion get the better of her self-control. *Doctoring is about mercy, not politics.* "These rebs," he said, locking eyes with Billy, "they're too full of themselves to listen to reason. Damn shame they're hell-bent on learning the hard way." He stepped back. "We're done here. You, Corporal, keep that arm higher than your heart at all times, hear me?" He turned to Sophie. "A few bandage changes and we'll be rid of him. Thanks for your help, ma'am. Any time you want, you're welcome to lend us a hand. We could use it." No longer sure of her own endurance, Sophie hesitated, and he walked away.

"He'll see soon enough." Billy's eyes followed him to another injured rebel across the room. "You're mighty sure of yourself, Miss Sophie, I dare say. I find it remarkable, such quick, profound thinking from a Northern beauty."

Sophie knew he saw the surprise on her face. She composed a sharp retort, but he continued, offered his right hand.

"No disrespect, ma'am. None t'all. You are a ray of sunshine and I thank you."

She thought he intended to kiss her hand, so she shook his. *Perhaps the reputed Southern gallantry is real.* "Thank you for your compliment... well, your intention at least, Corporal Billy, but—"

"Be honored if'n you'd just call me Billy."

"Um...I can do that. Billy. In fairness, you may call me Sophie."

"I do thank you, ma'am, but a fine lady as yourself is to be respected, so I declare *Miss* Sophie to be most proper."

"You just keep that arm laying up there and hold it still, and before long you'll be back with your regiment. So...I wish you well, Billy."

CHAPTER SEVENTEEN

Sophie listened to Billy chuckle as she wound her way out of the parlor. Crossing outside to the summer kitchen, she lingered to breathe in the clean, albeit muggy air, then wiped her face with her apron. The quiet felt heavy around her, as if puffing up for a mighty blow. She hoped it wouldn't, at least not anytime soon.

Turning in place, she took in the lengthy line of the Union's little fires, watched them wink whenever soldiers passed in front. *Might you be sitting fireside, Coop? Are you along the line or was that you fighting on the hill tonight? Are you well?* Riders traversing the ridge distracted her, and occasionally she detected a glint of steel in the firelight.

Behind her, the Confederate line offered practically a mirror image. From somewhere along Seminary Ridge, a fiddle's sweet high notes reached her.

They are all soldiers, but first they are fathers, sons, brothers, lovers. Above all, they are as alike as kin.

She wondered if either side ever pondered the other this way. Her heart ached for them, for their families in towns she'd only heard or read about, homes where these displaced soldiers all were missed.

We are truly surrounded, she thought, and stared through the darkness at her distant neighbors. They, too, probably have military guests by now, and have been stripped of their tranquility.

She scrubbed at her face as if to awaken from this dream. There were linens to boil and loaves to retrieve from the oven. She sighed because tomorrow most likely would begin early, end just as late, and involve more of the same. She took a mental inventory of their stores of flour, butter, sugar, coffee beans, peach and apple jams, along with whatever meats hadn't yet been stolen from the smokehouse. And water. Dwindling fast, all of it, and somehow she had to make it last.

"Er…Miss Sophie?"

The sight of a rebel officer took her back. Looking to be about her age and rather dashing in a spotless uniform, complete with gold embroidery on his sleeves, he doffed his broad-brimmed hat just outside the doorway. He must have followed her from the house, but how long had he been standing there? Did Dr. Taylor, himself a Union captain, know of this rebel's presence? And, if so, couldn't he do something about him? Sophie felt the rising temptation to send him away.

"Yes, soldier?"

"Captain, ma'am," he corrected her, bowing slightly. "The Yankee doctor has asked for you to come back."

Sophie pulled the last loaves from the oven, gave the new pot of linens a vigorous stir, then walked past him without a glance. He could still be standing in the yard for all she cared, but sensed he wasn't far behind. The mixing of Union and Confederate wounded was one thing, but having enemy officers under the same roof felt quite tenuous.

"Sorry, we have to call on your assistance again so soon," Dr. Taylor said, leading her toward Billy. From what Sophie could tell, the rebel appeared chipper now, surveying all the goings-on from his new spot on the floor.

He offered a broad smile. "Ah, my Gettysburg savior has returned. Hello again, Miss Sophie."

"I hope you're behaving yourself." She looked to Dr. Taylor. "He seems quite—"

"Not the reb," he said, pointing to the unconscious Union soldier next to him. "This Yank over here."

Sophie turned and knelt beside him, took in the dust- and wheat-covered uniform, the jaw and chin darkened by dirt and soot. The sloppily applied bandage around his head forced his cap nearly over his eyes. But she recognized him.

"Oh, good heavens!" She reared back, fingertips at her mouth.

Dr. Taylor crouched at her side. "What is it? Do you know him?"

Nodding rapidly, as if convincing herself of what she saw, Sophie felt her heart leap into her throat. "This, I mean, it's—yes. Yes, I-I do."

"Well, then." He set a tin tray of supplies by her feet. "Could you take care of him on your own? We could use the help. Are you up for that? It's just a gash on the head, I believe. Needs to be cleaned up, fresh band—"

"Oh, yes. Yes, of course. Absolutely. Right away." She hardly noticed his pat on her shoulder as he rose.

Coop. Oh, my. Won't you be surprised when you wake?

Carefully, she cupped his head and peeled off the hat. She marveled at how his hair had grown, probably past his shoulders, if freed at the base of his neck.

His eyelids flickered but failed to open and immediately they went still. A guttural moan preceded a turn of his head, to the left and then right, and, as eager as she was to greet him, Sophie knew he needed more time to rise from unconsciousness.

She admired his graceful eyelashes, the slight eyebrows, and was tempted to trace the one that arched and lent a dash of attitude to his look. Clean-shaven as usual, but so dirty. His long jawline, squared chin, and sharply cut nose all now so shadowy with gunpowder and grit over a complexion she knew had to be as bronzed as any farmer's. And she bit back a grin at the silly mustache of dirt that always seemed to sit above his lips. Lips that had kissed hers, lips *she* had kissed. The tactile memory tingled in her chest. *Six months. Where did they go? It's so fine to see you again.*

With a mental shake, Sophie sat back on her heels. He does the uniform such justice, she thought, glad to see he still had all the buttons to his frock, but the clothing had seen its share of wear. Caked with dust and speckled with chaff, Coop still wore the ragged signs of the Fredericksburg fight, the scars on his frock and trouser leg now joined by threadbare elbows and knees. Even his battered cap looked more brown than blue.

"What happened to him?" she asked, unable to look away from his peaceful face.

"Oh, um…" Dr. Taylor snatched papers from his coat pocket. "Grazed by a shot to the head. Nasty one, I'd say, but he's a lucky man. Death missed him by a hair."

Sophie released a heavy, relieved breath. "So, a concussion."

"Very good. Yes, most definitely. The notes say he hit his head when he went down, which didn't help in the least. I imagine he tried to tough it out and dizziness finally did him in."

Sophie stroked loose strands of hair from Coop's forehead. "That sounds like him. He's not one to give in easily."

"With luck, he needn't be with us long, but it's hard to tell with concussions. First that bleeding has to stop and his brain has to settle."

Sophie leaned over Coop and examined the bandage. "I'll need more wrap than what's on the tray here," she said, and stood, eager to fetch necessities. "I'll get more from Nurse Johnson. And I'll make sure he has some coffee and bread when he comes around."

"Excellent. I'll leave Private Samson in your care, then."

She heard Billy rustling on the floor as she hurried off. Dr. Taylor told him to lay back down, then threatened to report him to the gold-braided captain. She hoped Billy wouldn't become a nuisance. The last thing she needed, with Coop here at last, was trouble from some obstinate, headstrong Confederate.

Before she risked another attempt at opening her eyes, Coop knew where she was. The smell alone told her, and the dangerously familiar sounds said her awareness was improving. It made identifying this location easy. Panic began to tighten her gut. She should not be here. Her breathing grew short in the stifling air, and perspiration blossomed along her legs, back, and chest. Moisture prickled her face.

As subtly as possible, she slid her hand against her side and felt her frock still in place. *My head. My head is why I'm here. They won't need...*

She hungered but dreaded to see. A medical tent, just where she *didn't* want to end up, damn it all. Gather your wits, she told herself, and your strength to keep away any well-intentioned hands.

Someone loomed close by, she could sense it. Then came tentative touches to her head, to that bandage Tim had wound at a tough angle around her head.

Regardless of whether the room continued to spin, she had to determine her location, assess herself well enough to move, and get out.

She was lying on something hard, probably a wood plank. A field hospital. A multitude of footsteps scuffed a surface that sounded sturdy, solid. A real floor, perhaps, and she recalled that wood-frame farmhouse nearby when they'd sent those rebels running.

Coop almost shuddered. She had to get out, get back to her regiment, and quit risking exposure like this.

She took a breath for courage and blinked until she felt confident enough to keep her eyes open. The world, the *house* around her slid into intermittent focus, doorway, windows, fireplace. Oil lamps cast everything in a buttery glow and made the room appear as hot as it felt. It was night, she remembered that much. And here, a woman, not an army nurse, knelt at her side, turned away to gather some implement.

Coop noted the flowing blond hair and its lopsided blue ribbon at the nape of a slender neck. She wanted to see more, but her head weighed too much to lift. She could tell, however, that a full apron covered the woman's dress and pooled around her knees on the floor.

"Pvt. Cooper Samson. Welcome to Gettysburg."

Leary of that damned jabbing pain in her head and cautious about her focus, Coop raised her eyes and fell into the lure of a lush spring day. *No, this really isn't her.*

But wasn't this beauty too close *not* to be her? The sparkle in that gaze, the curl of those lips…How many times since January had she pictured them? *So many, you think they're right here before you. Seriously, don't make a fool of yourself.*

Coop's nerves hummed beneath the woman's examination and caution bells clanged in her head. Her top priority *had* to be portraying Cooper, not Catherine, Samson. Every ounce of effort and strength had to go to ignoring the dizziness, headache, and unreliable vision, and getting out of these close quarters before *Catherine* became the Army of the Potomac's latest scandal. *Concentrate. Get a bandage and you'll be good to go. Concentrate.*

"Coop?"

There was that smooth voice again, speaking her name with familiarity. Fingertips rested on her cheek, a most delicate touch, intimate. Then pain seared through her head and her eyes slammed shut. *Ignore it and stop fantasizing. Be good to go. Sit up, look alert.*

Gentle urging at her forehead. "No, please don't try to lift your head. Coop, can you hear me?"

"S-sure. Just woozy, is all." She had to take this plunge. She forced her eyes open and her heart leapt. There was no doubt who leaned over her with such intense focus. "Sophie."

The worry on Sophie's face flashed into happiness. "Yes! Oh, Coop. I'm so glad to see you!"

"I can't believe… It's hard to trust the eyes, when—"

"Hush. I'm sure they're giving you trouble, but you *can* trust them." She took Coop's hand and held it to her chest. "You're going to be fine. I'll make sure of it."

"I'm not still dreaming?" Sophie shook her head and Coop risked a quick look at the scene beyond her. "Where am I?"

"In my home along the Emmitsburg Road." Sophie squeezed her hand and set it down. "I need to start on this mess you've made of yourself."

She turned to the tray and Coop blinked repeatedly. Nothing seemed to sharpen her vision whenever that fuzziness arose, and she tried not to worry. She still had to project decent health to ensure a prompt release. But…here was Sophie. *This borders on cruelty.*

With both hands, Sophie cautiously tipped Coop's head to the side. She leaned closer, studying, and finally began removing the bandage. "You know," she began, "when we were down in Falmouth, I don't believe we agreed to visit like this."

"I should never have tried to stop that bullet with my head."

Sophie grinned as she cast the bandage aside. "And you're not to attempt that again." She lit a small candle on the tray, poured water from a pitcher into a bowl, and then slid everything close to Coop's head.

"No, ma'am."

"This is an ugly slice," she said, holding the candle above it to see. "And there's lots of blood down here." She probed the back of Coop's head. "And beyond, beneath your collar, to your shoulder, I think. Heavens, you've bled a lot." She drew Coop's collar away from her neck. "I can't quite see how far it's gone."

When she moved to unfasten the top uniform button, Coop snapped up her hand. "No. It…It's okay."

Sophie looked puzzled. "I need to clean you up. Let's open this—"

"No need to bother, really. My—my head is really all that needs tending."

"Oh, come now. You're roasting in this. I'll just clean you up and we'll get on with it." She reached for the button and again, Coop took her hand.

"No. Honestly, Sophie. You needn't bother."

"But it's no bother, really. In this heat, you—"

"I'm used to the heat." *Wow, my head hurts.* She winced hard.

Sophie withdrew her hand, frowning.

Coop swallowed. In dreams, she'd melted beneath Sophie's hands, eagerly removed far more than a frock, but reality was another matter, more of a nightmare at the moment. She wasn't the man Sophie wished to dote upon here and couldn't afford to let her or anyone else know it.

"Stubborn Yankee, you are, Cooper Samson." She shook her head. "Very well, then."

Coop's anxiety eased when Sophie started addressing the wound, moving Coop's hair aside, and washing away the blood. The tentative strokes were soothing, and Coop tried to relax but couldn't close her eyes. Occasionally, pain made her squint, but she refused to lose sight of Sophie's arm and bosom, so near as she worked.

"Did your regiment arrive here today? Is that why you're so remarkably filthy?"

"Round Top, in time to miss supper."

"I'll get you something to eat as soon as we're done here." She sat back and Coop looked up at her, knowing she again failed to hide her discomfort. "Try this," Sophie said, and wet a cloth in the pitcher. "Close your eyes."

"But I...I've only just laid eyes on you."

Sophie brought her grin close to Coop's face. "I'm not going anywhere, and neither are you. Now, close them. That's an order." The words echoed in Coop's head as Sophie laid the cloth over her eyes. "There. Leave that alone for a while."

Coop remained a good patient. She lay motionless, listening to Sophie tinker with items on her tray, still stunned to be here with her.

"Whatever you have there smells like it could set my head aglow."

"Oh, my. You could be right. I never considered such a thing," Sophie said, and Coop enjoyed her feigned alarm. "Seriously, though, the beeswax in the cerate is critical and that's what you smell. Thankfully, this wound is longer than it is deep and won't require much packing. I'm just putting cerate on this lint and holding it in place with some adhesive plaster. We can only hope it sticks to your thick hair."

"Will I get my cap on over it?" Coop hated the idea of sticky muslin strips on her head.

"Well, that could take a little doing, with the wound on the side of your head. The top of your head would have been more convenient."

Coop grumbled as Sophie worked scissors through the coated muslin. "I'll remember that, next time I'm under fire."

"But you'll try to avoid that, Private Samson."

"Yes, ma'am."

Coop lifted the cloth off her eyes. It had warmed quickly in the hot house and she used it to rub the grit from her eyes and lashes. Focus returned, although still slow and soft around the edges, and she hoped improvement would hurry. She needed that acuity to shoot, to really *see* Sophie. She inched her elbows back and dared to raise herself a few inches off the floor to watch her work.

Those sure, soft hands manipulated a length of bandage over the candle flame, warming and activating the adhesive. Coop blinked repeatedly to drink in the sight of her, and didn't mean to voice her thoughts.

"You're such a beautiful woman." Embarrassed, Coop took a breath. Sophie's cheek flexed and Coop wondered if she was biting her lip in that adorable way. "Forgive me for such a forward remark." She lay back, wincing, but watching Sophie's every move.

Her eyes on the bandage, Sophie moved promptly to Coop's head and carefully pressed the strip into place. "You always take my breath away," Sophie whispered. "Thank you, but I'm hardly presentable in the least." She sent Coop a sideways look. "Obviously, your vision has yet to clear."

Coop placed a hand on her arm. "You're beautiful inside and out, Miss Bauer. I'm recovering just being with you." She winced again and kicked herself for revealing her discomfort. "How soon do you think they'll release me?"

Finished with bandaging, Sophie blew out the candle and handed Coop a cup of coffee. "Do not guzzle," she said. "Are you looking to leave already?"

Up on one elbow, Coop forced down welling nausea to drink the coffee. Its strength and stout flavor took her taste buds by surprise and she suppressed a cough. Her head throbbed. "Thank you for this. And, no, it's not that I *want* to leave, of course, but..." Unsteady in this position, she wavered and took a breath at another pain. "I-I just assume they'll be collecting me as soon as possible. I suppose I'd be okay to go."

"Oh, do you, now?" Sophie shook her head. "Here. Please eat as much of this bread as you can." She placed the large chunk on Coop's chest. "I'm going to find you something for a pillow. You shouldn't have your head on this floor."

And she was up and hurrying away. As much as Coop longed to watch her, she couldn't risk much movement. The half-empty coffee cup now weighed ten pounds. She set it on the floor and took a huge bite of bread. Crusty and fluffy, exquisite. She devoured the rest despite her mounting headache. The pain and dizziness just might do her in, and she didn't trust the weakness in her limbs. She did have faith in Sophie's skill, however, that the bleeding had been stemmed, and tried to convince herself that she would soon regain strength enough to leave.

A little more patience.

"Here we are. This is better than hard wood." Sophie knelt close by again. "It's just an old jacket Karl has outgrown. I'm sorry it's all I could find." She folded and plumped the jacket.

"I'm grateful. Thank him for me. And thank you for the coffee and this bread. It's very good."

"Greta's specialty," Sophie said with a prideful smile, and cautiously lifted Coop's head and slid the jacket into position. She wet the cloth again and wiped soot and grime from Coop's forehead and face, cupping her chin to stroke her cheeks.

Coop relished the tenderness and cast her eyes down.

Sophie sighed. "You have the loveliest eyelashes."

Coop could feel the blush in her cheeks. She'd swapped her wardrobe for her brother's long ago, cut away the long braid that once drew the admiration of many, and today wore shoulder-length hair gathered by a strand of leather, but there'd been nothing she could do to disguise her eyes. She kept them lowered and swallowed the last of her bread.

Sophie must have noticed her reaction, even in this poor light, for she stumbled over her words. "Oh, I-I've embarrassed you, haven't I? I beg your pardon. I simply couldn't help but notice."

"Um...My mother's."

"Then I imagine she was a lovely woman." She laid a hand on Coop's shoulder. "I'd so much rather stay with you, Coop. Heaven knows, I would, but...you know, I-I promised to look after some of the others."

"I understand." Coop tried to read her eyes, to see a reflection of her own longing, but focusing hurt. Frustrated beyond words, she rubbed her eyes with her hands.

"It's important that you rest now, anyway."

"Thank you for all you've done. Come back soon, please?"

"As soon as I can. I don't want them snatching you back to duty without me knowing." She leaned down and squeezed Coop's hand. "Rest well, Coop. Don't roll your head onto your wound."

Sophie disappeared from her line of vision and Coop's tension eased. *Lovely eyelashes.* She pinched her eyes. They were strained, like the rest of her, and despite the concern that she'd be released soon, she tried to nap.

But motion to her right disturbed her. Another uncomfortable wounded comrade, she thought, and wondered if he was from her unit or even her army.

Chapter Eighteen

H ey, Yank. You awake?"

A damn reb. Coop cursed her luck. Heal quick, she told herself.

"Who's asking?"

"She's a pretty one, the nursemaid. Could you see that much?"

"'Course I could."

"You know her?"

"I do. Lay off."

"She and I made friends already, so don't get your hopes up."

"Gettysburg lady has no interest in your kind, Johnny Reb."

"Name's Billy. Heard you're Cooper."

"Not making conversation with you."

"Looks like we laid you out like cake on a griddle."

"Just a nick. You rebs can't shoot for damn."

"Was thinking the same about you feds. Just took a chunk out of this ol' arm. Nuisance is all it is."

"*That* we agree on."

"So, Doc says you're from hifalutin Massachusetts."

"What of it?" Coop asked, already weary of this exchange, especially considering she wasn't able to roll over and look him in the eye.

"Well, 22nd Virginia right here. Corporal to you, Private."

"We all bleed the same, corporal or private, Yank or reb. Black or white."

"Whoa, now. Don't be spoiling our social time with that talk."

Knew that would get you.

"Like I said, don't want to make conversation with you."

"Now, you listen up. We're both stuck here so's no reason we can't be polite."

Coop considered rolling onto her other side. That might shut him up. But if those dizzies came back, they'd end up prolonging her stay. Still, the idea of conversing with this Southerner soured her mood.

"Now, Cooper. Y'know we have some things in common, you and me. We're in this town to have at it, once and for all, we're both shot up, and we have us the prettiest nursemaid any man could want. But know what else?"

She refused to take the bait and stared up at the thick—fuzzy—hand-hewn ceiling beams. *Please just shut up and let me rest, let me think.*

"Well, I'll tell ya anyway. Doc said we have the same surname. Samson."

Coop caught herself just as her head twitched in his direction. *What are those odds?* "Bum luck."

He laughed. "Thought so, too. You spell yours with a 'p'?"

"No." She closed her eyes.

"Same here. Say, whereabouts you from in high 'n' mighty Massachusetts?"

Although surprised, Coop wasn't that curious. And she was drained. "No matter."

"Well, see, you might say I did some time up there." He cleared his throat, as if what he was about to reveal stuck in his windpipe. "Actually, I grew up there."

"Y'don't say." Now, Coop's curiosity level rose.

"I do. Hate to admit that a heartfelt loyal Virginian such as myself lacks pure Southern blood, but…but it's a fact. Born and raised in your state, but I thank the Lord I saw the light when I grew old enough."

Coincidence rattled her, made the fine sticky hair on the back of her neck tingle. She longed to see his face.

"Know what else, Private? Can't be very many Cooper Samsons in Massachusetts, so you know what I think?"

Fate could not turn on me this way, could it?

Coop tried to brace herself. Sonny, after fourteen years? Would he see in her the dead brother she now pretended to be? Or would he recognize his sister? How vivid was his memory? Her vision might be sketchy, but she itched to see if she recognized him.

Coop tried to think, to decide if she really wanted to know. So many memories came to mind. Oh, how they cried while he ranted that last day. Had to be a "man of his own making," he shouted at their father, to be somewhere that offered better weather, an easier life, and more appreciative ladies. And today, Sonny was the family's last surviving son, and entitled to the property she claimed as her home.

If he identifies me...

She faked sleep, snored a few times, and heard him grumble as he settled himself again.

Except he hadn't.

A firm jab to her arm forced Coop to open her eyes. He knelt at her side, leaning over her chest, so close her lack of focus didn't matter. Heavily bearded, he stared straight down at her with deep, dark determination. Coop nearly shivered. He had the family's broad shoulders and long face, the only child of the three to win Father's wide ears. And that cocky attitude, the aggressiveness she remembered from childhood.

There's little doubt. He has none, either, but which twin does he see?

"I can't let you sleep," Billy stated, frowning. "I need to know where you're from." His wiry beard bounced as he spoke. "And, God as my witness, you're looking familiar enough to me here and now to be my brother. So, out with it. Then I'll tell you where I's born 'n' raised."

The clouds that filled her head these past hours dissipated instantly, and Coop thought fast. *Better to be the brother he believes he still has, than the sister he'll expose.* She widened her eyes and let her jaw drop.

"Sonny?"

"Whoa, Lord above!" He fell back as if shoved, his look matching hers. "Yessir, it's me. And it's *you*!" A smile broke across his face. "Look what's happened to the wispy lad I taught to ride? I hardly recognize ya, boy!"

"Looks like the south has been good for you. You're bigger—and hairier—than I ever thought I'd see, Sonny."

"I go by Billy now."

"You're Sonny to me."

"Yup, we're kin. Damn stubborn Samson. I've gone by Billy for the past ten years, so you'll use it."

"Don't have to like it."

He laughed as his eyes roamed along her cheek to her chin. "With dirt all rubbed off now, I see y'still got Mama's face. Can't grow one of these?" And he tugged on his chest-length beard.

"Corporal Samson!" The rebel captain stalked across the floor. "Git yourself down on that blanket! Keep that arm up. Can't be sparing you much longer."

"Cap," Billy tried, hustling into position as ordered, "see, this here's my brother. Lot of years it's been, Cap."

The captain barely glanced at Coop before sending Billy a scowl. "Don't give a damn if'n you two is Davis and Lincoln. We got lots of brothers fightin' brothers. Keep your mind straight. You forget this is war?"

Apparently satisfied, he stormed away.

"He's new. All full of vinegar," Billy whispered.

"Any good?"

"Oh, he's all right. Knocked senseless in Fredericksburg but learned his lesson about parading around on his horse." He yawned. "Can't believe this. It's really you. After all this time. Bet Mother and the old codger sure hated to see you go, being the last man on the farm, and all." He chuckled, then. "And Catherine must've bawled her eyes out, losing her twin spirit. She married yet?"

All of sudden, you care?

Coop took her time formulating an answer. It was difficult, brought on a whole different type of pain. *She* had cried for days when the souls of both parents and Cooper *left her.* When the old barn collapsed on them, where had Sonny been then? How she had luxuriated in that hour-long buggy ride home, until she turned onto their property and found them. She was alone as of that moment and had been since. He'd abandoned them from the start, only ever sent one vague letter home. He didn't deserve many details.

"They all cried," she finally said. "Like that day you left." She knew he didn't want that subject revived. "And no, Catherine hasn't married." She added that fact out of pride.

"Hm. Well, I always doubted she would. Such a stubborn streak in that girl, just like you."

"She's a woman, Son—Billy. Not a girl. Smart, with a mind of her own. You, of all people, should respect independent thinking."

"You gotta admit, by now she should've seen the need to marry. Is she aiming to live off you once the folks are gone? Funny, I never saw her as some withered ol' spinster."

Coop tamped down her irritation. "She can make her own way as she likes. She's plenty capable."

"A woman still needs a man to provide for her, a house 'n' home, and little ones. It's not smart for a woman to get all independent, not proper. They shouldn't be roaming about, putting down roots wherever they choose."

"In your mind."

"Pretty sure old Massachusetts has laws about it, Cooper."

"Says the Confederate ignoring the president of our United States."

"Don't start that now. Southern independence is a whole different—"

"I need to sleep." Coop closed her eyes.

Billy fell silent for a moment and Coop gave thanks. Just as contrary as ever, contentious, and she knew he'd react in the extreme if he ever saw through her facade.

"We have so much catching up to do, Coop." His voice was distant now. "Hey, how about you come visit once this is over?"

That thought made her stomach turn. "You should give that invite more thought. There's lots to consider."

"Hm. I reckon maybe you're right."

Coop went quiet and listened to her heart pound in her ears. So far, so good.

A rebel dumped firewood into the corner of the summer kitchen, and Sophie recognized her farm's fence rails and the red-washed color of the chicken house. Bit by bit, the homestead was coming apart and she was helpless to stop it.

Helpless and toasting to a crisp. She wished she could let their stove go cold. Already, she perspired as linens boiled, biscuits baked, and a huge pot of corn mash cooked down. Greta had to use both hands to stir the latter and when she nearly tumbled off the footstool at the stove, Sophie took over.

"Enough, honey. Why don't you go up now, try to read some of your book?"

"But you told us Coop is here. Won't you take me to meet him?"

"There'll be plenty of time for that—I hope. Right now, it's terribly crowded in there with sights not fit for young eyes, and, besides, I don't know how he's doing this morning. Now, you be careful going back to the house, and go directly upstairs."

"I'm looking forward to meeting him too," Papa said from the doorway.

Karl stopped stacking the firewood to comment. "Me, too."

"There'll be time to meet him later," Sophie told them all, hardly sure of it.

Papa nodded with approval and wiped his brow. "Awfully early to be this hot. Going to be brutal today." He peeked into the pots. "I'll walk you back, Greta. It's probably not as peaceful out there as we think."

He eyed Karl's stacking job, and Sophie wondered what went through Papa's mind, seeing his hard labor reduced to firewood. He gave Karl a pat on the back. "In a bit, we'll take a look at the well and then see what's left in the smokehouse."

"Just please take care out there, Papa. By the sounds of things, a stray shot could come from anywhere at any time." She selected two warm biscuits from the basket nearby and set them in his calloused palm. "For each of you. This mash is almost done, so I'll bring it in after I deliver the biscuits and coffee."

"Have Karl help you, Sophie." He put a fingertip to her shoulder. "You pace yourself, young woman. Yesterday was a very long day and I don't like the feel of today."

"Well, it does have an odd feel about it."

"Be prompt with your deliveries in there and try not to get too roped into all that nursing work. I know you will, but... Well, there's a lot of men now and only one you. I think you catch my thinking."

"We have enough to worry about, Papa." She kissed his cheek. "Don't worry yourself about me."

Loaded with food and drink, Sophie and Karl walked briskly to the house and into the foul breath of the parlor. She hoped he wouldn't witness anything traumatic. Karl crinkled his nose and Sophie longed for the day they could air out their home. *It will take weeks.*

Inside, she found the scene calmer than last night, but with new additions that took up precious walking space. As Karl made room on a table for their biscuits and pots of coffee and mash, Sophie filled trays with cups and bowls on medical crates.

"Morning, Miss Sophie, Karl." Dr. Taylor looked as though he hadn't slept. Sophie couldn't imagine where he would have, anyway. "My, the Bauer family has been hard at it, I see. Thank you. Thank you. Thank you."

"Seems this is a quiet moment, Doctor. Where should I start?" Handing him the first cup, she scanned the room and noticed the addition of an operating table, formerly the door to their keeping room. She sighed. *At least it's not in use.*

"Nurse Johnson will show you," he said. "Most of them can take drink, at least."

"Okay. Karl, you can go help Papa, if you'd like."

"But he said I should stay with you on account of the men being—"

"Well, you're both sweet, but you can see things here are under control."

He scratched his head as he looked around for himself. "If you say so." He hurried away.

Dr. Taylor stood by sipping steadily, watching Sophie ladle coffee. "You have a wonderful family. We're so grateful."

"We're proud to do what we can, but what does it say about us when our young ones must confront the terrors of war? It's a sad day for us all."

"I do understand."

Sophie lifted the tray and turned to locate nurse Johnson. "I'm afraid our supplies won't last much longer, so maybe hostilities will end soon."

His face sagged. "Our supplies are lacking, too, and I'm sorry to say, I fear hostilities have yet to reach their peak."

Sophie shook her head, thought it best to concentrate on the task at hand. Following Nurse Johnson's direction, she inched her way to the rear of the room and began distributing coffee.

"Ah," Billy said as she neared, "my Gettysburg angel. Morning to you, Miss Sophie."

"Morning." She handed him a cup. "No, please take it with your good arm."

"Naw, this one's feeling much better."

She held the cup away. "Your *good* arm. Look, now I can see blood coming through your bandage. Not the progress the doctor hoped for today."

"Eh." He used his right hand to take the coffee and slurped as he drank. "Pardon my gluttony, ma'am. This sure is fine."

She glanced behind her at Coop.

"He's still sleeping it off," Billy told her. "Say, I have big news."

"And what might that be?"

He gestured with his cup. "Cooper over there, him and me, we're brothers."

Sophie straightened. "No."

That she hadn't expected. Details of a conversation last winter came to mind. *You are the long-lost brother?*

Billy nodded with enthusiasm. The reunion obviously pleased him. "Been some years, but we recognized each other last night." It appeared just as obvious that brothers now being mortal enemies didn't upset him.

Sophie couldn't see a shred of resemblance between them.

"You two talked and you're certain?"

"We did and we are. Taught him to ride and shoot when he was, maybe, five. He was just a boy when I left home. Haven't seen him in years. Ain't it something?"

"Certainly is. I must say you do not look alike."

"I know we both could use a good scrub, but that wouldn't help. We never did. He takes after our mother. Do you know he has a twin sister? Spittin' image."

"Yes, he's told me." *Told me far more than he has told you, apparently.*

"Hm. So...you and him...you two are, well, pretty *familiar?*"

Sophie straightened at the insinuation. "It really isn't your business."

"Eh." Billy flipped his good arm out with dismissal. "He tell you how he and his sister confounded everybody, even me on occasion? They made great fun of it, although Catherine was the instigator. Mother would get plenty mad at the teasing. Catherine would stuff that braid of hers up into one of Coop's hats, put on his clothes, and have Mother running in circles. She blamed Catherine, Father blamed him." He grinned at Coop. "Said Coop shouldn't let Cath run or ride as fast as him, or shoot better, but Coop always had Mother's soft side, so..."

Sophie studied Cooper's face, turned away in profile, and tried to picture a female version. For a fleeting moment, she saw a woman with neatly trimmed dark hair, aristocratic nose, smooth cheekbones, and wiry figure. The concept of a female Cooper intrigued her, definitely had appeal, and Sophie caught herself before lapsing into a familiar fantasy.

"Well, thank you for sharing a fine story, but I must move along."

"Do tell me you'll be back."

"I'm telling Dr. Taylor about your bleeding." She hesitated before turning away and nodded toward Coop. "I have some breakfast to give out, and he needs to eat. Yes, I'll be back."

"Soon, I hope," Billy said as she left.

Still facing away on his side, Coop grumbled. "You never shut up, do you?"

"Morning to you, too, brother."

"Y'think she's got nothing better to do than listen to your tales?"

"You always wake up so pleasant? I guess some of Catherine's feistiness wore off on you over the years."

I have to wake up to this.

Coop rolled onto her back and focused on the ceiling, glad to see the beams in crisp definition. She risked raising her head a few inches, and when that drew no pain or dizziness, she propped herself up on both elbows and looked around.

"Lord, look at this place."

"The doc caught up on everyone, so it's gone quiet."

She counted nine Union soldiers and seven rebs, including Billy and herself, then spotted Sophie in the doorway, speaking with a Union soldier, his hat in hand. *Tim!* He turned and picked his way across the floor to Coop.

"Samson," he yelled ahead. He looked tired and battle worn, but his goofy smile was literally a sight for her sore eyes. "Finally managed to get back out here. That *is* you beneath that headwear, isn't it?"

"My disguise isn't working?"

He chuckled at that and crouched at her side. "Sorry I'm late getting to you. Lot of preparations under way. Pickets are still hot, so I had to keep my head down to make it out here."

"Thanks for coming. You here to haul me back?"

"Sarge sent me and I just tried with the doc. Guess you're not fit yet." He looked over his shoulder in Sophie's direction. "But you've got plenty of reason to stay. Guess who I just found." He shook his head. "You have the damnedest luck, Coop, I swear. *Sophie's* house of all houses?"

"Hey, I had no say in where I ended up, remember. Surely can't complain, though."

"Well, you're the luckiest dog I know. How's your head?"

"Peachy." She didn't let on about the rising nausea, just being propped up like this. "What's happening out there? I was in and out last night, heard a lot of noise, but lately…"

"Everyone's maneuvering." He lent Billy a surreptitious glance. Leaning closer, he put his cap to his cheek to shield his hushed words. "General Meade arrived in the middle of the night and he liked what Hancock set up. We've been digging in and playing mason for hours now. Y'know, if I never see another stone wall, it'll be too soon."

"Where'd we set up?" she whispered.

"At least for now, we're centered along the ridge wall, just south and back of the 20th. There's movement on both our flanks so things could start there, on the hills. But, meanwhile," he jabbed his thumb westward, "Anderson's division sits right over there, looking straight at us."

"Meade's going to wait him out?"

Tim nodded. "The thinking is Anderson's going to come straight at us. We're in a mean hurry to collect all our men out of these farmhouses."

"Anderson would advance right through here?"

"No doubt, judging by where he's sitting. I expect we'll form up here along the Emmitsburg to stop them halfway. Things could get bad right here, Coop."

"Maybe the doc will release me in time. I'll push him for it."

"Good. But if you don't have any luck, keep your head down 'cause there's going to be hell to pay. Lot of units along their line, but we think there are lots more we can't see in their woods. Plus, artillery's set up along each ridge, so the lead's going to fly." He took a moment to survey the room. "Not much for cover in here. Maybe get yourself over to the wall and under that table."

Sophie and the family should know.

"I'll do my best."

He patted her knee, wedged his cap onto his head as he stood. "I'm counting on you to come out of this scrape, y'know."

"You watch yourself, too." Pain slashed across her eyes when she looked up at him. She winced and laid back tentatively. "We all need to come out of this in one piece, my friend."

"You remember that," he said, and winked. "Remember Sophie, too."

CHAPTER NINETEEN

"You should put more in your stomach than coffee, Coop," Sophie tried. "Here, eat a biscuit if you don't want the mash."

"My stomach's a little queasy. I don't want to risk it," Coop replied, not happy to disappoint but afraid to go too far. Back up on her elbows again, the nausea was awful. Just looking at the food was dangerous. She much preferred looking at Sophie, her relatively clean apron and rose-dotted dress, her satiny hair brushed and in place with a fancy comb, her face bright and aglow with morning energy.

"I'll take his if he don't want it," Billy said, and reached across his body for the biscuit.

"You mind your business, Corporal," Sophie said. "I can see the blood on your bandage from here. You may take the biscuit but lie down with that arm up. I'll change your dressing when I'm done with his."

She took away Coop's empty cup and began inspecting his bandages. "Looks like your wound has finally surrendered, but you mustn't press on it. No wearing your cap."

"No, ma'am. Not until I'm released. You think today?"

"How eager you are." She had to admit it hurt a little. "I first should make you eat a biscuit or two."

"Please no!"

"Don't worry. I won't, but Dr. Taylor says your dizziness still needs to fade further. When he examined your eyes earlier, I guess he knew. He says your disagreeable stomach is part of it."

"A man's got to do his duty."

"Oh, please. Do not tell a woman about duty, Private Samson."

"Well, I can't be coddling my stomach when I—"

"It's far more than your stomach and you know it."

"I've never let a foul stomach keep me from my work, and I'm not about to now."

"You *will* eat before going anywhere. Don't argue with me. My, you're obstinate today."

"I have a job to do."

"You want to go out there, stagger around, and get shot? Get your fellow soldiers shot when you can't do your part?" Coop snapped her mouth shut, glad to think she'd sounded like the average soldier. "Good," Sophie said. "Stop trying to be a hero." She set a biscuit on Coop's chest and resumed her inspection, a resolute expression on those alluring lips. "When you *are* released, you'll need some sustenance and you know it. In this heat, you will keel right over."

Reluctant, Coop ate and replayed her own words in her head, evaluated the performance. *A common soldier's attitude, an adequate portrayal, one Sophie would expect to hear.* Determined to reinforce her persona, particularly with Billy eavesdropping nearby, Coop vowed to be more deliberate with her words and tone.

"Things could pick up, Sophie, so you need to take care. Pretty sure we'll be finishing things soon, so I need to get back at it."

"Uncle Bobby's army may have something to say about that," Billy injected. "You best lay low, little brother, or you won't be getting back to anything. Pretty sure the family needs you." With a snicker, he added, "Bet Catherine's taken charge by now."

Coop flicked her eyes up to Sophie's. *Please don't correct him.* Sophie held her gaze for a long moment, maybe confused, maybe just surprised, but the look made Coop's stomach clench. *I have my reasons. Please trust in that.* She hurried to advance the conversation.

"Well, I can't have things get out of hand while I'm gone."

"Catherine's a real go-getter," Billy informed Sophie, "and not one to stay inside doing women's work for long."

Knowing Sophie observed them keenly, Coop turned just enough to see him.

"I recall the brother who used every excuse known to man to avoid *his* work."

"Not true."

"Yes, true. Whenever Father couldn't find you, guess who had to work twice as hard?"

So many times, I worked to help Cooper in your place, and did my chores for Mother as well. Every day, for years after you left.

"The work made a man out of you."

Coop considered delivering a literal blow to Billy's manhood.

"Here, now," Sophie said, and held up a palm toward each of them. "True brothers. Stop bickering." She drew rolls of bandage and lint from her apron. "Time to redress your arm, Billy. Hold it up."

He lifted his arm, and as Sophie packed and wrapped the wound, he grinned at Coop.

"Fine lady so hard at work, on the floor, no less," he said. "You'd never see such a sight in the South. A decent man would never allow it." He shook his head. "Tragic thing, I tell you."

"Hush," Sophie ordered him.

"Lady such as yourself is deserving of finery and luxury, enjoying sweet tea on the veranda, working her needlepoint with other gentleladies, not a care in the world. Now, can't you see yourself in such a life, Miss Sophie? I know you can."

Coop sighed. "Will you shut up?"

Sophie continued to work, undaunted. "Sorry to shake loose that dream of yours, Billy, but this farmer's daughter wouldn't last an hour."

"Why, certainly you would. Gentlemen callers bringing flowers, trinkets, courting you. They'd fill your sitting room, be lined up out the door for the attention of a lady as lovely as you."

"Have we mixed up our patients here?" She cast a wonderous look about the room before finishing with his bandage. "Why, *you* must be the soldier with the head trouble."

Coop laughed and the pain forced her eyes shut. Her stomach roiled and she put a hand over it.

"Now, the both of you be still."

Billy popped up on his good arm and watched her leave. "She likes me."

"Told you before. Gettysburg lady wants no part of Johnny Reb."

Billy laid back down, his bad arm straight up beyond his head, his good one tucked beneath it. "Well, I could sway her. Working a farm, keeping house, the cooking, cleaning, washing…All this work she's doing she'd never have to do at home."

"Oh, because you'd be right by her side, helping."

"No need, my brother. We have darkies for that."

Coop's rage simmered and she clenched her fist. *If I didn't think I'd fall over, I'd...* "You want to start that argument?"

"Why do you think I left?"

"We all know why. Father was so ashamed."

"Ashamed? I remember him eating up every word those big-talking politicians spouted, refusing to see reason, always professing how states should give everything to stay united. Didn't matter to him what Southerners cared about. Hifalutin Yankee ways. And then, when he'd start in about 'Negro freedom'?" He shook his head at the memory. "Simple common sense tells ya darkies ain't suited for that. Bet Father still works himself to the bone not seeing reason. Made no sense then and don't now."

"And here you are, seeing war as the solution."

"Because here *you* are, pushing that same nonsense." He rolled onto his side and pointed at her. "Pushing that nonsense onto others, Lincoln making laws to force it...Like a disease, I tell you. You can keep it up north. We're here to stop it spreading south."

Coop closed her eyes and rubbed her angry stomach. "Long as I live, I'll never understand how we can be related."

Sophie's heart sank to see that someone, no doubt a soldier, had drawn nearly all the fresh water from the summer kitchen's reservoir tub. Papa's cautionary words about their well immediately came to mind and she feared the worst. If they ran out of water...

She cut the last strips of fabric from the old skirts, petticoats, and sheeting Greta had collected upstairs and stuffed them into water just used for boiling bandages. Everything had to be reused now, supplies were disappearing fast, including kitchen supplies. She even swore when she found her favorite skillets gone.

Karl lugged in a bucket of water, staring at it as he moved with quick, abrupt steps. "I tried not to spill any, but it was hard to hurry—"

"Oh, Karl. You're a saint." Sophie rushed to help him and emptied the bucket into the tub.

"Papa will be right along." He wiped his perspiring face with his arm. "Buckets take a long time to fill. He said the spring's going dry."

"I know. Help me move the tub before he adds any more water." She pointed to the corner. "Behind the table, underneath it."

"We're hiding it, aren't we?" he asked as they dragged the tub across the floor.

"We are. Out of sight, out of mind." She raised the hem of the tablecloth and they slid the tub under the table, then lowered the cloth to conceal their treasure. "Soldiers are taking everything back to their camps and all of us, especially those wounded men in need, will soon be left with nothing."

"Papa said the rebels are a greedy bunch."

"They're so far from home, their supplies have to be low if not gone, and our army isn't letting Southern trains up this far."

"Well, the rebs busted up *our* train tracks, but Papa thinks there's a huge Union wagon train way down the Baltimore Pike. So, maybe we'll get some supplies from that."

"I suppose it's possible. That would be wonderful, wouldn't it?" Sophie stroked back his hair. "But it's a long haul to farmhouses out here on the Emmitsburg. We can't count on it."

"I miss our chickens, too. Eggs would be nice. You think they have eggs on the supply train?"

"Hm. They might."

"The rebs will steal anything, won't they? They even took Penny, a cow not yet prime."

"We all miss Penny, honey."

Papa arrived with another bucket and Sophie and Karl moved the table aside for him to access the tub. "Darn shame we have to resort to this," he said. "Good idea, nonetheless. How's Dr. Taylor situated for water?"

"Probably due any time now."

"I'll try to squeeze another bucket out of the well, but that may take a while. And our friend Cooper? How's he getting on?"

"Some mending to do still. You know, he's had the most confounding coincidence occur."

Papa let out an exhausted sigh. "Just what the poor wounded fellow needs right now."

"So true." Sophie appreciated his compassion. "He's met the brother he hasn't seen in fourteen years."

"His brother? Wow!" Karl exclaimed.

"My, my!" Papa set his hands on his hips. "Now, *that* should help his healing process. How wonderful for him."

"It would be if the brother hadn't aligned himself with the wrong side."

"Oh, no. Brother against brother?"

"You've already made the brother's acquaintance, Papa, that first rebel we had here. Billy's his name. The Virginian corporal."

"No! He's a big fellow, too."

"Do they look alike?" Karl wanted to know.

"Does *who* look alike?" Greta asked, hurrying in.

"Coop's brother is here," Karl announced, "and he's a reb!"

Greta's eyebrows peaked closer together. "Oh! Poor Coop."

"Exactly," Sophie said. "His brother abandoned the family long ago."

She returned to pondering Coop's pleading expression when Billy broached the subject of family. She could sympathize with Coop's animosity toward him, but why hadn't he told Billy about the tragedy?

Maybe Coop believes a brother who shunned the family doesn't deserve to know.

"Coop isn't particularly thrilled about this reunion. In fact, they've already started arguing."

"Typical brothers," Papa said.

Greta turned excited eyes to Sophie. "Now, I really want to meet Coop. Please, will you take me to see him? Please? Now?"

"Not now, Greta. He's been sleeping most of the afternoon, so I need to check on him—and the others, of course, and bring them something to drink."

"I'll help you."

"Thank you, but the parlor's no longer a place for children, I'm afraid. When Coop's allowed to walk around, test his balance, I'll arrange for this grand meeting."

Greta pouted and spun away. "Hope it's soon."

CHAPTER TWENTY

The scream of a thousand screech owls woke Coop with a start. The god-awful rebel yell. She knew it well.

Guns began firing, a scattering of shot that blossomed into a prolonged exchange. Cannon fired and the farmhouse shook. Very close by, she deduced, could be rebel guns. Then a blast hurt her ears.

A twelve-pound ball tore through the side of the house, and everyone who could, yelled something. A tall oak hutch behind Coop rocked back against the wall and, looking straight up, she watched it topple in her direction. She threw herself onto her good side and heard it crash behind her, glass, dishes, and bowls shattering on the floor. Billy howled in pain.

Coop swallowed the bile rising in her stomach to crawl to where he lay beneath the large shelving unit. Limited to one good arm, Billy lacked the strength and leverage to free himself, so she hoisted one side, fitted her shoulders beneath it, and rose on her knees until enough space opened for him to slide out. She went to all fours again and lowered the hutch to the floor.

Billy sat up and stared at the slanting sunlight now beaming through the wall. He snorted as a cut across his forehead bled into his eye. "Who in hell hit the house?"

Coop sat beside him, settling her stomach. Her vision could be better, but at least her head wasn't spinning. "Late afternoon sun's coming in. What's that tell you?" The setting sun said the shot had come from the west and the Confederate line.

"Hope we correct that quick," Billy muttered.

A minié ball pierced a shutter and its window with a pop. Coop and Billy ducked instinctively as it slammed into a beam behind them. Outside, the firing rose to ferocious volleys. The thudding sound of running soldiers could be heard inside.

"Skirmish fire," Coop mumbled, fearing it preceded far greater action.

"Eh." Billy wiped his eye with his sleeve. "Who knows what they're up to." He groused at his arm, at the blood seeping through his bandage. "This thing's gone and started up again."

Cannon fire then sounded from south of the house, a serious barrage, soon complemented by another, from the north. Like many other wounded nearby, they turned their heads from one side of the building to the other as the noise heightened.

"They're going at it on either end of the lines," Billy said.

"Which means this skirmishing around us here in the middle is either distraction or prelude."

"Best get over to that side. Might be safer."

Coop took her makeshift pillow and Billy grabbed her blanket, and they crawled to a niche in the corner.

"You use it," she told him as they settled down. "I'm just glad to have this for my head."

"Thanks. And thanks for getting me out, back there. You doing all right?"

"Well, my eyes, they're...peculiar. And my stomach wants to kick that biscuit back up."

"I suppose you ought to lie down. Don't be hurling nothin' up on me."

The front door banged open and a Union soldier helped a comrade inside. Blood ran steadily from the stump of the wounded man's arm as he was half dragged across the room to Dr. Taylor.

"From your unit?" Billy asked.

Coop shook her head.

A bullet ricocheted off the opened door and a rebel steward dared to go and shut it. Another zipped through a shuttered window and the one-armed soldier at Dr. Taylor's table spun out of his comrade's grip and dropped, shot in the head.

"Damn it all," Coop said. "Keep low. It's all we can do." They stretched out on the floor and listened to the rising tumult of cannon and rifle fire.

Solid shot, distinctive when it pounded into turf, landed directly outside and the tremor vibrated through the floor and into her back. Knowing the cannonball most likely would bounce, she and Billy exchanged a glance and waited for the final crash. She heard some building on the Bauer property shatter.

If only gunners and infantry stayed on target, she thought. Here, this incoming Confederate artillery fire seemed mostly random and faulty, long-distance attempts falling short of the hills, but infantry riflery from both armies spoke of closer action. She knew the house had just begun to suffer the consequences of its location.

"Wonder where Sophie went," Coop muttered.

"Saw her and the father talking and then leave pretty quick."

"The whole family should head for the cellar."

Billy surveyed the crowded, chaotic room. "House may not hold up for us, either."

Sophie preferred the safer confines of their summer kitchen with its robust stone walls to the wood-frame house, but most definitely preferred either to being outside. With five loaves of bread wrapped in a towel atop a basket of clean bandages, she stepped over the pair of wounded rebels in the doorway and dashed the ten yards to the house. Mid-stride, she spotted Papa scrambling to his feet near the barn.

She stopped, praying he hadn't been hit, and then yelped when a cannon fired from somewhere very close by. Through the ensuing smoke, she cried, "Are you all right, Papa?"

He waved her onward. "Get inside, Sophie! I'm coming."

"Hurry!"

She waited for him at the back door, and nearly swooned with relief at his brief smile.

"I'd just left the barn when the door exploded. Knocked me clean off my feet, stole my breath. Those boys ought to shoot better than that."

"A cannonball has clipped the peak of our roof," she told him, and pointed up. "Karl wanted to check the damage, but I sent him to the cellar."

Papa took the pile of bread off her basket and led her toward the parlor. "Let's pass these on. Time we looked after ourselves." They winced when multiple cannon boomed in the yard and he stepped closer to be heard. "A whole Union battery has moved up to just outside. Five guns. They'll be a target now, so it's going to get bad."

"I'll bundle up whatever I can spare back out in the kitchen."

"Not sure if we'll still be called upon, Sophie, but I'd prefer you were in the cellar with the children."

"You go down with Greta and Karl. I'll hurry. There's not much left out there anyway. That rebel captain *did* stop two of his men from taking our pots, but they'd already made off with the kettle and two skillets. He's started filling the room with wounded, by the way." She set the basket of linens on the table and he piled the bread beside it.

"Earlier you said the smokehouse is empty?"

"They've taken what remained, Papa. I'm sorry."

They jumped when shots peppered the house. Papa appeared to suffer the pain personally. Sophie tugged him closer by his shirt. "I reserved us some smoked beef and pork. It's already in the cellar. The children shouldn't go without."

As he left for the stairway, Sophie felt a nudge to her shoulder.

"Miss Sophie? Might you possibly spare us a couple minutes?" Dr. Taylor implored her with fatigued eyes.

Sophie studied her surroundings, thankful the doctoring tables sat momentarily idle, even as a new rebel steward mopped blood from around them. A handful of Southerners had joined the bustling personnel since she'd last visited the parlor, and the neutrality of the place struck her as both welcomed and sad.

Uniforms of blue, gray, and butternut intermingled on the floor, and now she could see a few in the keeping room, too. Her heart ached for them, for her home. This was her parlor, violently inverted with its shattered windows, the perfectly round hole in the wall. She gasped at the sight of her mother's prized hutch overturned on the floor.

And then she noticed the absence of the Samson brothers. A moment later, she spotted them in the far corner, and realized she had worried about their departure, had thought she'd lost the opportunity for more time with Coop.

"There are four who could use attention." Dr. Taylor pointed in the brothers' direction. "Including those two scoundrels."

"Have they been trouble to you, Doctor?"

"Oh, not really," he said with a sigh. "The Yank can be a tad gruff, but I've found their interactions something of comic relief. A sad irony, their situation. They'll have to part ways soon."

Sophie observed them from afar, both now sitting up against the wall, Billy talking non-stop, and Coop, with both hands on his stomach, looking quite disinterested. Perhaps he was distracted by the shadow that now fell over them through the hole in the wall. His solitary gaze appeared just as arresting from this distance as when she had knelt at his side.

"You'll release them soon?"

"The Yank, probably not until daybreak. The reb, maybe in a few hours. If you could see to that arm of his, we'll know better."

"I'll do that."

"There are two others, Yanks, also along the wall. Neither should make a peep. One is out cold with a head wound and the other has a broken jaw." He quickly assembled a tray of utensils and equipment and presented it to her. "We're taking some blows now, could take more at any time, so please watch yourself. You're quite special to us, Miss Sophie."

Just as she reached the brothers, Billy lurched aside and Coop emptied his stomach onto his own chest. Sophie stole a towel off a nearby table and hurried ahead.

"Coop!" She knelt at his side. "You were wise not to eat much, weren't you?"

"Damn mess. Sorry." He frowned heavily and took the towel before she could begin cleaning him up. "Thank you for this."

But Sophie didn't let go. "I'm going to help you," she insisted. "How's your head?"

He tugged the towel loose. "Thank you but you needn't concern yourself with this. I can take care of it. Why aren't you taking cover? Do you know we lost a man standing right over there?"

"Easy, Coop. Your worry is touching, but please, you mustn't stress yourself. Now, I asked about your head."

"Hm. It's fine."

"Mostly," Billy injected. When Sophie looked back at him, he shrugged. "*I* wouldn't say it's fine, would you?"

Growing more irritated by the minute, Sophie turned to Coop, watched him blink several times as he tried to clean debris from his uniform. "Listen to me, Private Samson." She snatched the towel away. "Dr. Taylor is expecting to release you later and your stubbornness isn't helping your cause in the least." Coop paused and rested his head against the wall, defeated as he closed his eyes.

"Lie down right now," Sophie commanded.

Billy said, "He's been insisting he's—"

"And you," Sophie turned on him, "you move away and do the same. Give me room to work." She waited until both men settled down. "Billy, your bloody shirt has to go, at least that disgusting sleeve." He stared at it, as if sad to part with it, and then ripped it off. Sophie almost grinned. "Time for this new dressing."

"Have at me, Miss Sophie," he said, offering his arm. "I'm all yours."

She removed the stained cloth and cleaned the wounded area. "At least you're the cooperative brother."

"Oh, for you, I most certainly am. Not the grumbly one."

"Just the talkative one," she said, and tied off the bandage.

She sat back and looked from one brother to the other. "You're both certainly determined to be your own worst enemy."

"Anything to bring such a vision to my side," Billy said.

Sophie peeked beneath Coop's bandage. "This looks good, but Dr. Taylor won't like what's happening elsewhere." She flashed a look at the door when a minié ball knocked. Then a cannon right outside fired and shook the house. Her ears rang. *Good heavens.* Raising her voice, as if Coop had difficulty hearing, she yelled, "Are you still dizzy?"

"Hardly at all," he answered. His resigned, calm tone steadied her.

Billy added, "Ask him about his eyesight."

"If you don't keep quiet back there," Sophie said, "I'll have that arm tied across your mouth."

"Yes, ma'am."

Coop scrunched his eyes and popped them open. "Eyesight's no worry."

Sophie raised an eyebrow, doubting him, then ducked when two cannon fired in succession. Deciding to stay low, she wiped the towel across Coop's uniform front several times until Coop lifted her hand away.

"Coop," she sighed, "don't start this again. It's just a little mess and won't take any effort at all."

"I can do it."

"Put your head back down this instant." She pulled herself free of Coop's grip. "Lord, but you're difficult." She resumed brushing the cloth over Coop's frock. Beneath the wool, his body provided broad, firm resistance, and she pictured him to be very fit, his stomach flat and hard, his chest slightly rounded and muscular.

Coop interfered again. "Looks good enough to me," he said, stealing the towel and peering down at himself. "I appreciate it."

"Very well." Frustrated by his unreasonable persistence, she gathered her equipment on her tray. "Neither of you may be leaving when Dr. Taylor predicted. Just so you know."

Coop took her hand. "Do you have a root cellar, a storm cellar you can get to? This is rattling you now, Sophie, but what's ahead—"

"Thank you for asking. Yes, the children are there. Papa, too, and I'll be joining them soon. Promise me you will stay down."

"You be safe."

Sophie offered him a smile and wished she could take him to the cellar as well.

She tended to the others along the wall, looking back at the brothers often. Billy somehow slept, despite the booming outside. Coop lay staring at the ceiling and Sophie tried to imagine what had captured his thought. Something made him the loner he appeared to be, resistant to personal attention, eager to leave for far greater jeopardy.

She considered the plight of a twin. Such a severed connection as his would nag at her own soul, she thought, were she in his place. Sophie pondered his sister's look and demeanor, curious about similarities, differences, the feistiness Billy described. She concluded that Coop's twin had to have been as attractive, as independent as her brother.

Back in the summer kitchen, there was hardly room to walk around the Southerners and the two stewards who fussed over them. She collected the last of the biscuits she'd wrapped and hidden in one of Papa's boots, pulled a jug of water from beneath the table, and grabbed a lantern at the door as she ran back to the house. The lid to the cellar stood raised off the floor, and her father waited at the top of the steps. He waved her down to the cellar, said he was going to retrieve Greta, who had run upstairs in search of a blanket. Sophie emptied her load into his arms and ran after Greta herself.

Cannons began firing in earnest as Sophie hurried up. The sound was deafening, heart-stopping, and concussions thundered against the house. Explosions sounded overhead followed by battering against the walls and Sophie remembered the significance of "shot" and its cluster of lead balls. She remembered the devastation they wrought. The window at the top of the stairs shattered, causing her to jerk aside, shield her face with her arm.

At last, she found Greta half inside a trunk, bedding strewn about. "Greta! Let's go. Now! Whatever are you searching for?"

"Mama's favorite quilt," she said in a squeaky panic.

A shell burst outside, and the crash of disintegrating wood reverberated throughout the house. Greta screamed and Sophie pulled her into her arms. Some part of their home had shattered. *The parlor?*

"Be brave, sweet girl. We're going to the cellar now. Papa and Karl are waiting for us. Come."

Across the hall above Papa's corner bedroom, a shell snipped the roof and the concussion knocked Sophie and Greta sideways, bouncing them onto Greta's bed. They shrieked in unison, and just as Sophie was about to give thanks for the soft landing, a blast of solid shot smashed through the wall and split the massive log beam supporting the floorboards. Sophie and Greta, bed and furniture, plummeted to the first floor.

CHAPTER TWENTY-ONE

Coop sat up, coughing in the dust. Like many around them, she and Billy brushed themselves free of splinters, shards, chunks of wood, and tried to assess the damage. The front porch had exploded just moments before, and that had broken all remaining windows and even kicked out some bricks from the chimney. But having part of the second floor collapse over the keeping room was bad.

Dr. Taylor, Nurse Johnson, a rebel nurse, and the handful of regimental stewards scurried around, flinging off debris, checking wounds, old and new. Coop pointed to the cloud of dust still wafting out of the corner room.

"What the hell are your boys shooting at?" she asked Billy, shouting over the din inside and out.

"Has to be new men. A few batteries have fresh recruits. That's all I can imagine."

"Well, damn," she said, grunting as she struggled to her knees. "They've done some *real* damage now. Two of ours and one of yours are in there." She slapped his shoulder and staggered to her feet. Her stomach complained and she pressed her hand to it. "Get up, Johnny Reb. We need to get in there."

They weaved paths through the rising dust in the room, careful of their footing as they climbed over planks, roofing, and pieces of furniture. Two rebels with head wounds and Nurse Johnson joined in the search, helped pull apart the debris pile and toss it aside.

"At least we'll get good firewood out of all this," one reb said to Billy, and Coop grabbed him by his shirt front.

"Stinkin' reb! S'matter with you?"

"Git your hands off me!" He shoved Coop away. "Face facts, stupid Yank."

Coop stepped back into his space. "All you see here is firewood?" She clenched a fist but thought better of risking a swing.

Billy pulled the rebel out of her reach. "The wounded were over there. Let's go."

They all concentrated on unearthing the wounded trio, but found one had passed on, impaled by a section of roof joist. Billy and the reb managed to drag him through the parlor to the yard. Coop and the others helped the remaining wounded pair to precious spaces on the parlor floor.

Still steamed about that stupid reb, Coop hustled back to the keeping room and hurled debris into a heap in the corner. A family's home, a family that's given all it could, she thought. So much flooring, sections of drawers, a slice of mirrored glass, a bedpost. Whose bedroom was this?

A meek groan came from farther into the room, beneath more rubble, and Coop abruptly stopped. She straightened so quickly, her dizzies returned, but then faded just as fast. Unsure if she'd heard anything at all, she took another carefully plotted step.

"Help! Someone help!"

Coop lunged at the pile. The second reb joined in. Together, they hauled long sections of oak flooring off the top, pulled out a mangled bed frame, and a girl's teary face appeared.

Both Coop and the rebel drew back with a start.

"Lord above!" the Southerner exclaimed.

"We're coming," Coop said in a gush, pawing through the mess, her head throbbing now. "Can you move at all?" This had to be Greta.

"M-my legs h-hurt!"

"Don't cry, now. We're a-comin'," the rebel said, and glanced at Coop as they worked. "This just shouldn't be."

Greta paused between sobs, heaved in a breath, and cried out. "Sophie! Where are you?"

Coop jerked to attention. "Sophie's here?"

"She has to be here somewhere!" Greta shouted.

The rebel hoisted her free of the rubble and she cried uncontrollably, staring down at the debris.

Coop tore into the pile, shoved aside two layers of flooring by herself, and exposed a folded feather bed. She thought she saw it shift but didn't trust her vision. She steadied her feet on the debris and peeled back the bedding. Sophie lay face down on the bedding's other half, thankfully cushioned through her fall, but Coop feared what she'd find under her.

"Sophie." Coop leaned down, almost atop her back. "Sophie?" Gripping Sophie's shoulder, she ignored the intense pounding in her brain and lowered her head to Sophie's ear. "Wake up, Sophie. Please answer me." She stroked her hair aside and pressed two fingertips to Sophie's throat. *Thank God.*

Sophie groaned and her hands crept up to her face. "What…?" Coop edged back. "Oh, my Lord," Sophie said, looking around and then up at Coop, her eyes filling immediately. "You're here!" Then shock hit her. "Greta!" She thrust herself upright, wincing at some pain, and spotted Greta in the rebel's arms. "My God, Greta! Are you all right? Can't you stand? Are your legs—"

"She's all right, ma'am," he assured her and set Greta on her feet.

Coop offered her hand to Sophie and guided her out of the debris to Greta. As the tearful sisters united, Coop appreciated their resemblance. Greta already was growing to be as beautiful.

"Are you two hurt?" she asked, amazed to see only a few superficial cuts.

"I-I'm fine, I think," Sophie managed. She held Greta at arm's length, inspected the small cuts on her hand and legs, and brushed off splinters and dust. "I think we both are, it seems." Greta poked a finger through a tear in Sophie's sleeve and the sisters smiled at each other in nervous relief.

"Was anyone else with you?" Coop asked.

"No, and we were just leaving when this happened." Sophie looked up at the gaping hole in the second floor, and beyond it, the smaller hole in the roof. "Good heavens. Our poor house." She surveyed the debris around them. "The bedding must have saved us."

"Come away from all this." Coop led them through a doorway on the other side of the room. "Evidently, this is your main kitchen?" She moved several crates to use as chairs. Only used for eating meals during the summer, the large space offered just a sink and dormant cast iron cookstove, but now also stacks of medical supplies, and what looked like Dr. Taylor's personal encampment in the corner. She watched Sophie stare at the two stewards setting up accommodations for more wounded and couldn't fathom the despair as hospital service crept through still more of what remained of her home.

"Yes, for most of the year, this is our kitchen. Dr. Taylor said I—or they—probably will have to bring it into service, now that the summer kitchen is filling with wounded, but…" Sophie looked around as if trying to figure out how. "Looks like there soon won't be much room here, either. Even if there was, the stove would make it terribly hot."

Sophie finally sat, looking more defeated than Coop could ever recall. Greta slid her crate closer to sit against Sophie's side, and Sophie slid an arm around her shoulders.

"Would you like some water?" Coop asked. "I'll try to find you some."

Billy bolted into the room and stopped short, his bad arm clutched against his chest. "My Gettysburg angel?" Coop rolled her eyes when he dropped to his knees before Sophie. "I don't believe this. You're okay?"

"Yes, Billy. My sister, Greta, is as well, and we thank you." She nudged Greta.

"Appreciate you asking, sir," Greta said, although her sour face said she didn't mean a word.

"Pleasure making your acquaintance, Miss Greta," he offered. "Cpl. Billy Samson, 22nd Virginia, at your service." That didn't win a smile from Greta either.

"Samson? Are you Coop's brother?"

"I am."

"Does he look like you?"

Leaning against the wall across the room, Coop grinned.

With his hand to his heart, Billy said, "No, miss. Coop looks every bit like his twin sister, you see, not like this handsome devil before you." He winked at Sophie. "Now, allow me to be of assistance to you ladies. I'll… um…I'll get you water." He darted off.

Sophie gave Greta a squeeze. "I think it's time for the introduction you've been waiting for." She turned a weary smile up at Coop. "Not exactly the way I envisioned it, but… Greta, this is my dear friend, Coop Samson."

Greta's eyes widened and she practically jumped up from Sophie's side. "*You're* Coop?" She overcame a little stumble as she curtseyed. "I'm Miss Greta Bauer. How do you do?"

Straightening to attention off the wall, Coop rapidly assessed her dizziness and risked a chivalrous bow. "It is entirely my pleasure to meet you, Miss Bauer." She grinned and whispered, "Feels like we know each other already, doesn't it?"

Greta giggled and slapped both hands to her lips to contain it. She nodded instead and sat.

"You're feeling better, Coop?" Sophie asked.

"A building coming down upon you has remarkable healing properties."

"Indeed. I suppose Dr. Taylor will be seeing to your release momentarily, then."

Coop set a palm to her wound. "Not without reason, I suppose."

"Your vision is clear? How's that disagreeable stomach?"

After all Sophie had just endured, Coop mused, she concerns herself with others. *Truly, a strong, remarkable woman. If only I had more time in your company.*

"Both are improving. More importantly, you're sure you two are all right?"

Billy returned with two tin cups of water and handed them to Sophie and Greta. "With the good news of your well-being comes the sad news of our parting." He glanced at Coop. "The doc is booting me out."

"Your arm is well enough? No sling for you?" Sophie asked.

"Can't let a sling get in my way. Besides, it hardly bleeds anymore," he said, "and the cap'n told me I'm needed."

"Well, I'm glad for your recovery, Billy." She offered a handshake.

Coop watched Greta's expression harden as Billy kissed the back of Sophie's hand.

Inching to the edge of her seat, Greta asked, "Are you going out there to kill our soldiers?"

Billy sent a look to Sophie, and then one to Coop, who only smirked.

"I'm a soldier, Miss Greta," Billy said gently, "and soldiers follow orders. I'm mighty grateful to you all, though, especially your sister, for all the fine hospitality and nursing. I thank you kindly." He took her hand, attempted to kiss it, but Greta pulled away. He stood and shrugged at Coop. "Guess I need to find my gear in that pile in the parlor."

Coop watched him go, unsure if she should accompany him, or what she should say. He was her brother, gone many years, but blood nonetheless, and theirs was a shared childhood, a shared family. But he'd chosen a very different path in adulthood. *Does that matter, as we head into battle, perhaps to our own deaths?*

"Papa!" Greta raced across the room to the ragged farmer in the doorway. Having come through the debris-filled keeping room, and with a tow-headed boy stumbling along in his shadow, he stood dazed until Greta revived him. He raised her in a hug, and Sophie moved to his side.

"There you two are!" he said, his eyes teary. "My word! Are you well, Greta? Sophie?"

"Oh, Papa! Me and Sophie, we…You won't believe it, we—"

"I do believe it, Greta." He cupped the back of Sophie's head. "The Lord is on our side and I am more thankful than I can say." He drew Sophie to them with one arm.

"You must meet the soldier who helped us, Papa," Sophie said, and gestured to Coop. "I want you to meet Pvt. Cooper Samson."

"*The* Cooper Samson? This is Coop?" His happy surprise warmed Coop to her core. She didn't even worry too much about passing inspection under his full-body glance. When he extended a handshake between his daughters, she again straightened to attention, swayed a moment when the dizzies threatened, stepped forward, and shook it.

"Honored to meet you, Mr. Bauer, sir."

"Likewise, Private." He glanced up at Coop's bandage. "I'm grateful for your effort, braving your own troubles. We so hope you fare well."

"Thank you, sir. The same to you and your family."

"Hi, Coop!" Taken by every aspect of Coop's uniform, the boy finally smiled up at her and stuck out his hand.

Coop obliged. "You must be Karl."

"Yessir!"

"I'm glad to meet you, too. You're taller than I imagined."

"Tall as Greta now," he boasted. "Will you come visit us once you get rid of the rebs?"

"First chance I get."

"A nine-year-old's backhanded invitation if I ever heard one," Papa said with a shake of his head, "but heartfelt, I know. You're welcome here any time, young man."

Sophie touched Coop's arm. "Dr. Taylor hasn't released you, too, has he?"

"Not yet, but I expect he will give me the word at any moment." She set her hand over Sophie's. "I won't leave without saying good-bye."

CHAPTER TWENTY-TWO

Coop searched the parlor for Billy. She fully expected Dr. Taylor to approach and release her, but he either didn't see her or was allowing her this moment with her brother, who currently struggled with his knapsack at the door.

Overwhelmed by a reticence she couldn't explain, Coop helped slide a strap up his bad arm to his shoulder. He turned to face her, floppy felt hat askew on his head.

"Didn't think we'd bother with good-byes," he said, placing a hand on her shoulder. "But guess I am glad of it."

"Amazing that we met up."

"Would you...ah...Look, I know they may not care anymore, but would you pass along my greetings to the family? I do think of them, y'know."

Coop forced down the lump in her throat. The family had always cared a great deal, prayed for his well-being, and would today, if they were still of this earth. Here, she again wrestled with the notion of sharing her news. Indeed, since meeting him here, she had even considered telling him that *she* was all that remained of his family. But, perhaps now, with duty calling and their own mortality hinging on every ounce of concentration, this wasn't the best time. Then again, perhaps this would be the *only* time.

"They missed you from the first," she said, and winced at a sudden pain in her head.

He nodded. "Sure wish you were on the right side here, Coop. Seeing you after all these years has brightened my days, but, well, you know." He tipped his head toward the battlefield just outside.

"No place for a reunion. I understand."

"Maybe we'll find a way to meet up once this is done."

"Not likely, but…" Her hand seemed to extend of its own accord and his eyes darkened as he grasped it.

"Cooper. You take care, now, hear me?"

"Good luck to you, Billy."

He stopped at the door, chose a rifle from the rebel stand along the wall, and turned and saluted her. She saluted back as he ducked out into the chaotic twilight.

For some time, she stood pondering the exchange, their lives, the wisdom of the decision that lodged in her chest. That's where it had originated, after all, not in her rational mind but in the heart he had wounded so long ago. He had transfused family blood until nothing remained but the fading shadow of a stranger she once knew.

Two relations, neither with a family, each making that choice. You chose your road long ago, and I've chosen mine now.

Dr. Taylor called for her help. She figured hers probably was the first available body he spotted. More wounded needed to be arranged in the kitchen and the keeping room debris had to be cleared promptly because the space was sorely needed.

She rubbed her stomach, trying to squelch the uneasiness, and stepped carefully over the wounded. Scattered like kindling, they made for precarious walking. Dr. Taylor said he had acquired a surgeon, nurse, and steward from another regiment, but Coop couldn't imagine that being enough. *At least he's giving me more time here. He can't still doubt my suitability for duty.*

She set about reorganizing supplies in the main kitchen, dragged and hefted crates to make room, while nearby, Sophie worked with her father to bring their stove out of its summer hibernation. The house would soon heat up hotter than Hades, but boiling water and some form of edible sustenance were necessities. She hoped Dr. Taylor soon would send both Bauers to the cellar with the children, away from danger.

Coop cordoned off half the floor space for additional wounded and helped a rebel steward carry in four soldiers. The burden grew heavier with each man and actually caused some throbbing at her wound, so she was glad to move on to the keeping room issue. She and a Vermont private spent the next hour working up a drenching sweat, breaking open the windows and throwing debris outside. Forced to pause several times to let dizziness pass, Coop feared all this stooping and straining in this stifling heat were taking their toll.

When she doubled over and heaved up nothing from her stomach, Coop collapsed to her knees. The Vermonter yelled for help, and she squeezed her eyes shut when two men lifted her by the arms and sat her in the corner.

Someone gripped her chin and when she opened her eyes, Dr. Taylor stared back through a strange instrument.

"Hard to read concussions," he told her. "Some take longer to settle than others. You need longer than I thought. Lay flat another few hours." She lay back on the floor and saw him turn to the steward. "Bunch up his frock under his head."

Every muscle in Coop's body clinched when the steward reached for her buttons. "No. Wait." She put both hands on her stomach. "Just let me stay. I'm not feeling...Right now, moving could be messy."

The steward withdrew and, on Coop's promise to remain still, she was left alone in the dusty room. She stared up at the broken ceiling and beyond. Stars peeked through the roof. Fuzzy dots of light. Her vision was acting up again, which meant this afternoon's labor and excitement had set her recovery back substantially.

She listened to the relentless cannon fire, the rifle shots, and couldn't pinpoint their directions. She wondered what Sophie was doing, if someone would tell her that Coop lay in the other room, compromised once more. She tried counting the stars, but smoke from the battlefield frequently blotted them out. Finally, she closed her eyes. Some things were easier to see this way, she mused. Billy's big frame filled the farmhouse doorway, pack on his back, long gun in hand, that bright new bandage on his bare arm. Brothers fighting brothers.

By the time reality struck her, Coop knew someone was unbuttoning her frock. She lurched upright. Through the blur, she saw Sophie kneeling at her side, working intently.

"Sophie. Eh...no." She slapped a palm over her chest. "You needn't do that. I'm—"

Determined at her task, Sophie shook her head and picked Coop's hand away. "Lie down and stop fussing please." Coop quickly covered the remaining buttons, but Sophie pried her fingers between Coop's. "You're not in charge here." Grimacing against Coop's strength, she eventually slipped each button through its hole. "There! Now lay down."

Sophie blew a breath up to her forehead as she watched Coop settle back. Beads of perspiration slid down his cheek and his eyes belied his discomfort—and apprehension.

"Sophie. You know you needn't go through all this trouble."

Sophie gritted her teeth and pushed Coop's hands aside. She laid his frock open, and exposed the buttoned white shirt, yellowed and soaked with sweat, spotted with soot down the front where dirt and gunpowder obviously had worked their way between the buttons. To her surprise, the flimsy fabric revealed another shirt beneath it, and both clung to Coop's upper body like a second skin.

Sophie reached for the top button. "You definitely need to cool down."

"Stop." Coop seized Sophie's hands. "Please."

Sophie sat back on her heels. She'd assured her father she would follow him promptly to the cellar, but felt compelled to inquire about Coop, if he had indeed left without saying good-bye. She hadn't expected to find him like this. And now here she was, exasperated beyond belief, her goodwill, shaken.

"Why won't you let me help you?"

"I'll be just—"

"Are you afraid?"

Coop cocked her head, apparently struck by the question. "What would I be afraid of?"

"Maybe of a woman's attention to your personal needs."

"Hardly. Rest assured I've had plenty of women's attention in my day."

Sophie had wondered about that. She tried again for the top button. "Then you won't object to showing some of yourself."

"Oh, but I will!"

"Coop!" Sophie swiped at the perspiration now trickling down her own cheek. "Look at you. This shirt is stifling you, and you wear an under garment that looks as tight as this one. Surely our army can find you better fitting shirts. These are far too small."

"Eh…They keep my muscles tight and strong."

"Fine. And in the meantime, you swelter and pass out." She rushed her hands to Coop's throat, popped open the first button, and had her fingers on the second before Coop could stop her. *Why am I bothering with this man? I've never allowed one to test me this way.*

Coop coughed and winced but refused to move his hands. He suffered still, it was clear, yet would fight to his last breath to remain fully dressed. He must pose a formidable foe on the battlefield, she thought.

"I-I'm sorry, Sophie, but I'm doing better, and you've been through enough today. Your fortitude, your generosity humbles me."

"Compliments will neither heal you nor stop me, Cooper Samson. You are correct, that today has been the most frightening of my life, and I do *not* need further struggle. So, grant me this effort and I'll leave you be, which seems to be your preference."

Coop set his hand on her arm. "I wish you well, is all. It's far safer downstairs. You must know I don't want you to go. No man in his right mind would, and I-I am no different, but—"

"Then why?" Sophie searched his tired eyes, pondered their depths, and wished he could recognize her sincerity, this peculiar insistence she had to tend to him. "You don't trust me."

Then his eyes flickered shut. He dropped both hands and sighed hard. She momentarily thought he'd lost consciousness.

Finally, he muttered, "Trust is cautiously granted."

"Trust is earned, Coop." She set her fingers on the next button and waited for him to react. When no objection came, she unbuttoned it and then the rest.

The broad muscular chest Sophie expected to see lay bound beneath a thin, tarnished cotton undergarment, a shirt so tight it flattened Coop's small—*feminine*—breasts.

Sophie recoiled. Unsure of what she saw, she stared at the softly rounded mounds, and knew they hardly resembled a man's well-exercised chest. No, she wasn't mistaken.

She yanked the overshirt closed. Her heart now throbbing in her throat, she looked about, relieved to see they were still alone, and gazed up at the soldier she thought she knew. Coop lay staring at the ceiling.

"Coop, I-I...Um..."

"Please don't be angry." Coop's eyes closed.

"Angry? I'm not sure what I feel, actually, but it's not anger."

"I'm so thankful for that. Honestly, I have never been comfortable, keeping this from you. I never should have, considering all we have shared."

Yes, Sophie thought, we have shared a great deal. *So many confidences, touches—and kisses. Between women.*

"Well, I am shocked. Definitely shocked. I can guess why you hid from the army, but...Coop." She lowered her voice. "You kissed me."

"How could I not? It was Christmas Eve and everything felt... Controlling my emotions in your company had become extremely difficult, and we were so comfortable together. I-I didn't think about it."

"I remember every glorious moment. Everything I dreamt about for years became real in those moments—and I didn't know."

"I was too afraid of a lot of things."

"You? Afraid? Of what? That I would report you? I would never do such a thing."

"Well, at first, before we came to know each other, yes, that was at the back of my mind. But after we'd enjoyed time together—"

"And kissed."

"Yes, kissed, it felt…almost too late. I wasn't the man you thought I was. You had every right to resent me, feel humiliated, and hurt. Plus, I couldn't bear it if attentions from the real me repulsed you because… you're in my heart now." Coop took a breath. "I-I just never expected that you…"

Sophie reached for Coop's hand and entwined their fingers. "That I what? That I, like you, prefer a woman's touch?"

Coop's eyes moistened. "And *you* kissed *Cooper Samson*."

"Oh, I did. And honestly? *Never* have I been more confused. And our intimate parting at Christmas meant too much to spoil it with confusion. And now I know why."

"I wish I had had the courage to trust you from the start."

"My months of self-doubt would have passed far easier, if you had, so consider yourself duly scolded. But I understand completely."

"The army would dismiss me, send me home in disgrace."

Sophie struggled to think through her fluster, the excitement blooming in her heart. She found it so unjust that the army would oust such a skilled and devoted soldier, regardless of gender, but she knew it would. Shortly after the war began, she'd read about the discovery and discharge of a woman in uniform. Once aware of the woman's deception, townspeople shamed her as a harlot trickster and banished her from town.

Coop was violating all the rules.

Sophie stared at the shirt, then up at Coop. The ruse had been flawless.

"Billy didn't recognize you. Truly amazing, how you've hidden yourself all this time."

"Women have just as much to defend as men. This is our country, too."

"Oh, I agree, but you've risked everything, Coop, your very life. You certainly don't deserve disgraceful treatment. I believe your honor and character are beyond reproach." She promptly buttoned the shirt and draped the frock closed.

"A woman's honor and character mean nothing when it comes to soldiering, Sophie. Being a woman is a terrible offense." Coop winced when a shell exploded directly over the house. She tugged Sophie away from a floorboard falling from above.

"This is unbelievable." Sophie fanned away the dust. "This house…" But she knew she now had to cope with an even larger issue, and it lay right before her. "You know, after two years and all you've been through…to not need serious medical care until now, to have never been, well, exposed…" She shook her head.

"One of the lucky ones. That's what I keep telling myself. Only some minor wounds. I've had plenty of close calls, though, where I just managed to hide in time or cover myself, fording rivers, bathing, that sort of thing."

"How you managed to persevere and constantly stay on guard. It's simply stunning."

"If the army ever found out and sent me home, I always knew I'd have to sell the farm and move to a new town. I thought I would reenlist there, maybe join a cavalry unit."

"You're determined to fight, aren't you?"

"Living a life I choose means that much to me. I'm sure freedom for all means a lot to you as well. We must never allow anyone to break our country apart, Sophie. Its principles are righteous, too important." Coop shrugged. "I sound like my father."

Sophie almost smiled. "The army doesn't know what it has in you, Private Samson."

"It has everything Cooper and I always hoped to give it, and that's plenty."

"So…It's Catherine, isn't it?"

The heavy sigh answered her question. So did those delicate eyelashes, the sleek complexion, the sensuous lines of those lips. And the tingling warmth, the cushiony depths of their Christmas kisses.

Shocking discovery and its ramifications aside, Sophie acknowledged a growing, albeit curious sense of relief. Like a restoration of faith in myself, she mused, an unraveling of the emotional twist this attachment to Coop had wrought.

Intuition knew long before I did.

"Cooper and I had always been alike, but what he carried in gentility, I guess I made up for in gumption. Choosing to do this wasn't as hard as you might think."

"You didn't tell Billy before he left, did you?"

"No. It wasn't an easy decision, but I stand by it."

"Would he have reported you?"

Coop shrugged. "Would be one less enemy soldier."

"Hm. Well, *Cooper,* your secret is safe with me." She leaned closer. "But you must promise to survive this wretched war."

"I'll do my best."

Sophie tried to think over her heart's insistent clamor. The endearing though gnawing, confusing affection she'd developed for this *man,* now began to glow freely for this *woman.* She couldn't deny the butterflies in her chest. And because she had spent years forthrightly dismissing it, with all practicality, desire rose welcomed and thrilling.

Leary that her voice might quiver, she managed, "Promise me."

Because you must come back to me.

Coop rose on an elbow and cupped her cheek, drew her near until their foreheads met. Sophie felt her heart skip as Coop brought their lips together. "I promise, to my dying breath."

CHAPTER TWENTY-THREE

G et out!"
  Propped in the corner of the keeping room, Coop awoke to Dr. Taylor's command in the parlor. Around her, wounded men lay moaning, calling for aid from a rebel steward who hustled from one to the next, trying to keep up. Outside, gunfire had grown sporadic and she wondered how long she'd been asleep. She saw stars through the roof hole. Clearly.

"Lieutenant!" Dr. Taylor yelled again. "There's no taking cover in here! Get your men out!"

Coop didn't know if Union or Confederate soldiers were bothering him, but they'd obviously become a problem. She couldn't imagine the crowded horror scene in that room by now.

A scream came next, from a patient in the parlor, followed by someone's shout for chloroform. An amputation. A blast of solid shot rocked the house, and something upstairs crashed. Instinctively, she looked up again and her thoughts swung in a different direction.

Sophie, please be in the cellar.

The secret that is no more. The kiss. The promise.

"Samson?"

Drawn from her wonder, Coop stood without swaying, without a throb in her head. "Good to see you, Sarge."

He looked her over and nodded. "Doc says you're good to go, so head back to the unit. It's almost dawn."

"Yes, sir."

He left for the parlor and Coop went to the kitchen. She hoped she wouldn't find Sophie hard at work, hoped she was safe in the cellar with her family. But she yearned to see her, now more than ever.

Two Union and two rebel soldiers lay on scattered hay, bleeding and barely conscious, but otherwise the steamy room was empty. Near the door, a patch of flooring suddenly swung up and a rebel appeared from below, rifle slung across his back. He wrestled with an armload of goods, a crate filled with packages and a pistol on top.

"Heathen!" a man bellowed up at him.

"How *can* you?" came a desperate plea. Sophie's voice.

Coop sprinted across the room and snatched up the pistol.

"Low-life reb," she growled, pointing it at his sooty face. "Put the box down."

"All's fair in war, Yank. Outa my way."

Coop cocked the pistol and prayed it was loaded. Surely as she stood here, she'd shoot him.

"There's decency in this home," she said, "none in you, but here, yes. Put it down and head out."

The rebel shifted the load in his arms and snorted. "Now, I guess this is as good a place as any to be shot."

Grinning, he stepped around her and Coop slammed the gun to his head. He collapsed against her and she caught the crate as he hit the floor. Thankfully, the pistol hadn't discharged randomly into the room.

From the bottom of the cellar steps, the Bauer family peered up at her.

Coop just shook her head as Karl cheered and Greta clapped. Their father hurried up.

"Now, *that's* a soldier for you!" he exclaimed, and slapped Coop's shoulder. "Good job, man!" He took back the crate. "Thought we'd lost everything for a moment. Thank you, Cooper."

She handed him the gun. "Wasn't loaded, was it?"

"Hadn't had the chance. I'd just managed to get to it as he came down the stairs."

"Well, go on back down and load it."

"I will," he said, and edged down the steps. "I definitely will."

Coop dragged the rebel outside and came back to the top of the stairs. Sophie looked up.

"Time for me to go," Coop said.

Sophie gathered the hem of her dress and climbed the steps.

"Things aren't too bad out there anymore, are they?" Her concern flashed from Coop's face to the dimness of early dawn visible through a shattered window. "Will you be all right? How are you feeling?"

Coop smiled. "Which question should I answer first?"

Sophie grinned back. "How about, 'Do you remember your promise?'"

"I do, Miss Bauer. I remember everything."

"Good." She stroked Coop's cheek. "You mean a lot to me, Cooper Samson."

Coop set her palms on Sophie's shoulders. "And I can't say as anyone's ever meant more to me." She wrapped her arms across Sophie's back, and cherished the feel of her. She let the perfect—honest—union of their bodies penetrate to her bones, knowing she would carry this thrill to her last moment on earth. Sophie squeezed her in return, a tight lengthy hug. *Was that a blissful sigh?*

Coop turned her face to Sophie's ear. "I'm keeping you in my heart, Sophie. I hope you don't mind."

"Mind?" Sophie sniffed as she leaned back in the circle of their arms. "You've been in mine from the first and I do believe you're there to stay. I hope *you* don't mind."

Look at us. How could I mind?

Coop brought her mouth to Sophie's for a tender, lingering kiss that made her entire body hum. Sophie's soft lips melted Coop where she stood. There were holes in the walls, stars on the ceiling, and war raging outside and in—even a family watching from the cellar—but she didn't care. Everything swirled around them and she didn't want any of it to stop.

Sophie uttered a soft moan as she returned the kiss, and her eyes were slow to open.

Coop saw the welling tears. "Please don't cry. If you start, I'll start."

Sophie tried to laugh. "Soldiers don't cry, do they?"

"This one might."

"I'm afraid for you, Coop." A tear trickled down her cheek.

"Sh. You're not alone, beautiful lady. We're all afraid. Only a fool isn't." She wiped away the tear with her thumb. "Will you take care of yourself? For me?"

Another tear escaped when Sophie nodded. "For you."

Coop kissed her lightly and inched away. "I want a million of those," she whispered, "so I'll be back."

Coping with what felt like a "love-struck daze," Sophie spent the entire morning going through the motions of boiling pots of bandages and coffee and heating the house to an unbearable degree. Having a special someone who made your heart race and dreams come true certainly felt like *that word.* She wondered if she dared acknowledge it, and, if she did, what would happen to her day's work when her mind soared off into the clouds.

Focus.

This work was *so* far from the family's typical pre-holiday preparations. No picking vegetables for platters, no wrapping packages of cookies, no helping trim out the horse and wagon for the festive parade in town. Tomorrow was the Fourth of July holiday, or at least for Northerners it was. She assumed Confederates wouldn't honor the day.

"Please, let today see an end to hostilities," she thought aloud, because so many had been injured yesterday and the day before. *How many more must die, be maimed in such ghastly fashion? Did artillery wagons really hold an endless supply of ammunition? Surely would be grand if we won on Independence Day.*

In the main house, only a meager space remained for kitchen duties. Every room sat filled to overflowing with wounded. Weary from uncomfortable and restless sleep, Sophie struggled to tend to the soldiers, and to keep from seeing Coop in their places. War was hell when she *didn't* know anyone particularly well, but now, she knew a soldier, knew her heart was invested, and that made all of this sheer torture.

Devastated bodies, overpowering smells, incessant wailing, all preyed upon her harder than ever before. Wounded men filled the summer kitchen and blanketed the patch of yard next to it. Outside the parlor's side window, surgical assistants amassed a grotesque pile of severed limbs. Earlier this morning she spotted Union graves being dug beside the front porch, and rebels burying their dead behind the barn.

Sophie strictly limited activity for her siblings and forbade them to venture out. There were no more crops or animals to tend, and exercise had to be forsaken. Addressing one's personal hygiene took place behind a blanket curtain in the cellar, not in the now-disgusting privy off the kitchen or the one just outside, if it was even still standing. She hoped that the fighting currently raging on the hill to the north would close the battle, although a quick look around said there was no way to predict the victor.

She shooed Greta down the steps with a loaf of bread and followed her down with a tray of coffee and condensed milk she'd acquired from the army. The small space had grown stuffy, but at least it was far cooler than upstairs and definitely better than the merciless heat and danger outside. And it wasn't even noon.

"I prefer that you stay here now, Sophie. You're worn to the bone." Papa's heavy eyes studied her as he drank his coffee. "Last time I was upstairs, I saw plenty of stewards. They'll just have to handle things."

Lying on the bench along the wall, Greta plumped the blanket beneath her head. "They could stop fighting today, couldn't they?"

"It's possible," Papa said, "but doesn't appear that anything's been decided."

"Do you think the Robinsons are safe?"

"Cannot even guess, Greta. We can hope, however."

"Mr. Robinson should have stayed down here with us."

"Well, we should wish the best for them with all our might. We mustn't fault Eldus for wanting to get back to his family. Could you imagine his torment, being here, not knowing about Rose and Tassie?"

Greta frowned at the floor. "I suppose if he'd been here with us, that heathen rebel would've taken our belongings *and* him."

"But Coop would have come to the rescue," Karl said. "Wonder where he is now?"

"Back with his unit, son, like the good soldier he is."

Sophie caught Papa's glance and nodded. Gunfire had ceased and she had been picturing Coop clustered with comrades, with Tim, maybe cleaning guns or digging rifle pits. *A woman surrounded by unsuspecting men.* She worried about Coop having enough water, if she'd had a chance to eat something. She left the house at dawn, so hopefully she had the opportunity.

"I can't wait till he comes back," Karl said. "I think he's a nice fellow."

With a sly smile, Papa gestured to Greta. "I think I know one young lady who's rather sweet on the handsome soldier."

"Papa!" Greta turned her face into the blanket.

"Oh, come now, Greta," he added. "There's another lady here who wholeheartedly agrees with you."

Seeing Greta lift her head, Sophie turned to their father. "Oh, Papa!" she said on a gasp, and winked at Greta.

He reached from his stool and patted Sophie's knee. "It warms my heart, young woman, seeing you two so taken with each other. I believe he's a good man for you."

"Very special, indeed," Sophie said, leveling as much sincerity at him as she could. "We care a great deal for each other. Unfortunately, what the future holds for either of us can't be known."

He nodded and gave her knee another pat. He understood the cost of war, the tenuous nature of survival. And Sophie prayed he eventually would understand so much more, that a woman could be an outstanding soldier, anything she wanted to be, including a loving partner with another woman.

Would Coop want them to know?

She sipped her coffee, trying to imagine the family's reaction to *Catherine* Samson. Despite the swell of pride that rose within her, she knew it would shock them mightily. Karl's idolatry would shatter, along with Greta's adolescent crush. Both would evolve, but Papa was another matter.

Disapproval of Catherine is disapproval of me.

The entire family witnessed the affectionate scene at the top of the stairs, so there was no denying her feelings. Not that she would or could. To her own surprise, she felt quite the opposite, and almost snickered because she had barely admitted her feelings to herself.

She dreaded the possibility of shattering Papa's dream for her, that someday she would marry a "good man" and build a family. The last thing she wanted in life was to see his heart broken yet again. Although fond of Coop, he would have a difficult time accepting Catherine, and would likely see Sophie's declaration as his personal failure.

Nevertheless, Sophie could feel her hope expanding as if drawn by fate. A relationship with Coop could be worth all her effort, more meaningful than social acceptance or even family. She finished her coffee, feeling purposeful, confident, and aligned to her course, and indulged herself with a vision of everyone living happily ever after.

CHAPTER TWENTY-FOUR

Her cartridge and cap boxes refilled, Coop settled on the rocky ground beneath the sun shelter Tim erected, the half-sheet of canvas supported by their rifles bayonetted into the dirt. The sun bore down and heat and humidity shimmered up, driving every soldier along the battle line deeper into mind-numbing lethargy. Those without shade moved only by instinct or habit, silently playing cards, gnawing on biscuits, writing letters. Like everyone else, Coop wondered when the call would come to advance across the mile of steaming field and settle this once and for all.

Exhausted and oppressed by the heat, she laid back, head on her knapsack, and closed her eyes. "Wish Hancock had put us on that ridge instead of this one," she mumbled. "Rebs have trees."

"I agree," Tim said. "Can hardly see them for the haze, but that green horizon looks awfully tempting. Just nice to imagine, mind you, not tempting enough to stomp all that way over there. My feet are swimming in sweat."

"Another stretch of canvas and we wouldn't have our shoes sticking out, frying."

"Our boys in that copse of trees just up to the right, look at them." And Coop sat up. "See them lounging? They sure got lucky. Pennsylvanians. Maybe New Yorkers."

Coop gestured west, directly forward to their battle line. "No surprise the Harvard boys got lucky, having a piece of stone wall. It's no cover from the sun, I know, but at least it's some defense. The 15th Mass, down the other way, they have nothing, just like us back here."

"Hm. I don't think I like being rear of the front line. No wall, no fence, no trees, just the educated backsides of the 20th."

"And artillery at our hip to blow our ears out." She chuckled as they watched cannoneers water their horses nearby. "Will you listen to us? Moaning and groaning? At least we're luckier than all those in that Spangler hospital way back." She frowned hard. "You know, they say there's a pile of arms and legs six feet tall. Sorry state of things."

"That's from yesterday. Fighting took a mean toll all around while you were at the Bauer house. Hand-to-hand on both hills, and we had company right up to the wall. Bet you didn't know the 13th Vermont was practically at your door, taking back guns from those damn Georgians. Must've been loud in the house."

"It was. There's a lot of damage. The whole family's in the cellar now and I hope they stay there."

"Theirs is still a busy place," he said, pointing. "Such comings and goings. Rebs at the back door, Yanks at the front." He tapped Coop's leg. "But I'm surprised it didn't take a provost guard to drag you back here."

"It was hard to leave. The family's tired and afraid, the little ones and the father, too. Makes you wish you could do *something*."

"And Sophie?"

Coop gazed out at the farmhouse, the isolated island between encampments. "Never met a woman so strong. There's no end to her generosity, the effort she gives for others."

"Bet she gave you her finest effort."

"Hey. Seriously. The way she treats everyone, family included, and blue or gray, doesn't matter. She's good at doctoring, too, you know." *Everything about her is fine.*

"Not surprising. Being at Antietam and Fredericksburg probably taught her a lot, like it did all of us."

"I suppose staying busy helps her keep from dwelling on the situation she's in, while she's getting squeezed out of a home that's slowly being blown apart."

"I wouldn't want to be stuck out there in the middle of this mess. Why didn't they leave like so many other farmers did?"

"Probably thought they'd care for their home. I can't see Sophie or her father abandoning the place. I think the Bauers are cut from stiffer cloth. Got to respect people like that."

"You're coming back for her, aren't you?"

Coop rubbed her eyes. They were clear but weary, and she longed to be sitting in the shade with Sophie talking about anything, holding hands, stealing kisses. There was something in those kisses. Hope, maybe promise. Whatever it was, it made her heart beat loudly.

"I don't know what kind of future she wants."

"Why didn't you discuss it when you had the chance?" He waved a hand in futility. "She could be looking for you to sweep her off her feet, and you have the perfect place just waiting for you." He laid back, grumbling at her.

"I doubt she would leave her family. Massachusetts might be too far from them." She mulled the subject to shreds these past months, especially in recent days, and still didn't know what to think. "Anyway, there should be some serious love first, and right now, this is all pretty new."

And here I am, leaning that way, when it's unwise to conjure such grand dreams. I think she feels as I do, but strongly enough to join me in my deception—as a bride, to ease the minds of family and friends? Or strongly enough to become Catherine's spinster companion, which though not uncommon, could dishearten, bring dishonor upon her family?

Tim abruptly sat up. "I think you're chicken. The 19th's ace rifleman is scared to find out. I'd blame the crack to that rock-hard head of yours, if I hadn't wondered earlier. You've dragged your feet from the start, pussyfooted around her 'cause you're afraid she'll hook you, that she'll say yes. Aren't you?"

"Stop harping. It's a big step to take, so—"

"So, nothing. Does she at least know you're seriously sweet on her? Tell me she knows by now."

"She does. And she's…" She found it freeing to say aloud. "She's sweet on me."

"Well, hallelujah, Jesus! The man's finally admitted it to himself."

"Quit it. Yes, I've admitted it to myself, but there's more to it than just being sweet on somebody. And this is a horrible time to be turning your life inside out."

"Did you ever think this could be exactly when she needs to hear from you?"

How difficult can life get?

Coop squinted at the Confederates along Seminary Ridge, a battle line considerably longer than her own, motionless, and barely visible through the trees. The quiet pressed in on her, heavy and unnerving.

"Feels like the heat's risen so much, everything's just going to—"

A puff of cannon smoke at the southern end of the ridge caught her eye a split-second before anyone heard the boom. The deep unexpected sound seemed to linger, snared by the thick, humid air. Less than twenty yards to Coop's right, the cannonball landed amidst a battery and blew a cannon off its wheels, flung gunners to the ground, ricocheted and cut two legs off a horse still harnessed to its team.

Coop, Tim, and the 19th jumped to their feet and grabbed their gear as a second shot sounded.

"Signal shots," Tim said, disgust in his voice. "No more quiet time."

Coop looked about, tense, anticipating the landing of that second blast. A young lieutenant stood and spit the dregs of his coffee, just as the shot struck his chest. She spun away, bent over, breathless, hoping she wouldn't vomit.

Units scrambled, some rushing to help the wounded, others to safety farther back, and as they expected, shots then came in earnest. Confederate artillery cranked to life, picking up speed and booming across the plain, rapid and relentless. Coop looked back at the sight. Dozens upon dozens of cannon fired at will, easily two miles of them, spewing smoke along the entire length of Seminary Ridge. Repetitive, overlapping thundercracks became insufferable within a minute. Hovering along the ridge, a white-gray cloud thickened, pierced only by flashes of yellow muzzle fire, and the rebels disappeared from view.

Looking up, Coop could see the Confederate message arriving in a hellish rain. Rebel gunners overshot the Union front to levy serious chaos and damage upon artillery, munitions, and any troops staged to the rear. Where some of her comrades sought refuge tucked against the wall, Coop knew that she and others with her had no place to hide.

Solid shot slammed into caissons, cannon, animals, sun shelters. Running soldiers were plowed off their feet, many losing limbs as they were hurled about. Screaming shells, their iron shards and lead balls, and exploding stacks of munitions claimed soldiers in all directions and slaughtered tethered horses and mules.

As Coop and her company ran to the aid of the New York battery, she could tell Tim was complaining about something, but discerning curses from panicked cries or shouted commands had become nearly impossible in the din. She glanced at him as they ran, saw he was keeping up, and decided he hadn't been hit.

Booming echoes pounded in her ears, and when Union forces began returning fire, the ungodly volume increased. With a flash of worry, Coop noted the throbbing in her head. She knew that adding the heavy pulses of their own cannon to the already merciless noise surely would test her stamina. Blast waves fluttered her frock and pants, and she had to reset her feet.

The hundreds of cannon created an apocryphal scene, hell rising from the ground and smashing everything and everyone down into it. As a storm of sulfur smoke darkened the sky, Coop watched an ocean of golden crops ripple beneath the percussion. Shells and shot of all types crisscrossed overhead, some she could trace to their targets, and oddly she hoped no birds dared interfere. Ironically, she then spotted a small flock leave the copse of trees and struggle in the turbulence. The earth vibrated.

With Tim and several others, Coop held the crippled cannon by its stock while gunners frantically replaced each wheel. To her side by only ten yards, solid shot plunged into the ground and the sickening tremor reached her feet. Occupied as she was, she could only stare at the hole and try not to let the near miss rattle her. Not the safest place to be, she pondered as the gunner hurried his work. She heard Tim comment and, over the load they bore, she queried him with her eyes. He looked at the hole and then up to the heavens.

Finally, everyone wheeled the cannon into firing position, and, with her rifle slung across her back, Coop ran to the limber and scooped up ammunition. Heading back, she staggered when a shell blew apart what had been her sun shelter. Pushing on, she heard the dreaded whistle overhead and dove beneath a wagon just as it shattered around her. She crawled out from beneath the mess, ears ringing, and managed to deliver her goods. Seconds later, the New York cannon joined the action.

Minutes passed like hours, until Tim grabbed her by the shoulders. "Can you hear me yet?" he yelled into her face.

"I can. It's coming back," Coop said, jiggling a finger into each ear. "At least *our* guns have stopped. We're playing coy, if you ask me, holding munitions in reserve."

"Good old Henry Hunt's not the most generous general. He's holding back, all right. The rebs will shut down if they think they've pounded us to dust."

Coop looked around at the bodies and heaps of debris, remnants of wagons, guns, animals, and supplies. She picked up a lost pistol, glad to see it was loaded, and tucked it into her belt. They stepped aside as an ambulance wagon hurried to the rear.

"Glad they can't see what great shape we're in."

They dashed to a safer spot at the heightening sound of a shell and took a moment to catch their breath. Oblivious to the random waning fire, a cluster of mounted officers approached, assessing the battle line.

"Here comes something you don't see often," Tim said. "Staff meeting on horseback." He slapped his dusty cap against his thigh and reset it properly.

"Brigade commander has division commander's ear, I see." Coop swiped dirt and splinters off her arms and legs. "I'd guess Hall's taking Gibbon for a tour, but…with assistance from Devereaux, Macy, and Mallon?"

"At least we're represented. Devereaux will get in a good word for us, even if Macy starts bragging about Harvard again. But Mallon?" He shrugged. "Well, he's New York Irish, so I guess he's okay."

"But I wonder what it means for our illustrious 3rd Brigade," Coop whispered as the officers neared.

Accompanied by a divisional color-bearer and the general's adjutant, the little parade slowed through Coop's area, and she and Tim stood at attention and saluted. The officers returned the salute in unison, and Coop thought they looked quite sharp doing so.

"Bravery under fire, gentlemen," General Gibbon told them, and turned in the saddle to address everyone. "Police this area on the double and collect yourselves. Stay sharp now."

Devereux acknowledged them with a nod as the parade shifted west, toward the front line and the 20th Massachusetts, and then back north, paralleling the stone wall. Coop, Tim, and all soldiers along the route watched until the parade disbanded at the copse of trees.

Joining others collecting abandoned rifles and gear, Coop said, "Maybe Gibbon's going to change Hall's alignment on the wall." She leaned five guns into each other and moved on to arrange another stand. "Think they'll move us up from reserve?"

"We'd miss all this fun back here," Tim said as they stood their collections into one stand. "Did you know Jeff Davis appointed Gibbon to West Point?"

A shell exploded just past their position and knocked Cooper off her feet. She slammed into Tim's chest, and both crashed to the ground.

Flat on her back, she clawed for air, tried to focus, to concentrate on regaining her composure. *Easy. Steady. Breathe.* Finally, her lungs relaxed and Coop threw herself onto all fours and sucked in the foul air. "Damn. I hate those." Dizziness threatened and she swayed. The ringing in her ears returned. "Too close. You okay?"

Tim sat up and shook dirt from his beard. "Enough to know we were lucky."

"Let's try to stay that way," she answered and rose tentatively to her full height.

Tim mumbled as he stood. "Where was I? Oh, yeah. It's true about Gibbon and Davis, really."

Coop cocked an eyebrow. "Is that all you care about?"

"I think it's a pretty curious thing. Having our division commander beholden to the president of those Confederate states is worth some thought."

"Not for one second is John Gibbon beholding to Jeff Davis." She shook her head. "You've been in the sun too long."

Tim followed her to the pile of rubble that used to be their shelter. "You're wobbling. Sit down a minute."

Coop slid out of her knapsack, crouched, and closed her eyes. She had to put fingertips to the ground to prevent toppling over. "It'll pass soon."

Tim, meanwhile, rummaged through their debris. "He could be tempted, you know."

"Who?"

"Gibbon."

"Will you quit this?" She retrieved her tin cup from the pile and tied it to her knapsack.

"No. Really, he could be tempted. Did you know he has three reb brothers?"

Coop pondered that as she shrugged into her pack.

"Tim, my good friend." She sighed, turning to face him. "I have one, too."

He shrank back, eyes wide. "What?"

"Remember, long ago, I told you about the brother—"

"Oh, I do. The one who left. You met—He's a reb?"

Astonishment on his wooly face almost made Coop laugh. "We met at the Bauer house."

"No!"

"He's a corporal, 22nd Virginia, and a die-hard." She shook her head at the ground. "Trust me. Having a reb brother hasn't changed my mind any."

That stopped Tim's gossip and Coop was glad. She'd managed to relegate Billy to the back of her mind and now she had to do it again. It wasn't easy. Her brother was out there, through all that smoke along that ridge. Rebel guns now had fallen silent, but he was out there with his own gun, waiting, and she was in no hurry to reconnect. Ever.

Swinging her canteen off her hip, she considered the possibility of pouring it over her head. How glorious, she mused as she popped the cork. She gazed over the canteen as she drank and watched the smoke on the plain drift away. Activity swarmed around the Bauer farm like bees at the hive.

How bad is it inside, Sophie? Please still be safe downstairs.

Sunshine flooded the landscape, and immediately sweat slithered down her back. She closed her eyes and drank more, letting the water and the memory of Sophie's kiss refresh her. But when she reopened her eyes, every muscle in her body froze.

CHAPTER TWENTY-FIVE

Albany," Greta answered.

Karl shook his head. "It's New York City."

"No, Albany." Greta turned to Sophie for confirmation and munched on her lunch, the last of their bread with apple butter.

"Greta's right, Karl. Papa, your turn. The capital of Rhode Island?"

He rubbed his bristly chin and exaggerated his thought process. "I...think it's...Philadelphia."

Karl rolled his eyes. "No, it's not."

"Raleigh?"

Karl had to think about it.

"I know!" Greta slid to the edge of her bench.

Sophie grinned at them, pleased they'd found another game to occupy their midday hours. Constant footsteps in the main kitchen above said tending to the wounded carried on without her, but now that quiet apparently had arrived outside, she fully expected the call for assistance to come from Dr. Taylor.

"It's Concord," Karl blurted out.

"That's in Massachusetts with Lexington," Greta said, and turned to Karl as he helped himself to more butter on his bread. "Remember the minutemen?"

Sophie held up a finger. "But it's also the capital of New Hampshire."

"Oh."

Papa leaned forward. "How about Providence?"

"Ah-ha!" Sophie grinned. "Papa knows."

A distant cannon blast brought Greta up short. "They're not going to start again, are they?"

"Hard to say, honey." Sophie sent a look to Papa. "Whose was it, theirs or ours?"

"Too far away to tell, but it sounded like it came from down around Sherfy's."

A second cannon fired, and all heads turned toward the south wall.

Karl looked confused. "But they already fought down there yesterday, Papa."

"Well, they fought to the north on Cemetery Hill yesterday, too, and didn't we hear them fighting there again this morning?" Karl nodded. "Not all battles are won in a day, son."

Another cannon boomed, then two more almost simultaneously. Then several practically at once, and then even more until they continued nonstop. The noise grew deafening and the ground practically rolled beneath their feet.

"Confederate guns," Papa said with volume, as artillery fired faster and faster.

Greta covered her ears. The trap door at the top of the steps rattled.

Sophie set her shoulder to Papa's and hoped he'd hear her whisper. "They're shooting all around us, aren't they?"

He nodded toward his shoes. "And over us." He met her eyes. "Sounds like they're using everything they've got."

Moving to sit halfway up the steps, Karl raised his voice to be heard. "I wish we could go out and watch." He beamed expectantly at Sophie.

She frowned and waved him back. Disappointed, he stood, and a deafening bang just outside sent him tumbling to the floor. They all jumped and Greta shrieked, as dust floated from the ceiling.

Sophie brushed dirt off Karl's back and lifted his chin. He looked more than a bit shaken. "I best check for broken bones, huh?" She squeezed her way up one arm and down the other, then squeezed his knee. He grinned and twisted away.

"I'm okay." He hurried back to his box seat. Cringing beneath the incessant noise, Greta gathered her blanket and sat close to Papa.

"I'm sure that explosion was an accident," he said in his most soothing voice. "Doesn't serve anyone to strike at an innocent farmhouse."

Suddenly, the trap door opened, and sunlight flooded the room, overpowering their candlelight.

"Miss Sophie?" a man yelled. "We sure could use a hand, please?"

Standing in the middle of the room, Sophie looked down at Papa.

He shifted his wary eyes to the steps and shouted back. "Amidst all this racket?"

Sophie glanced at each of them, not keen on leaving her family or their sanctuary, certainly not with all hell breaking loose outside.

The man yelled again. "Doc says you make fast work of things, Miss Sophie. He said for me to ask 'cause we got a houseful in need, ma'am."

I'm sure you do. My house full.

She took a heavy breath. "No doubt I could be of assistance," she said, looking from Greta to Karl to Papa. "And you *did* make a good point about that accidental shot. I'm sure none of them intends to injure us." Their blank stares had Sophie wondering if she was trying to convince them or herself. "I-I'll try not to be long, okay?"

She kissed each of them on the cheek and whispered to Papa. "I'll get a look at the condition of the house, at least." She hurried up to the Union steward holding the door.

"We're grateful, ma'am," he said, and shut the door after her. "Doc's this way."

She surveyed the kitchen before following him to the parlor, dismayed to see some dozen soldiers of both armies covering the floor. Only an open rim some two feet deep surrounded the stove, and she figured no one wanted to be any closer in this confounded heat. Her two large pots boiled on the surface, steam thickening the humidity.

The parlor had taken on a terrible air in her absence and she rubbed her nose. Wounded were everywhere, propped against walls, prone on the floor, pressed together to such a degree that stepping between them looked dangerous. In the near corner, Dr. Taylor left the amputee on the bloodied table for his assistant to finish and maneuvered to where she stood.

Another serious bang in the yard made everyone flinch. Broken glass shook loose from a nearby window and he slid it aside with his foot. How he carried on mystified her. He probably hadn't slept in days.

"Ah, Miss Sophie." He leaned to her ear. "Reb gunners need better teachers." He tried to grin, but his expression soured. "We're trying to move these boys along, to get those waiting outside in here, but we're just too shorthanded." He dipped his hands into a basin of bloody water, rubbed them together, and dried them on a disgusting towel. *From my kitchen.* "I suppose," he continued, "if those shots don't stop falling out there, we won't have many fellows left to worry about, but we have to stay positive. Don't we?"

Optimistic? The image of helpless soldiers being splattered all over the yard turned her stomach.

He assembled bandages and equipment onto a tray. "You don't know how much I appreciate your help." Handing it to her, he scanned the room.

"I'll do what I can, you know that, but my family needs me as well."
He didn't react and she hoped she'd spoken loudly enough.

The noise had intensified, and those "accidental" bangs shook
the house more frequently now, so frequently that she began to doubt
artillerists' intentions. Then again, it was more likely that Union cannon
were firing back. *They can make mistakes, too.*

"Hm?" He glanced at her. "Oh, yes, of course." He looked back at the
room. "There he is." He pointed toward the fireplace. "Nurse Mather. He'll
get you started."

Sophie stepped away, respecting his mournful imperative. She
searched the fireplace area, a sea of tattered blood-stained gray and brown
uniforms. A rebel crouching over a comrade stood and beckoned to her.

"Right here, ma'am." He flashed a quick, nearly toothless smile and
feigned a salute. "Cpl. Hanlon Mather, ma'am, 7th Louisiana. You must be
Miss Sophie. I'm mighty pleased to meet you."

"How do you do, Corporal." Sophie couldn't tell if the smell assaulting
her nose originated in the room as a whole or with all these ragged rebels.
There was little doubt this one hadn't bathed in too long. She wondered
how he came to his role as a nurse. Another explosion rocked the house
and she ducked instinctively.

"Sorry about the noise, ma'am. Yanks gotta be more careful." He
turned in place and indicated the assortment of wounded at his feet. "These
boys should come around soon, I reckon, but a few are bleedin' pretty bad.
If you could see to their needs, I'd be obliged."

"I'll do what I can." She stooped where she stood and checked the
nearest soldier. With a "Thank you, ma'am," Nurse Mather edged around
her and moved on.

Her patient groaned in his stupor. Blood trickled steadily from a
savage wound in his thigh and pooled on the floor. She knew it soaked
through the meager layer of hay beneath him, and fleetingly, she considered
the fate of her precious rug. She set about cleaning the wound, flinching
again as another explosion occurred too close to the house.

Then another came, deafening when it burst directly overhead.
Shrapnel peppered the roof as if a hundred carpenters were hammering.
Screams came from the keeping room and she remembered the earlier
destruction that had opened a hole to the sky.

Coop, are you safe? Are you watching all this?

She bent lower, praying the parlor ceiling stayed where it was, and
concentrated. The noise in the bedroom above her, *her bedroom*, gave her

something new to fret over. Who knew what was happening in the room she adored? The possibilities made her cringe.

You may not recognize this place anymore, Coop. Whole sections are crumbling. A glimpse of your smile, the touch of your hand surely would help right now.

She pondered that truth as she worked, taken by desire that seemed to heighten every hour since Coop's secret upended her world. Sleep had been so sketchy last night. Exhaustion had barely prevailed over her excited heart's constant play, and those vivid imaginings crept to mind again. We danced among friends at a town fair, she told herself, you dusted me with flour as you kneaded that dough, and we kissed by the candlelight of the Christmas tree.

But where? We were alone in our harmony, with no sign of where. Does fate point me to your farm? Perhaps here or, someplace new we might find together? The adventurous concept of starting a life with Coop in an entirely different place made her pulse quicken. *But you have gone to such lengths to live the life you choose in your own home, and I respect that too much to expect you would consider living elsewhere.*

Sophie sighed and helped a wounded rebel drink from his canteen. She saw Coop agonizing on the floor of some medical tent, parched, bleeding from a chest wound, as this rebel did. And she saw a steward rip open Coop's shirt. Sophie blinked hard to dismiss the image.

The relentless pounding outside lessened, and as she made a third trip through the maze of wounded for more supplies, she dared to think hostilities were winding down. Maybe now she could check on Papa and the children.

A cannonball plowed through the parlor wall and the crash knocked Sophie to the floor. A sharp breath chirped amidst the shattering of debris, and she needed a moment to realize it hadn't originated with her. Casting aside the shards of wood, she climbed to her knees and found the disfigured body of Nurse Mather, thrown across two dead Union soldiers.

CHAPTER TWENTY-SIX

"Tim!" Cooper pointed to the field.

"Holy... Will you look at that."

To the left and right, as far as she could see, rebels emerged from the trees along their ridge and advanced in several well-trimmed lines, elbow to elbow. By the thousands.

Someone yelled. "Here they come! Here comes the infantry!"

Comrades in the 19th gathered to stare. All along the wall, soldiers rose, gaping at the sight. Rear units rushed up for a better look.

Coop muttered, "Have you ever seen anything like it?" Tim just shook his head. "Me neither. That's impressive, for sure."

"I'll give 'em that."

Maybe because of pride in her 19th Massachusetts, a unit often recognized for its precision maneuvering, Coop had never considered a more striking presentation until now. The Southern uniforms were a hodge-podge of gray, brown, and butternut, but strung out like this, in perfect linear march, each man with rifle glinting on his shoulder behind hundreds of banners, the rebel ranks commanded admiration.

Tim asked, "How many, you think?"

Coop scanned left and right again and gave up trying to count the color-bearers. *Could there really be twelve or even thirteen thousand?*

"Too many colors to count. I'd guess two divisions?"

He swore under his breath and Coop couldn't blame him. The Union line seemed vastly outnumbered.

Batteries around her came to life, officers and crews yelling, sighting their guns on the advancing rebel lines. Cannon opened fire and, again, clouds of smoke began to obscure the numbing sight. Bolstered by reserve batteries, the Union line unloaded from all points along Cemetery Ridge, including the heights of Little Round Top to the south and Cemetery Hill to the north. Devastation poured onto the fields.

Like all Union troops, she strained to see their artillery's impact. Exploding shells and solid shot punched holes in the lines, flattened soldiers by the dozen, and to Coop's amazement, no one retreated. Rebels immediately closed ranks and kept on.

"Can't tell if that's stupidity or bravery," Tim said.

"Maybe something else, entirely," she answered, taken by their devotion to their cause.

The Union skirmish line, out along the Emmitsburg Road, a position Coop knew well, held strong as its rebel counterpart approached, only withdrawing when those imposing lines of Southern infantry caught up. Directly out from the center of the Union battle line, rebel pioneer squads pressed closer, dismantled some sections of road fencing, but the bulk of the Confederate lines was forced to climb over or through the obstacles. And now volleys of Union riflery caught hundreds indisposed.

When rebels dropped over the fence onto the sunken roadbed, they disappeared, and Coop noted that some never reappeared to tackle the parallel fence, the one she'd used for cover less than two days ago. Rebels who did were slow to reform and once again Union infantry and artillery took full advantage of the ideal targets. With a determination Coop found nearly incomprehensible, Confederates marched on.

She shook her head as thousands advanced, now on her side of the Emmitsburg.

Coop glanced at the Bauer farm and a wave of helplessness rolled up to her throat. Rebels, in rows thousands of men wide, now trudged past on both sides of the barn, the house, wrapping a human target around the farmstead. Coop stared, unable to move.

Cannon fire cut the rows of marchers into sections large and small with solid shot and percussion shells. Bursting locus-like clouds of case shot spattered the ground. Bodies spun in place, collapsed mid-step, whirled through the air as easily as leaves in a gale. An errant shot drove in the roof of the Bauer's summer kitchen, and Coop's heart skipped. She *had* to stop envisioning Sophie administering to the wounded in any of those buildings.

Through the smoke around her and that on the plain, she saw the rebels close ranks again and shook her head in disbelief. To her right at the copse of trees, regiments rose from their prone positions and fired.

Their wall of lead slammed into the rebel line, followed by another and another. She could hear Confederate officers' desperate commands now, the screams of the wounded. She hated to think of what the Bauer family heard.

Sophie, stay below.

"They're coming straight at us," Tim said, then nodded toward their left. "Might be my imagination, but seems like *they're* angling toward us, too." He snorted. "Getting all jumbled up with each other, trying to turn this-a-way."

Coop nodded, observing the Confederate southern flank perform a poorly executed turn in their direction. "Are those Vermonters down there?"

"Yup, I think. Some of them are new, but oh, they did mighty fine work yesterday. They're not going to let those rebs waltz across their front."

Coop looked to their right. That Confederate flank also had begun to shift toward them. "Is every damn reb coming our way?" She flashed him a wary look. "They're converging from both ends on our center."

"Well, same fate's awaiting those rebs, I bet." He no sooner spoke when an infantry unit's riflery joined the artillery fire coming from Cemetery Hill. Hit from the side and front as they shifted, rebels to the north dropped by the score. Most turned and ran, leaving the bravest to risk joining their comrades who marched ahead. "That's an Ohio unit all strung out up there," he added, pointing. "They're making it one rough day for those Johnnies, I tell you."

The way Coop saw things, it was going to be *everyone's* roughest day.

Incoming cannon fire now hit Union stores and munitions with too much regularity, and explosions forced troops to dodge or fall flat for safety. Coop hoped the batteries were replenishing their supplies because she'd already heard their calls about running low.

Enhanced by infantry rifles, northern guns that just earlier had concentrated on the Confederate ridge now wreaked havoc on the fields, to the left, right, and center. Still, the rebel force advanced as if being squeezed toward the Union middle. *Can we keep pace?* Hundreds of dead and wounded dotted the fields in the rebels' wake like newly sprouted crops, and Coop noted many a Southerner running for his life. *But still they come.*

She turned an eye to the Bauer farm again and gasped when a percussion shell flattened part of the barn. Like too many others, Sophie's farmstead would endure wholesale damage before all this ended. Already, a small structure, possibly a privy, sat ablaze not far from the barn. A scattering of rebels sought refuge in the house and made Coop wonder just how much room remained, how Sophie was coping, where she was.

None of this seems real. A woman steps out of my dreams and is enveloped by horror and death. Thousands of able-bodied men fervently march to their own demise. We clamor to deliver mayhem and destruction, cheering as we make widows of wives, orphans of sons and daughters. While I watch. What remains of one's country when we've finally destroyed each other? How can a nation ever heal after such human ruin as this? Who have we become?

Confederate shots dropped everywhere onto Cemetery Ridge as Southern artillery tried to cover its advancing troops. Gathered in their reserve position, Coop and the 19th crouched in a unified flinch and waited, collective anxiety soaring as the scene unfolded.

Nearby, the Rhode Island battery withdrew, too damaged to remain in position. The New York battery rolled forward, then lost most of its crews to a shell, and Coop heard an officer assign some of the 19th to replace those missing. She wished a different regiment had been chosen because their ranks had already seen their share of loss to date, probably numbered fewer than one hundred fifty souls. That was a far cry from the nearly four hundred who mustered out of Boston two years ago, and now, on top of today's losses, sending more than two dozen off for artillery duty compromised their depleted strength in a major way.

She sighed hard at the sight of her 19th brothers hurrying off to occupy what, for the enemy, was a highly coveted prize. *Not the safest place to be.* She reminded herself that she was lucky to avoid that duty, to remain here at the ready.

But ahead in the fields, where thousands lay out of action and just as many retreated, it seemed unfathomable that an equal number still approached with deadly intention. She'd seen regiments devastated by single shells, one South Carolina unit completely erased, but however diminished, the rebels seemed undaunted. Hundreds upon hundreds drew closer, picked up their pace.

Tensions heightened along the wall. Troops grew frantic. Coop could feel it; breathing came hard. She spared a glance at Tim and wondered if she looked as fearful. As rebel shells screamed in, she checked her rifle by rote, made sure the cap was in place, ready to fire. The call to action could come at any moment and, as she blinked sweat from her tired eyes, she summoned strength to maintain aim, her reflexes to lend her speed.

Comrades at the front fired at a frenetic pace, desperate to stem the incoming tide. They alternated in rows, stepping back to reload as a second line stepped forward, all while Union cannon blasted over their heads. Shells with shortened fuses sprayed clusters of iron balls at closer range and devastated rebels by the dozen. Coop heard urgent voices in the New York battery scream to double the load of the cannister. The buckshot-like ammunition, at very short range, cleaved massive sections of Confederates from the multitudes.

Coop's chest tightened at the sight of their faces. She could see them clearly now, wide-eyed, reddened, feverish. Victory propelled the Confederates into urgent frenzy, and, unleashing their screeching rebel yell, they broke into mobs and charged the wall.

Papa met Sophie at the top of the steps, fright for her well-being distorting his already haggard features. He took her by her arms. "Thank heavens."

"I'm all right, Papa. Rattled but all right." They stepped aside as a rebel dragged a comrade to the kitchen. He laid him half atop another, for lack of space. "The house is taking a most horrendous beating," she said. "It's not safe for these men."

Papa urged her toward the cellar. "Nor for us, not up here."

"I can't leave without first speaking to Dr. Taylor. You go down and tell—"

"Downstairs, young woman. An artillery fight like they just had could bring down the wrath of the Lord. Never thought I'd say such a thing, but there's a city of soldiers on either side of us, Sophie, and they're out there for a reason. And I fear it's not just to wale on each other from a mile apart."

"Yes, that was hell on earth, Papa, but it's over and—" Cannon began firing again. The whistling of shells almost had become familiar.

"See?" he insisted, running his gaze across the ceiling. "East to west, Cemetery to Seminary ridges. We're taking it to them again." He sighed. "Oh, Sophie. We've lost so much already." He took her hand and his defeated expression tugged at her heart. "Come, now." He gestured to the kitchen. "Mostly Southerners here now, anyway. No need to risk yourself for these treasonous—"

"Papa, please. I promise to be down directly."

His fatherly stare bored into her. "You mustn't allow that charitable nature of yours to do you in, my girl."

"Let me handle this." She patted his cheek. "I'll be as prompt as I can be. Now, please." She turned him by the shoulders. He implored her with a look, but reluctantly complied. Before closing the door after him, she blew a kiss to Greta and Karl who had been watching from the steps.

Papa was right, she thought, probably should have retreated to the cellar long ago. And yes, rebels outnumbered Yankees in the house, but that didn't seem to bother the indefatigable Dr. Taylor or his crew. *It shouldn't bother me, either, but it's hard to imagine those Southern belles tending to our soldiers like this.* On second thought, she supposed they did. Despite all the vengeance and horror in evidence, there *had* to be some humanity left in this world. *It won't do to think otherwise.*

Sophie stretched her back, listening to guns boom and the explosions they wrought land closer and closer. Far closer than before. Quickly retying the ribbon in her hair, she assumed—with considerable anxiety— that Union artillery had a target nearby.

With a heavy exhale for courage, she peeked through the hole in the kitchen door. Sunshine made her squint, but she had no trouble discerning the world of Confederates overtaking her property, Virginians all. The sight stole her breath. Never had she seen so many in one place. Everywhere she looked, rows of them advanced, disassembling to round the barn, carefully crossing the carpet of their own wounded around the summer kitchen, and reforming as they passed her door, so close she could touch them.

Captains led the way, their embroidered sleeves as brilliant in the sun as their forward-tipped sabers. Thousands of bayonets and rifle barrels sparkled with reflected light. The glittering steel seemed to brighten the hundreds of flags in a macabre festival of colors. And with all this military propriety, ragged, often bare-footed men with solemn faces eyed the horizon. Occasionally, one would speak to another, but their focus, their pride was evident, and their courage, far too great to measure.

A shell burst above the yard and at least a dozen soldiers crumbled. The percussion staggered Sophie in the doorway. She watched in awe as their comrades closed the gap and hardly missed a step.

The whirring of another shell made her crouch and, once the blast shook the kitchen walls, she looked out to see half the barn in shambles. Billowing smoke drew her attention to what remained of the outside privy.

Rifle fire then joined the fray, and rebels dropped as if they were nothing more than targets in a county fair skill game. Shells poured like rain and still the force marched on, leaving a trail of comrades in her flattened wheat and rye.

The magnitude of the march gripped her, led her to wonder about its scope. Sophie opened the door and stuck her head out. *Is the entire Confederacy passing by?* Absently, lost in curiosity, she slipped outside and crept against the house to the front, until she could peek across the half-mile to the Union line. Cannon smoke connected those north and south hills in a roiling cloud and wafted from explosions all over the plain, from what had been families' sustenance for the year to come. Glimpses she had caught of yesterday's battle bore little resemblance to what enthralled her now.

Rebel troops emerged from the other side of her house and from much farther to her left, all angling toward the Union center. Immediately, they fell under fire from the north. Shielding her eyes, she rose on her toes to look southwest, and found more rebels angling in a similar way. Clouds of smoke indicated they were receiving the same treatment.

Meanwhile, the spectacle in front of her played out in fictional fashion. The grandeur, the mesmerizing reality of it all defied her comprehension.

How can they just walk right into that? So much devotion to country is required, not only to take a life, but to leave family, a forever love, and give your own. How deep in one's heart such devotion must live. Is this the measure of a soldier?

She searched the cloud-covered Union line, wondering where Coop was, what she was thinking in the face of this onslaught. *Catherine Samson, you are a soldier. Your devotion is immeasurable...but please come back to me.*

She watched the steady, ever-shrinking Confederate lines edge closer to the Union center. Bodies staggered and dropped, jerked violently, heaved off their feet. Singularly and in groups, their numbers diminished rapidly. *A shooting gallery.* She fought back tears for all of them.

Sophie never heard the horse until it appeared at her side. She fell against the house in shock, squinting up at the most refined officer she had ever seen.

From his gold spurs to his gauntlet gloves, he dazzled. A double row of brass buttons sparkled up the center of his crisp, spotless gray uniform, and curls adorned the tips of his drooping mustache and the end of his modest beard. He doffed his cap to her and smiled, and with a slight bow of his head, his hair swung in ringlets to his shoulders.

"Pardon my hurried approach, madam. Sincere apologies for startling you. Major General George Pickett, division commanding."

As if his abrupt arrival wasn't surprising enough, his rank took Sophie aback. *Such a dandy! But Southern generals don't wear caps.* Then she noticed the stars on his upright collar.

"Um…Well, hello. I-I was…" Completely caught off guard, embarrassed, she fumbled for words. "How do you do, sir?"

He looked her over with a keen gaze. Sophie figured her bloodied apron explained her presence in the middle of the battlefield.

"Is this your farm, madam?"

"It is, sir. This is the Bauer farm."

"Then, on behalf of the grand Army of Northern Virginia…" He slapped his cap to his heart. "Please allow me to extend our most profound gratitude for your service." A shell screamed overhead and exploded beyond the barn. Sophie jumped, but Pickett never flinched. Neither did his horse. "Now," he said, resetting his cap and backing away, "I respectfully ask that you remove yourself to safety inside at once."

His manners didn't escape Sophie, but neither did the air of Southern superiority, and it irked her. She took a step toward the kitchen door but turned back, a hand on her hip. Seeing her about to speak, Pickett removed his cap again.

"General, I *do* thank you for your concern, but my home hardly provides safe haven anymore. Perhaps it might, if only you all would sit and work through your differences—and include a woman's perspective, I might add—instead of killing and maiming, and blasting families' farms to splinters."

"Point taken, madam." Pickett bowed deeply as his horse pawed at the turf.

"Good day, sir."

CHAPTER TWENTY-SEVEN

Through a tempest of cannister fire, a rolling sea of Southern fury crested at the wall. Flurries of Union lead slammed it to a stop. Coop held her breath, could only watch with the rest of the 19th, as hundreds of Confederates who'd survived the devastating gauntlet across the field swelled against the Union line.

Coop tensed where she stood. She scanned the length of her front, left to right, northward up the gentle rise to the copse of trees, and willed every ounce of her energy to comrades there, fighting for their lives. As fast as humanly possible, they sent volley after volley into the rushing horde. So many in blue fell, weren't fast enough. The rebel dead and wounded literally fell in piles, replaced immediately as the unrelenting surge stepped over them, on them to breach the Union line.

Chaos reigned at the copse, and, still held in reserve, Coop, Tim, and the rest of the 19th bristled in helpless frustration. She identified flags from North Carolina, Tennessee, Alabama, Virginia now among the Pennsylvanians and New Yorkers. She could see more coming. What remained of a Union battery cried out for ammunition and settled for ramming shell fragments, bayonets, rocks, anything it could find down the muzzles. About to be overwhelmed, Union infantry had no time to reload and grabbed spare rifles, then resorted to pistols if they had them, to bayonets, then to using their rifles as clubs, and finally, to knives and fists.

"My God. This is insanity," Tim said on a breath.

Some Pennsylvanians retreated and Coop really couldn't blame them. Officers drew revolvers and sabers and sent them back, then ordered another home state unit into the fray.

To her south, Union forces labored behind very scant cover, and Coop pointed along that stretch of the line. "Vermonters out there to the left are helping, but everything's leaning this way."

Colonel Devereux rode up to the outskirts of the 19th and Coop wondered what possible orders could make him hold their regiment in reserve like this. At his other side, the 42nd New York itched to move as well, and Silas Benning, the harmonica player, haplessly threw his hands at her in silent agreement. Tim bumped Coop and tossed his head toward Devereux, daring her to question him. She rolled her eyes in response.

Union action definitely had begun to slant northward, swaying right along with all those incoming Virginian flags, countering their approach. Tim snatched off his cap and shoved a hand through his hair. She could relate to the unbearable anxiety.

Dripping sweat stung her eyes and she rubbed it away. *Cursed heat.* She tried shifting inside her frock and shuffled her roasting feet. Her hands grew moist, the grip of her rifle, slick. *Too much watching and worrying only leads to fear. And far too much waiting.*

Another glance south showed the 15th Massachusetts, and Maine and New York regiments now firing as they ran up the line to oppose rebels angling ever closer. Straight ahead, the thinning Harvard ranks struggled to hold their own, as they, too, drifted toward the copse. Next to them, the Michigan unit began to buckle.

With an elbow to his arm, Coop directed Tim's attention toward the copse. "The 7th is falling."

Adding to their horror, the 59th New York, the next and last unit before the copse, broke wide open and rebels poured over the wall.

Tim spat. "Dammit to hell."

Her friend Henry raced his Harvard men to the copse but, even joining with the belabored 69th Pennsylvania, it was evident to Coop and her comrades, that the effort wouldn't be enough to overpower the growing Confederate thrust.

She watched a Virginian general, somehow still on horseback, weave into the throng and take a bullet to the throat. Yet another Virginian general, this one with his hat impaled on his saber, climbed fearlessly over the wall and into the melee. A screaming rebel claimed the wall with his regimental colors.

One too many Confederate flags on our side, Coop thought, and she whirled to Devereux, unkind words at the ready. But, of all people, the commanding general on the field, Winfield Hancock, had just ridden up, and though she missed Devereux's words to him, Hancock expressed his in typical fashion, loud and definitive.

"By all means, man! Get in there, quick!"

Coop hefted her rifle and exchanged a look with Tim. "Here we go."

He nodded hard. "'Bout damn time, if you ask me."

Drawing his saber, Devereux spun to them, his mouth open, and no one heard the command over the soldiers' roar. The 42nd New York men cheered like hungry hounds. Coop didn't see their Colonel Mallon and was surprised to see them prepare to step off on Devereux's order. Someone somewhere then called for a "right wheel," and both units turned and dashed to the copse.

Midway up the rise, both regiments fired on the run. Coop and other skilled shooters managed to reload with barely a pause and took out more rebels at the trees. A company stopped, pivoted to the front, and cut down rebels trying to jump the wall. Reloading just fifty yards from the maelstrom, Coop knew this could be the last shot she'd have with the Springfield.

A bullet pierced her canteen. The high-pitched scream behind her said the 19th's youngest member, a Dorchester boy she knew to be only sixteen, had taken the hit. Furious, she pulled up, took aim, and shot the first Confederate she saw in the forehead. She reloaded. *Hurry. Almost too close.*

Having been positioned north of the 19th, her companion New Yorkers were first to charge into the copse. Coop's wave of soldiers arrived next, guns loaded, bayonets leveled.

She banged aside a rebel rifle, knocked the soldier out with a jaw-breaking uppercut of her gunstock, and spun in time to deflect a bayonet with her own. But the Confederate pressed his considerable bulk onto their locked rifles, snarling mere inches from Coop's face. She spat into his eye, he twitched awkwardly, and Coop, quicker and more nimble, drove her bayonet into his chest. She had to grit her teeth to free the blade. *Pray that I never grow accustomed to this grisly deed.*

A comrade collapsed against her, and spilled Coop into another Yankee as he fired. Stunned by the blast near her ear, she stumbled—out of the direct path of a bayonet. Coop felt the left sleeves of her frock and shirt split and blood run hot from her bicep. *Collect yourself or you're dead.*

Her ears rang but didn't blot out the cacophony of screams, guns, curses, hurrahs, and cannon. She willed her senses to steady just as a punch slammed the side of her head. Sparks flashed behind her eyes. Her stomach lurched and she wobbled, fell to a knee, supported only by her rifle. Chaos convulsed around her and bounced her in all directions. *Get up. Get up, dammit all!*

Someone seized a fistful of her frock at the shoulder and hauled her onto her feet.

"Don't make it so easy for them!" Tim shouted.

Coop blinked and almost whimpered with thanks when her fuzzy vision cleared. Yes, she mused, the tickle behind her ear probably meant her wound had reopened, but she *was* on her feet. Thanks to Tim.

Grappling bodies separated her from him now, but she caught a glimpse of him delivering a punch—and of another rebel taking aim at his head. Someone fell against her legs and she staggered, almost went down again, and she cursed the untimely distraction. The danger of Tim's shooter remained. She managed to raise her gun in the crush of bodies, knowing she could wait no longer than a beat for opportunity to open. In that moment, she leveled the long gun and pulled the trigger.

A screeching rebel, his gritty face fiendish with rage, fell upon her then, took her by the throat with both hands and pulled her close. He aimed to use his shoulder strength to crush her windpipe and was doing a fair job. Coop's head throbbed mercilessly. Blood rushed in her ears. She gasped and saved the breath.

With all her strength, she yanked her Springfield upward but couldn't break his hold. She had no room to drive it against him, so she tried again. He unleashed the rebel yell as he tightened his grip. Then Coop slammed her knee into his most delicate place. He recoiled and, in that moment of relief, she whipped the rifle barrel across his face.

Coughing, desperately gulping air, Coop staggered in the tussling crowd. Ahead, one of her sergeants seized the colors of the 19th Virginia at bayonet point, and she took strength in his success. Triumphant, he shouted his intention to cover its insignia with that of their own 19th.

But next a rebel cheer rose over the din and Coop seethed to see the Virginian general claim a Union cannon. Around him, Confederates roared, but a Pennsylvania unit then charged, shot the general, sent his men running, and tore after them. Coop and many others cheered them on, and she took heart that this madness might soon end.

She also rejoiced when remnants of the 15th Massachusetts arrived from their southern posts, along with comrades from the 19th Maine and 82nd New York. Together, they joined with the stalwart 69th Pennsylvania to form a crescent-shaped defense, extending out from the copse, and began the difficult repulse.

Elbow to elbow, face to face, bodies clashed and fell, wounded, dead, and just unable to rise in the crush. Coop jumped when someone on the ground fired and grazed the top of her shoe. Stepping on a dead rebel's chest, she thrust her bayonet into a burly foe and dodged a swinging rifle in time to send her bayonet into that rebel's stomach.

With all the whirling, dodging, and forward stomping, Coop found herself closer to the stone wall, where most guns had been turned into clubs and fists were flying.

She knocked a rebel's gun from his hands and jammed her rifle butt up under his chin. Then, caught with her gun almost above her head, Coop took a punch to the stomach. Air gushed from her lungs and she doubled over. Kicked in the head, she fell and darkness flickered. *Get up! They'll finish you right here!*

Struggling to her knees in the tumult, Coop swallowed bile and blinked hard. Jostling bodies shoved her this way and that, which didn't help clear her dizziness. In the seconds required to stand, she realized the Springfield was lost, and that turned her stomach ever further. She slapped a hand to it and discovered the pistol she'd picked up after the cannonade still tucked into her belt.

When a bugler ordered the 19th to turn to the wall, she had to wrestle and shoot two rebels to get there. A Confederate's old rifle turned out to be a lucky find, and, tucking the pistol away, she snatched it up greedily, thankful to find it capped and ready to fire.

Dozens of rebels still hustled doggedly forward, though Coop could see they were the last of their lot. They reached the wall, climbing, vaulting, screaming. Union bayonets went up and leaping rebels landed upon them. Guns swung wildly, smashing together, breaking apart until men fought with the pieces. All remaining Union rifles fired at point-blank range, Cooper's included.

Her victim toppled toward her, over the wall, and yanked her gun from her hands as he went. Coop drew her pistol to greet the next onrushing rebel.

Seeing his rifle rise in her direction, she extended her arm and took aim at the shabby uniform. He aimed as well, sighting along the barrel, his finger on the trigger. Pointed at her face, the muzzle of his gun gaped like the mouth of a cannon, and Coop's heart pulsed in her throat. A long, peculiar second passed as she exhaled smoothly to steady her nerve, acutely aware of the trigger waiting beneath her finger. Then, she spotted the bloodied wrap around his naked arm. At the far end of his gun, his eyes widened beneath the classic floppy hat.

Her blood chilled and the pistol trembled in her hand.

Billy stopped not twenty feet away. His rifle still on her, she saw it shake. An entire day seemed to pass, or perhaps years, *their* years. Coop desperately wanted to be anywhere but here in this moment.

At last, his finger slid off the trigger and the tip of his rifle dipped.

Coop cleared her throat and stiffened her arm. She *had* to keep her composure.

"Y-you are my pris—"

A bullet snapped his head sideways. Coop saw what burst from the other side. Frozen in place, she lost her breath as his lifeless form crumbled to the ground.

A comrade gave her a shove. "Shoot, y'damn fool!" He fired into the last of the rebel charge.

But most Confederates now were in withdrawal, and sections of wall swarmed with gray and brown uniforms heading back across the mile of desolate, morbid fields. They intercepted stragglers still seeking to attack and turned them back. Around her, many zealous Yankees continued to fire, some hopped the wall in pursuit.

Pistol lowered to her side, Coop still stood in place. The sight of her brother kept her there, while hurrahs rang out from one Union regiment to the next, until those atop the hills and every Union soldier between them shouted, fired their guns, tossed their caps in victory.

She forced her feet to move and leaned over the wall, searching for a place to step, a patch of ground not covered by bodies. From this vantage point, to the north and south along the wall, from the Union camp behind her to the distant Seminary Ridge, there seemed to be nothing but.

With the blessed end of shooting, Coop realized the ringing in her ears had faded. There was relative silence now. A painfully profound, *dead* silence. And from it rose the blood-curdling moans, the desperate, gut-wrenching cries of thousands of wounded.

She knelt at Billy's side. He stared up at her with vacant eyes, coppery brown like their father's, and blood from his wound trickled silver in the light. But it would stop now. Sunshine bathed his sweat-slick face, neck, and arm, and she mourned the sad irony of it all. The tragedy. He had given his life for a cause she could never defend. But he wouldn't shoot his brother.

"Or your sister," she whispered.

His eyelids were warm to the touch as she lowered them. Tears blurred her vision. He was gone, never to tease or rant or cajole again, never to see the old home place, even if he did seem not to care. He'd hurt his family irreparably, abandoned those who loved him for strangers who might. She knew she'd never forget that, but, for the sake of her parents, Cooper, *and* herself, maybe one day she would forgive.

Coop sniffed, swiped at tears as she fought back a sob. His new life had brought light to his eyes and he had shared a hint of his former, joyful self with her. She believed those few hours together would always be both a pleasant and tragic reminder.

"Rest in peace, Sonny."

CHAPTER TWENTY-EIGHT

Sophie swung aside the shoddy, rain-soaked blanket that hung in place of the kitchen door.

"Coop!" Through a haze of tears, she threw her arms around Coop's neck, ignored the press of Coop's drenched uniform to her dress, and kissed her madly. "Oh, I-I'm just so glad to see you!"

"Sophie. Finally. The most glorious sight on this Fourth of July." Coop squeezed her tightly with one arm as she shouldered a bulging sack over her rifle.

Mindless of the steady rain, Sophie held Coop away by the shoulders and inspected her from top to bottom. "You're all right?" She cupped her cheek as Coop nodded. "Oh, Coop!" She closed them in another hug. "Come in." She tugged her inside. "Come in out of this rain."

Sophie backed in, refusing to take her eyes off her. Ever since fighting ceased yesterday afternoon, she had wondered how or if she would learn of Coop's fate. The fretting, the lack of sleep, the nightmare her home had become, all had sapped her remaining endurance and strength, and the not-knowing had ripened into agonizing heartache.

Coop tucked her wet cap into her belt as she crossed the threshold, then dropped the sack to enclose her fully. "To see you, to feel you at last." She kissed her way along Sophie's cheek to her lips.

"And I've been so worried, s-so afraid you—"

"I've never felt so helpless, along that line watching this place, knowing you were in the middle of it all." She kissed Sophie's forehead. "Please tell me you, everyone is well."

"We are. Yes. Somehow."

Coop dropped her forehead to Sophie's. "That walk just now, Sophie, across the plain...I swear, through hell itself. My God, Sophie, how fate tests us." She raised her head to look into Sophie's eyes. "And how fate rewards us." She kissed her, long and deep.

Sophie drew back, breathless. Undeniable, she thought, this hunger to feel Coop's presence, to put hands to the wet uniform, her back, shoulders, arms.

"I'm afraid there's still a lot of hell remaining in this house, Coop. Orderlies have another trip or two before they've removed all the supplies. The last of the wounded were carried out just an hour ago. They've been working since last evening."

Coop stiffened as she looked around, and Sophie realized just how accustomed to the scene she had become these past three days. The stench of the heated house had to be overpowering, and the ramshackle kitchen and parlor entry were self-explanatory. *You haven't seen anything yet.*

She rubbed some of the grit off Coop's cheek. "How are you, really?"

"Comparatively speaking? I am well. As you said, *somehow.*" She gathered the sack and led Sophie by the hand into the kitchen. "Enough hardship, I say." She set her rifle against the wall.

With a careful swipe of her arm, she pushed everything on the table to one side, put the sack in place, and peeled open the blanket. She chuckled when Sophie's jaw dropped.

"Courtesy of the United States Army," Coop announced.

The provisions and gear Coop had collected left Sophie speechless. Only minutes ago, Papa had whispered with despair about their lack of goods, unsure of how to provide for Greta and Karl. Without crops, gardens, or livestock, and with their home in tatters and secret supplies nearly gone, she knew they faced a horrible struggle in the days ahead.

"My good heavens, Coop! There are all kinds of things here." Floored by the pile of goods, Sophie turned to her and whispered, "You robbed the sutler, didn't you?"

Coop laughed lightly. "No, although I might someday. He deserves it."

Sophie gazed at the pile. "Coop, I don't know what to say. We're s-so grateful. You humble me, Private Samson." She sniffed. "We're in your debt."

"You definitely are not, Miss Bauer. I knew you wouldn't have much of anything left here, so I, well, I rounded up some stores. Tim helped, too. Our support trains were allowed to come ahead once the fighting stopped, so the army has plenty."

Sophie looked from the pile back to Coop. "But all this—"

Seemingly just as excited, Coop placed a hand on Sophie's back and beamed at the treasures with her. "There's flour, oats, corn, beans, and sugar in those little sacks, and we grabbed as many vegetables as we could carry. There's coffee, too, and tea, and those paper wraps have spices and even some decent meat."

Sophie located the items as Coop rattled them off. "I can't believe my eyes." She picked up each one, hardly sure it was real. "And combs? Toothbrushes? Oh, Coop. Soap, candles, and apples? Socks, too?"

"All from the quartermaster, the sutlers, and the Christian Commission. But those new blankets," Coop added, pointing to them, "you'll have to torture me to learn how I got them."

Tears trickling along her cheeks, Sophie grinned. "Well, now. Isn't that an appealing idea?"

Coop moved closer and her gaze fell upon Sophie's lips. A spark flared deep within Sophie's chest, heated her loins with demanding fire. The temptation to dissolve into Coop's kiss beckoned, irresistible, magnetic.

"Cooper!" Greta raced across the kitchen and swung her arms around Coop's waist.

"Greta," she said, returning the hug. "It's good to see you, too."

Sophie wiped her eyes. "Aren't we lucky he's safe, Greta?"

"We sure are." Greta retreated a few steps, collected herself, and looked down and then up along Coop's frame. "You have new bandages on your head."

Sophie leaned closer to see for herself. "Forgive me for not noticing before now. Those aren't my bandages. Did you...?"

Coop shrugged. "A kick to the head, that's all." Pointing to a slice in the arm of her frock, she told Greta, "There's a fair cut in there and more bandages, but that's it."

"What's going on *now*?" Papa trudged up from the cellar, Karl on his heels. "Cooper!" He strode forward, hand extended, and Coop shook it. Karl offered his small hand next and Coop shook that, too.

"Good to see you all," she said.

"We are *very* happy to see you, too," Papa said. "Relieved you survived the madness."

"Did you shoot plenty of rebs?" Karl asked, and Coop nodded with great solemnity. "And did they shoot you?"

"No, although they surely tried."

Karl grinned. "They're not as good as you."

"Well, thank you for that, Karl, but luck might have had something to do with it."

"Hey, look at all this!" Greta was up to her elbows in goods on the table. Karl rushed to see, and Papa looked over them. He turned knowing eyes to Coop.

"You are a special fellow, Private Samson." He offered another handshake and enclosed Coop's within both of his. "I'm not a man who takes charit—"

"It's not charity, Mr. Bauer, not when one friend cares for another."

Obviously humbled, Papa lowered his eyes and pumped Coop's hand.

"You know," Papa began, "after what's just happened in this town, with all the scars of it in this house, out in those fields, only a special someone could deliver a dose of sorely needed humanity. I thank you, sir. My family is eternally grateful." He finally stopped shaking Coop's hand and promptly returned to the cellar.

Watching him go, Sophie stepped close to Coop and set a palm on her chest. "You've touched him in a divine way. *I* thank you, for that. For everything." She kissed Coop's cheek again, lingered before drawing back. "You are a *very* special someone."

"I'm eating this now," Karl declared, and chomped into an apple.

"We need to organize everything," Sophie said, "maybe bring all this to the cellar until there are clean places to put things. We still have," she glanced around the remnants of the kitchen, "well, we still have work to do."

"I'll start taking things down to Papa." Holding the apple with his teeth, Karl began collecting items in his arms.

"I would gladly stay and help," Coop said, "but—"

"You can't leave yet." Greta took her hand and pulled her toward the parlor. "You have to see what happened to everything."

"Greta," Sophie tried. "Coop's seen enough destruction."

Greta sent a pleading look up to Coop. "But this is our *house*."

Coop nodded. "Of course." She glanced at Sophie as Greta led her away.

One glimpse of the parlor had Coop again looking back for Sophie. The transformation from what she remembered was staggering. How Sophie, any of them, coped with this boggled her mind, and this was only one room.

"We've started to clean up, sweep, so we can scrub everything," Sophie explained.

Coop could hardly bring herself to walk into the room. Dirty sheets and blankets flapped in every window, at the front door, over holes blasted through the walls in three places. Broken furniture sat in a crumpled heap by the door, ripped to pieces for firewood. She was amazed to see that the hutch had survived scavenging soldiers and its memorable crash. An image of Billy beneath it flashed to mind, and then one of his empty stare on the battlefield. Thankfully, Greta's tug on her sleeve set that memory aside.

"Look at the floor, Coop. All the spots are disgusting. They're—"

Sophie pressed a hand to Greta's shoulder. "He knows, honey."

Coop said, "The rug you made. I-I never had the chance to see it."

Sophie pointed to it, rolled up, unidentifiable in the corner. "Once I dare go outside, it's going in a pile to be burned. I never want to see it again."

Coop scanned the telltale signs of war. The stained floor was littered with swept piles of soiled hay bedding, discarded shoes, scraps of darkened bandages, strips of blue wool and butternut cloth, sawdust, brass buttons, bent saw blades, shards of wood. The keeping room door, now stained a black-red, leaned against the wall alongside empty crates that had supported it as the operating table.

Greta moved ahead of her as Coop wandered into the keeping room. *Great revelations happened in here.* Several old pots sat in a puddle and she looked up through the second floor. Rain struck her face.

"Papa says to catch as much as we can," Greta said. "We could only find this many pots."

Sophie added, "Even if Papa dared to climb onto the roof, and I won't let him, it's too big of a hole for him to patch. There's nothing to patch it with anyway."

Coop nodded. "I wouldn't trust the second floor, Sophie. The beam supporting it…"

"As a matter of fact, I *did* try, over on the far side, over the parlor, but only for a moment. I just had to see what they did to my bedroom." She flicked a despondent look at Coop and turned away.

They returned to the kitchen, with its own share of refuse and blotches. A towel covering a hole in the wall blew open and Coop twisted a bent nail over a corner to keep it down.

"You're all staying downstairs for a while, right?"

"We are. Bit by bit, we'll clean the place, and hopefully capture enough rain before it adds to the damage. We really need to get outside, at least to check on the well, and to see if there's anything left in the barn we can salvage." She glanced at Greta and seemed reluctant to continue. "But just going outside…"

"Please avoid it at all costs." Coop caught Greta's eye. "You and your brother stay inside where you can be the biggest help, all right?"

"I've looked out there and it's scary."

"You're absolutely right, so no more peeking. And don't let your brother look, either. Maybe for a few days. Think you both can do that?"

Sophie hugged Greta to her side. "My sister's stronger than she knows."

"Can't you stay, even for a little while?" Greta asked.

"I'm afraid not. I should head back before they need me to—"

"But we need you, too," Greta cried, and hurried to hug her.

Coop bent and drew her closer. "I think we could all use a good cry, Greta. Please don't feel that you're alone. But we have important jobs to do now."

Greta's sobs waned but Coop continued. "And after that good cry, we take a breath, maybe a few, and we face all this work waiting to get done. We stare it right down and then we jump on it. We're courageous. We don't let it get the better of us, no matter what." She held her at arm's length. "But, first of all, will you *please* organize the mess I left on your table?" Greta wiped her eyes as she nodded, and a grin slowly appeared. "You know," Coop added, "you Bauers make a powerful team, brave and strong. Can I rest easy, knowing you'll rescue your home?"

"Yes, sir."

Coop gave her another squeeze and Greta went to the table but turned around. "Promise you will come back? You won't get shot up?"

"I'll do everything in my power," Coop answered, a palm raised to take the oath, and wandered back to the parlor. Sophie followed and Coop turned to her. But Sophie spoke first, a tremor in her voice.

"Coop, thank you…for Greta. You are so…I cannot bear to let you go ag—"

Coop touched a fingertip to Sophie's lips. "If there was any chance I could stay, please know I would. I want to be here for you, *with* you."

Sophie nodded and a tear slid along her cheek. Coop leaned in and kissed it.

"This is a trying time for everyone," she said. "This place, for all its destruction, calls me like a sanctuary, because you are here and that brings me peace. I have to admit I could use some now more than ever. Yesterday was beyond description out there, Sophie, a blood-letting animal frenzy so wild, it's not healthy to remember a single tragedy among the many."

Sophie smoothed a palm over Coop's wet hair. "I imagine there isn't a single sight that escapes your memory."

There is one that never will.

"Sonny—I mean Billy's gone."

"Oh, Coop. No."

"We…There wasn't time," she said as Sophie took her hands. "There was craziness all around, everything was happening so fast. Billy…" She lowered her head. "He didn't suffer."

"Then, he is at peace, Coop." Sophie pulled her into an embrace. "And your heart can be at peace for his soul."

Tucked into Sophie's hold, Coop felt the protective barrier she had constructed against the loss begin to give way, and she tightened her grip around Sophie's waist. "We knew, I mean, we had just recognized each other." She cleared her throat. Suddenly, talking was hard. "At first, it… it was so sudden, being face-to-face with the wall between us. Before we knew, we even aimed at each other, but then when we…" She rubbed a tear away on her upper sleeve. "There just wasn't time."

"Neither of you fired."

Coop shook her head. She could see the result too clearly to speak.

"Be thankful both of you will always have that." Sophie pressed her cheek to Coop's. "And he may not have known it was you, my sweet soldier, but he did know family was there when his time came."

Coop dropped her forehead to Sophie's shoulder and exhaled hard. She had sought to lend Sophie hope, reassurance, and now she was in need. She squeezed Sophie to her and kissed her neck.

"I could linger on this spot till I'm old and gray." Sophie's fingers in her hair forced her eyes closed.

"And I would welcome it, if the army promised not to jail you for desertion."

"Oh." Coop straightened and saw the misty twinkle in Sophie's eyes. "You're right. I *do* have to get back." Pure longing pounded in her chest and thinking past it felt impossible. "It's important you know what I've heard."

In her arms, Sophie waited, graceful features so compelling, her gaze so attentive, enchanting, and Coop struggled to remember the crucial news.

"I heard talk," she began softly. "Our stores, rations, the army will be distributing them to farm folks soon and for some time to come."

"Really?"

"Take anything and everything you can and stash it away."

"Okay."

"And at least for the next few days, there will be burial details, stretcher-bearers, ambulances everywhere, and heaven knows who, all around this place. Already, there are families here from afar, out there searching the fields for grave markers of loved ones they want to take home—and there are hundreds not yet buried. Hundreds, Sophie. We started burial shifts yesterday evening and the numbers just numb the mind. You all must try, really try, not to go outside. It's not healthy to see *now*, let alone after more hot summer days."

Sophie wished more than ever that Coop could stay. Hearing the scenario described out loud almost made her shudder. "We'll do our best."

"I don't mean to upset you," Coop added. "I just want you to be as prepared as you can be and know what to avoid. I hate knowing that you, all of you, must cope with something so shocking. It will become vile, Sophie, because it may take weeks to collect...everything." Coop took a breath. "The smell outside, well, last night, we began collecting and burning pyres of animals. That will take a long time. Do you have any peppermint oil or perfumes to help fight the smell?"

"There might be some in my bedroom." Coop started to shake her head and Sophie touched her arm to reassure her. "It's safe. Greta's room is gone, but mine seems safe. I'll go slowly, lightly. I won't stay long."

"Please be very careful. Your side of the house might be stable, but it's possib—"

Sophie stopped her with a light kiss. Coop's lips trembled against hers and Sophie hugged her close. "I worry just as much about you."

"Forgive me for going on. I just don't want anything to happen to you. Thoughts of you accompany me like a guiding light everywhere I go, Sophie, every moment of the day."

"I don't want you to leave." *Ever.*

"It's the last thing I want, too." Coop clasped Sophie's hands. "I think we're striking camp soon. It could be as early as tonight, although I'd rather not march in mud, but soon. I may not be able to visit again until..."

Sophie's heart skipped. "Until when?"

"Well, I don't know, really. I don't know where we'll be or when I'll be granted leave."

"But...Might you leave Pennsylvania? Surely, you won't return to Fredericksburg, will you?"

Coop entwined their fingers. "I hope not. Please cross these lovely fingers because we all have too many bad memories of that area. The only real happiness I can recall there was time with you." Sophie fought back a sob when Coop placed a kiss on her hand. "But, I'm sorry, Sophie. I have no idea where we'll go. Everyone in the regiment believes Lee is preparing to pull out and that General Meade will have us run him down and finish him. So, I can't predict where that will happen."

Sophie stared at their hands, fitted perfectly together by what felt like fate.

"It's going to be hard starting over," she whispered. *Without you.* She exhaled slowly to maintain composure. "We'll get through it, I know, but I'll miss you terribly."

"I will try to write every day." She cupped Sophie's face in her hands. "It breaks my heart to leave. I-I want to be at your side. I want you at my side." She kissed her slowly, deeply, and Sophie threaded her arms around Coop's neck and kissed her just as passionately.

Clutching her close, Coop kissed her cheek, ear, and neck, and Sophie tried unsuccessfully to stop the tears. She clung to Coop hard, absorbing every inch of her that she could.

"Return to me, Coop Samson," she whispered against Coop's cheek. "Can you feel my heart pounding?"

Coop squeezed her tighter, stroked her back. "Is that your heart or mine?"

"I know mine is very demanding." Sophie ran her fingers into Coop's hair as she kissed her.

Coop slipped her mouth along Sophie's jaw, whispered between light kisses. "I want that heart, Miss Bauer. I've waited all my life for your heart. I'll gladly give my own for it."

CHAPTER TWENTY-NINE

Coop sat with Tim, watching their cookfire flare beneath drops of salt pork grease. Her thoughts kept returning to Sophie and what she might be concocting from the sack of goods for the family's supper. Better to dwell on that than the living conditions Coop had left behind.

"Never imagined I'd want to march," she said, her voice distant, "especially march like this."

"Ah, the lesser of two evils, my friend. Burial detail is enough to convince anybody." Tim wiggled his feet in the dirt. "But my dogs are killing me already. Kinda makes you wonder who's really on the run, here."

Coop nodded. Having dug graves and buried corpses through the night of July fourth and its violent thunderstorm, and on through most of the fifth, she had barely caught a night's sleep before II Corps struck camp. Others remained behind to finish, and she knew they'd have a much harder time of it. Days of rain had only just relented, but the steamy temperatures hadn't, so each summer day wreaked more havoc on already bloated bodies on those fields. Thankfully, she dreamt of Sophie these past nights, and not that horrific carnage.

"I bet she cooks them something amazing for supper."

Tim chuckled as he inspected his meat. "She's a farmer like you, so she can make something out of anything." He glanced at her and added, "Good to see them, though, wasn't it? Out there when we left?"

Coop had to smile. She would remember that sight for a long time, all four of the Bauers just outside the kitchen door, waving and cheering, a blanket spanning their heads in the steady rain. Karl saluted her. Sophie blew her a kiss.

"See?" Tim added. "That's what you need to keep in mind, to cheer up. Remember them that way."

"You're right. Thank God that part of their property had been cleared and they stayed close to the house. But I hope they went directly back inside with eyes front, especially Greta and Karl. The farm is…ghastly. I almost wish they hadn't come out to see us off."

"But they did. You mean that much to them." He blew on the tip of his pork and bit off a piece. "They're going to see it, Coop, and probably have nightmares. Nothing anyone can do about it. All those rebs will get buried last." He shook his head. "How Lee could just up and leave thousands for us to…Well, it confounds me."

The sight along the road *was* ghastly. Corpses on the Emmitsburg made marching difficult, Coop recalled, bodies draped upon each other, slain in rows where they'd fallen climbing the now nonexistent fences. And they surrounded the farmhouse and barn, and beyond, bodies and body parts stiff and swollen in the trampled, muddy acreage.

"I know, once everything's cleaned up, the farmers will all join together, help each other with repairs, but there's so much to be done and nothing to work with. They better get what they need somehow, before too long."

"Don't forget we heard the train as we came in this afternoon. A good sign, having it back running."

"True," she agreed, even if it was loaded with wounded for the big hospitals here in Frederick City. Coop hoped trains were bringing lumber, livestock, and other essentials *into* Gettysburg, along with shop inventories that had been stowed out of town. "None of the farmers on that plain have wagons—or beasts to pull them." Coop waved her meat at him. "How do they even go to get what they need?"

"It'll surely take some time. Months, maybe." He snorted and threw his stick into the fire. "On top of all that, the town's getting swamped with lookers, gawkers. Who'd have thought?"

"I heard General Howard had a devil of a time pushing Eleventh Corps into town. I guess rounding up all the rebels was a bigger chore than expected, but then all the folks arriving turned things messy. Families want to find their boys, I know, but they shouldn't be on the battlefield like that, wandering around. Can't understand how they stomach it."

"The scavenging has started, too. Those wretched buggers can't wait to roam the fields. How many weapons did we collect? Thousands, I say.

Them scavengers, the looters, they'll go after everything they can find, anything they can dig up, too."

Coop shook her head in disgust and tossed away her stick. The thought of families strolling across the plain, protected by umbrellas as they peered into blackening faces for recognition, delved into drenched pockets for identification, it all soured her stomach. Would a desperate father find his son's name on a board sticking out of the mud, and paw his way down to the body? Would scavengers and souvenir hunters fill baskets with brass buttons, belt buckles, caps, spectacles, shoes? Would they rip an officer's epaulets from his shoulders? Run off with rifles, pistols, and bayonets? *The provost guard had better be policing that ground.*

Coop stared into her tin cup, disappointed to see her coffee gone. "Slow leak." She leaned sideways and looked to the far end of their tent row. "When is there *not* a crowd at the quartermaster?"

"Get a new one tomorrow. My guess is we'll be off and running again, so best make it early." Tim stood and stretched. "I'd love to know what Meade knows, where those damn rebs have run off to."

"Last I knew, Lee moved four corps back over the Antietam," she said, rising stiffly beside him. "We'll either head west and catch him in the mountains or south to keep him away from Washington. That's my thinking. Like before Gettysburg, only backwards."

He sighed. "I need to write to Mary. Kinda short-changed her with my last letter."

"At least you told her you're okay and we won."

"But that's all I had time for. I'm sure she wants more." He tugged on his beard. "Guess, I want to say more, too."

"That's a good idea." Coop went to her knapsack in the tent and came back with paper and pencil. "I need to talk to Sophie."

Papa hammered the board in place and climbed down the ladder where Sophie, Greta, Karl, and several neighbors applauded. Sophie released a heavy breath of relief and hugged him, glad to have him on the ground, and the last basic house repair completed. A similar community effort already had helped fix the barn, rebuild the broken walls and roof, and, although rubble still sat in the far corner, it provided full shelter for the cow and chickens that arrived by rail last month. She hugged each neighbor and Papa shook their hands.

"I'll be glad when the wagon's fixed, now that we have wood," he said, wiping his forehead as they entered the kitchen. "Don't care to keep on borrowing like this."

"Then we can buy a horse, right Papa?"

"Yes, Karl."

"Okay! I'll help you work on our wagon tomorrow."

Papa ruffled Karl's hair. "Good boy. We'll need the ladies' help, too," he added, looking at Sophie.

"Say the word, Papa. Greta and I could do with some sunshine. We'll all get the wagon done tomorrow."

As much as she looked forward to a change of scenery from the house, Sophie still had reservations about working outside. Birds had returned, contaminated wells finally ran clean, and human remains no longer were visible, but as far as she could see, the scars upon the once vital, healthy acreage broadcast vivid memories.

Fences had disappeared and toppled stone walls lay scattered across the ground, leaving no one's property delineated, no means to corral livestock that farmers were starting to reacquire. Deep artillery tracks, burial mounds, and huge swaths of mud interrupted the land, along with a steady stream of people seeking remembrances of the battle, endlessly searching for loved ones, even disinterring bodies. Sophie could hardly gaze upon it all, and certainly didn't want Karl or Greta doing so. She thought the imminent return of school a very good thing for both of them.

July through August had been a horrendous period, and Sophie wrote as much to Coop in letters twice a week. She withheld news of mistakes and minor injuries, the frustration and stomach-turning despair, and instead recounted the work and achievements of each family member.

Sophie also filled letters with news of working again with the Ladies' Aid Society, this time in her own town. She sent along tales told by the wounded to whom she administered aid, and of helping organize train loads of donations and supplies that flooded Union hospital camps and storehouses in town. This was far less frenetic work, she wrote, but she had to include that the recovery of their farm, all area farms, and the town itself, still required months of effort.

In the summer kitchen, she prepared ham from a neighbor and set Karl to work, making his specialty for their supper. She marveled at how often she gave thanks these days, and wrote to Coop about all of them, the neighbor's gift of ham, Papa's patience in letting Greta and Karl assist with the roof repairs to this little building, the courageous work of Union soldiers and Negro crews who ultimately removed all the Confederate remains. She scrubbed the floor, walls, stove, and tables, and remarked to Coop about her surprise that each of them still existed.

Papa had just placed a helping of biscuits and ham on Karl's plate when the Robinson family arrived, looking weary but relieved. A two-wheeled cart heaped with belongings sat near the summer kitchen.

Greta threw back her chair. "Tassie!" She raced out to hug her.

"Eldus, Rose," Papa said, and shook the man's hand heartily. "Come in and join us."

"Goodness! Thank you, no," Rose said. "We just stopped to catch our breath on the way home. We're powerful sorry to interrupt your supper."

"Nonsense," Sophie said, trying in vain to wave them in. "We've been wondering about all of you for weeks. Everything is well?"

Eldus nodded. "Finally making our way home." He gestured to the cart behind them. "Started out this afternoon, and it's a mighty long haul, but not too far now."

"Then you can come in and rest," Sophie insisted, knowing Eldus had towed the cart for miles. "Have some of Karl's wonderful supper." She bent to Tassie. "Your belly wants supper, doesn't it, young lady?"

"Yes, ma'am." She quickly looked to her mother for approval.

"It's settled," Papa stated. "Greta, fetch the bench and make room 'round the table."

Karl darted toward the summer kitchen. "I'll get more biscuits and milk."

Within minutes, the Robinsons had the Bauers transfixed with stories of their escape from the rebels in Gettysburg and their stay in Taneytown. Sophie hated having to apprise them of what they would find in town, the battered condition of their home, and the devastation that probably existed inside. Karl spared her the effort.

"They busted your fence up. We saw it a while back on our first trip to town. Rebs took wood from everywhere for cooking and building."

Sophie sent him a look. "Our soldiers took it, too, Karl, remember."

"A lot of fences like yours, pickets," Papa said in a more delicate tone, "they ended up as grave markers. I'm afraid you'll see lots of different ones all over, shingles, cracker box pieces, names carved into trees. They're hard to miss."

"Don't be surprised if they set your house upside down," Greta added as she watched Tassie eat. Sophie knew Greta had reason to be worried for their friends. "It took us weeks to clean our house, right, Sophie? And that was on account of the wounded here, not just rebel heathens turned loose."

Rose nibbled on a biscuit and looked somberly upon Tassie.

Eldus wiped his plate with his last bite of biscuit. "We've been preparing ourselves for what we find, but it will be good to be back home, safe."

"We are bracing. No doubt it's been torn asunder," Rose added. "Folks came to Taneytown with stories hard to believe. The Trembleys..." She shook her head.

"I saw him," Greta said, "saw the rebs take Mr. Trembley."

Rose looked from Papa to Sophie. "We heard Mrs. Trembley done run off to save herself and them rebels did frightful things to the house. They burnt furniture right in the sitting room, tore up books, shredded the featherbed, even mixed up feathers with flour and water and poured it on the walls, down the stairs. Miserable...just miserable."

Sophie placed her hand over Rose's. "Your home could..."

"I know. I imagine everywhere there's still lots to be fixed." Sophie's heart broke, seeing the forlorn look she sent Eldus. "You should have no trouble finding work," Rose advised him.

Karl slid his empty plate aside to put his elbows on the table. "For a carpenter good as you, Mr. Robinson, people will be lining up."

"The lad's right, Eldus," Papa added. "There's need all over town. We may never see the end of telltale signs, but if and when you need a hand, we'll be there to help. Lots of folks will." He put the last biscuit on Tassie's plate, then leaned toward Rose and Eldus. "Be prepared for all the embalmers," he said carefully. "They are a bit repulsive with their tents everywhere, competing for business. So many folks are looking to ship remains home."

Karl inched forward, evidently with important knowledge to impart. "Costs five dollars to do a private."

"Karl?" Sophie snapped, amazed he knew such a thing.

Papa turned to him. "We don't need that talk at the table, son."

"No, sir."

"The hotels and shops are open," Greta said, attempting to brighten the mood. "Still lots of wounded in places, though, and ambulances and such, but all sorts of people everywhere." She finished her meal, muttering, "Hard to figure where so many find lodging."

"You should be able to get what you need for repairs," Papa said. "But you remember to call on us when you're ready for help."

"I'll do that. Sure good to have friends," Eldus said. He stood and his family followed him to the door. "We thank you all for your kindness, for the fine supper. Most delicious, Karl." He tipped his hat to him. "We have a ways yet to go, so, while we still have the sun…"

"We'll help you with the cart," Papa offered, and gestured for Karl to follow. "We can at least spare you for some distance." Eldus politely declined the aid, but Papa and Karl donned hats and went out anyway.

With Tassie and Greta chatting on the porch, Sophie spoke confidentially to Rose in the doorway. "You all are okay, truly? You weren't harmed hiding in the cellar?"

"No. Tassie and I were so lucky. We heard them upstairs, knocking things around, hooting and hollering, but no one reached the cellar. An officer called them to move on, probably just in time. It was much later when Eldus found us." She forced a little smile. "I near to fainted when he threw open the door. Like God's gift, I tell you, having him back with us."

"I can't imagine your joy."

She hoped Karl and Greta were learning something in all this, something uplifting and lasting. The Robinson family's love and bond equaled their own, and its friendship and support, its vitality, were things to be treasured and respected.

Rose touched her arm. "And you, Sophie. What of your soldier friend you've talked about? Cooper, is it? With all we heard of the battle here, you must have seen him."

"I did. Coop arrived here by great coincidence, wounded, and we were surprised to find each other." A suspicious twinkle in Rose's eye made Sophie smile. "Thankfully, he survived without further injury. Before the army left, he brought us a vast assortment of goods that helped us manage through the awful days that followed."

"A solid, honorable man, your soldier. I am happy for you, Sophie. Your papa approves?"

"He likes Coop very much. So do Greta and Karl. We all hope he returns soon."

And often. Will she visit more than once? How long will she stay? And, oh, what do I do with these feelings for her?

Rose took a ponderous step over the threshold just as Eldus called for his family. "It is time for us to go, but… A bit of advice from this long-married woman?"

"I cherish your advice, Rose. You know that."

"One never knows which way life will turn, so do think on this… this friendship with Cooper. You are a fine woman, Sophie, and deserve happiness. I wish that for you."

Sophie bit her lip and Rose smiled broadly as she left to join Tassie, crossing the yard. With Papa and Eldus at the handles, and Karl pushing, they rolled the cart to the road. Sophie and Greta watched the little entourage make its way along the Emmitsburg for some time. *One never knows which way life will turn.*

CHAPTER THIRTY

A re you going to write to Coop now?" Greta asked, grinning up at Sophie as they returned to the house. "I heard Mrs. Robinson say you deserve happiness. She means with Coop, doesn't she?"

"Yes, I believe so." Greta said nothing as they collected supper dishes and Sophie grew concerned about thoughts that might be brewing in that little blond head. "What do you think about it, Greta, my friendship with Coop?"

Greta shrugged. "If you married him, would you move to Massachusetts?"

Sophie nearly dropped her stack of plates. *Two concepts I've yet to reconcile. Not that either hasn't crossed my mind, but such is fantasy. Or is it?* Greta waited for an answer.

"Well, that's taking our friendship quite far, don't you think?" She set the dishes in the sink and Greta began pumping water. "We've become fast friends, Greta, that's true, but I don't think—"

"Sophie. I've seen you two kissing. Do you love him? I think he loves you."

Sophie's pulse quickened. She knew she'd have to deal with her feelings at some point but didn't expect her little sister to initiate the process. Rather overwhelmed at the moment, she resorted to truth.

"Difficult questions for a girl to ask, you know."

"Well?" Greta stopped pumping.

"Well..." She drew out the end of the word, her mind racing. "I think...maybe."

"Maybe? I don't believe 'maybe.'"

"Oh, you don't? Well, what if I said yes? How would you feel about that?"

Heavens. What's happening?

"I guess I'd feel happy," Greta admitted, pumping water again. "Love is a good thing. People *do* need to love each other more."

"That's a very grown-up statement, Greta."

"I know there's different kinds of love, too, like when you love animals or a sunny day or Mrs. Sherfy's peach pie."

"And friends, like my friend Elizabeth or your friend Tassie."

"But your friend, Coop, that's different." Greta's point landed directly and she knew it. She grinned when Sophie stopped washing dishes and met her eyes.

"Are you sure you're only twelve?"

"You *do* love him. I knew it!"

Sophie had to chuckle at a twelve-year-old's triumph. "All right, so it could be true."

Her heart skipped at the admission. *It's hard to face the facts when they lead to so much uncertainty.*

"So, what if he wants to get married and live in Massachusetts? Would you go?"

"Greta, please." Sophie dried her hands and gave her the towel to start on the dishes. "I have no idea. I-I haven't thought about it." She kicked herself mentally for the lame answer. Greta obviously had given it thought.

My thoughts go only so far before they involve heartache. How could I leave the family when we're rebuilding the farm? Or leave Papa to raise two young ones? On the other hand, could I watch Coop—Catherine—leave forever, take with her the chance for happiness I never dreamed I'd find?

"Is his farm like ours? With crops? Does he have cows?"

"I think so." She knew she had to address the subject because Greta gave no sign of changing it. "Our family needs all of us here, honey, so…I suppose I wouldn't go." *Did I just make a decision?*

"So, you wouldn't marry him? It's because of us, isn't it? Me and Karl. I know it is."

Sophie lowered her head to catch Greta's attention. "I'd be dishonest to deny it, honey, but that's only part of it. Have you looked outside lately?" And she tried to grin. "There used to be a farm out there. We have more work ahead of us than we've ever seen."

Greta stacked the last dried plate, and Sophie pulled her into a hug.

"I want to see a smile on that pretty face, Miss Bauer."

"But I know you would be sad, Sophie."

It's called heartbroken.

❖

October 6, 1863
Dearest Sophie,

Curious, how I am drawn to write so often these days. What could possibly be my motivation? I smile as I scribble away on this rainy night, as visions of you always warm my heart.

Are you well, my dearest Sophie? Being as we are in October, are Greta and Karl settled into school routines and doing well? I am sure your toiling with your father each day has assured there will be some winter crop to harvest. Did your garden produce the late growth you hoped for? Have you picked the pumpkins yet? You are such the diligent worker, Sophie, I trust you sleep well, and I hope you dream of someone who is dreaming of you.

Of course, we are still in Virginia, continuing cat-and-mouse action with Lee. We fell back to Centreville today and II Corps, as is often the case, covered the retreat. Consensus among us is that General Warren is an able commander, not a Hancock, but quite proficient as his temporary replacement, and thus far there are few grumblings about his decisions. The rebs are close now and at times it is hard to determine cat from mouse in this confounded game, although so frequently assigned rear guard duty, we can guess.

Weather turned on us last night, almost "Fredericksburg cold," as many said. I thought of your gardens, of the replanting in Gettysburg, and hope all of it escaped a frost.

I was glad to hear of the intended postings in town and trust that the notifications being erected will put an end to the grave robbing, the constant unearthing of bodies. How shameful, no matter the reason, to manhandle and desecrate the dead. For your family's sake, may it not bear witness to such things. An organized and supervised plan will be good to reinter those soldiers properly in the new cemetery, but it is bound to be a daunting task.

Although I saw none of it during the battle, I am excited to see the area and the town revitalized and look forward to doing so, arm in arm with you. We have no indication of where we will bivouac for any length of time, so I cannot predict when furloughs will be granted, but know I will be first in line to apply. I am desperately eager to see you again.

I have been beyond lucky as a soldier, and not just in battle as only you know. I have passed army muster in service to our great cause, but passing in your home has caused me much consternation. I surely do not wish to soil your character with deception, Sophie, nor inflict upon you the disparaging gossip of others. You have acted already on my behalf, and for that I am immeasurably grateful. However, I am torn between honest living and the deceit that enables us to share this beautiful bond so freely. I have come to believe that ours is a sincere courtship, one I deeply treasure, but I wish you to know that, if you cannot see a way forward for yourself or us, I will somehow come to understand.

Please, by no means, think such resignation would be easy or that it is my desire. To the contrary, my heart believes that a means must exist by which we can flourish, weather social and familial storms together. I have lent days and nights to this thinking and have concluded that if being forever bound to this guise is such a means, then so be it, for my life would amount to little without you.

As always, I miss you, and do so yearn for your deepest thoughts, the silkiness of your cheek, the union in our embrace. They empower me each day. Know, my dearest Sophie, that, should I fall, my last thought will be of your sweet kiss.

The sober nature of this letter surprises even me, and there is much food for thought, I realize. Kindly forgive this soldier's literary venture. How I long for our coffee chats in camp, to look into your sparkling eyes and speak heartfelt words face-to-face. Someday soon, I hope. In the meantime, take care and please write when you can. I remain, always,

Your kindred soul,

Coop

CHAPTER THIRTY-ONE

Sunshine and a steady, refreshing autumn breeze flooded Sophie's bedroom, an invigorating start to the day. She shook out Coop's blanket across her bed and caught herself smoothing the wrinkles with lingering, searching hands.

She sat and drew Coop's most recent letter from her nightstand drawer and read it for the fifth or maybe this was the sixth time. Today was a writing day. She always wrote to her on Fridays, but she had no idea where to start.

Thankfully, Coop's words were familiar now because the tremor in Sophie's hands made focusing on the fluttering little pages difficult. She knew she really didn't need to read them, the words imprinted onto her very soul, and knew another reading would set her mind adrift for the entire day. Again.

But she scanned the written words again, in desperate need of the courage Coop imparted, yet saw it only in stark contrast to her own. "So much for standing firm to live my dream," she whispered. "When the question is put, I falter, while you are so brave, so willing to sacrifice...to mold your very existence to mine so that we, that I..."

This is love, what I've always wanted, she told herself as a tear started down her cheek. And to face what it really means, what it costs, what it asks of a woman, I must find the strength.

Wiping away the tear, she raised her head into the breeze, let it dry her face as she stared out at the fields. Many acres away, several farmers were already at work, and she tried to envision Catherine—or was it Coop—alongside her and Papa, doing the same. But the vision was of a dark-eyed soldier in blue, not a woman in dress and apron, bonnet shielding her from the sun.

Sophie smiled at that concept. Almost theatrical, she thought, so out of character, and believed Catherine would keep to a man's attire for practical purposes and might even choose to keep Cooper's name. Sophie considered the courage such decisions would require and couldn't help but marvel at the woman she loved. And that woman, whether Catherine or Cooper, always fought for her dream.

Lowering her head in self-doubt, Sophie asked herself if she, too, possessed such strength. She could sense Catherine awaiting her reply. In her bones, she knew Catherine would share her dream, live freely with a woman as her partner, or at least as "dear friend" companions, as some women did. *But am I as courageous?*

The repercussions at home then bore down. Greta and Karl would be shocked but intrigued to learn about Catherine, while Papa would…would what? He'd come to regard Coop with the highest esteem, and that just might serve their relationship well. The possibility of Catherine asking her to come to Massachusetts caused Sophie's mind to spin, rationalizations came so quickly. Greta and Karl were almost old enough to be responsible and helpful under Papa's guidance, and he was healthy, skilled, and considerate. Neighbors were reliable friends. *After all, how long do I live, purely exist, as substitute mother and housekeeper?*

Either way, in Gettysburg or Massachusetts, openly as partners or companions, Sophie knew that courage was in order, and began to wonder if she could be shortchanging herself. Hadn't she displayed plenty of courage since Mama passed? During this difficult year? Just this hellish summer?

She exhaled with relief, feeling fortified, now knowing what to write.

A gunshot cracked the blissful serenity outside. Sophie hurried to the window and spotted Greta running from the barn, screaming. Sophie bolted down the stairs and out the kitchen door, and Greta threw her arms around her waist, hysterical.

"P-papa! Oh, Sophie! P-pa—"

"Greta! What? What happened?"

Greta fought to catch her breath, heaving sobs onto Sophie's chest. Sophie looked beyond her, desperate to see Papa or Karl. She yelled for them, but neither responded.

"Greta. Greta!" She held her at arm's length. "The barn?" Greta could only nod. "Show me." Sophie turned her in that direction, but Greta tugged away.

"I-I c-can't!"

Sophie looked to the barn and back. "Go into the kitchen, honey. I have to go." She raced into the barn and needed an extra second to adjust her eyes in the shade.

Papa lay prone in the corner rubble and Karl knelt at his side, his small hand on Papa's arm. She saw the dark blotch on Papa's chest just before her vision blurred. She expected to faint.

Breathless, she ran to them. "Oh, dear God! Papa!" She fell to her knees, noted the long rifle at his feet. Blood seeped from a hole in his breast and immediately, she slammed one hand on top of the other over it to stem the bleeding. Tears fell from her face and she blinked repeatedly.

"Karl." He knelt frozen in the hay on the floor. "Karl! Run, Karl. From the pasture, wave, yell to the neighbors for help!" Finally, he rose, unable to take his eyes off Papa's blank expression. "Go!" He pivoted and streaked out of the barn.

Skills she never thought she would need again rushed to the fore. Her hands dripping with blood, Sophie ripped a swath of cotton from her dress. "Papa! Oh, please, God. Papa?" She wadded the fabric and pressed it into the wound. "Papa! It's Sophie! I l-love you, Papa!" She leaned on both hands, harder, held her breath, strained to see through her tears. "Come on, Papa! Look at me! P-papa!"

But she knew the signs. His eyes had emptied. His gruff, worn body lay perfectly still.

Her chin dropped to her chest and a torrent of sobs began. Still holding the material on his wound, she shook with despair.

"No," she muttered, sagging back onto her heels. She lifted her dress to her face and cried into it. "Papa, no."

Karl's heavy breathing at her side led her to look up, his innocent features knotted in confusion, pain. Unmoving, he stared at Papa.

Greta ran up behind him and began crying into her hands.

Sophie turned and drew them both down into her arms. "Easy, now. Easy. Let's breathe." She swallowed hard and managed to stop her own tears for the sake of her siblings. "Papa's...He's gone now."

"No!" Greta cried.

"Sophie, the-the Sherfys," Karl tried, still unable to look away from Papa. "They were the only ones I saw. They're getting an ar-army doctor. I ran really fast, as f-fast as I could."

She turned Karl's face to hers. "I'm sure you did. No one could have gone faster, Karl. No one." She knew that, even on horseback, an army surgeon could not have arrived in time.

"But...but the doctor won't m-matter now, will he?" Greta said between sobs.

"No, honey." Sophie squeezed them tighter. "Papa went right to Heaven, straight away. There's nothing anyone could have done."

"That gun did it." Karl pointed at the old Enfield rifle-musket most often used by Confederates. "We were cleaning up this corner. Papa was pulling out boards for me and Greta to stack, and...and..." He backhanded a drip from his nose. "We never saw it in the pile." Looking expectantly at Sophie, his reddened eyes welled with tears. "It just went off."

A horse and wagon came to a dusty stop outside the barn. An armed soldier positioned himself at the door and two silhouettes ran in. Their progress slowed once they saw the scene.

"Miss Sophie."

"Nurse Johnson? Your familiar face is a most welcome sight right now."

His eyes on Papa, he crouched and set a hand on her shoulder. "Ma'am. I'm real sorry."

Sophie fought back a rising sob. "This is my brother, Karl, and sister, Greta." She looked from one to the other, relieved to see both withholding tears. "Nurse Johnson spent a lot of time in our house."

He tipped his cap at them and moved around Sophie to check Papa for vital signs. He tilted his head to the officer kneeling at Papa's other side. "This is Captain McGowan of the provost guard."

McGowan lifted his cap briefly. "Officially, the Patapsco Guard, ma'am. Arrived just the other day. We, er...Just a formality, ma'am, you know, with...with shootings." He watched Nurse Johnson work. "How did it happen?" he asked, examining the rifle, and Sophie recounted what Karl said.

McGowan nodded. "They tell me it happened a lot, back in the summer especially, guns going off everywhere, too many civilians taking souvenirs." His eyes narrowed on Karl. "Heard one little boy found a rifle just like this and pretended to shoot his brother. Well, the gun was loaded and the brother died. Don't you or anyone you see mess with these things. Okay, boy?"

"Yessir."

McGowan stood and left with the rifle. He was back promptly with a blanket and covered Papa.

Nurse Johnson urged everyone to step outside. "If you'd allow me, Miss Sophie." He removed his cap. "I'll personally see to it your father is properly prepared for burial. We'll assist you any way we can. The army's in your debt."

She had no words for such kindness. If she ever needed assistance, it was now. She nodded and tears started again.

In a soft voice, he continued. "We can recommend a good undertaker, and I know there's a shortage of coffins in town, but I can get one. A good one."

"Thank you. I-I don't know what to say."

"After all your family has given to the United States Army, ma'am? I'd be honored to do this."

Sophie just bowed her head and cried. Greta and Karl each put an arm around her, and she held onto them desperately.

All Coop could think about was the unopened letter she'd stuffed into her shirt. Not the holes in her shoes, the extra cartridges in her pockets, or the view someone in the 42nd New York got of her posterior this morning when she relieved herself. Not even this rush into attack formation. Just Sophie's letter, which came precisely one minute before assembly sounded and all hell broke loose.

Damn war, she thought, as the 19th quickstepped along the Orange-and-Alexandria train tracks at Bristoe Station. But, to their collective soul, everyone in II Corps wanted to settle this score and ambush the Confederate III Corps, led by Gen. Ambrose Hill. His rigorous divisions contributed to the nightmare at the Gettysburg copse of trees, and everyone remembered his name.

"Underestimate our Second Corps at your own peril," Tim said, breathing hard.

"I know we always seem to be stuck guarding retreats, but this will be worth it," Coop answered, "getting to knock around A.P. Hill—or at least his General Heth." They halted along the bottom of the railroad embankment and settled in.

Tim squinted, then frowned into his canteen. "Did you know he's General Pickett's cousin?"

She shook her head at him. "And they say women love to gossip."

"Hey, you read your letter yet?"

Coop patted her stomach, could feel the envelope. "No. And if I try now, you just know we'll be moving."

Less than a minute later, the 19th and every regiment along the embankment received the "all quiet" order.

Tim leaned closer and whispered, "Somebody just said Heth's coming after Fifth Corps and doesn't know we're bringing up its rear." He grinned devilishly. "Ol' Henry is in for a surprise."

In short order, Heth did come along, and Coop grinned at Tim's knack for newsgathering. She could see the tips of North Carolina flags dancing by on the other side of the raised tracks, and listened to horses snort, and artillery creak. On command, she, the 19th, and a dozen other regiments stood and unloaded. The battle was on.

As many rebels seemed to fall as run off into the woods. Union cannon fired high, sprayed case shot over the scattering Southern regiments. A Confederate battery struggled mightily to establish a position as its gunnery teams began to fall. Coop chose them as her targets and took down several rebels before things became sketchy off to the right.

Heth's men breached the 42nd New York and rushed down the embankment any way they could, some on their backsides, firing as they came. Coop and the rest of the 19th closed in from one side and the 19th Maine from the other, and beat them back in stout fashion.

Several companies, including Coop's, chased them up and over the tracks and she now found herself sliding down the far side of the embankment, firing, rolling to the ground and scrambling to reload. They dashed ahead, eyes on the battery of seven Confederate guns.

The slim trees hardly provided much cover, but she dodged forward, steadied her aim against tree trunks, and fired successfully, once, twice, three times. Cannon activity began to slow for lack of manpower, one actually sat abandoned. She, Tim, and others from the 19th and now the 1st Minnesota advanced, forcing the battery crews to haul on their guns, withdraw as they fired.

"Don't let them run!" someone shouted, and a Yankee cheer rose above the noise.

She staggered when one of the guns burst apart, probably overloaded, its entire crew slain in the conflagration.

Running now, bayonets level, they descended on the battery, and most of the overwhelmed rebels surrendered their guns. Coop's heart pounded with relief and joy. A huge, prestigious prize in a victorious Yankee ambush. She turned and aimed at the gunners running off, tempted. One rebel fired harmlessly, high over his shoulder. *They never go quietly.* He twisted to look back and fired again.

The bullet struck Coop's left forearm with a crack and sent her rifle tumbling from her hands and her to the ground before she felt any pain. Stunned, she blinked up at the clouds, tried to recall the previous second. Then the pain arrived like someone peeling the skin off her arm. She screamed as lightning coursed up her arm and she writhed uncontrollably to quash it.

"Hold still!"

Tim's voice. He was ripping her sleeve open at the bullet hole. *Damn, that hurts!*

A lone, resentful shot sounded from the woods.

"Miserable rebs," Tim groused, then yelled at them. "You're done! Quit firing!"

Her eyes crushed closed, she spat out words. "My arm, I-I can't—"

"There are worse places to get hit. Lay still, damn you!"

"I can't...I can't feel my fingers!"

He swore when another hidden rebel fired. "We have to get after them. Look, Coop, the arm's a bit crooked."

Squirming, she growled through her teeth, low and long. *It's broken.* "Tim—don't...don't let them take it! Don't—"

He put a hand on her breastbone and held her to the ground. "If you don't quit thrashing, I'll sit on you!" She stilled, though not completely. Searing pain made that impossible. "Probably just a normal break," he said "like when I fell off my horse as a kid. Stop thinking the worst. Was a pistol bullet, not a minié. Big difference."

Another random shot came from the woods, followed instantly by a massive explosion of cannon munitions. The ground beneath her shook and Coop covered her face with her good arm as shrapnel whizzed around them. Comrades wailed. Tim fell across her chest.

His weight pushed the air from her lungs, but shock had already seized them.

"Tim!" She reached across his back and grabbed a fistful of his frock. Her broken arm screaming in protest, she pulled with all her strength, and rolled him over her and off, onto his back. "Tim!" Blood poured from a huge gap in his throat, the work of an iron fragment.

"Good, Jesus!" From her knees, her deadened arm at her side, Coop clapped her hand to the opening, but blood bubbled around her fingers, ran freely beyond the heel of her hand. Hers simply wasn't big enough.

She shouted over her shoulder. "Help here! Need a stretcher! Doc!" A frantic scan of the area showed soldiers racing into the woods in pursuit, soldiers writhing on the ground, and no medical personnel.

"Hold on, Tim! Hold on!" *I won't lose you!* She let go long enough to grip her limp arm, and knowing what was to come, took a breath. In a blink, she hauled it onto his chest and her numb hand onto his wound. Pain sent a flash of black across her vision and bile rose up her throat, but she put her good hand to the gash as well and pressed, trying to close it. "Hold on, my brother." Again, she looked up and screamed for help.

"Come on, Tim. You can do this." *Please. Please. Not Tim.*

"C-coop." His voice, barely audible.

Her eyes filled. "I'm here. I got you."

"Mary."

"I know, Tim. Rest easy. D-don't talk." She blinked to glance around again. "Help here! Stretcher!"

"Love her," he said through a gurgle of blood. "Always." His eyes fluttered.

"She loves you, too, Tim. Forever."

"You…Sophie…"

You're thinking of me at this moment? Such a beautiful soul you are, Pvt. Tim Doten.

"Sh. Quiet now." Coop snapped her head to fling off tears. Her hands were lost in his blood. "Help here!" she screamed long and hard.

He started to gag, and his chest heaved beneath her limp arm. "Deserve…" He coughed. "Love Sophie…forever."

A sob jammed her throat. "I-I'll try, Tim. P-please keep quiet."

"Do it." He blinked, coughed, and his eyes opened wide, full of urgency and wonder. "You," he managed through a gurgle, and coughed again. Blood pooled at his lips. Forcing out words, he sent it streaming from the corner of his mouth. "Secret…long time."

Coop's breath caught. *Couldn't have heard correctly.* A sob escaped. "You're the finest of m-men, Timothy Doten. I love you, m-my brother."

He gagged, convulsed, and Coop blinked as hard as she could, desperate for decent vision. Then a hard and final cough seemed to clear his airway. "Love y-you, Coop…brave s-sister."

CHAPTER THIRTY-TWO

Coop swayed in the wagon, coddled her broken forearm in its sling, and considered her life now to be as circuitous and challenging as this road north to Frederick City. With any luck, and she knew she was brassy to expect more, she'd be healing at home in a week or so, and she trusted the salty ocean air, the familiar fields in their mid-October finery to revive the spirit that had empowered her these past couple of years. A spirit sorely in need.

She pinched the fingertips of her left hand but felt nothing. If the nerves healed, she might start feeling things in a few months, according to the doctor, but he offered no guarantee. Although she was lucky to have the limb at all, the diagnosis still stung, especially when topped by the heartache of losing Tim.

He knew so much more than he showed. A brother as close as Cooper had ever been.

And then there was Sophie's letter. None before had laid Coop so low. Finally reading it last night, during her stay at the aid station, Coop felt a second devastating tragedy sink her already-leaden spirit to new depths.

As if the Bauer family hadn't endured enough sorrow this summer. Coop's heart broke again, for Sophie and the children and their family's love for each other. She remembered Sophie's father fondly, had looked forward to more time with him, and sensed that, ultimately, he would accept Catherine in his daughter's life.

Sophie wrote of her family's spiritual grief, how all three of them cried constantly. But she also confirmed her affection for Coop, said she envisioned a shared, loving future, and wrote how she had been eager to travel—until tragedy struck and committed her to the farm and her siblings.

Coop struggled to reassess her dream of the two of them in her homestead, a place of their own. Tragedies now weighed down her thinking: the loss of a true friend, the passing of Sophie's father, the acquisition of what probably was a permanent impairment, and Sophie's intentions.

Bumping along, the wounded around her in the wagon moaned, some dozed, others read, and she watched the sunny countryside pass, trying to see a way forward. She dug Sophie's letter from her knapsack and reread the last page.

...As one who has forever dreamed for a heart to chime in harmony with mine, I yearn for your company and tenderness, Coop, in every way. Your beautiful words, your affections humble me, touch me deeply. How they warm and awaken my heart's desires. I read them at least once each day, for they are a balm to this struggling soul.

You are courageous beyond my words here. Your heart is wonderous and true, and memory of it beating with mine in our embrace provides strength I so dearly need. I dream of us sharing every day, no matter where, no matter the activity, and no matter the opinion of others, for my heart belongs to you.

Here now, however, amidst my family's great loss, it grieves me to say that dreams must remain dreams. I relate to your longing for your dear family home, and I am so very proud of your fight to preserve rights we all cherish. You have bravely taken fantastical measures to remain true to yourself. No one respects, treasures, that effort more than I. But as for me, fate has decided that I provide upbringing and security for Greta and Karl through their tender years, here on our farm in Gettysburg. I still work to accept this and can only hope that your selfless and kind heart will do the same.

I miss you madly, my dearest Coop. Please do secure the very first furlough possible because time is interminable without your company, your exquisite kiss. With great longing and anticipation, I look forward to our next glorious embrace.

May safety and good fortune accompany you at every step, my darling kindred soul.

Yours truly,
Sophie

"That face of yours says you ain't writin' back any time soon."

Coop looked down at the soldier lying beside her. The 42nd New York's Silas Benning had one less leg now, lost during a failed rush to save his commander, Colonel Mallon. His graying hair reached out from beneath his torn cap, his haggard face overgrown by an unkempt mustache and beard. She doubted he was as old as he looked and wondered how he played the harmonica through all that hairy growth.

He raised bushy eyebrows and held up a whiskey bottle. She accepted.

"I'll write when we stop tonight," she said. The harsh spirits burned in her empty stomach. "Sometimes, it's hard to know the right words."

"Y'love her?"

Coop stared at the pages, her thoughts racing. *I truly do. My heart leaps at the very thought of her.* She nodded, took another drink, and returned the bottle.

"Then you'll find the words eventually. We all do, don't we?" He snorted and drank. "Have y'told her yet? 'Cause you better. Women need to hear it. A lot." He paused before taking another swig. "The wife's farewell advice."

"Not just women who need it." She glanced down at him again, saw he'd drifted away in thought. "Sorry about your wife."

He shrugged and handed her the bottle. "I s'pose I could've shown more caring, done a bigger part for our future, but...Men are pigheaded, y'know? And here I lay. Gonna be a lonely peg-leg printer now."

"You're one strong cuss, Benning." She drank a smaller amount this time before giving back the bottle. "You can run a press on a store-bought leg. All things considered, you're a lucky man."

He shrugged again. "You, too, not losing the arm. It's broke?"

"Pistol shot. The break will heal, but nerves to the hand probably won't. Doc wasn't hopeful."

"That's tough, too, bein' single-handed." As an afterthought, he backhanded her knee. "But, y'know," he grabbed his privates, "y'only need just one."

"You *are* the dog everyone says."

He laughed as he pulled himself into a sitting position. "What do you do back home?"

"Hay and wheat, mostly."

"Hm. Gonna need a hand with that." He chuckled at himself. "So, marry the lady, Samson, tackle those crops together."

Coop stared out at the roadside again. *Cooper Samson marries Sophie Bauer. Uh-huh. I'm too much of a realist to imagine such a thing. Not in this century, anyway.* Actually, she cursed her inability to devote heavy thinking to any one issue because so many crowded her brain, rushed around, vying for individual attention.

She *did* know, however, that what she felt for Sophie could not be forsaken. A powerful force inside said she must not—*could not*—simply enjoy some time with her and move on with her Massachusetts dream, regardless of how loudly it called. There would be agony in that for both of them. She could feel the edges of it already. Still, the life and farm of her own design now beckoned from within her reach.

Coop tucked Sophie's writings inside her shirt and sat back. A shadow darkened the dream. It widened a hollow in her chest, cast doubt on her capabilities and the measure of her heart, especially now that Sophie's letter had faded her from view.

Would it be best to write our good-byes? We each have a calling, as imperfect and difficult as it is. I could no more ask her to leave her home than she could ask me to abandon mine. And neither of us deserves the torture of that one last kiss.

She feigned a yawn, pinched the bridge of her nose to discreetly rub away tears.

I'll find the right words. Tonight.

She sat back and closed her eyes. *Maybe a short rest won't come with dreams this time.*

But the short rest became three hours and ended with the abrupt call to disembark.

Coop straightened her legs where she sat. As she rose, she checked on Benning, snoring on the floor. She nudged him with her toe.

"Hey, peg-leg printer. Wake up."

He grumbled at her and she smiled at his temperament as she hopped off the wagon and headed for the overnight shelters in the field.

In short order, all the wounded were situated in the flimsy tents and cookfires had the aroma of soup drifting across the encampment. Orderlies directed the walking wounded into a food line and brought trays to the immobile.

Coop ate sitting cross-legged in her shelter and studied the arrival of twilight. Days grew so short. She shrugged inside her frock. The chill would become outright cold soon and she hoped she could keep warm enough to write.

She rummaged through her knapsack until she located matches, a nub of paraffin, and her wrap of paper, envelopes, and pencil. Lighting a match single-handedly proved challenging, but after considerable cursing, she lit the candle and stood it in its own drippings on the backside of her plate. Exhaling hard, she realized how exhausting even the simplest chores would be now.

She needed a writing surface. The only fairly firm and flat item in her possession was the precious family tintype, a small, thin piece of lacquered iron encased in a folded paper mat. Coop couldn't help but spend a minute with the image. She opened it on her knee, tilted it toward the light, and lost herself in the family she once had.

Wearing obedient, frozen smiles, the four of them stood with arms around each other, Cooper, Mother, Father, and herself, looking for all the world like farmers fresh from the barn. And Coop stared beyond them to that distant structure, so in need of repair, the barn that took her family when it fell.

Coop tore her eyes away and examined the image of herself with flowing tresses and layered dress and apron. "Such a lady you were, Catherine Samson." The absence of regret or yearning to return to that persona didn't surprise her. Who I am today, she thought, is the real Catherine.

She shook her head at how the image showed her dark eyes, nose, and long-jaw smile as perfect matches to her brother's. *Uncanny. How he would have ranted, seeing me in his uniform.* Their relentless teasing, even as adults, came to mind, and she wondered how his soft heart would have reacted to meeting Billy after all these years. *None of you will ever know.*

Behind the gathering in the image, their home stood steadfast and patient, and she knew today it must look so very empty. Like herself. *Perhaps, not for much longer.*

October 15, 1863
My dearest Sophie,

I send heartfelt sympathies to you, Greta, and Karl on the loss of your beloved papa. Such a shock it was to read of this tragedy. I cannot conceive of the pain you all have withstood and wish these words could convey an embrace sufficient to relieve all the suffering that still weighs upon you.

I apologize for the delay in my response. We were roundly victorious at Bristoe Station, this week, but the engagement proved especially brutal for me.

A rebel pistol delivered a most problematic wound, breaking my left forearm and canceling all feeling in my hand. The break is expected to heal, but the doctor is far less optimistic about the restoration of sensation in my fingers. I hold onto hope that someday it will return.

Hardship then grew to heartbreak for me with the loss of my finest comrade, Tim Doten. The night I spent in the aid station was most trying, suffering more from his passing than my own condition. On his dying breath, he imparted to me a shocking revelation, that he had seen through my guise long ago and thought me quite brave. I was stricken dumb by this, humbled, that such a decent, honorable man should know "me" even to a minor degree. Further, I believe you will be as moved as I to know he wished us happiness together.

My time with the 19th has been suspended and I have been ordered home to recuperate, after checking in at the Frederick City hospital. My thinking is that, unlike with my injury last spring, the army has little hope for my hand, and, therefore, little use for a one-handed soldier. Although my enlistment extends for another nine months, I believe this injury brings a premature end to my service.

From your gracious letter, I see that your decision to care for Greta and Karl has been made with great consideration and love, and no one, least of all this feigned soldier, should dare question your resolve. Admittedly, I had hoped (quite presumptuously) that we might venture along a new road together, but, as you have written, the fates now lead us elsewhere. Nothing in my life has posed as great a test of my soul, for my heart and my reasoning are at war. I am caught amidst this battle, battered until weary, a solitary farmhouse between colliding forces.

As eager as I am to see my home again, to take healing comfort in those surroundings, I wish to accomplish one thing first if you will allow me. I plan to stop in Gettysburg to spend a time with you. The fates may fume, but a reunion matters more. If you prefer I forego this visit, please do respond quickly, as I hope to arrive soon.

Your correspondence of any nature is always welcome, of course. The sight of your script alone brings a smile. And always will.

Sincerely,

Coop

CHAPTER THIRTY-THREE

Sophie emerged from the summer kitchen with a basket of squashes on her arm, a glass of tea in her hand, and two decently sized pumpkins balanced in her other arm. She set them on the table in the shade of the barn and waved for Eldus to join her.

"Sit. You, sir, are going to drop if you don't rest." She rolled two chunky logs off the nearby pile and sat them upright to use as seats. "I'm going to find some way to thank you, Eldus. I feel terrible, you finishing our barnyard. Heavens. I'm sure Rose is wondering if you're snoozing somewhere."

He laughed. "Oh, she knows I would lend a hand if I saw you in need, Miss Sophie. Can't just deliver her apple crumble and run off, now, can I?"

Sophie shook her head, pleased to see him drink, pleased just to have his company, possibly because he brought forth such pleasant memories of Papa. Since his passing two weeks ago, many neighbors had stopped by, but Eldus owned a special place in her family's heart.

And here, today, he had delivered another of Rose's masterpieces and then spent three hours splitting rails and angling them into a fence out from the barn—three hours that would have translated into three weeks for her and Karl and Greta, or far more than she could afford even if she'd found a company from town to do it.

"Now you won't waste your day chasing after those cows," he said, and pointed at one meandering off the Bauer land. "You just get that one back with the other two in their new yard and then you can put the children in charge. Save yourself."

"I look forward to that," she said, eyeing the cow and trying to summon the energy to go after it. "Thanks to you, Eldus. Greta and Karl realize now that animals aren't just pets, and they appreciate how much Papa did around here. More responsibility at their age is good for them." She leaned against his shoulder. "Especially with all those chickens."

He chuckled again and finished his tea. "They are good children, learning and helping, but you send for me if you need help." He reached for the handle of his little wagon, but Sophie set a hand on his beefy shoulder and stopped him from leaving.

"Eldus. Good gracious, thank you. You've already helped with so much around here. I never want to take advan—"

"No, no, no. Me and your Papa, we had an agreement from the start. He calls it a 'mutual assistance,' I believe, means we always help each other. Just 'cause he's gone now doesn't mean I break my part. No, ma'am."

Sophie took a deep breath, as subtly as she could. The sweetness of this man could make her cry.

"Well, then. Now that I've learned about you men and your 'mutual assistance'…" She extended her hand. "Bauer women don't break their agreements either, sir." He smiled broadly as they shook hands. "As soon as that garden over there brings us some money, I'm paying you for every hour you've given us." She put the pumpkins and basket of squashes in his wagon.

He removed his hat, looked out to the fields and the now-distant cow. "That's thoughtful of you, Miss Sophie, but we're getting by okay. Thank you."

"You're welcome, but," she elbowed him, "I got an apple crumble *and* a barnyard! *I* thank *you*." She watched him wipe the glisten off his ebony cheeks with a bandana. "Truly, Eldus. Papa surely could judge character and he picked a fine friend in you."

"Like family, Miss Sophie." He settled his hat on his head and moved off, towing his wagon.

Sophie trotted into the field, still a cautionary act. Papa already had turned over several acres for planting, but many more remained blemished by brown blotches of earth, signs of souvenir hunters, scavengers, and ghoulish graverobbers. To both north and south, she spotted little clusters of people and wagons, adding more scars to the land as they exhumed soldiers for interment in the new cemetery. Only begun a week ago, the government's task was monumental.

She slowed and stroked the cow's hind quarters as it munched on trampled grass. It had been months since she'd ventured this far afield from the house, halfway to Cemetery Ridge, and the image of thousands of men marching, shooting, dying right here gave her pause.

The fields were quiet, save the scattered workers too far away to hear, and she felt the profound stillness seep into her bones as surely as gallons of blood had seeped into this ground.

The majesty of their deeds deserves the highest honor. May soldiers never endure such horror again.

The tactile memory forced her to look down. A minié ball sat inches from her shoe. She picked up the piece of lead, rubbed her fingers over the conical shape, and somehow sensed the fear and determination of the soldier who'd last touched it. She dropped it into her apron pocket because she could not simply cast it aside. It landed with heft and she tried not to imagine it plunging into flesh.

Coop had escaped such pain, although a pistol round had broken her arm, and Sophie sighed at the return of a subject that tore at her heart. The letter had left her despondent, much to Greta and Karl's frustration, and she only dared recall Coop's words when she could submit to more tears.

Coop, I couldn't advise you not to come. I just...I couldn't bring myself to respond at all. Probably not wise of me, because how will I ever let you go? How will I control the sadness? Dare we agree to meet on occasion? And what if someone new...I don't want anyone to take your place, or mine.

"Too much pondering," she thought aloud, and wiped away welling tears with her apron. "How many times a day must I go through this?" She swatted the cow's rump and shooed her around toward the house. "C'mon, Lulu."

She cast an eye northward, to the cemetery bustling with activity atop the hill. A lone soldier left a gathering of the hired workers and began walking down the slope toward the field. *They could search this plain for years and never find every trace of every man.*

Sophie tapped Lulu's hind quarters to keep her in motion. The beast enjoyed this excursion and Sophie couldn't blame her. The sunny breeze taunted Sophie's bonnet, so she drew it back, off her head. Such crisp air, rejuvenating—and clean, finally. With a look back, Sophie cringed to see the soldier walking directly toward her, maybe a quarter mile away now. *Sorry, soldier, but I'm weary of the army's requests and inquiries—and bold advances.*

Lulu's moseying eventually brought them onto Bauer land again, and Sophie wished the family's first order of business after the battle had been to reerect perimeter fencing. Aside from a few restacked stone walls, very little had gone up anywhere. Every neighbor was hard-pressed to recover. Sophie had no idea when she'd have the money for all the labor and rails.

The soldier still approached. He carried no rifle, so his business had to pertain to the interment work underway. But she now could see he wore a knapsack and canteen. And one arm hung in a sling.

Sophie's heart lurched. Vacantly, she slapped Lulu on the rump and sent her into the barnyard. Turning toward the field, she clasped her hands in front of her and tried to calm her breathing.

She exhaled with great deliberation. Her feet tingled, and she thought they begged to run to Coop for all they were worth. She wrung her hands and studied the uniform, the glint off the brass buttons, the trim fit of the frock, the spotless sky-blue trousers. And, as always, Coop's face was lost in the shadow of her cap.

The stark white sling bounced against her chest with each step. Considering all the horrific wounds Coop could have suffered, a broken arm was a relief to see.

Coop inched her cap higher and called out. "Good afternoon, Miss Bauer!"

The tears started. That smooth alto tugged her forward. The smile Sophie knew so well shimmered into her chest as the distance separating them closed.

Coop swung her sling aside and reached for her. Sophie ran into the outstretched arm and wrapped hers around Coop's neck, as the strength and surety of heaven swept her off her feet.

"Coop!" She buried her face in the warm blue wool and sobbed.

"My God, Sophie. I've missed you so." Coop squeezed her tighter and breathed heavily against her neck. "How I miss my other arm, too!"

Sophie leaned back to find the face she'd seen in every dream. "I don't care how many arms you have." But that one arm clutched her so close now, so perfectly close, and Sophie pressed up on her toes to kiss her.

She trembled when Coop lowered her mouth to meet hers. The tender, satiny lips Sophie remembered so vividly spoke of desire equal to her own and left her cognizant of nothing but this moment. Drawing her closer, Sophie deepened the kiss, and Coop reached for more as well. Her lush, eager kiss grew firm, ardent, until she broke away, as if catching herself.

"Sophie," she breathed, and the brim of her cap bumped Sophie's forehead.

Sophie nodded and edged back, lowered her hands to Coop's shoulders, and acknowledged that, as with grief, overwhelming emotion was hard to handle. The very idea that sheer desire could take such control, usurp every conscious act and thought, almost made her shiver.

Complete surrender.

She took Coop's hand and they walked to the house in silence.

Sophie stood in the doorway to Papa's bedroom, a hand on the doorframe as if relying on its support. Coop thought that was possible. She felt more than a bit shaky just hanging her cap on the bedpost. What lay ahead for each of them seemed sadly predestined, and withering beneath a desperate, insistent passion wasn't making this reunion easy.

She carefully withdrew her arm from the sling and knapsack and dropped them on the bed. A forlorn sight, she thought, this room so tidy in his memory. She hoped she would be able to sleep here, considering.

"Would you enjoy a bath? I can prepare one for you," Sophie said. "Greta and Karl won't be home for a few hours, so you have the time and freedom to relax. You probably haven't…I mean…" Her cheeks flushed.

"No, I haven't in a long, long time. It sounds like a glorious idea. Thank you." She laid her frock across the arm of a chair and caught Sophie reviewing her in just shirt and trousers for the first time. "You know, I prided myself in being the regiment's cleanest soldier. Teased brutally because of it, but I've rarely been ill." She winked. "I turned my personal care into a clandestine art."

"Someday, you'll have to tell me how you managed."

Coop smiled sadly. *We need to plan a someday before "we" is left behind.*

"If you'd like, I could wash those clothes while you're in the bath."

"Oh, Sophie. No. I will not have you waiting on me like a servant or maid."

Sophie set a hand on her hip. "Do you have a second set of clothes?"

"Well, my…my underthings, I do. And trousers, yes, but shirt, no, which is the opposite of the usual. Like me."

Sophie's smile brightened her entire face. "Then, I'm rather 'opposite of usual,' myself, aren't I?"

Yes, you are. We match.

She watched as Sophie deliberately ran her eyes the length of her frame.

"The 'opposite of usual' looks very fine on you," Sophie said at last. "It suits you."

"Thank you. I appreciate that." She bowed slightly. "This surely doesn't feel 'opposite.' Never really did, I suppose, not even when Cooper and I confused folks with our tricks. Actually, I'm just comfortable this way." Looking down at herself, she added, "Not bad, you think? Only a little dust, no gunpowder or grease, no dirt or—"

"Or blood."

"Or blood. Enough blood." She glanced at her cuffs, hoping the stains of Tim's blood would never fade.

Sophie approached, reaching for her shirt. "I imagine this is difficult with one hand." Coop gave her free rein and slid an arm around her waist. "You realize, I hope," Sophie continued, working the first button free, "that I was not speaking of your cleanly appearance, before. My reference was to your…your…Well, the absence of femininity."

Coop drew her in and kissed her cheek, her neck. "I think you need to be closer."

"There's no way I—No way I can concentrate on these buttons."

"Perhaps you should concentrate elsewhere." She kissed her way up Sophie's throat, relishing the silkiness, the fresh taste of her. She mourned her broken arm, ached to enclose Sophie completely and imprint the feel of her on her soul. She kissed her chin, the tip of her nose, her closed eyes, soft touches to even softer skin. "You are precious to me, Sophie Bauer."

She cupped Sophie's cheek and claimed her mouth, let delicate kisses finally linger. Sophie's lips quivered and she moaned, threaded her arms around Coop's neck, and leaned against her.

Suddenly, Sophie lunged back, panic-stricken. "Your arm!" She placed both palms beneath it, supported it gingerly. "I hope I didn't—"

"Sh. No." Coop stroked the mussed flaxen hair, committing the touch to memory.

"But, Cath—"

"Sh." Coop executed a lazy salute. "It's Pvt. *Cooper* Samson, ma'am."

"Oh. Yes, of course. I-I don't know what I was thinking."

"For as long as I'm here."

The light in Sophie's eyes dimmed. "For as long as you're here."

Coop lifted Sophie's chin. "Let's make the most of this time, shall we?" Sophie only nodded. This was hard for both of them. "Why don't we heat some water for the tub?"

Sophie cleared her throat. "The summer kitchen, then." She flashed a small smile before leading the way downstairs, a meager smile that reflected a resignation Coop shared, one that advised her not to prolong the inevitable.

But she found herself struggling to stay awake, one large galvanized tub and many buckets of hot water later. Scrubbing with one hand wore her out, or maybe it was just the long-lost luxury of time and soothing heat that sapped her energy. She awoke after another quick doze and spotted her knapsack and frock on the table. Sophie had come and gone who knows how many times, and probably had taken who knows how many looks at this boney body in the soapy water.

Really not unfamiliar to her, but certainly not my preferred introduction. And, yes, I would have gazed at yours, Miss Sophie Bauer. For a very, very long time.

Her head back on the rim, she studied the patchwork ceiling, the specks of sunlight peeking through what no doubt had been a hurried repair project. Buckets in the corner probably caught the rain. Whitewash on the stone walls looked just as haphazard, missing here and there around the room, and Coop figured they'd been scrubbed hard. Like the floor, light—and dark—spots stood out. *Blood. Sophie would never have had her siblings help clean this. Guaranteed, the army didn't.*

Coop's curiosity slid into concern about repairs to all the structures, the crop acreage, the fences. She recalled seeing only a few scattered stone walls on her trek from Cemetery Hill. *How does she keep the cows in check?*

Sophie had written that their friend Eldus continued to help the family, and she had lamented her inability to pay him as much as she wanted. Coop knew that had to prey on Sophie's kind nature. With a family of his own to support, he was lucky to have real clients who could pay.

Besides, he'd already made so many urgent repairs. The kitchen had a real door and window again and he'd put quality work into the second floor, including the bedroom she had been lent. But makeshift fixes had been put to so much else, the holes in the walls, most doors and windows, the floors, probably by Sophie's father on his own or with the family, or maybe just by Sophie and the children after he passed. Valiant efforts, for sure, but not of the substance to last and provide security and protection against the elements.

Overall, she thought, the burden Sophie now bore without her father had to be insufferable. Most women in her position married hurriedly for the support, but Sophie definitely was not most women.

How much money do I have?

Coop dunked her head, scrambled the last of the soap from her hair, and dried herself as promptly as she could. She really had no idea of time and now wondered if Greta and Karl had arrived from school or were due momentarily.

Count the money.

She stepped into her drawers and then her trousers, thankfully having mastered pulling them up with one hand and half an arm. She maneuvered into the thin undershirt, and was as winded as she was relieved by the time she finished pulling the tight garment down over her torso.

Some cash for Robinson could help resolve the biggest Bauer issues, like this roof and holes in the house, maybe fencing. She steadied her billfold on the table with the heel of her hand and plucked out the paper money, a treat to look at, all fanned out. The sight of it still gripped her, after living with military-issued paper script and using Confederate dollars to light cookfires. She'd squirreled away nearly three hundred dollars during her service, even had another seven dollars in her pocket.

She pushed one hundred dollars into a pile and managed to work the rest back into her billfold. *Now to convince Sophie to accept it.* "Please let me do this for you."

"Do what, Private Samson?"

"Sophie! Oh, um…" *No time like the present.* Coop folded the pile neatly with a roll of her fingers, a talent polished in too many card games, and extended it to her. "I'd like—"

"Oh, no. Absolutely not."

"It's not a lot, Sophie, and won't solve the problems of the world, but it will help. *I* want to help."

"You've been helping me since the day we met. I cannot take more from you. You defied death for that money. Thank you, but I will not accept it." She turned in the doorway, hands to her face.

"I never risked anything for money," Coop tried, now close behind her. "Bounties lured many soldiers. Money was all they cared about, and quite a few paid a price for being bought, but I fought to keep us free to live as we choose."

"And you are restarting your life so every cent is important."

"We're all starting over, Sophie." Coop urged her to turn back. "It's not easy for any of us. And I *choose* to help you."

A tear slipping from her eye, Sophie put a palm to Coop's cheek. "Why must you be the most noble person I've ever met?"

Coop kissed Sophie's palm. "I need to know you all will be secure, that you'll be safe and warm and have what you need. November's almost here." Without looking, she slipped the money into Sophie's other hand.

Sophie pushed the money back into Coop's trouser pocket. "I sincerely appreciate the gesture, Coop, but..." She waved a hand, flustered. "And, please, do *not* leave it for me to find after you've gone." She gulped a breath and hurried back to the house.

Coop watched her go. *Such stubborn pride.* She couldn't leave without convincing her.

Chapter Thirty-four

Coop labored into socks and shoes, captured her hair in a noose of leather string, and then found her clean shirt hanging on the new clothesline just outside. *And you won't let me do anything for you.* Eventually, she fastened most of the buttons, reminding herself that she no longer needed to dress exactly to regulations, and tucked herself in as best she could, then slid the useless arm back into its sling. She thought the least she could do was make her frock as presentable as possible and went to brush it out on the table at the barn.

The routine work set her mind to wander, as it always did, except that, on service, the escape had been welcome, often deliberate. Today, thoughts grew from nagging to demanding.

If you don't take the money, Sophie, I'll go crazy not knowing how you are. The cows will disappear without fencing. Those windows will leak and patches on the walls will cause rot. Rain, snow will blow in. You'll sit around in blankets trying to stay warm. There is only so much you can do by yourself, Sophie. Please. Take it for Greta and Karl, at least.

And she saw herself at home, warm, secure—and pacing in front of the fireplace, hungering for letters, leaning on the porch rail composing telegrams in her head, ending each day's field work staring into a soup bowl.

"Now, that's pathetic. As if I won't have enough to keep me busy." And she chortled. "The old place probably needs plenty of its own fixing by now, anyway, so I won't have time to worry."

Good God. I'm losing my mind.

She straightened and rolled her shoulders. Leaning back against the table, she took several long, invigorating breaths.

And her eyes settled on the plain. The broad expanse flooded her mind with memories. Hundreds of acres of dead, dormant, and missing wheat, rye, oats, hay, corn, all of it gone until next spring delivered *life* to a place of immeasurable death. *But it will recover.*

In the distance, a wagon made its way into the cemetery, and farther south, another began the same journey along the ridge. She thought there had to be an actual road there by now, carved by those wagons of corpses, the carriages of sightseers and scavengers. A road over all the footprints and blood left there nearly four months ago, her own included.

Her frock draped over her shoulders, she walked beyond the barn to the Emmitsburg Road to the spot where she had been shot. The fence rails she'd sighted on had long-since been shattered or taken to cook a soldier's supper. She hoped that future travelers along the road would know that a logjam of devoted soldiers once occurred here.

"From here to the house," she said with wonder, scanning the distance she had no recollection of being taken. "Such a sight to behold you were, Miss Bauer. You lifted my heart that night, even if you were fuzzy around the edges." She warmed at the memory, of struggling to focus and finally *seeing* that creamy complexion and welcoming expression gazing down at her.

Like it was meant to be. And still feels that way, especially here. Should we ignore it? Two lives closing in on each other, Sophie, and here's where we stop.

She turned completely around, took in the ridge again, the old position of her Union line across the far edge of the plain. "Devil himself fell upon us that day."

Thankfully, healing will come, to the land, to survivors, to families... us, too, Sophie. You are such a part of that healing, a part of me. Oh, what I wouldn't give...

Coop stopped. The completion of that thought filled her with as much angst and awe as she'd felt behind that line in July. The realization hit hard, what she *wouldn't* give for a life with Sophie.

There is nothing I wouldn't give.

She moved forward, ghosts of that staggering Confederate march aligned to her left and right, escorting her as she debated her future. Sophie had the daily honor of this view, she knew, and bowed her head to the unflinching courage and fidelity sacrificed on this ground.

It's in all of us, Sophie, that strength. You show it every day to those you love. To me. Let me be strong for you in return.

Ruts left by artillery challenged Coop's footing, and she stepped over minié balls, ramrods, scraps of sun-bleached cloth. Iron shards appeared everywhere, the weeds of the field, ragged bits of shell impaled in turf instead of soldiers. Respectfully, she circumvented the patches of dirt where bodies had been exhumed, the massive ash piles of horses' remains, and the occasional gentle mound, six feet in length, that had yet to be disturbed. Farmers dealt with all of this every day. They would for seasons to come. Coop's spirit twisted.

She arrived at the Union's stone wall, surprised she'd walked so far, surprised to be within reach of it. Again. It never had been very high, she recalled, just high enough for the Pennsylvania, New York, and Harvard boys to lay behind. Even shorter now, with stones blown aside by shells and cannonballs, scattered in a maelstrom of men madly pushing for leverage, falling, clamoring.

She surveyed the length of it, her perspective a rebel view of the Union front, and a chill came over her at the realization of where she stood. *The heaps of blue and gray.*

Down on one knee, she pressed her hand to the ground.

"Sonny Samson. You up and took off on me again, my brother."

She sniffed and blinked back tears.

So hard to see Billy in you, when so many memories remain. Our fights in the hay, how you chased me up trees, told those scary stories by the fire...I hope they brought you the happiness they bring me.

"Family lived in our hearts then, Sonny." She wiped her eyes with her sleeve. "I guess it still does. It's one of those things that takes root and never really goes away, isn't it?"

The heart doesn't waste a beat on opinion or uniforms or where you call home—or, for that matter, skin color or even gender.

She rubbed her fingers into the dirt until she clenched a fist full of it and wondered if rebels had taken him back to Virginia or if he had been buried here in Gettysburg.

"Maybe we'll find each other again someday." She let the dirt filter through her fingers. "Never feel alone here, Sonny. You're with family and in the company of many brave souls."

Karl threw his schoolbook on the kitchen table as he ran into the parlor.

"Hey, Sophie! Sophie? What's the soldier doing out by the barn?"

Greta walked in behind him, and not seeing Sophie, turned and yelled up the stairs. "Are you up there?" She went back to the kitchen and squinted out the window. "I think…he's wounded?"

"He's wounded?" Karl asked, running to look with her. "Hey, Sophie! I'm going out. Maybe he'll show me where he got—"

"You'll do no such thing!" Sophie yelled back, now hurrying down the stairs. "He's wounded, yes, and he's our guest, so he is welcome to stroll around and come in when he's ready. That's how it works. You can talk with him then."

"How come he's our guest?" Karl asked, eyes still glued to the window.

"Karl, please come away from there. Give him some privacy."

Greta sat and took off her school shoes. "What's his name?"

"He'll be in soon enough and we can all talk, okay?"

"But what's his name?" Greta insisted.

"Yeah," Karl added, "and is he going to sleep in the barn?"

"Of course, silly," Greta told him. "You think Sophie would let a stranger sleep in Papa's room?"

"We have our chores to do, don't forget," Sophie said, "so let's change out of those school clothes. I'll wait for you because we do our best work together."

They ran upstairs and Sophie went to the window. Coop stood along the road, a considerable distance beyond the barn, and looked to be taking it all in. Sophie couldn't fathom a soldier's reaction to revisiting this battlefield. The army had grown accustomed to crossing the Potomac and Rappahannock, fought twice in Fredericksburg, tromped up and down Virginia's valleys too many times to count, but *this* place amounted to a trauma unlike any experience.

Coop was walking now, out into the middle of it all, and Sophie wanted nothing more than to be holding her hand. *How carefully you step. There's so much to avoid. Thank heaven, you left when you did, the sight was unbearable then. You're going all the way, aren't you?*

She sighed, taken by the courage required.

"Can I make supper when we're done with chores?" Greta asked, now in her favorite faded dress.

"Sure you can. That would be wonderful. We have plenty of bread, and there's chicken and potatoes. Maybe we can still find a few carrots in the garden."

"Do you think our guest will like my cooking?"

"He's going to love it, Greta."

Karl checked out the window before speaking. "He's a ways out now." He picked up on Greta's topic. "We don't have any ham, do we?"

"No, sorry, honey, and I can't wait until we do, because your supper is excellent. Now, let's go."

They went their separate ways in the barn and Sophie's thoughts ran from Coop on the battlefield to Coop in Massachusetts. Coop's offer of charity would have Papa rolling in his grave. She knew whatever they did with such money would remind her forever of love lost. But Coop had been right about its importance, and Greta and Karl deserved as good a home as Papa would have provided. *I will have to take it.*

Beyond everything, however, the prospect of Coop's imminent departure chipped away at her heart by the minute.

She hasn't said how long she'll stay, and I can't bring myself to ask.

By no means could she fault anyone for wanting to return to a homestead. The only house Coop had ever known, it held the memory and spirits of family, and had added to her purpose for enlisting. Sophie could relate and had to admit, she'd have the same drive, but the life of a solitary farmer didn't *feel* appropriate for someone so warm and thoughtful. Coop deserved a *home* not simply a house.

Images of Coop tilling a field, cooking, eating, reading by the fire, struggling to do all of it with one hand—and alone, grew too vivid, excruciating when Sophie realized how much she yearned to provide companionship. She forced herself to focus on other things, this farm work, Karl herding the cows, Greta singing to her chickens, a family enjoying a meal in the kitchen.

When all the images blurred, she stopped sweeping and straightened.

I know what it means to you, Coop, what you've fought for, but I'll miss you so. Would you...consider staying?

She leaned heavily on the broom and shook her head. *I can't give up this place even if you did ask. And, sharing it with us...What soldier who fought on this land would care to actually live on it? Would love make a difference?*

She returned to sweeping. "Hope it won't hurt to ask."

"Hey!" Karl hurried past her to the doorway. "He's coming this way!"

She heard Greta running to join him and set her broom aside. Through the open doors, she saw Coop enter the barnyard and adjust her cap to see ahead in the slanting sun. That smile preceded her by a mile, and Sophie felt her heart skip.

Every time.

Greta spun back at her with wide, excited eyes. "It's Coop!"

Karl hopped in the doorway and ran out, tossing his hat in the air. "Hoorah!"

They raced through the barnyard, cheering and calling her name. Leaning against the door, Sophie let the warmth of the moment soothe her heart.

CHAPTER THIRTY-FIVE

"Y ou know he's wearing your cap to bed," Sophie whispered as Coop poured more wine, a delightful surprise Coop had brought from Frederick City.

"You allowing him to wear it at the supper table was big."

"Confidentially," Sophie added, leaning on the arm of Coop's chair, "Papa might have allowed it, too. This is a big occasion, having you with us. If we'd had ham, Karl would have fixed his wonderful biscuits and ham for you."

"I'm touched. A boy who can cook is a rarity, especially talented." Crackle of the fire in the fireplace drew her attention, appeared to give her pause, and Sophie stole the moment to enjoy Coop's sharp profile and deep tan. She envisioned her marching endlessly on a steamy dirt road, could still see her gazing into the cookfire on that snowy Christmas Eve in Falmouth...and lying in this room, covered in wheat chaff and grit.

"When I was growing up," Coop continued, "my brothers hardly were allowed in the kitchen. Likewise, I lost half my free time being kicked out of the barn."

"But you obviously made the most of it."

"Well, thanks to Sonny, rest his soul, I learned to ride and shoot at a young age—and keep up with Cooper. Did you know that Karl asked me to teach him to shoot?"

"Already? The boy's quick. He's quite taken by the romance of soldiering."

Coop raised an eyebrow. "In light of what went on here four months ago, inside and out of the house, I'm surprised he still feels that way. There's nothing romantic about the military and I'll tell him so."

"That might discourage him."

"But, you know…" She eyed Sophie sideways. "I would do it all over again, if need be. I wouldn't hesitate."

"Oh, please don't tell him that," Sophie said with a smile. "Things are difficult enough with a twelve-year-old girl fawning over you."

"When she cut my chicken for me, I didn't dare speak."

"You did look a bit flustered."

"They're both so sweet, you know, Sophie. You've done such a great job with their raising. How old were you, when…?"

"Fourteen. Greta was just a toddler. Papa had a hard time, though, worrying about each of them because two babies had passed after I came along. But he helped at every turn, not a doting father, but dutiful for sure."

"They seemed excited that you lent me his room. Sleeping in the barn would have been a luxury for me, so I feel extremely honored."

"Well, Greta put her foot down at first, didn't approve of a stranger staying in the house at all. Then she found out it was you." Sophie waved her hand in grand fashion. "And *everything* changed."

She stood and prodded life back into the coals. Their quiet time must not end soon, and it was quickly slipping away with all this skirting around the topic they needed to discuss.

How do I ever broach the subject?

"Coop, I…" She sat and finished her wine. "I, well…I don't know where to start, quite honestly."

"Neither do I." Setting her wine aside, Coop drew her chair to face Sophie's, knee to knee, and with one hand, gathered both of Sophie's. "But I want to apologize if I insulted you with the money. It was inconsiderate of me, not thinking you might perceive my offer that way, but my intentions were honorable."

"You are an amazing woman." Sophie stroked back a strand of Coop's hair. "You could never be dishonorable. I just saw the gesture and…and all I could think of was…you leaving."

"Sophie, I—"

"I didn't stop to consider my responsibilities, providing for Greta and Karl. And that was selfish of *me*. I just felt…Well, I felt something new and didn't know…" When Coop reclaimed her hand, Sophie blew out a breath. This wasn't going as well as she'd hoped.

Frustrated with herself, nervous about her choice of words, Sophie couldn't sit any longer. When she moved to the fireplace, Coop moved with her.

"Coop, there's…You…What I mean is, I've—"

"Sophie. I love you."

Sophie's heart skipped. Lightning flashed through it and she felt her jaw drop, knew her eyes had opened wider. With her breath stalled in her chest, words failed her.

"Sophie, I do. I know I'm in love with you as surely as I've ever known anything. I don't want us to go through life apart." She looked down, spoke softly as she entwined their fingers. "You might feel differently but I really hope you don't." She shrugged. "Not that I'm sure what to do about it all." She lifted her head and Sophie saw hope, sincerity.

"Oh, and I love you," she said finally, and stepped closer. "I've never said those words before. I-I wasn't sure if that's what they call this…this feeling I have for you."

"Are you sure now?"

"Yes, I'm quite sure."

"That smile has never meant more." Coop leaned closer, her eyes lowering to Sophie's lips.

Sophie leaned toward her as well, reaching for Coop's shoulders, and closed her eyes as Coop kissed her. A gentle calloused hand cradled her cheek, moved into her hair, and cupped her head. Sophie heard herself moan, a surrender she issued gladly.

Coop withdrew and spoke against her lips. "*You* have been my life's dream, Sophie Bauer. Whatever it takes, in whatever way I can make it happen, I won't let you go. I want us together, forever, if you'll have me."

Sophie kissed her hard, with desire she hadn't known she possessed. Arms laced around Coop's neck, she swallowed joyful tears and reveled in their union. She wanted more, all of Coop's passion, every kiss, every touch to every place. The yearning rocked her, shortened her breathing, even weakened her knees.

And when Coop wrapped her arm around Sophie's waist, kissed her again as she drew their hips together, Sophie feared she might drop to the floor, as legless as a sack of flour.

She clung to Coop's strength, squeezed them even tighter together. "Please don't leave," she breathed into Coop's ear. "I couldn't bear it."

Coop inched back and set her forehead on Sophie's. "I couldn't bear it either."

"Will you stay?" Tears now ran down Sophie's cheeks. "I-I'm asking a great deal, I know, but I have to ask. Will you stay here with us?"

Coop kissed her tears and Sophie stopped breathing. *She has to say yes.*

"There are big things to consider, Sophie, my homestead, who I am to Greta and Karl, to your friends, to the army," she brushed her lips across Sophie's, "but yes, wherever you are is definitely where I want to be."

Sophie set the candle lamp on the dresser. "I imagine Karl and Greta will be up early," she whispered, and turned down the bed covers for Coop. "They'll be excited all over again to see you, have breakfast with you. I know they'll fly through chores, so you might even find them sitting outside your door when you get up."

Coop watched her flitter about the room, busy herself checking that all was in order for Coop's stay. The mellow candlelight softened the shadows of her curves, the rosiness of her dress to a deep blush, and the sunshine of her hair to a warm bronze. Coop found it difficult to stand in place and not go to her.

Coop removed her sling and flexed her stiff arm. She could hold it against Sophie's side, at least offer something of a full embrace, despite the useless hand.

"There's water in the pitcher," Sophie said, almost too quietly, "and, oh. I meant to fetch you…" She left promptly and, curious, Coop went to the doorway, then down the narrow hall to the dim glow now coming from Sophie's room. She found her rummaging through a hope chest at the foot of her bed.

"Sophie." She stepped in and softly closed the door. "You're fussing way too much."

"There's a quilt I wanted to put out for you."

"Stop, please." Coop set a hand on her shoulder and urged her upright. "Everything is perfect."

"No, I want you to be comf—"

Coop lifted her chin and kissed her. "Just having you right here, *that* makes me comfortable."

"I guess I'm as excited as Greta and Karl that you're here."

"And I can hardly believe we're here, together." She kissed her again and drew Sophie to sit beside her on the bed. Her lips to Sophie's neck, Coop felt her tremble, heard herself utter words she thought destiny would never let her say. "You are my dream come true. I cherish you, Sophie." She moved her lips to Sophie's, on the verge of shaking as Sophie welcomed them, and dissolved into a tender, luxurious kiss. "Everything I've ever wanted and more."

"You...You're a special gift to me, Coop." Sophie kissed the tip of her nose, and Coop fought back tears when Sophie grazed her lips across her mouth. "Love like ours is so impossible to find. And after all our hard times, to find you...to find love..." When she slid her arms around Coop's shoulders, Coop kissed her down onto the bed.

"I never want you sad or worried or fearful again," she whispered into Sophie's shadowed eyes. "I want happiness for you always. I swear I will do all in my power to see you sparkle with life every day."

Sophie drew Coop's mouth to hers with both hands. She slid the tie from Coop's hair and the dark, ragged curtain draped their faces. She slipped her fingers through it, held it back at Coop's ears.

"This could not feel more right," she said in a hush, "us here like this, your weight on me, our kisses." Coop kissed along her jaw, down her neck, and Sophie invited her caress by tilting her head. "Your mouth is so warm."

Coop kissed across her shoulder to the piped collar of her dress, lifted the edging with her nose and kissed as far beneath it as she could reach. Sophie tugged it a bit farther away to help.

"I want to cover you with kisses," Coop whispered, rubbing her cheek against the satin of Sophie's bare shoulder. She hungered for more, wanted to release Sophie's arms from the sleeves, to lower the dress, kiss her full breasts, taste her.

Sophie urged Coop back and sat them up. Her palms trailed from Coop's shoulders to the buttons of her shirt. "I need to feel your heart beat against mine." She peeled the shirt off Coop's shoulders and helped her out of it. "I do so remember the stubborn soldier who refused my attentions not so long ago."

"Not so stubborn now. Had we done this back then, I wouldn't have made it through that horrific next day. My concentration..." And it faded as Sophie fingered Coop's thin, tight undershirt.

Yes, I will bare my soul to you.

She helped Sophie pull it over her head, withdrew her good arm, and carefully slid it off her bad one. Sophie clasped the shirt to her own chest, and, to Coop's wonderment, Sophie leaned forward and kissed between her breasts.

"May you, one day, never bind yourself so." She set her palm between them. "And never from me." Sophie kissed her deliberately and Coop shuddered at the concept, the *feel* of freedom.

Sophie sat back and unbuttoned her bodice. She met Coop's eyes, held her gaze, but temptation stole Coop's occasional glance as she undressed.

Sophie nudged her dress off her shoulders and arms and stood to let it drop to the floor. When she started on the corset hooks, Coop reached out to assist and Sophie stepped closer.

Coop looked up and grinned sheepishly. "I have never missed wearing this contraption."

Sophie appeared to stifle a laugh, her fingertips to her mouth. Watching Coop release each binding, she whispered, "Then, I shan't be shy about asking you to hurry."

Corset aside, Coop fingered the long, cottony chemise that draped from Sophie's shoulders. She moved her hand across Sophie's stomach and squeezed her side. "Have I told you how your beauty moves me?"

Sophie lowered her chemise and stepped out of it, and Coop's heart thundered in her chest as loudly as during any charge she'd ever made. Her gaze lingered on each breast, each pert nipple, and rose to Sophie's anxious expression.

"I want you more than anything in this world," she said, standing, and tugged free the tie that held Sophie's drawers.

Coop slipped her hand up and down Sophie's back, lost in the exquisite feel of her skin, stroked along her spine and over the plush softness of her buttocks. When she squeezed, Sophie inched closer, pressed her palms to Coop's nipples, and Coop kissed her hungrily. Desperate desire heightened to urgent need.

Sophie grazed a hand along her side and Coop felt those slim, sure fingers tuck beneath the waistband of her trousers. Inwardly cursing her injury, she released her dreamy hold on Sophie's buttock to unbutton her trousers, then yanked loose her drawers.

Please, never let this moment end.

As Sophie locked her arms around her neck, Coop drew her in and felt the warmth of their bared skin combine and ignite. She groaned into their kiss, at the euphoria that surged through her. A world that surpassed all others. At last.

She turned them, lowered Sophie to the bed, and carefully situated herself on top, her broken arm at her side and a thigh nestled between Sophie's legs. The intimate connection, the snug fit evoked a sigh from Sophie, and Coop received it as glorious confirmation, reassurance that such an advance was welcome.

She relished the gentle writhing beneath her, Sophie's supple form so responsive to her slightest touch. She kissed her throat, her chest, cupped a precious breast to her mouth. She kissed the nipple, took it between her lips, slowly ran her tongue over the pebbled surface, and sucked.

With a muted groan, Sophie drove her fingers through Coop's hair. She drew a leg over her hip, opened herself farther to Coop's thigh, and rocked against it. Captivated by the treasure in her mouth, Coop responded by rubbing her thigh harder, deeper into Sophie's moist heat.

"Coop. Coop, please…"

Coop kissed her way to Sophie's other breast, driven by a craving that surprised her. She doubted she could ever be satiated by this woman. She sucked firmly, needily, and listened to Sophie moan with pleasure.

She trailed her palm over Sophie's stomach, her abdomen, flexed her fingers into the lush skin as she went, and slid her hand between Sophie's legs.

Sophie took a sharp breath and her hips shifted. She pulled Coop's head up to hers, kissed her as if she would never stop, and Coop returned Sophie's kiss with just as much abandon.

Sophie's body reacted to every stroke, every press of a fingertip, and Coop drew back to watch her shudder, pant Coop's name, and struggle to remain quiet. The power of touch, a woman's sensitivity, how they were exalted by love, how she gave herself to Coop.

Sophie's hips rose and shook. She flailed at the pillow, hauled it across her face to smother a cry. Coop set her cheek to her stomach, reaching deeper, feeling Sophie stiffen and vibrate beneath her, around her fingers.

Coop stopped, heard the breathy exhale, and smiled against her abdomen. With a twitch as Coop slowly withdrew, Sophie dropped a hand onto her shoulder.

"Never in all my days…" She ran a finger around Coop's ear. "I do love you so."

Coop hovered over her, leaning on an elbow. "Sophie, I—" Pain lanced through her forearm and she inhaled sharply and dropped onto her shoulder. "I'm sorry."

"Oh, Coop. *I'm* sorry for your suffering. You have absolutely nothing to be sorry about." She kissed Coop onto her back, moved with her until she straddled her hips. "You just shook the world single-handedly, Private Samson. No one is more humbled than I."

Coop pulled Sophie's head down. "This soldier wants more of you," she whispered, and kissed her.

Sitting back on Coop's thighs, Sophie relished the look of the sinewy frame, the pale skin glowing warmly in the poor light. She dragged her hands to Coop's chest.

"Well, this woman wants more of her soldier." She plucked at Coop's nipples and grinned to see her cringe. She covered them with her palms and squeezed. "It fascinates me, how you hid yourself."

Coop lifted her head enough to look at her own chest. "Eh. There's not much to hide, really." She cupped Sophie's breast. "Hiding *this* would have been impossible."

Sophie nearly swooned at the feel of Coop massaging her breast, wanted the sensation to last at least forever. She rolled Coop's nipples in her fingers and tasted them, the hint of her own lavender soap wafting back to her off Coop's skin. She smiled at that, such a contradictory fragrance for a soldier.

She rubbed Coop's ribs, traced each one, and vowed to feed her everything she could several times a day. *You will not fall ill and waste away on me.*

Sophie edged down along Coop's legs, and the slim waist gave way to narrow hips and well-defined bones that had Sophie shaking her head. She flexed her fingers into Coop's thighs, muscle evident, but that was all.

"There isn't an ounce of fat on this body."

"Don't know. Been too long since I cared to look at it."

Sophie laughed. "Well, *I* care to look at it." She twirled a finger through the tuft of hair at the juncture of Coop's legs. "*All* of it. And for a very long time."

She kissed Coop's hip bone and made her sigh. Eager to please, to thrill, just as much as she craved this glorious contact, she slipped her fingers between Coop's legs. Stroking, gliding into her depths, seeing Coop yearn for her, Sophie thought her own heart might stop. *To realize a dream.*

Coop quaked beneath her and clutched at the bedclothes with her one hand. Sophie drove Coop's hips off the bed and her legs hardened to stone. Awestruck, Sophie watched her surrender unconditionally.

"Sophie." Coop reached for her and Sophie stretched out along her broken arm, draping her own arm and leg across her. "If you are a dream, Miss Bauer, if this is a dream, please don't wake me." Coop drew her in by the chin and kissed her.

"It *is* a dream, my love." Sophie wiped perspiration from Coop's forehead with the sheet. "It's a dream and we are going to live it."

Chapter Thirty-six

Holding a fistful of red, white, and blue streamers high above her head, Tassie shouted Greta's name as she raced through the crowded festivities in the center of town. Sophie noticed her first.

"Tassie. Good to see you. Your mother and father are here somewhere?"

"Yes, ma'am." She pointed into the throng, then turned to Greta. "I got us these. They were free." She passed her a streamer and reached around her and handed one to Karl, who wrapped it to his belt. Abruptly, Tassie looked up at Coop and dropped her eyes. "I'm sorry I didn't get more. I didn't think…"

"Don't you worry," Coop said, and tweaked Tassie's chin. "You might say I'm already wearing my streamer." Tassie stared at the uniform and nodded.

"Coop, look." Karl tapped her arm. "Soldiers are marching in over there." He bobbed his head to keep them in sight. "Come on. Maybe you know them. We should go see."

"Check their colors," she told him.

Karl studied the flags. "Pennsylvanians!"

"Very sharp of you, Karl."

Preoccupied attaching the streamer to her hat, Greta sighed. "Me and Tassie want to go that way." She tipped her head toward the opposite side of the diamond.

"Tassie and *I*," Sophie corrected her.

"Tassie and *I* want to go to the magic show. See the sign on that wagon?"

Karl looked from Sophie to Coop. "I think I'll go with them instead."

"And when it's over," Sophie said, "we'll all meet in this area."

Coop leaned down to whisper among them. "Always watch the magician's hands. You keep the keen eye, and don't let him trick you."

The trio took off. "We won't!" Greta yelled over her shoulder.

"Well, gracious me! Miss Sophie Bauer, how lovely to see you!"

Mrs. Eliza Schmidt of the Ladies' Aid Society strutted toward them and gave Coop the once-over, grinning from ear to ear. Coop removed her cap politely.

Sophie extended both hands and they hugged. "Mrs. Schmidt, how are you on this lovely November morning? It's been quite some time."

"It has, indeed. I thought I might see you in my shop one of these days, but I completely understand. I was so saddened to hear of your loss. Your father's passing was such a shock. My deepest sympathies, my dear." She glanced at Coop and her sling and Sophie wondered what she would say next. "Now, I know my recollection doesn't serve like it used to, but might you be the soldier we saw so often down in Falmouth?"

"The same, ma'am. Pvt. Cooper Samson, 19th Massachusetts." Coop offered a slight bow. "A pleasure seeing you again."

"Well. I declare it is fine, being away from all that business, isn't it? Will you heal quickly?"

"I'm hoping so, ma'am, although my hand might have other plans."

"Now that's a shame, but you still have it, Private. There is that."

"I am grateful."

"So where did it do you in?"

"Bristoe Station, ma'am."

"Do tell. Up from Chancellorsville?"

"Down from Gettysburg."

"Oh." She straightened and put her fingertips on Coop's sling. "My, didn't the Lord beat down the devil that day? You boys surely made us proud. Was the foulest of battles. I hear they have yet to finish moving all those poor souls into the new cemetery."

"We just strolled through," Sophie said, "and there is still so much to be done after today's commemoration."

Mrs. Schmidt turned to Coop again. "Do you expect to reunite with your regiment at this event, Private Samson? Or, dare I ask if a certain fine eligible lady has drawn a handsome Gettysburg veteran back for a visit?"

"Last I heard, the 19th was nowhere close, so I suppose I'll represent the boys by myself today." She sent Sophie a smile. "As for your other question, ma'am, well…" She leaned closer, confidentially. "I've yet to meet *one* handsome Gettysburg veteran."

Mrs. Schmidt giggled behind her hand.

"Oh! The band has started," Sophie injected, and stepped away, urging Coop to follow. She waved vigorously to Mrs. Schmidt. "So good seeing you! I promise to come by the shop and we'll chat longer."

"Fine, dear! Please do."

With a slight bow, Coop edged back. "A pleasure talking with you, seeing you again, Mrs. Schmidt."

"You take care now, Private Samson."

"Yes, ma'am. Thank you." She settled her cap on her head. "Enjoy the day."

Sophie waited just inside the crowd, an eye on Mrs. Schmidt, who still had her eye on Coop.

She figured Mrs. Schmidt saw Coop as a conundrum, hard to decipher in a civilian setting, especially spit polished and scrubbed clean. Sophie gave thanks that Coop's crooning alto and strong bearing served her well and confounded those curious enough to wonder, which was exactly what Mrs. Schmidt appeared to be doing.

Until Coop mustered out next summer, Sophie adamantly believed, Coop's secret would be preserved, in honor of that gallant service and the uniform. They'd discussed it at length these past weeks, and she conceded Coop's point, even though she was proud and willing to stand beside—and, maybe, flaunt—her female companion. But, as Coop pointed out, with the hope for her full recovery came the possibility of a return to active duty, and if her hand healed before next July, *Pvt. Cooper Samson* needed to be back in the ranks.

Seeing Greta and Karl squeeze their way through the crowd, Sophie reflected on the difficult and unfortunately necessary decision to withhold Coop's identity from them. She and Coop firmly believed Greta and Karl would respect what Coop had done, marvel at the accomplishment and accept her, but saw too great a risk in allowing Coop's service to hang on the promise of an excitable young girl and boy.

Knowing this train of thought threatened her high spirits, Sophie concentrated on Coop's return to her side. Coop offered her elbow, in practiced gentlemanly fashion, and Sophie gladly accepted as Greta and Karl arrived.

"He was boring," Greta said, and Karl nodded, more interested in his peppermint stick. "Me and Ta—I mean, Tassie and I figured out his tricks, so we left."

Sophie turned to Coop. "My sister's a smart one, you know. No one's fooling her."

Greta grinned up at Coop and Coop winked back.

Sophie took great pleasure in that exchange. Her siblings worshipped Coop and Sophie was immeasurably grateful.

She squeezed Coop's arm to her side, and with Greta and Karl leading, they walked among the thousands following the parade out of the diamond along the Baltimore Pike.

Greta stopped short and pointed. "I see him! There he is!"

People surged farther onto the road, narrowing the parade to a crawl, and Karl struggled to see between bodies. Coop drew him to a tiny opening in the crowd and bent to his ear.

"There he is," she said, and he sighted along her extended arm. "President Lincoln's on the chestnut bay."

Karl hopped with excitement. "I see him, too! There's his top hat!"

From atop Cemetery Hill, a cannon boomed a salute, and Coop twitched. Sophie patted her arm. A minute later, another fired, and then each minute thereafter as the crowd escorted the president's procession up the slope.

"This way," Coop called, and threaded them through the mass of people to a decent viewing spot in front of the speakers' platform.

As they watched President Lincoln take his seat among the politicians, generals, and dignitaries, Coop wondered if those around him, chatting so casually and smoking their cigars, had any conception of what transpired on this hill or in this town. Everyone else seemed to.

To her bones, she knew all this hoopla amounted to far more than a rally for a president desperately in need of support. After all, folks stood so appreciatively through band music and prayers, and then withstood two hours of the famous orator, Edward Everett, as he described the battle and its cost, its purpose.

Maybe the bigwigs understand now—assuming they were paying attention.

She hoped Lincoln would tell them in his deliberate, powerful way. She'd read plenty of his speeches and couldn't wait to hear his eloquence drift over this land. She knew the crowd would pay attention. People came from far and wide for his Gettysburg address, to hear him commemorate this place on behalf of a grateful nation.

Right after this hymn.

Sophie stroked her arm and leaned close. "I'm so thankful that we're here together."

Coop lowered her lips to Sophie's ear. "Today and always, my love."

She clutched Sophie's arm closer to her side. Straightening her shoulders, she smoothed a palm down the front of her frock and was glad she'd given it an extra brushing for this auspicious occasion, buffed extra shine onto the buttons.

Coop looked at the expectant faces, men and women of all ages and races. Turning, she also took in the tranquil, familiar landscape beyond the hill, the ridge leading south from here, the one parallel to it a mile away, and that extraordinary plain in the middle.

She wondered if it would always be this easy to see the advancing Confederate force, the lattice of projectiles overhead, the acres of bodies. Or to hear the painful cries and the echoes of victory. Or to *feel* the recognition in Sonny's eyes. She knew the answer as surely as there would always be that farmhouse. And Sophie.

The crowd around her began to murmur and Coop turned back as the master of ceremonies bellowed, "Ladies and gentlemen! The president of the United States!"

GETTYSBURG ADDRESS

November 19, 1863

Four score and seven years ago our fathers brought forth on this continent, a new nation, conceived in Liberty, and dedicated to the proposition that all men are created equal.

Now we are engaged in a great civil war, testing whether that nation, or any nation so conceived and dedicated, can long endure. We are met on a great battlefield of that war. We have come to dedicate a portion of that field, as a final resting place for those who here gave their lives that that nation might live. It is altogether fitting and proper that we should do this.

But, in a larger sense, we can not dedicate—we can not consecrate—we can not hallow—this ground. The brave men, living and dead, who struggled here, have consecrated it, far above our poor power to add or detract. The world will little note, nor long remember what we say here, but it can never forget what they did here. It is for us the living, rather, to be dedicated here to the unfinished work which they who fought here have thus far so nobly advanced. It is rather for us to be here dedicated to the great task remaining before us—that from these honored dead we take increased devotion to that cause for which they gave the last full measure of devotion—that we here highly resolve that these dead shall not have died in vain—that this nation, under God, shall have a new birth of freedom—and that government of the people, by the people, for the people, shall not perish from the earth."

THE END

About the Author

Having retired from careers in telecommunications and community journalism, CF "Friz" Frizzell devotes her time to creating lasting characters in memorable settings. *Measure of Devotion* is her sixth novel for Bold Strokes Books, four of which either have received top honors or been shortlisted by the Golden Crown Literary Society. To date, ventures into historical fiction have garnered the Debut Author Award (*Stick McLaughlin: The Prohibition Years*) and a Best Historical Fiction nomination (*Crossing the Line*); in the romance genre, she has received a Best Contemporary Romance Award (*Night Voice*) as well as a competing nomination (*Nantucket Rose*). Friz credits powerhouse authors Lee Lynch, Radclyffe, and the generous BSB family for inspiration. She is into history, New England pro sports, and singing and acoustic guitar, and loves living only an hour from Provincetown with her wife, Kathy, and their chocolate Lab, Chessa.

Books Available from Bold Strokes Books

A Turn of Fate by Ronica Black. Will Nev and Kinsley finally face their painful past and relent to their powerful, forbidden attraction? Or will facing their past be too much to fight through? (978-1-63555-930-9)

Desires After Dark by MJ Williamz. When her human lover falls deathly ill, Alex, a vampire, must decide which is worse, letting her go or condemning her to everlasting life. (978-1-63555-940-8)

Her Consigliere by Carsen Taite. FBI agent Royal Scott swore an oath to uphold the law, and criminal defense attorney Siobhan Collins pledged her loyalty to the only family she's ever known, but will their love be stronger than the bonds they've vowed to others, or will their competing allegiances tear them apart? (978-1-63555-924-8)

In Our Words: Queer Stories from Black, Indigenous, and People of Color Writers. Stories Selected by Anne Shade and Edited by Victoria Villaseñor. Comprising both the renowned and emerging voices of Black, Indigenous, and People of Color authors, this thoughtfully curated collection of short stories explores the intersection of racial and queer identity. (978-1-63555-936-1)

Measure of Devotion by CF Frizzell. Disguised as her late twin brother, Catherine Samson enters the Civil War to defend the Constitution as a Union soldier, never expecting her life to be altered by a Gettysburg farmer's daughter. (978-1-63555-951-4)

Not Guilty by Brit Ryder. Claire Weaver and Emery Pearson's day jobs clash, even as their desire for each other burns, and a discreet sex-only arrangement is the only option. (978-1-63555-896-8)

Opposites Attract: Butch/Femme Romances by Meghan O'Brien, Aurora Rey, Angie Williams. Sometimes opposites really do attract. Fall in love with these butch/femme romance novellas. (978-1-63555-784-8)

Swift Vengeance by Jean Copeland, Jackie D, Erin Zak. A journalist becomes the subject of her own investigation when sudden strange, violent visions summon her to a summer retreat and into the arms of a killer's possible next victim. (978-1-63555-880-7)

Under Her Influence by Amanda Radley. On their path to #truelove, will Beth and Jemma discover that reality is even better than illusion? (978-1-63555-963-7)

Wasteland by Kristin Keppler & Allisa Bahney. Danielle Clark is fighting against the National Armed Forces and finds peace as a scavenger, until the NAF general's daughter, Katelyn Turner, shows up on her doorstep and brings the fight right back to her. (978-1-63555-935-4)

When in Doubt by VK Powell. Police officer Jeri Wylder thinks she committed a crime in the line of duty but can't remember, until details emerge pointing to a cover-up by those close to her. (978-1-63555-955-2)

A Woman to Treasure by Ali Vali. An ancient scroll isn't the only treasure Levi Montbard finds as she starts her hunt for the truth—all she has to do is prove to Yasmine Hassani that there's more to her than an adventurous soul. (978-1-63555-890-6)

Before. After. Always. by Morgan Lee Miller. Still reeling from her tragic past, Eliza Walsh has sworn off taking risks, until Blake Navarro turns her world right-side up, making her question if falling in love again is worth it. (978-1-63555-845-6)

Bet the Farm by Fiona Riley. Lauren Calloway's luxury real estate sale of the century comes to a screeching halt when dairy farm heiress, and one-night stand, Thea Boudreaux calls her bluff. (978-1-63555-731-2)

Cowgirl by Nance Sparks. The last thing Aren expects is to fall for Carol. Sharing her home is one thing, but sharing her heart means sharing the demons in her past and risking everything to keep Carol safe. (978-1-63555-877-7)

Give In to Me by Elle Spencer. Gabriela Talbot never expected to sleep with her favorite author—certainly not after the scathing review she'd given Whitney Ainsworth's latest book. (978-1-63555-910-1)

Hidden Dreams by Shelley Thrasher. A lethal virus and its resulting vision send Texan Barbara Allan and her lovely guide, Dara, on a journey up Cambodia's Mekong River in search of Barbara's mother's mystifying past. (978-1-63555-856-2)

In the Spotlight by Lesley Davis. For actresses Cole Calder and Eris Whyte, their chance at love runs out fast when a fan's adoration turns to obsession. (978-1-63555-926-2)

Origins by Jen Jensen. Jamis Bachman is pulled into a dangerous mystery that becomes personal when she learns the truth of her origins as a ghost hunter. (978-1-63555-837-1)

Pursuit: A Victorian Entertainment by Felice Picano. An intelligent, handsome, ruthlessly ambitious young man who rose from the slums to become the right-hand man of the Lord Exchequer of England will stop at nothing as he pursues his Lord's vanished wife across Continental Europe. (978-1-63555-870-8)

Unrivaled by Radclyffe. Zoey Cohen will never accept second place in matters of the heart, even when her rival is a career, and Declan Black has nothing left to give of herself or her heart. (978-1-63679-013-8)

A Fae Tale by Genevieve McCluer. Dovana comes to terms with her changing feelings for her lifelong best friend and fae, Roze. (978-1-63555-918-7)

Accidental Desperados by Lee Lynch. Life is clobbering Berry, Jaudon, and their long romance. The arrival of directionless baby dyke MJ doesn't help. Can they find their passion again—and keep it? (978-1-63555-482-3)

Always Believe by Aimée. Greyson Walsden is pursuing ordination as an Anglican priest. Angela Arlingham doesn't believe in God. Do they follow their vocation or their hearts? (978-1-63555-912-5)

Best of the Wrong Reasons by Sander Santiago. For Fin Ness and Orion Starr, it takes a funeral to remind them that love is worth living for. (978-1-63555-867-8)

Courage by Jesse J. Thoma. No matter how often Natasha Parsons and Tommy Finch clash on the job, an undeniable attraction simmers just beneath the surface. Can they find the courage to change so love has room to grow? (978-1-63555-802-9)

I Am Chris by R Kent. There's one saving grace to losing everything and moving away. Nobody knows her as Chrissy Taylor. Now Chris can live who he truly is. (978-1-63555-904-0)

The Princess and the Odium by Sam Ledel. Jastyn and Princess Aurelia return to Venostes and join their families in a battle against the dark force to take back their homeland for a chance at a better tomorrow. (978-1-63555-894-4)

The Queen Has a Cold by Jane Kolven. What happens when the heir to the throne isn't a prince or a princess? (978-1-63555-878-4)

The Secret Poet by Georgia Beers. Agreeing to help her brother woo Zoe Blake seemed like a good idea to Morgan Thompson at first…until she realizes she's actually wooing Zoe for herself… (978-1-63555-858-6)

You Again by Aurora Rey. For high school sweethearts Kate Cormier and Sutton Guidry, the second chance might be the only one that matters. (978-1-63555-791-6)

Coming to Life on South High by Lee Patton. Twenty-one-year-old gay virgin Gabe Rafferty's first adult decade unfolds as an unpredictable journey into sex, love, and livelihood. (978-1-63555-906-4)

Love's Falling Star by B.D. Grayson. For country music megastar Lochlan Paige, can love conquer her fear of losing the one thing she's worked so hard to protect? (978-1-63555-873-9)

Love's Truth by C.A. Popovich. Can Lynette and Barb make love work when unhealed wounds of betrayed trust and a secret could change everything? (978-1-63555-755-8)

Next Exit Home by Dena Blake. Home may be where the heart is, but for Harper Sims and Addison Foster, is the journey back worth the pain? (978-1-63555-727-5)

Not Broken by Lyn Hemphill. Falling in love is hard enough—even more so for Rose who's carrying her ex's baby. (978-1-63555-869-2)

The Noble and the Nightingale by Barbara Ann Wright. Two women on opposite sides of empires at war risk all for a chance at love. (978-1-63555-812-8)

What a Tangled Web by Melissa Brayden. Clementine Monroe has the chance to buy the café she's managed for years, but Madison LeGrange swoops in and buys it first. Now Clementine is forced to work for the enemy and ignore her former crush. (978-1-63555-749-7)

A Far Better Thing by JD Wilburn. When needs of her family and wants of her heart clash, Cass Halliburton is faced with the ultimate sacrifice. (978-1-63555-834-0)

Body Language by Renee Roman. When Mika offers to provide Jen erotic tutoring, will sex drive them into a deeper relationship or tear them apart? (978-1-63555-800-5)

Carrie and Hope by Joy Argento. For Carrie and Hope loss brings them together but secrets and fear may tear them apart. (978-1-63555-827-2)

Death's Prelude by David S. Pederson. In this prequel to the Detective Heath Barrington Mystery series, Heath discovers that first love changes you forever and drives you to become the person you're destined to be. (978-1-63555-786-2)

Ice Queen by Gun Brooke. School counselor Aislin Kennedy wants to help standoffish CEO Susanna Durr and her troubled teenage daughter become closer—even if it means risking her own heart in the process. (978-1-63555-721-3)

Masquerade by Anne Shade. In 1925 Harlem, New York, a notorious gangster sets her sights on seducing Celine, and new lovers Dinah and Celine are forced to risk their hearts, and lives, for love. (978-1-63555-831-9)

Royal Family by Jenny Frame. Loss has defined both Clay's and Katya's lives, but guarding their hearts may prove to be the biggest heartbreak of all. (978-1-63555-745-9)

Share the Moon by Toni Logan. Three best friends, an inherited vineyard and a resident ghost come together for fun, romance and a touch of magic. (978-1-63555-844-9)

Spirit of the Law by Carsen Taite. Attorney Owen Lassiter will do almost anything to put a murderer behind bars, but can she get past her reluctance to rely on unconventional help from the alluring Summer Byrne and keep from falling in love in the process? (978-1-63555-766-4)

The Devil Incarnate by Ali Vali. Cain Casey has so much to live for, but enemies who lurk in the shadows threaten to unravel it all. (978-1-63555-534-9)